Graveyard
Of The
Greats

Graveyard Of The Greats

MOKBEL ALMAYLAA

ARPress
45 Dan Road Suite 5
Canton MA 02021

Hotline: 1(888) 821-0229
Fax: 1(508) 545-7580

Ordering Information:

Quantity sales. Special discounts are available on quantity purchases by corporations, associations, and others. For details, contact the publisher at the address above.

Printed in the United States of America.

ISBN-13:   Paperback   979-8-89356-646-8
                eBook   979-8-89356-647-5

Library of Congress Control Number: 2024903479

Table of Contents

Dedication vii

Beginning Steps... ix

An Opening xi

CHAPTER 1   Age of Insanity 1

CHAPTER 2   Death is a Necessity 12

CHAPTER 3   A Mysterious Crime..................... 21

CHAPTER 4   Meet and Greet 33

CHAPTER 5   Who Does the Skull Belong To?............... 45

CHAPTER 6   Five Hundred Dollars................... 51

CHAPTER 7   Cherry Juice................................ 66

CHAPTER 8   Playing with Fire 84

CHAPTER 9   Who Might He Be?...................... 93

CHAPTER 10 The Murder Weapon................... 110

CHAPTER 11 A Democratic Solution 115

CHAPTER 12 An Ice Storm Hits the Graveyard 127

CHAPTER 13 The Yearning of a Whale 145

CHAPTER 14 Blue Smoke................................ 157

CHAPTER 15 For Love of Metal and Fire...... 173

CHAPTER 16 Provocation................................ 180

CHAPTER 17 An Apology................................ 187

CHAPTER 18 A Stay in the Ocean 199

CHAPTER 19 A Call to Arms.......................... 203

CHAPTER 20 Heart Ache................................ 218

CHAPTER 21 A Hornets Nest........................ 232

CHAPTER 22 The Heart of a Janissary 252

CHAPTER 23 An Eye for an Eye..........256

CHAPTER 24 The Skull's Scenario..........265

CHAPTER 25 A Red Spot..........288

CHAPTER 26 Two Roses to Look At..........309

CHAPTER 27 A Place under the Sun..........312

CHAPTER 28 Appearances can be deceiving..........326

CHAPTER 29 A Shoe Flies at the U.N...........342

CHAPTER 30 Who Rules the World?..........354

CHAPTER 31 An Unidentified Person of Interest..........371

CHAPTER 32 A Gold Lighter..........378

CHAPTER 33 Red Light..........396

CHAPTER 34 Prized Game..........410

CHAPTER 35 Rocky Mountains..........425

The Final Chapter   Hot Ice..........437

Conclusion..........460

Dedication

To men and women of honor,
who plant lilies in humanity's garden.
Who work to put an end to war,
And spread peace between all peoples and nations.
With love, and best wishes,

Mokbel Almaylaa

Beginning Steps

It's common for us to chitter-chatter about movie stars and famous people. We like to ramble on about their lives, emulate them, look up to them, and to keep posted as to their comings and goings. We all have our favorite celebrity. If any of us is lucky enough to get an autograph from one of them, to say that we would be excited would be an understatement. For a while you'll have no other care in the world, and your friends and colleagues won't hear the end of it. That miserly piece of paper is liable to make you famous with people near and far. And if your lot is such that you were able to get a picture with said celebrity? Forget about it.

In this respect, I'm no different from anybody else. Well, not completely. See, I'm a coffee lover – a coffee *fanatic*, even. No one has a better appreciation for its unique taste than I do. The only thing that could make the experience even more pleasurable is if I could have coffee with one or two people.

Special people.

I was once asked, if you could have coffee with anybody in the world, who would it be? Who better than the greats of the twentieth century! In fact, I *have* had coffee with them. That's right: I descended into their graves, met with them, listened in on their conversations, and had coffee with them. They were a lovely crowd.

I got a sense for the way their hearts pulsed at a peculiar time in man's history. I took down their fingerprints. The record of that meeting is encapsulated between the covers of this novel.

An Opening

Human beings are distinct from other beings by virtue of their intellect. The intellect drives them to search for the truth and to love knowledge. This distinction has in turn had the fortuitous effect of leading to the discovery of many of the most well-guarded secrets of this magnificent universe. Needless to say, many more secrets remain to be discovered.

Humans begin their lives on this Earth with tears – a baby's all too famous first cry – and *end* their lives with tears – this time the tears being shed by others. But between birth and death humans experience life, a life that confounds them by constantly reminding them of the frightening prospect of death. Death is foreign to us, a phenomenon yet to be discovered and explored, save perhaps in the world of eschatology. It is important to keep in mind, however, that not having sufficient knowledge about a thing is no good reason to deny the reality of that thing.

At the raw emotional level, death is almost always attached to sadness and mourning – after all, in its apparent form, death is viewed as little more than the absence of life. Just as we suffer the first few hours of the night before we are permitted to take our nightly rest, so does life pass – swiftly, uncontrollably – before our mortality catches up with us. And just as the windy breeze scatters fallen leaves from one place to the next, so does death carry souls from one mode of existence into the next. In a sense, death is a gateway, a right of passage.

Many theories have been proposed to explain the phenomenon of death. The Abrahamic religions propose that death is a form of recompense: humankind is held to account for its worldly deeds by means of death. Good deeds are rewarded with entrance into paradise, bad deeds punished in the hellfire that never ceases to burn.

Ancient philosophers also denied the ephemerality of the soul, limiting mortality to man's physical body, which alone experiences death and undergoes decay. The soul, on the other hand, is eternal, and continues to correspond with humanity at some level. Yet even with this in mind most people are loathe to think of death, the very thought of which fills them with revulsion, fear and dread. It's no wonder, then, that the promise of resurrection – resurrection of the dead – constitutes a very real motivator for people to do good in this life.

In this novel, *Graveyard of the Greats*, we take a brief sojourn into the world of the dead. Here, we converse with those long-gone greats, shed some light on their worldviews, and uncover the truth of who they really were. It's a literary intervention, rather than a philosophical or theoretical one. It's an attempt to navigate the abyss that lies between existence and non-existence, and experience the twin phenomena of life and death simultaneously. It's an attempt to penetrate the guarded secrets of the twentieth century, a time in which humanity has progressed – through a series of manmade technological breakthroughs – beyond anything previously thought possible.

It's an epoch marked by a desire for freedom and liberation, in which the world underwent two of the bloodiest and most extensive wars in its history, resulting in the formation of the League of Nations and the independence of most nations in the world. Later we saw the second wave of nationalism take shape, as well as the spread of democracy and the triumph of capitalism. But in the midst of all this, our sense of culture came to be distorted, much of this distortion a result of the very same technological advancement we've grown to champion. Our notion of civilizational values turned awry. We witnessed the emergence of communism, Nazism, and fascism. Then came imperialism, which irrevocably transformed the colonial enterprise: the desire to acquire wealth – the essence and end-goal of capitalism – became transfixed with the use of economic exploitation as a tactic designed to plunder poorer nations and deprive them of their resources. In the end, colonialism enveloped all: either you were a colonialist, or one of the colonized.

As a result of these divergent (and often times clashing) ideologies, wars ensued, catastrophes occurred, and the people's sense of culture began to be restricted to matters of leisure and recreation. Culture lost all meaning, and descended into mere merrymaking. People became intellectually and spiritually malnourished, and everyone became preoccupied with the corporeal and the mundane. The acquisition of wealth became the end-all of existence.

Man's greed made exploitation lawful and silenced the voice of conscience. Thereby, he turned himself into a commodity, in which values are ready to be bought and sold for dirt cheap.

Graveyard of the Greats is not a historical novel, even if it seeks to depict events of the twentieth century, and even if its main characters were instrumental in the formation of history. Each of these characters pushed for the ultimate triumph of their own ideology, even at the expense of a human enterprise which lost millions of people in the process, not to mention millions more – including the elderly, the women and the young – who were left injured and debilitated.

The events of the twentieth century require tens of volumes to record and interpret, and at any rate the libraries are filled to the brim with volumes that relate the story of what happened. This novel is solely a literary effort, focusing on the twentieth century, and more particularly with the events that defined that era.

CHAPTER 1
Age of Insanity

At dawn, the village roosters began to crow, announcing the promise of a new day. The villagers would arise from their deep sleep, rushing headlong into their fields to carry on their interminable toil. In the midst of all this, something extraordinary was happening in the graveyard of the greats. The graveyard lay atop a secluded mountain foothill that embraced it lovingly and tenderly, from which descended a stretch of silk meadows that led the way to the city, which was built in such a way as to represent all of the major capitals of the world, without exception. Surrounding the graveyard was a colossal fence that had been constructed out of white stone, polished with care and precision, which had come with the passing of time to be overtaken by a slew of plants and algae. The end result looked something like a very pleasant painting, the green blending splendidly with the white.

A far-away place, with nothing to be heard but the chirping of the birds. The calm silence was occasionally broken by the living who had come to visit the graveyard, seeking thereby to honor in perpetuity the memory of their ancestors. On occasion, the sound of women wailing, weeping, and prattling would rip through the graveyard, sending fear and terror into the world of the skulls and skeletons that rested peacefully beneath the earth.

The morning light began to spread gradually over the graveyard of the greats, casting out the gloom of darkness and allowing the graveyard's lofty gate to shine in all of its glory. The gate towered over a garden whose appearance was like music to the eyes, its grounds covered by a carpetlike expanse made up the most exquisite green verdure, in the midst of which was a floral clock, whose numbers were made up of foliage and its hands adorned in the choicest flowers. Adjoining the clock was an enchanting display of roses of various hues and colors. With every tick the clock would startle the greats buried therein.

Standing adjacent to the graveyard stood a mountaintop, from which descended a bustling river. The river travelled far and wide, across the plains and fields depositing its waters into the ocean. A small rivulet broke off from the main river, and took its path towards the graveyard's garden. On both sides of the rivulet grew a string of populous trees that stood watchfully over the terrain. A succession of soft morning breezes would penetrate through the trees, accompanied by the delightful sounds of the water's dribble that trinkled about in the nearby waterfall.

The water's surface was clear and transparent. The rays of the sun would reflect off the top, producing an illumination so bright so as to serve as a beacon and a guide for all the thirsty birds that passed through on many a heated summer day. The birds would alight to drink of the rivulet's waters and to take a moment's rest on top of the branches of trees that stood so stately and resplendent, scattered across the garden's grounds. Off in the distance, geese and ducks swam in an artificial lake, around which were built a few benches made out of stone.

Pine trees shrouded the dead in shade; as for the eucalyptus trees, which were planted on the western edge of the graveyard, their fragrance constituted something of a natural remedy that protected the dead from various ailments, particularly the common cold and other forms of nasopharyngitis.

Along the road that led to the graveyard there were stands dedicated to the sale of flowers, laurels and basils, which were eagerly purchased by visitors to the graveyard who would then present them as gifts to the dead, as a token of remembrance and the will never to forget. Next door were the workshops dedicated to the manufacture of coffins and caskets of varying shapes and sizes, as well as others who specialized in the cutting and polishing of marble tombstones. Other services offered included the engraving of the stones with creative decorations that gave each tombstone its own character. Every tombstone was engraved with the name of the deceased person buried underneath, not to mention the dates of birth and death. All other funerary accoutrements needed to help the dead make the transition into their final destination were also readily available, each of them appropriate to the cultural and religious subjectivities of the time.

Class discrimination had made its way into the graveyard. The graves of the poor resembled ancient ruins, a place so despondent that owls and ravens built their nests in their midst. On the other hand, ostentatious displays of opulence could be clearly seen in the graves of the wealthy, like five-star hotels lining the Las Vegas Strip.

Each nation had its own national graveyard, which it called "the graveyard of the martyrs." The other graveyards took on names of a commercial nature, like "The Graveyard of Eternal Rest," "The Graveyard of the Olive Trees," maybe even "The Graveyard of Eternal Bliss," and so on.

As for the transnational "Graveyard of the Greats," it was a graveyard whose walls were constructed out of concrete blocks reinforced with iron pegs, so as to be strong and durable and to protect against the possibility of the walls caving in over the graveyard's residents and wiping out any trace of the latter's presence, and, ergo, of the history that they made. The graveyard was well-guarded, equipped with all the latest gadgets and the most developed communication systems, including high speed internet, and watched over by officers commissioned by the United Nations wearing blue helmets. The United Nations took it upon itself to guard the graveyard as they deemed it to be the preserve of humanity as a whole, housing the greats of all nations without bias in favor of a particular ideology or prejudice for a specific race. Death is the ultimate truth, the scale of justice that protected the Earth's rights. For on the Day of Creation, the Earth grieved its plight to its Creator, saying:

My Lord! You created the Heavens, and deprived it of nothing. Yet you created me, and deprived me.

The Lord responded:

By my Majesty and Glory, I will return them all to you, virtuous and wicked alike.

It replied: "I swear by your Majesty, that I will wreak my vengeance upon those that disobeyed You," – a reference to man, who was created from the Earth (like the old Ash Wednesday saying, "You are from the dust, and to dust you will return"). All men are equal in this respect: they return to the Earth's embrace, irrespective of the strength or greatness they enjoyed in life.

Above every grave was a tombstone made of marble stone, which pinpointed the location of the deceased. Over here there is a tombstone of polished black marble, upon which was inscribed in golden case letters in French: "General Charles De Gaulle (1890-1970)." Four meters away was another slab of pearl white marble which read "President John F Kennedy (1917-1963)." Between the two graves was a dais, upon which stood a small statute of the Virgin Mary, her hands laid out in supplication before the Almighty, and behind the statute was a tombstone that read, "Winston Churchill (1874-1965)." Nearby there was a grave made in the shape of the hammer and the sickle that carried the name "Joseph Stalin (1879-1953)."

Next to it was another grave, with a tombstone of diminutive proportions, indicating the stone mason's sense of shame in having taken up the job and with deliberate intent to diminish the stature of the man to whom it was dedicated. Upon the tombstone in German was read: "Adolf Hitler (1889-1945)." At the southernmost point of the wing, under a triangular, pyramid like structure was another grave upon which was inscribed the opening chapter of the Qur'an: "In the name of God, the Compassionate, the Merciful. To God, the Lord of the Universe, is due all praise. God, the Compassionate and Merciful one, the Magistrate of the Day of Judgment. It is you, Dear God, that we worship, and it is from you that we seek aid. Guide us along the Straight Path – the path of those with whom you are pleased, not that of those who have incurred your Wrath, nor those who have gone astray. President Gamal Abdel Nasser (1918-1970)." Continuing on there was another grave upon which was inscribed in prominent letters another Qur'anic verse: "In the name of God, the Compassionate, the Merciful: Dear human soul, sound and at peace; Return to your Lord, pleased with Him as He is pleased with you; Enter into the ranks of my servants, in a paradise of inestimable bliss. Sultan Abdul Hamid II (1842-1918)." On the trunk of a sandal tree planted nearby was inscribed in Gujarati: "The Mahatma Gandhi (1869-1948)." On the eastern side of the wing there stood a lone, spacious grave whose marble tombstone was imported on special order from the stone quarries of Italy. The grave was constructed in the shape of a big steamship, and the engravers – acting on a written testament from the deceased himself – printed the letters of the deceased's name in large, imposing letters that were coated in pure gold. The letters, rather than being printed as was the case with the other names, was written in the most beautiful cursive that was fitted well with the numerous rose bouquets that surrounded the gravesite. The bouquets were brought along by the heirs of the deceased during their numerous visits in the first few months after the deceased's passing. Later on, the heirs gradually began to get distracted by the massive fortune they inherited that their late father had left them and stopped visiting in tot. "Aristotle Socrates Onassis – Millionaire (1906-1975)."

The other graves belonged to some of the most famous names the world had known: Lenin, Roosevelt, Napoleon Bonaparte, Mao Zedong, Kemal Ataturk, Lumumba, Simon Bolivar, George Washington, Ernesto Che Guevara, Muhammad Ali Jinnah, and others.

An extraordinary event was underway in the third wing. The wing had poor air circulation, which had the effect of creating a suffocating, despondent atmosphere to reign upon its downcast and dejected residents. Buried underneath in a grave as comely as it was spacious was a skull that had been pacing back and forth with the swiftness of a vehicle that accelerates into a crowded street, but with no horn to warn other residents who come in its way. It stops for a moment, then proceeds in its way and collides with the feet of a skeleton that laid restfully in the grave's roomy accommodations. Startled, the skeleton jumped to its feet at once, protesting: "What is with you, guy? You can't sleep, so nobody else can either?!"

"All due respect, Mr. Skeleton," the skull said as he continued to pace, "you've been sleeping for sixty years now. Haven't you had enough?"

The skeleton replied, "Even a lifetime of sleep is not enough. At any rate, what is so important that you feel it necessary to disturb my rest and awaken me from my sleep after all these years?"

The skull was too preoccupied to answer.

"Why don't you answer me?" The skeleton demanded.

Still no response.

"If anybody sees you pacing like this, they'd think you were trying to win a marathon."

The skull began to run around in circles, seemingly at random, which drew the skeleton's ire to no end.

"Son of Adam, I understand that a healthy mind needs a healthy body. But this running around of yours is certainly no exercise!"

The skull, now annoyed enough to respond, hollered back, "I'm not in the mood for your jokes right now! I'm not exercising! I'm in a bit of a bind here, and I need help! I don't understand why this keeps happening to me! I feel all alone here!"

The skeleton grumbled.

"Leave me alone. I want to go back to sleep."

"You're just going to leave me here?!" the skull appealed to the skeleton.

"Come on, we're neighbors! Throw me a bone here!"

The skull's plea had a noticeable effect on Gandhi's ashes, bearing the distinct scent of frankincense and sandalum, whereupon they immediately transformed into their pre-cremation state. Gandhi snuck a peek at his neighbors, who were attentively following the skeleton and the skull's exchange.

"I gotta find some ear plugs. That'll do the trick," replied the skeleton haplessly.

The skull needed to find a way to provoke the skeleton out of its slumber.

"You are cold and heartless!" the skull finally summoned.

"Don't try to induce me into feeling sorry for you. I've been dead for sixty years, after all. I forgot all about life on the outside and all the human emotions that came with it. Might

I remind you, sir, that you were the one who disturbed me. So, would you at least explain what you're up in arms about?"

"There's something going on inside my head. I don't know, maybe it's the turbulent events happening outside that have awakened me from my death."

"Death on the outside is quite different from death in here."

"So you haven't been hearing what's going on just outside our doorstep?"

The skeleton pounced upon a cotton ball he had found near the millionaire's casket.

"Hey, be a pal, help me put this thing in my ear."

"You're insane, you know that?! You think putting a cotton ball in your ear will protect you from what's going on outside?"

"You're right. But I'm not the one who's insane. This century's insane."

The skull had had enough. The sound of the resulting commotion – knocking into walls, rolling around the floor uncontrollably – seemed to stir a reaction in the skeleton.

"Ok, calm down! Calm down! Stop rolling around. Let's try to figure something out, ok?"

The skull struck a repose almost immediately, then looked to the skeleton. The skeleton continued, "Ok, now we can hear each other out."

"I'm a General. Call me General!"

The skeleton gaped in surprise. "General?"

". . .You're not Adolf Hitler, are you?"

"Why would you think I'm Hitler?" the skull asked in disgust.

"No one disturbed his neighbors as much as he did."

"Relax. Hitler was a corporal, not a general."

"Thanks, General. That's a relief."

Suddenly, the skull went back to running around and causing a ruckus.

"We're on the verge of crossing into the twenty-first century and everybody's still cursing Hitler's name."

Hitler jumped to his feet upon hearing the insult, his voice rattling out angrily from one of the corners of the wing.

"Who dares insult the Fuhrer?"

The skeleton stared anxiously off into the distance from which the voice came.

"Who are you, his lawyer?" The skeleton stammered.

"If you had the slightest intelligence you would know who I am. I am the Fuhrer. I am Adolf Hitler."

The sound of Stalin coughing came barging from the very same corner of the wing.

"Don't speak roughly to him, Hitler! You've caused the blood in his veins to freeze, and he didn't even do anything to you, you lowlife," Stalin protested.

Hitler, shocked from the unexpected attack, responded in kind:

"And who are you to dare call me a lowlife?!"

"I am Joseph Stalin, the man you backstabbed in days past."

"Necessity has its own rules, dear friend," replied Hitler, his sense of calm restored.

"Shut your mouth! Don't you dare call me your friend! What do you know about friendship!" Stalin retorted.

"Take it easy, gentlemen!" interjected the Mahatma, hoping to put an end to the fight.

"Haven't you two ignited enough wars in life? Must you two continue your shenanigans down here?!"

"It's all Hitler's fault," said Winston Churchill, lighting up a cigarette.

"He's the one who broke his pact with Stalin and invaded the Soviet Union."

"He's right," General De Gaulle let out with a yawn. "Hitler is to blame for everything. His military occupation of French lands is just one of his many unforgivable sins."

"Get off your high horse, General!" exclaimed the skeleton.

"Let's hear what his neighbors have to say!"

"Silence, you skeleton!" snarled Hitler. "Don't get involved in matters that don't concern you!"

The skeleton moved back cautiously and implored the general once again:

"Please, stop moving and come sit next to me."

"You coward!" Hitler told the skeleton while waving his fist menacingly.

"You want the general to protect you? Ha! This proves that brute strength is how you get what you want in this world."

By this time, John Kennedy became annoyed by all the insult hurling and the shouting.

"A kind word and a diplomatic temperament go a long way, gentlemen."

"That's true," retorted Abdel Nasser, "but the transgressor must be condemned!"

The skull continued to roll around on the court floor and then bumped violently into Sultan Abdul Hamid II, who had been soundly asleep.

"What is all this commotion?!" shouted Abdul Hamid, obviously disconcerted and disheveled.

"And what's that smell?!"

Suddenly, a noise is heard. It's the sound of steps belonging to someone from the world of the living. Silence filled the room, and everyone was overtaken by a stark mix of utter astonishment and debilitating fear. It's every man for himself. The skeleton rushes to put the cotton balls in his ears, and the skull rushed off to hide in the nearest corner.

Everyone knows who it is. It's the grave digger.

CHAPTER 2
Death is a Necessity

They called him Cain Goldstreak, an exceptionally tall man with a colossal build. His body sported a dense forest of chest hair, and his eyes, blue like an ocean above which white clouds hover, meshed uncomfortably with his gruff facial features and a perennial frown that marked the face of a man who never learned to smile. Everyone, the dead and the living, feared him. He was a gravedigger, the Angel of Death's emissary on Earth. Generous to a fault, he freely granted visas to the underworld, capable of picking off his customers regardless of time and place. He worked non-stop, day after day, night after night, having reached his peak level of performance during the twentieth century. Granting one-way, no return, permanent-exit visas was his business, and business was good.

The gravedigger had inherited many privileges from his grandfather: a brawny physique, strong and shapely muscles, and a love of travel. His grandfather aforetime had relocated to a vast and strange land, going to work first as a cowboy, then as a hunter who was famed for his boundless selfishness. Indeed, he was the first human to fence off a piece of land that he owned And say, "This is mine."

His father mined for gold in California's bounteous rivers and valleys, with only simple tools at his disposal. [Eventually] he managed to accumulate an exorbitant amount of wealth, enabling him to secure a [lucrative] coal production deal, and later moved on to drilling his first oil well in Pennsylvania in 1858 with astounding results. In time, he began to specialize in drilling and digging all kinds of things ranging from precious metals to individual or mass graves with an eye to accomplishing the goals he set out for himself. He had put all appropriate strategies to work in pursuit of these goals, taking advantage of whatever political and diplomatic leverage he was able to muster, playing nasty or nice, even going as far as to devise wars and initiate conflicts if the circumstances required.

The grave digger had seven sons, to whom he had bequeathed his craft and who were responsible for administering his affairs, hand-in-hand with his trusted associates. They spread out to the four corners of the globe, armed with advanced technologies of surveillance and communication, and taking as their base of operations areas of rich with crucial natural resources, particularly energy resources.

Just after two o'clock in the afternoon, the phone rang in the grave digger's villa, breaking his deep, restful sleep. The night before had been a lascivious one, distinct for its fancy vibes, dim lights, singing and dancing, and all manner of food and drink.

He picked up the phone. It was a phone call from his associate in New York City.

"I'm sorry to wake you, but things are moving quickly and we need to respond fast. We need your direction."

"The Russians won't just leave us alone ?"

"Actually, this time it's the Chinese. Their companies have just entered the African market."

"They sneak in from the eastern side?"

"Indeed they have!" The agent responded enthusiastically. "They began with Sudan, and now they're in Somalia. What do we do?"

The grave digger mulled it over for a bit, and then said: "Instability and volatility will be effective in preventing their incursion into the market." "Understood."

"The rise in oil and gas prices seems to have opened their appetite."

"We need to revise our pricing policies. Keep an eye on the stock markets. The banks must lower interest rates in order for exports to increase."

"Certainly."

"Ok, what's next?"

"These renowned statesmen. . .one of them's gotta go."

"That's fine, I'll get a place ready for him in the Graveyard of the Greats. Send me his information, and let me know about any and all updates."

His wife made him a hot cup of coffee while he was busy getting dressed for work. He was thinking about how to teach those Chinese a lesson. His coffee was bitter, just the way he liked it. The fax machine sounded off, and began to print the information [that he had requested] on pearl-white sheets of paper. Then he made his way to the Graveyard of the Greats, with a hemp bag that contained his pick and shovel over his shoulder and in his right hand, the sheets of paper with the information that he had requested. He walked up to the marble factory, which has begun operating twenty four hours a day in order to meet the hoard of requests that have accompanied the exponential rise in deaths in this century. The death of a great one, however, causes an entire country to grind to a screeching halt, and the world over to pause and take notice. As for the burial preparations, it was going to be something of a VIP treatment, to use the gravedigger's expression, who in the meantime had prepared a list containing his detailed instructions as to what he wanted inscribed on the tombstone. He edged ever farther away from that dreamful town with its posh residences and busy shops and continued his climb upwards toward the graveyard, that final abode of rest which he loved so dearly and which he looked after with so much care.

His heart jumped with delight as his eyes fell upon the graveyard's walls. He began to admire its stark heights and to suppress any fear he might have if one of the great ones awakening from his repose to escape back into the world of the living. He crossed into the cemetery, failing to notice the two guards who greeted him as he stood by the gate. The air in the cemetery was crisp and clear, the lush trees had cast their shadows over the cemetery lawn. A deep, majestic silence had taken hold over the vast courtyard. He walked to the center of the graveyard and, having laid down his hemp bag, took a seat near the water fountain. The exquisite scents that emanated from the cemetery lawn rejuvenated his heart like nothing else could. He cast a glance at the many tombstones that were planted atop the different wings of the cemetery, and then took a deep breath. He read the names inscribed on them, pausing to reflect on how those very names are what gave these gravesites their majesty and grace. He closed his eyes, and began to imagine a large tomb adorned with marble, upon which was written the name "Cain Goldstreak Gravedigger." He could see his wife holding a wreath of roses, pacing towards his gravesite, her heart ailing and the tears from her eyes flowing incessantly. In turn, Cain himself began to shed tears, and as the teardrops flowed from his eyes he muttered to himself, "I know she loves me. She'll miss me greatly." But then again, she most certainly will take great pride in her husband, buried as he is among the greatest men who lived. Suddenly, he wondered to himself whether the world would even allow for him to be buried here, and he was immediately overtaken with rage.

He shook his head, knowing that the answer was certainly in the negative. After all, I am responsible for the deaths of millions. The living are ignorant they don't see how valuable death is, they don't perceive its advantages, its charms. Is it not a godsend for those sick and ailing, who spend their days in torment, without any hope of relief?"

Is death naught but the ultimate truth?

Let's say death was eradicated at some point. How would the Earth be able to accommodate all these people?

Were it not for death, no human would know the value of life. It is through death that humans have come to know the satisfaction of sacrificing one's self for the sake of God, for the sake of one's beliefs, one's nation.

God created life, and has brought about death, so it must be a necessity.

Death is brought about in a myriad of ways through war, through ideology, through disease, though earthquakes and tremors, through volcanoes and other natural disasters. Through revolutions.

Were it not for the ideas of Voltaire and Rousseau there would have been no French Revolution (1789) and France would have never been liberated from the yoke of tyrannical kings backed by the authoritarianism of the church. When ideologies clash, wars break out. Wars, in turn, take their fair share of bodies and souls. The expansion of empires also led to wars, greed to the rise of colonialism and the exploitation of the masses. In turn, these masses rose up against injustice and tyranny and for the sake of liberty and dignity, and in the aftermath revolutions broke out. These revolutions led to battles and the shedding of blood. These revolutions led to death.

Isn't death better than life?

What every saint and every Sufi ever wanted in the world was to die, drawn by the idea of meeting their Beloved. Justice, freedom, equality, human rights all ideas and concepts that were consecrated and consolidated in the twentieth century, by means of death.

Everyone thinks I'm evil because they see nothing but the victims, the blood, the destruction, the wreckage. They are outraged by the deaths of women, of the elderly, of children. My sword cuts deep, and everyone is within my hand's reach. It's only in the nature of things that a few innocent bystanders get in their way, but that's a small – and necessary price to pay. The price of democracy was paid in blood. The price of freedom is innocent lives. The price of civilization and the attendant need to solidify the rule of law was paid in the souls that were sacrificed by the various nations of the world at one altar after the other. It is for this reason that nations seek to protect these ideas with all their might, and if someone or something tried to deprive them of these sacred cows then they are always ready to pay the ultimate price in blood over and over again until their rights are restored.

Given that death is the source of all this greatness, shouldn't I be considered among the great ones? The greatest of the greatest, even?

Death has done much for the majority of people. It has helped contribute to the formation of our present state of greatness, and helped to constellate the various ideologies that they sought to further with every resource at their disposal. They coerced mankind into serving their ideologies, and turned them into pawns. If need be, they were willing to wage an endless series of bloody wars, all in order to accomplish their intended goals.

I have my own ideology, and I work long and hard to see to its implementation. I'm as great as anyone is, and I haven't had to die to be great – death is no prerequisite to greatness.

If the graveyard of the greats is the proper resting place for those who changed the twentieth century, then I too, as a living person, have a place here. And I will go in death, and so will my children and grandchildren after I'm gone. We are alive, digging graves, burying the dead, all for the sake of our ideology. The best ideology is that which lasts the longest.

Long live my ideology! Long live the ideology of the grave diggers!

Cain turned his attention to the graves.

"Death is great. . .Yes, death is great! But I am greater than all of you! This is my graveyard – mine alone! This colossal wall is my fence, delimiting the boundaries of my domain!"

"I'm a grave digger, and I will dig the grave of anyone who threatens my domain! My greatness lies in my continued life. Yes, you are all great. But I'm the one who dug your graves, and I'll continue to do so, until I've eliminated everyone."

After emptying his chest, the grave digger breathed a sigh of relief. He convinced himself that he was great, and that his greatness necessitated his continued life. The need to continue his work reinvigorated him. He had a mission to accomplish and he was here to accomplish that mission. He picked up his bag and extended his hand unconsciously to his keychain to make sure it was still there.

He proceeded to the fourth wing, making his way through while mumbling a song that he had in his head. He carried his lantern in order to illuminate the caskets that were stacked up before him. The shelves were packed to the brim with coffins. Strangely, there didn't seem to be any open spaces. There was nothing for him here.

He shut the door behind him as he walked out, and the sound of the door squeaking irritated him. He locked the door with his key, and said to himself, "I suppose overcrowdedness is becoming a problem here too." Come to think of it, the dead faced a more harrowing plight than the living in this respect. After all, the dead don't leave the cemetery until Judgment Day.

Cain thought about mass graves. He deemed it a viable solution for the growing problem of congestion – for both the living and the dead. It can be done swiftly and with absolute discretion, and that will do away with the need for gratuitous ceremony. All that is needed is a couple of bulldozers to dig a big pit in which all the corpses can be cast, and then take the earth and put it back where it came from. Afterwards, all the grave diggers will need to do is wash their hands, and it would be as if nothing happened.

But for the greats, things are different. They need to be interred with the same degree of magnificence and splendor that they enjoyed in their worldly palaces. He opened the third wing, and the spaciousness that he found filled him with delight. He began to sing. . .

"Oh, what a night! And the future is bright!"

He beheld the sight of the bones that lay before him scattered and dry. He picked them up one by one and organized them carefully right next to the wall. He picked up the skeleton and noticed that it had cotton balls in its ears, which put an end to his singing. "Maybe this guy's family knew how terrible my voice is and decided to spare him the pain," he said with a grin. "My apologies, dear sir. We'll all end up where you are some day." He resumed singing.

"Oh, what a night! And the fut. . ."

He knew to handle the corpses of the dead with professionalism and skill. He had lost touch with his emotions a long time ago. He needed to make room for his new tenant. He took the bones that he had assembled next to the wall and placed them in his bag, followed by two skulls. As he extended his head to grab his shovel, it slipped from his grasp and came tumbling down on the grave floor, resulting in a thunderous noise. As if provoked, one of the skulls began to roll around on the floor, pacing back and forth. The grave digger was aghast, seemingly incapable of believing what was happening before his very eyes. He appeared visibly shaken. The blood in his veins turned cold and his heart was paralyzed with fear. His teeth began to chatter, and the pupils in his eyes began to expand. The hair on his head stood and turned to white, and all this time the skull continued to pace back and forth with terrifying agility. He began to sweat profusely. There was nothing he could do but run in fear. It felt like the graveyard was going to crumble over his head. He was going hell for leather, and yet he couldn't fight the feeling that the skull was behind him in swift pursuit. He didn't even bother to shut the door behind him. All he could do was shout:

The skulls are moving! The dead are rising! The skulls are after me!

CHAPTER 3
A Mysterious Crime

People are afraid of death. They eschew the very thought of it, hoping thereby to stay clear of its grasp. Death is a most unwelcome visitor – despised, rude even bringing nothing but sorrow and worry in its wake. It doesn't depart before leaving its mark. The bereaved – wailing and howling over their loss – search for consolation and solace, and they find no better place for it than in religion.

> We belong to God, and to Him, one day, we shall return (Qur'an 2:156).

> He that believeth in me, though he were dead, yet shall he live (John 11:25).

But then there are those who believe in metempsychosis. They hold that the deceased shall be born again instantaneously. As the body undergoes death, it disintegrates and withers away, and the soul is left to wander the skies in search of a new home. This it finds in the form of a newborn baby whose body – raw and unwilted – is an appropriate vehicle to lead the soul along the next stage of its journey.

Among peoples for whom metempsychosis is a reality, it is common for well-wishers to comfort the deceased's relatives by reminding them of this fact. Grief-stricken and hopeless, the mournful are warned that their dejection and bitterness may be spoiling the milk in the breast of their loved one's new mother.

For the grave digger, life after death was precisely what he was afraid of. Having witnessed signs of life in the skull, he collapsed and had to be transported on a stretcher to the nearest hospital. The most well-trained specialists were called to his side in the Intensive Care Unit. For precaution's sake, increased security measures were instituted inside the hospital and in its immediate environs. Despite the lengths gone to keep the situation under wraps, word of the incident had reached the news media, which dutifully shared the report with the various radio stations and television broadcast networks. The next day, the news was all over the front pages of all the major newspapers and magazines, with the various headlines worded in such a way as to reflect each publication's political slant and peculiar take on world events.

Grave Digger Violently Assaulted

New Terror Wave Strikes in the Heart of the Graveyard of the Greats

Grave Digger in the Critical Care Unit

Violence Erupts Between the Grave Digger and Unknown Terrorists

Grave Digger Bravely Defends the Graveyard of the Greats, Prevents Terrorists from Infiltrating

The World Nature Organization issued a press release condemning the despicable act. It noted that the terrorists had made a particularly big mistake in assaulting the grave digger, in that – in attacking the grave digger – they had acted rather short-sightedly: after all, once they are apprehended and handed over to the International Criminal Court, they will find no one to dig their graves for them. Instead, they'll be left to rot out in the open, where crows and other birds of prey will go about picking apart their corpses unhindered.

Rose bouquets of different shapes and hues made their way to the hospital, along with heaps of personalized cards congratulating the grave digger on the success of his operation and praying that he will rapidly regain his earlier state of health and vigor and go back to doing what he does best. Even the hospitals' terminally ill patients breathed a sigh of relief, comforted by the knowledge that their erstwhile fears of dying and having no one who would be able to bury them were premature.

The Security Council called its fifteen member states to hold an emergency special session to discuss a response to the crisis. It particularly urged the council's five permanent members – each of which represent the great powers of the world – to attend, noting the seriousness of the situation.

At its permanent headquarters in the French city of Lyon, the International Criminal Police Organization (INTERPOL) was on full alert. It issued a series of orange notices marked as high-priority bound for the regional offices it has spread out in all member states worldwide, and commissioned a host of special investigators to look into the matter and uncover the facts.

The United Nations rushed to dispatch a contingent of peacekeepers to the Graveyard of the Greats, and the White House made an official request to the twin intelligence agencies of the CIA and the FBI to investigate what happened and to publish their findings in a detailed report. The Pentagon – the nerve center of America's defense establishment – ordered that two fighting battalions be stationed at each of the four corners surrounding the graveyard.

World reaction to the incident varied greatly – some nations refused to comment on the matter at all and decided to suspend judgment until the results of the official investigations are released, while others had no qualms with condemning the attack on the grave digger as an act of aggression.

Slowly, Cain began to recover, and the day came when he would regain consciousness after having remained in a coma that lasted for three days. The doctors then permitted the lead investigator from INTERPOL to interview the patient. The investigator entered the room in which he was staying and asked everyone to leave.

They were finally alone. Cain's health was in great shape. Everything had gone back to normal, with the exception of Cain's stubborn hair, which stayed vertical and refused to be tamed despite Cain's many attempts at combing his hair, washing it, getting it blow dried and even applying different kinds of hair sprays and gels to get the strands to loosen up, all to no avail.

The investigator began walking towards the hospital bed. He had many years of experience under his belt investigating complicated cases like this. At first, the investigator had used his hand to cover up a smirk that seemed inappropriate given the situation at hand. Then he extended his hand to greet the patient, and took a seat across from the hospital bed and readied himself to hear Cain's version of what happened.

The grave digger obliged, and started to go over in the most intricate detail the course of events that led to his stay in the hospital. The investigator listened attentively, and although he could see that the grave digger's hair had turned grey from fright he nevertheless had his doubts about parts of Cain's story. He finished up his interview with Cain and proceeded to make his way out of the hospital room, intent on discovering the truth for himself.

The graveyard became swarmed with law enforcement personnel. The armed forces were also called in to secure the premises, and along with their munitions and supplies proceeded to form a ring around the graveyard and to impose a curfew on the residents of the townships that bordered it. Journalists and anchors flocked to the scene, followed by religious clerics who wanted to examine the situation for themselves. They all gathered for a meeting in the graveyard's reception room, whereupon each of them proceeded to give their take on the momentous event that had brought them all together. The atmosphere was palpably tense. For every moment of reasoned and polite dialogue there were ten in which tempers flared and blows were exchanged.

Helicopters roamed the skies above the graveyard with growing intensity, surveying the area and searching for remnants of the terrorist cell that carried out the attack on the graveyard, in hopes that they might still locate a few of them hiding in the lush tree covered hills that encompassed the graveyard. Nearby, army units were on stand by, prepared for any eventuality that might arise. Those following the news that night were terror-stricken.

News reporters gathered outside the graveyard's main gate with cameras and recording devices on hand. Each device was equipped with a label that indicated the name of the station that they worked for. Arguments ensued after armed guards prohibited the news reporters from proceeding to the garden area inside the graveyard's walls. Shortly thereafter the lead investigator arrived in a fancy car and the reporters flocked to meet him. The investigator waved the reporters away with his hand, preferring to check in on the security personnel stationed at the graveyard premises first.

A closed-door meeting was held with senior officers from all the major security agencies that were on call that night, and by the conclusion of the meeting they had agreed upon a plan. A Finnish Special Forces Unit – highly trained in the use of infiltration and storming tactics – will charge the graveyard's third wing. Strict orders were given forbidding the unit from using live fire to subdue the skull, as the plan emphasized the need to apprehend the skull while sparing it any damage. In the case of extreme necessity, the attack team would be permitted to shoot in the air in order to frighten the skull into surrendering. Zero hour had been set.

After much delay, and only after a thorough scrutiny of their bona fides, news reporters were finally permitted to enter the graveyard complex. The questions came flying:

What happened today at the graveyard?

Lead investigator:

– Out of concern for the success of the impending operation and with the interests of the world community in mind, I suffice with saying that everything is going according to plan.

– Is it true that we are witnessing the resurrection of the dead?

The lead investigator pointed his finger at the surrounding graves and tombstones and said, "Look around you. Everything is fine. The graveyard is safe and secure."

"Were any of the greats hurt in the attack?" one of the reporters asked guilefully.

"Rest assured, none of them suffered any harm."

"Did any of them rise from the dead?" another reporter asked inquisitively.

"They never died," replied the investigator, tongue in cheek.

"They will always be alive in our hearts. But we're probably going to need another twenty four hours in order for all of the facts to come out."

A slew of questions followed:

– What was the fate of the terrorists in the aftermath of the attack? What was the fate of the terrorists in the aftermath of the attack?

– How many of them were there? How many of them were there?

– What nationalities do they hail from? What nationalities do they hail from?

– Is it true the grave digger was killed in the attack? Is it true the grave digger is in actuality dead?

The questions began to multiply, and the only answer that could be heard was the sound of the questioner's echo. The investigator then concluded the press conference abruptly and left the garden area. The faces of the reporters betrayed their sense of confusion and worry. At this time, one of the reporters made their way to the graveyard's reception room, where religious clerics were debating the incident on their own terms. The reporter rushed to ask: "Is resurrection at hand, respected Imam?"

"Is this a joke to you?" The Imam replied with a mix of anger and sympathy. "Do you think the resurrection is simply a cinematic performance? It appears the situation is much more precarious than you are willing to admit."

"Indeed, our Lord Jesus Christ rose to life on the third day following his death," the priest jumped in. "So, this isn't the first time someone rose from the dead."

"Do you mean to say," one of the journalists shot back, "that the grave digger was right in suggesting that what we are witnessing here is the resurrection of the dead?"

"Did not the Christ tell his disciples, 'Verily, verily, I say unto you, The hour is coming, and now is, when the dead shall hear the voice of the Son of God: and they that hear shall live.' (John 5:25)," replied the priest in pious certitude.

The imam, his eyes closed and his tongue preoccupied with mantras glorifying the Creator, raised his hands as if to beseech God and asseverated, "On that Day, 'Faces shall be resplendent, looking towards their Lord,' (Qur'an 75:22-23). And the son of Mary will descend from the Heavens as a just ruler and a fair judge."

"I think it's safe to say, then, that the Final Hour is upon us," said the reporter, as if the delightful truth had finally dawned on him. "The resurrection is here, and justice shall at last reign supreme on Earth! Why, we can finally offer our congratulations to those people with hopeless causes! Everyone ought to be celebrating now! Things are going to be well from here on out!"

"Not so fast, my son," interrupted the imam. "Certain presaging events must precede the Announcement of the Hour."

The priest knew what the imam was talking about. "One nation will rise up against another, and a famine will ensue.

The rays of the sun will go black, as will the light of the moon, and the stars will come crashing down on the Earth."

The imam picked up from where the priest left off. "The moon will split in halves, causing a multitude of earthquakes to shake at the Earth's very core. Political and moral corruption will run the show, whereupon a heap of fire will rain down on the Earth and swallow it whole."

"Please, imam, no more!" the reporter pleaded.

"The sun will rise from the West," the imam continued on.

"Gog and Magog will emerge from the Earth, and three eclipses will cover the world in darkness. But then again, no one truly knows when the Hour will come save God. Magnificent is His Might!"

The reporter cast a daunting glance at the two religious clerics. He knew what he was hearing was no silly science fiction flick. For all their sparring and quarreling in bygone days, the priest seemed to nod his head in approval at the imam's descriptions. At this point, they seemed to be concurring on everything. The sense of accord was rather contagious, and in no small time the reporter caught himself nodding in agreement as well. He curtly ended the interview and fled from the room without bidding the clerics farewell or even thanking them for their time, and rushed off to grab footage of the sun rising from the West.

The atmosphere inside the graveyard's gardens was tense. An air of nervous, menacing silence. Zero Hour was here. The reporters took up positions behind the treelines and the graveposts, hoping to observe the operation from afar. The Finnish Special Forces Unit was making final preparations to storm the third wing. Their commanding officer was putting the finishing touches on what was legitimately an inspiring oratory performance. Fear was not something that could be countenanced in a situation like this. The gate of the wing had been thrust open, with the target of the operation only steps away. The members of the unit, even in the final seconds preceding the commencement of the operation, were still hoping that the operation would be called off. Their hopes were dashed when the commanding officer raised his voice and ordered his men to attack.

The unit took one step forward and two steps back. The commanding officer repeated his order, angrily this time. The members of the unit felt stuck. One of them summoned up the courage to pass through the main gates, his finger clutching the trigger, his voice roaring in a display of contrived valor. The officer was caught off guard by the sight of the skull rushing at him in full speed. Bullets started to fly all over the place, puncturing gaping holes in the wings sturdy walls. As bullets whizzed by, and with anxiety escalating into full-fledged panic, the officer lost control of himself. His comrades pulled him back, less out of concern for their lead man and more out of fear that his shooting in a rage would get one of them killed. Shortly afterwards, the officer lost consciousness, and he was handed over to Red Cross units standing close by. The sight was a harrowing one to the remaining members of unit, who though armed to the teeth got cold feet and ran away at the sight of one of their men down.

"There's no pulling back!" shouted the commanding officer, his eyes seething with rage. "You either apprehend the skull, or you die trying!"

"Now, attack!" he pointed to the wing. "Attack!"

"Attack! Attack!" the remaining unit officers repeated after him in a loud voice that sounded almost like a shriek.

They succeeded in storming the wing, even if only reluctantly. They managed to encircle the skull, and one of them pounced on the skull and managed to take hold of it. The skull jumped back and forth between his hands, which at this point were shaking tumultuously. Finally, the officer – scared out of his wits extended his arms, clasping together his two trembling hands, and stood still. A stammering, shaking voice broke out on the radio:

"We. . .go-ot. . .the. . .sku-ull. . .sir."

The officer held out the skull in his hands as the others stared on in amazement. The whole operation had been recorded and broadcast live. The officer's hand continued to shake nervously. Suddenly, a large rat jumps out from underneath the skull and lands on the floor. As fast as it had come it was gone, having escaped into a hole underneath the wings' walls. The officers' bodies froze, hysterical and incapable of comprehending the scene that had just passed before them.

The lead investigator made his way through to the officer witha smile. He was here to inspect the skull. Taking the skull in his hands he began to twist it to and fro, and was surprised by the discovery of a long screw that was lunged in the back of the skull. With the instinct of an expert who's been dong this for years, he realized that the rat got stuck between the skull's cranium and the screw, and as it tried to break free the skull began to move along with it.

The screw looked rusty with a greyish color to it. The investigator studied it for a bit. Finally, he dislodged the screw, which dragged along with it two small pieces of bone. He proceeded to wrap them carefully into a small piece of tissue that he had in his pocket. The media cameras stood right behind him. Afterwards, his eyes fell on the hemp bag that the grave digger had abandoned there during his escape. He edged towards it to put the skull in it. Then, he turned around, and ordered the swarm of people around him to leave. The operation was now officially over.

The investigator walked over to catch a glimpse of the misty waterfall that was nearby. His hands were squeezing the tissue in which he had placed the screw. The swarm that had gathered a short time before had now largely dispersed. He was lost in contemplation. That poor rat had uncovered evidence of a crime. An act of crime by means of a long, tall screw lodged into the back of the head. It was a cruel and unusual crime. Time could no longer bear to keep it under wraps. It was imperative to call in the grave digger for further questioning in hopes of identifying who the skull belonged to. More important than that, however, was to try to uncover the truth of what happened – and who the killer might be.

CHAPTER 4
Meet and Greet

They couldn't have returned to life, even if they'd wanted to. But life didn't leave them be. It went to them.

It stealthily entered into that graveyard in hopes of gaining insight into the causes of the raging political and economic crises of the day. It hoped to walk out with a plan to put out the searing flames of hate and war that threatened to engulf everything in its path. To spare the Earth and it's peoples the harrowing fate of annihilation and non-being, something had to be done.

Whatever eminence and distinction the greats might have enjoyed in life – or even after life had passed from them – their newfound home could not escape the suffocating humidity and the distinct scent of putrefaction that the dead are known for. The gorgeous garden area that lied without stood in stark contrast to this, from which only the sweetest and most intoxicating aromas can be beheld, dispersed generously over the garden's grounds with the help of the light gentle breeze that wandered over the garden's enchantingly radiant¬ expanse, a place befit for lovers and dreamers like.

The skeleton struggled to catch his breath inside the stuffy hemp bag, filled to the seams with scattered bone parts heaped together and stuffed in carelessly. He began to poke at the skull.

"What do we do now, general? I see you're short of breath. You must have been frightened, huh?"

"Even after a decorated life spent on the battlefield leading my men into victory after victory, I must confess. . .yes, I was very frightened."

"From who?"

"The grave digger."

"Let's get out of this bag."

They managed to escape, and the general breathed a sigh of relief.

"These people are crazy," he said. "Humans like to shoot at things without thinking. Look at the way they ruined the place."

"Are you one to talk, general? You forget how many battles you've led?"

"The battles I fought in were symmetrical ones," the general replied with a voice of pride. "One strong army against another. This is different. They were armed to the teeth. We were unarmed!"

"What were you going to do if you were armed?"

"I would have fought them and went home with another victory medal to my chest."

"Were you afraid of the bullets, general?"

"Yes, they caught me off guard initially. Naturally, I was frightened. But then, I must say, the sheer inundation of bullets coming one right after the other was like music to my ears. God, I felt so alive!"

"You're a strange man, you know that?"

The skeleton stopped to think for a bit, then continued:

"You know, you might be right. Had you taken a hit from the live fire, it might have put an end to this chronic pain that you keep complaining to me about."

The skull cast a smug glance at the skeleton and said, "You got me all wrong, skeleton. Even if they hit me with bullets, they couldn't do anything to me."

"I don't understand, general. Kindly explain what you mean."

"You see, skeleton," the skull explained matter-of-factly. "I'm a general who lost all his bones. All I have left is my skull. . .in fact, I'm not really a skull."

The skeleton gaped and his pupils widened, confounded by what he had just heard.

"You mean you. . .are not. . .you? Do I understand you correctly?"

The skull exhaled, letting out a long sigh.

"My enemies are many. Nations on every continent are at war with me."

"I'm an idea."

The skeleton began to fidget around for a bit, scrummaging for pieces of the cotton ball still in his ears.

"An idea?" he asked, seeking clarification.

"An ideology, if you will."

"An idea, an ideology, it doesn't matter – how did you lose all your bones?"

"That damn grave digger stole them from me."

"The grave digger? Our grave digger?"

"None other. It was a long time. He came once with a shovel. He was very tall then. . .he had to duck to keep his head from knocking into the ceiling. He was wearing gloves, like the ones doctors wear. He was gathering all the skulls and skeletons into his bag. But it got full before he managed to get me in there. He wrapped the bag and threw it over his shoulders, and left me hear, a skull without his bones."

"You got a tear-jerker there, general."

"Oh how it irks me to think of where my bones must be now. They're probably with another skull somewhere."

"I promise you, we'll look for them together, and we'll give them back to you."

"Why, thank you! Your generosity warms my cheeks."

"You mean. . .warms your heart?"

"Well, that's what they say, but I feel warmness in my cheeks. I don't have a chest. . .do I have to spell it all out for you?"

The skeleton let out a hearty laugh, exposing his bright white teeth. Suddenly, he remembered the special forces attack from the night before, and how the skull managed to escape unharmed. Then it dawned on him.

"Tell me, why did the inundation of the bullets impress you?" he asked with a grin.

"The sound of bullets whizzing gets my juices flowing. I'm just used to it. It's like a rhythmic symphony to my ears. It's. . .extraordinary!"

"How does your head feel?"

"After the shooting stopped, I was picked up off the ground. I remember there was a distinct smell of rich tobacco in the air. I was swinging back and forth. This guy – boy, was he dressed sharp – picked me up and turned me up side down. I actually got cross-eyed for a minute. He then pulled something long from the back of my mind. It felt like a metal rod, actually. It felt very hot. I was twisting and turning in his arms until, suddenly, the pain that I've had ever since I got here disappeared, just like that."

"And when did you grace us with your presence?"

"In 1917."

General De Gaulle woke up from a deep sleep. He seemed annoyed.

"Would you guys stop with the blabbering! You guys ruined a really good dream for me. I need some peace and calm. Who knows? Maybe I'll be able to finish my memoirs."

Gamal Abdel Nasser took this opportunity to stretch his limbs a bit. He began to remember the crowds, and the millions of people who walked in his funeral.

"My ribcage still feels bruised from how badly they were wobbling my coffin. You'd think they were doing a dance routine."

"Maybe they were dancing over your grave," Hitler remarked.

"More like the coffins dancing."

"The date the skull mentioned," said Stalin with a smile, "I love that date."

"It must have been the year you were born in," Abdul Hamid said derisively.

Churchill broke out in song.

"Happy birthday, Staaaalin! Happy birthday, cutey pants!" Everyone started to sing along with Churchill.

"Why I thank you all," Stalin said. "Really, from the depths of my heart. But no, this occasion is much more important than my birthday."

"We would love to enjoy this occasion with you, Mr. Stalin. But what is it?"

"Why, of course, Mr. Nasser."

Everyone drew close to Stalin, gathered together in a circle formation. Behind them stood a grave decked out in pearls. Stalin began his story with a sigh:

"At the beginning of the twentieth century, poverty and hunger were at their utmost. Diseases and epidemics spread rampant. The Russian people in particular fell victim to this sordid state of affairs. It could not be tolerated or withstood. It paved the way to the birth of the Communist Revolution, which saved Russia and it's people from the tyranny and torment which they had suffered as a direct result of the policies of Czar Nicholas II and his supporters."

"I know this man!" Abdul Hamid said ecstatically, rejoicing upon hearing the news that the Czar had fallen.

"He was such an overweening man. His father, the Czar Alexander III, was one of my worst enemies."

"He was a strong man, though," said Hitler, who was actually quite fond of the Czars.

"He was a tyrant!" shouted Stalin, waving his arm dismissively.

"All tyrants are strong men," Hitler said, waxing philosophically. "But not all strongmen are tyrants."

Nasser shot a glance at Stalin, with eyes that were begging him to continue his story.

"Please, continue, Mr. Stalin. We're all ears."

"I'm not going to continue until we are through with this ridiculous squabble," Stalin said in a protesting voice.

De Gaulle's calm response was timely.

"I don't know. . .your silence might lead this conversation down more absurd paths."

"When hawks fall silent," Churchill remarked, and then cast a glance at Hitler. "Parrots start to prattle."

Hitler was restless. He wanted to convey his rage at the humiliation Churchill had made him suffer. He threw his hands around in a fit of rage, striking the leg of Gandhi, who had been sitting next to him. Gandhi's thigh bone was now crushed beyond recognition.

"Oh, he sure is a hawk, this one!" Churchill raised his voice to grab everyone's attention.

"He's demonstrated that by attacking Gandhi's leg."

"Why find fault with the strength of my blows?" Hitler asked with boast and pomp. "Gandhi's the one with the weak leg. Fault him for that!"

His conscience got the better of him. "I didn't mean to hurt you, Gandhi."

"No harm, no foul," Gandhi replied tenderheartedly. "A small ice chip is all that is needed to remove the feelings of pain from my leg."

"Where's Mr. Diplomacy?" Abdul Hamid pout.

"I leave the diplomacy to my Secretary of State," Kennedy said blithely. Everyone started to laugh.

But not Abdul Hamid. "Well done, sir. Foreign ministers and secretaries of state personify the character of the men that they serve. Your secretary of state, then, must have been an astounding diplomat."

"It seems to me," the skull said, his laughter dying down, "that the Sultan doesn't know who any of you are."

The skull's words struck a chord with Abdul Hamid. "This skull's got a point," he said with a smile.

The skull felt snubbed by the Sultan's remark, and responded in protest: "I am not a mere skull! I'm a general. Your Excellency, a general!"

Abdul Hamid felt reassured, thinking himself in the presence of old company. "Ah! My regards, General. You did not let me down in the slightest. You must be the commander of my janissary armies. Well, go on then. Arrest them all, and send them into exile. Maybe they could learn a thing or two about diplomacy."

"I'm no janissary!" the skull replied angrily.

His words were a blow to Abdul Hamid. "You must be the General, Mustafa Kemal. God has caused you to transform into a transmogrified version of your former self, left to fend for yourself by currying favor with a sweet word here or there, as recompense for the evil that you wreaked against the Sultan and his people."

"Please calm down, Your Excellency," said Nasser, attempting to mollify the Sultan.

"How am I supposed to calm down, when you are all barging in here, storming my palace without my permission – without an appointment, even! Where is this diplomacy of which you speak?!"

"He thinks he's in Yildiz," said De Gaulle with a scoff.

"Guards! Guards!" Abdul Hamid called out in a loud voice. No one responded to his call. He then began to howl incorrigibly, "Where is my harem? What did you people do with my harem?"

Churchill took one look at the skeleton and saw an opportunity.

"Skeleton! Let His Excellency the Sultan take a good look at you. Maybe then he'll figure out where he is."

The skeleton walked over and stood right in front of the Sultan. The Sultan looked at him the way sultans look at their minions.

"Begone, skeleton! Come back when there are meat over your bones. Your appearance does not befit our lofty presence."

"Don't forget to wear a tie," Kennedy cracked.

"We are in the lofty presence of death, Abdul Hamid!" shouted Hitler, who had lost his patience with the Sultan.

Abdul Hamid was baffled by Hitler's remark. A sultan could never die. "Death?!" He asked in a tone that betrayed his bemusement. "I see, we must be in paradise, then! Where is that river of wine and milk I was promised? Where are the houris?"

"We didn't make it to paradise just yet," mumbled Nasser.

"I can see that. I don't recognize the 'radiance of delight' (Qur'an 83:24) in your faces."

"We're still waiting our turn," Gandhi said with optimism in his voice, "for them to let us in."

Abdul Hamid rose impatiently.

"You may all sit here and wait as long as you wish. I'm going to go see the gatekeeper. There must be some kind of mistake. I'm the Caliph, for God's sake!"

"You might consider submitting a formal written request," De Gaulle said playfully.

"Don't forget to put a stamp on it too," Kennedy added, his tone actually sounding serious for once.

"I am excused from having to pay any duties and fees," replied Abdul Hamid with a resoluteness befitting of a Sultan.

"The rules of the world are one thing," Gandhi reminded him with a smile, "the rules of the afterlife are quite another."

Abdul Hamid remained on his feet. His initial look of confusion had given way to a withering anger, which could be seen clearly in his facial expression.

"Why don't you have a seat, Abdul Hamid," asked Churchill.

"Why bother yourself with standing when you can relax?"

The Sultan took a seat.

"You're never going to hear back from them, Abdul Hamid," said Stalin.

"Thanks, that's reassuring!" he retorted back sarcastically.

"In here, justice reigns supreme," said Gandhi, his voice resounding with confidence. "Not like on Earth."

"I still don't know who you gentlemen are," noted Abdul Hamid calmly.

"You must all have come after me."

"Oh, pardon me, gentlemen" the skeleton volunteered. "I'll go ahead and introduce you to each other. I know you all very well. I remember just how much I kept track of your stories. I even published them in my newspaper."

"Glad to see we're back to diplomatic protocol," said Abdul Hamid, his angry temperament largely gone now.

"Please, continue."

"We are here in the 'Graveyard of the Greats.' The graveyard contains a number of wings. We here are in the third wing. The oldest residents of this wing are the General – that skull over there – then His Excellency the Sultan Abdul Hamid II, the most famous sultan of the Ottoman Empire." Abdul Hamid exulted upon hearing himself described in such a manner, which renewed his sense of majesty and glory.

The skeleton picked up where he left off, drawing everyone's attention to the leader of the Soviet Union.

"Mr. Stalin."

"Stalin?" Abdul Hamid inquired. "What does he sell?"

"Oh, nothing," replied Hitler sarcastically, then continued in fluent Egyptian Arabic, "just 'water in a neighborhood full of watersellers,' isn't that right, Mr. Nasser?"

"Ah, I get it! You mean he sells propaganda and cheap slogans to other politicians?"

"Ah, I see!" Abdul Hamid shouted, as if he'd split the atom. "You mean he's a book peddler?"

Kennedy guffawed loudly.

"Oh yes, literary masterpieces with beautiful red bounding.

Marx. . .Engels. . .Lenin. . ."

The skull decided to partake in the fun, shouting out loud as if he were an auction dealer.

"Going once, going twice! Any takers?"

"Enough buffoonery!" De Gaulle exclaimed angrily.

"The way you are all acting, you'd think we were in a working class café in Cairo."

Abdel Nasser recalled the fond memories he had had in Cairo's neighborhoods. He thought it would be nice to play along.

"Let me get a hookah, Gandhi! Don't forget the charcoal!"

De Gaulle was displeased with how the Mahatma was being treated.

"This is unacceptable, Nasser! Monsieur Gandhi is no waiter!"

Everybody thought of Mr. Gandhi as polite, not to mention weak. It wasn't right to pick on him.

"Oh, we're just fooling around!" Nasser pleaded. "Death has kept us silent for too long."

"Death can be quite boring without a sense of humor," Kennedy concurred.

Nasser shot a glance at Gandhi, and apologized in the only way he knew how – the traditional Arab way.

"As for Misyoooo Gandhi. . .ah, let me have them cheeks! I love this guy!"

He kissed his forehead in loving friendship. Gandhi's eyes brimmed with tears, having been moved by the gesture.

It was Stalin's turn to boast.

"I am Joseph Anatoli Stalin," he said, directing his speech to Sultan Abdul Hamid.

"The leader of the Soviet Union."

"Ah, a new Czar! Away with you! I can't stand the Czars!" "Pardon me, Sultan! I despise them just as much as you do!

I was the one who solidified the Communist state which brought an end to their rule and relieved the Russian people and their neighbors of their presence."

Abdul Hamid approached Stalin reverently and extended his hand to greet him.

"A pleasure to make your acquaintance, dear sir."

The skeleton continued to introduce the greats to one another, when all of a sudden someone began to knock at the door violently. Everyone was taken off guard. Frightened, the skull ran off and hid behind President John F. Kennedy.

"What's the matter with ya, pal?" Kennedy asked bemusedly, with a touch of sympathy in his voice.

"You know who it is," the skeleton replied. He was out of his wits. "It's gotta be the grave digger."

Silence fell upon the room. All that could be heard were the knocks at the door, which increased in violence and intensity.

CHAPTER 5
Who Does the Skull Belong To?

Thick, gloomy clouds heaved together in the skies above the French city of Lyon. September had come dragging the sorrow and volatility that it was all too famous for.

It was a scowling, miserable, lifeless day. The hustle and bustle of morning traffic passing to and fro and the rustling cry of city streets served to resuscitate it somewhat. Vehicles began to pull off to the side of the road to make way for a patrol car whose horn honked with a cadence most unsettling to the ears. The morning light, as colorful as the prism of a rainbow, stretched out to illuminate the long road which was still wet from the soft morning rain. A longwinded procession followed in the patrol car's tracks, stopping in front of an enormous building. Out comes the grave digger, donned with dark colored shades, surrounded by

four men with burly figures charged with the task of escorting the grave digger in his ventures.

Inside the head of INTERPOL had been waiting to receive the grave digger in his office. The building's façade overlooked a splendid vista, whose charms and captivating natural scenery extended as far as the eye can see. With an effortless glance a visitor may behold the glistening stream of a river whose waters gushed forth between two mountains adorned in serried conifers. The mountain's dashing peaks beamed up towards the sky, cradling the clouds in its warm embrace. The earth, dry and yearning to be touched, was due to be visited by continuous rain, and the wind was carrying the clouds along to whence they shall loosen their burdens, leaving in its wake a misty fog which gave the skies the appearance of smoke without fire.

With a gesture of his hands the investigator invited the grave digger to have a seat on the leather couch in the center of the office. The investigator had been busy packing his pipe with a richly scented tobacco whose vapors continued to invigorate the skulls' senses. He took a seat in the chair that was across from the grave digger, and immediately ordered that a cup of coffee be prepared for his guest.

"I'm sorry that I called you over here directly from the hospital, but we have some important matters that need to be taken care of immediately. Any information you can give us about the skull will be immensely helpful."

The investigator's question hit the grave digger like a rock. Fear and trepidation noticeably shot across his face, and for a moment it appeared as if the grave digger was going to take cover behind the couch. He had called to mind that dreadful night when the skull simply wouldn't stop circling around him.

"Ease up, man," said the investigator, scurrying to pacify him.

"Everything is under control."

The grave digger seemed doubtful.

"Really?

Then what happened to the dead?

Did Hitler come back to life?

Is Kennedy going to resume office in the United States?

And what about the living?

What's going to happen to us?"

"What's going to happen to us?" the investigator recapitulated, slightly taken aback by the strangeness of the question.

"Yes, us. We're not dead yet, so what are we to do vis-à-vis the resurrection?

"Resurrection? What are you talking about?" the investigator asked in earnest.

"Why, the resurrection of the dead! Where skulls run around and. . ."

The investigator interrupted the grave digger's frenzy with a hearty laugh.

"Oh, so you don't know about the rat that was moving the skull around?"

The grave digger had a disturbed look on his face.

"Why would a rat do that?"

"Oh, they just like to get under our skin from time to time," responded the investigator, obviously in jest.

"What brought him to the graveyard, you think? Curiosity?"

"Hunger perhaps," replied the investigator. He then lightly tapped the grave digger on his knee and said, "Drink your coffee. I'll explain what happened."

The investigator lit his pipe and took a deep draw, exhaling the smoke upwards in the direction of the office ceiling. The grave digger was listening attentively to the investigator's account, and a look of relief flooded his face.

"So that's what happened?!"

"That's what happened. You know, you seem to have reversed that Aesop's Fable. This time, a rat went into labor, and gave birth to a mountain!"

The grave digger breathed a sigh of relief.

"Boy do I wish I can get my hands on that rat!"

"Hey now, that rat ought to be a considered an international hero. He singlehandedly exposed a crime of murder that had gone unnoticed for centuries. He even helped us to uncover the murder weapon, a long screw which had been drilled vertically into the skull."

"A hero indeed!" exclaimed the grave digger sardonically.

"You guys ought to offer him a position here at INTERPOL."

"Really, I mean it. Even the best investigation teams couldn't have given us the kind of information that that rat was able to uncover for us. And don't you forget how kind he has been to you. Those days of respite in the hospital replenished your good looks. That hair of yours now has a stunning greyish hue worthy of your stature."

The grave digger hung his head in embarrassment. But the investigator wasn't going to let him mope.

"Please, do tell me what you know about the skull's owner." "It's been such a long time," the grave digger responded ruefully. "I'll make it easy for you."

"How so?"

"The skull's owner is one of the greats," the investigator said with a calm that indicated confidence.

"You seem sure of yourself."

"I'm definitely sure. The skull was buried in the Graveyard of the Greats, after all."

"You're quite perspicacious, I must admit."

"The skull's owner was probably some kind of president or king. Maybe even an emperor. Or perhaps he was an intellectual or an artist. Actually, I'm beginning to think he might have been a military commander, perhaps a general."

"Yes, yes he was!" shouted the grave digger.

"What's that?"

The grave digger placed his hand on his temple, as if to speed up the process of memory recovery. Then he scratched the back of his head, his nails penetrating the follicles of his copious white hair.

"I remember he had stars, military insignia made of metal. . ."

"The kind of insignia worn by generals!" the investigator responded vigilantly.

"He must be a general!" shouted the grave digger as if the very idea had completely eluded him until then.

The investigator cast him an astonished look. "Wait, wait. . .you say he's a general, but what reminded you of his stars?"

The grave digger altered his seating posture and went on to elaborate:

"A long time ago, when I was still new to this job, I used to handle the dead delicately and reverently. I remember this one time when I was busy cleaning up the place and interring whatever scattered bones I found in a bag. That's when I found the stars and other military insignia. I knew they belonged to the deceased, and so I preserved them together with the deceased's other remains as a token of my respect. But the bag filled up quickly, and so I left the skull behind, thinking that I would come back at a later date to reunite it with the deceased's other remains. But I guess my workload got too heavy and I ended up forgetting about it."

The investigator had been listening carefully.

"How do you remember this incident so well, given how long ago this all must have been?"

"I was angry that day. One of the stars had ripped through the bone-laden bag, and that's how I knew the star belonged to the skull."

"I tip my hat off to you, grave digger! You have quite the memory on you. Only high-ranked army officers of particularly noteworthy distinction are given those stars. The owner of the skull must have been one such officer."

"How can we be sure he's not some ordinary, low-level officer?"

"If he were so, he wouldn't have been buried in the Graveyard of the Greats."

"So we're sure he's a general?"

"Yes, I'm sure. The skull certainly belongs to a general. But which one? And who might have killed him?"

A plethora of questions started to fly around in the investigator's mind, which was busy searching for clues that might help solve the mystery. All the same, he stood up to bid the grave digger farewell. He urged him to keep in touch anytime he had new information to share that might help the investigation team crack the case. He also urged him to forget about his fears and to go back to digging graves as it was his wont to do. After the warm farewell, the grave digger departed INTERPOL headquarters with a heart firmly at rest, certain that his terrifying nightmares had finally come to an end.

CHAPTER 6

Five Hundred Dollars

The sound of knocking pierced through the stark, stagnant quiet like the beating of a drum, and began picking up pace. The skull – which had taken cover behind President John F. Kennedy – was beside himself, becoming more and more terrified with every subsequent knock. Through a series of gestures the President had tried to comfort the skull, but to no avail. Churchill was the only one to brave his fears, but only after discovering the source of the clamor: a coffin – decked out in gold and diamonds – shaking tenaciously in one of the corners of the wing. He then called out, addressing all in attendance:

"Everyone relax! It's not the grave digger."

Gamal Abdel Nasser sprung up and rushed towards the coffin, having also noticed that it was wobbling around.

"Everyone follow me! Me and Mr. Churchill have figured out where all the thrashing is coming from."

Poise and serenity began to warm the hearts of those in attendance, with the exception of the skull, which was still trembling on account of the frightening experience it had.

Hitler moved towards the skull and took it into his hands.

"At ease, General!" shouted Hitler.

"Or would you prefer I have you shipped to the concentration camps along with the Jews?"

"Damn you, Hitler!" replied the skull, squirming in the Fuhrer's hands.

"Do you really think you can go back to giving your callous and cruel commands!"

"Are you mad, General?! You're talking about my glories here! Have you forgotten the marvelous feeling of acclaim that comes with giving orders?"

General Skull knew what Hitler was talking about. Everyone proceeded to move in the direction of the tomb, the source of all the clamoring and the commotion. An empathetic spider had spun a web around it, hoping thereby to protect it from the general, who in his rage would have wished he could detonate the tomb and whoever was in it.

As Gandhi began to take the cobweb apart Stalin heard an intermittent voice emerge from the tomb and brought his ear closer to hear more clearly.

"I think I hear someone calling for help!" shrieked De Gaulle.

"Please, help me!" the voice groaned. "I'm stuck. I think I'm going to suffocate in here!"

"Hurry, let's open this damn casket!" shouted Abdel Nasser as he clutched the tomb with his hands. "Someone is calling for help! It is one of the most obligatory of Arab customs to give aid to the distressed!"

Hitler, skull still in hand, was standing next to Sultan Abdel Hamid. They, along with everyone else, were patiently waiting for Gandhi to finish cleaning the fabric. The inscribed engraving on the casket slowly began to reveal itself, and everyone read along:

"Died due to complications arising from myasthenia gravis. . .The renowned millionaire, Aristotle Onassis."

Everyone laughed in relief. Churchill was busy lifting the coffin's lid and succeeded in liberating the corpse that lied buried underneath. The corpse – already visibly terrified from the experience of having screamed his lungs out for ages without anyone seemingly bothering to notice – grew even more afraid at the sound of the boisterous, incessant laughter.

"Don't be afraid!" shouted the skull. "Wait, we're going to help you up!"

De Gaulle and Abdel Nasser took turns helping Onassis out of his coffin. In the midst of taking deep, heaving breaths, Onassis surveyed the men that stood around him. Their pallid faces and raggedy clothes drew the millionaire's astonishment as to their squalid state.

"You must be paupers. . .which neighborhood are you all from?" he asked.

"How much money you got?" asked Kennedy, answering a question with a question.

"Oh, you know, a few billion dollars," replied the millionaire haughtily.

"Well, as for us, dear sir," began the skull, with a mocking tone in his voice, "why, we don't own a thing!"

De Gaulle took an examining look at the casket.

"Why, that's not true. It seems you are only richer than us by $500."

The millionaire felt perplexed, unable to understand what De Gaulle was talking about.

"He means the cost of the coffin," Kennedy said with a laugh. "And to think we slabbed the streets with gold in order for people to step on it," said Stalin, wringing his hands angrily.

In a midst of rage, Stalin attacked the coffin with his hands, and in one fell stroke of his iron grasp the coffin shattered into four different pieces, each piece flying around in a different direction.

The skeleton laughed, noticeably pleased by the result.

"We are now, each and every one of us, once again, a classless society. Allow me to introduce you to your esteemed roommates. Stalin. . . De Gaulle. . . Churchill. . ."

The millionaire interrupted the skeleton's introduction and rushed to greet Churchill warmly.

"Mr. Churchill, my dear friend, how delightful it is to see you again! Please excuse me for not recognizing you at first. You've changed much since our last shared junket aboard the Christina some time ago."

"It's a delight to see you as well, Onassis. As for my appearance, I advise you to take one look at the mirror yourself, and you'll understand why I look this way."

"Do you gentlemen mind waiting till I finish?" the skeleton asked annoyingly.

"Abdel Hamid. . . Hitler. . . John Kennedy," the skeleton continued, pointing at each of the greats as he introduced them.

The millionaire inched slightly behind Churchill upon hearing John Kennedy's name. He recalled having spent many lovely years in the company of Mrs. John Kennedy, and wasn't interested in getting into trouble. As the millionaire's mind wandered the skeleton began wrapping up his introductions, with the word 'Gandhi' resonating in the millionaire's ear. Once introductions were over, the millionaire rushed to catch up with the skeleton and the skull who were sitting by the wing's main column. Stalin took a seat near Abdel Hamid II,

Hitler, De Gaulle and Abdel Nasser. Winston Churchill was blowing smoke from his cigar into the air, engaged in intriguing conversation with John Kennedy.

Little time passed, and Gandhi joined the millionaire near the column, while the latter took the initiative in engaging Gandhi in conversation.

"You must be the Mahatma Gandhi, then?"

"Yes, I am Gandhi."

The millionaire looked bashful.

"It would appear my death has been far more fortuitous than my life. Wealth accumulation had sidetracked me then, and I simply didn't have time to meet with you in person. But I am much delighted to be meeting with you now."

"Consider yourself at home – or, might I say, in your humble palace. Everyone of us welcomes you with open arms."

"Much obliged, Mr. Gandhi. You are every much of the gentle, tender, and gracious man that they said you were."

The millionaire then turned his attention to the skeleton.

"I thought I heard you introduce me to Stalin. Is that really him?"

"Why, yes, that is Stalin."

With the corner of his eye the millionaire tried to catch a distant glimpse of Stalin, who was still seated in the vicinity of Sultan Abdel Hamid.

"This man is as dangerous in death as he was in life," he whispered.

"He must have scared you out of your wits when he smashed your coffin!" said the skull gleefully, as if expressing delight at the millionaire's misfortune.

"Why, yes he is such a coarse man!" said the skeleton. "In fact, I do recall the last statement he released before his death.

. .I remember him saying, 'All systems grow old and wither. We must all stop to ponder the ends of history.' It's a random statement, but I'm sure he had some kind of ulterior motive in giving it."

"Actually, Mr. Skeleton," replied the millionaire.

"This statement was not a casual one. In fact, it kept the financial centers of the world preoccupied for three years, each of them trying to figure out what Stalin had meant by 'ends of history.'"

"Based on what I know of Stalin, he's a very perspicacious man," noted the skull.

Gandhi took a moment to think and then remarked, "He was talking about the disintegration of democratic practice and the need to give people breathing room."

"Why, what serendipity that he died before we went bankrupt," the millionaire thought to himself.

"Be careful," Gandhi warned the millionaire.

"You don't know what they might do if they hear you."

"Please, keep this a secret between us."

"And don't you dare let the skeleton in on what you're thinking," Gandhi advised.

"Why? Is he a KGB agent? A close friend of Stalin?"

"I don't think he's a friend per se. To anyone, actually. But he's always on the look out for secrets to surprise the world with. That's the thing with journalists, they're always striving to be the first to break the news."

"Thank you, Mr. Gandhi. With that said, it is my hope that we can be close friends from here on out." Their hands embraced, the handshake acting as a down payment for eternal friendship.

THE ARGUMENT heated up in the Sultan's circle, and everyone joined in to hear what the fuss was about.

"The nineteenth century was a period of stability the world over!" said Abdel Hamid.

"Well said, Sultan," De Gaulle retorted approvingly.

Churchill thought an explanation was in order.

"That was because of the equilibrium in the balance of power between the great powers."

"But the Russian Czar had gotten eerily close to breaking this balance when he waged war against you in 1877," Stalin noted, directing his words to Abdel Hamid.

"He supported the Serbs and Bulgarians in their quest for independence from the Ottomans. 250,000 Russian infantry marched forth to come to their aid, along with 600 cannons."

Hitler whistled in amazement.

"That's quite a formation indeed. I imagine you must have lost that war, oh Sultan!"

"But I remember reading that the Ottoman army fought with bravery and courage in that battle," remarked Kennedy.

"Thank you, Mr. President," said Abdel Hamid, receiving Kennedy's words appreciatively.

"Kind words from a handsome man."

"The war ended with the Berlin treaty, which was supervised by the German Chancellor Otto von Bismarck."

Abdel Hamid nodded his head mournfully.

"It was an inequitable and injurious treaty from our standpoint, Mr. Hitler. But we had no option but to accept it."

"What was the makeup of the great powers in that time?" asked the millionaire, seeking clarification.

"The twentieth century had dawned with six great empires battling it out for pre-eminence, the oldest of which was the Ottoman Empire. . ."

". . .and the British Empire!"

". . .and the French!"

"Don't forget the German Empire," urged Hitler.

"And the Russian Empire!" Stalin roared.

"There was also the Austro-Hungarian empire," the skeleton added.

"And where were the Arabs in this period?" the skull asked Abdel Nasser.

"We were subjects of the Ottoman Empire. With time, the British and the French took an interest in us. To protect us," replied Abdel Nasser, a scoffing tone in his voice.

"What about the New World?"

Kennedy took it upon himself to answer:

"You see, skeleton, we were at work repelling the brunt of Spanish imperialism from the American continent, particularly in Mexico, Nicaragua, Haiti and the Dominicans."

"Wars of liberation," rejoined Abdel Nasser derisively.

"A gift from the United States to the peoples of Latin America."

"The same way they 'liberated' the Philippines from the Spanish," De Gaulle added along similar lines.

"It was unfortunate that the Filipino people couldn't comprehend then that we were trying to liberate them," said Kennedy, defending the American position.

"It must be their backwardness that caused them to fail to see that," said Churchill, expounding on Kennedy's words.

Stalin began to clap his hands in a scathing attack on Churchill's erroneous interpretation.

"So that's why they fought you tooth and nail for fourteen years (1899-1914)."

"No good deed goes unpunished," the millionaire thought out loud.

Kennedy continued his defense, but this time more honestly.

"We were preparing ourselves to be the sole superpower in the world by strengthening our economy and building our armed forces."

"You Americans," Hitler murmured.

"Your intentions are always evil."

"Where's the evil in strengthening one's economy?"

"Hitler's right," Stalin said.

"My feelings about him notwithstanding."

"You all didn't answer his question!" Churchill demanded.

"Why were our intentions evil?"

"How else would you describe their attack on the Philippine islands?" responded Abdel Nasser.

"It seems," Hitler said with a smirk, "that the Americans were intrigued by the European imperial club, and so they sought to join it."

The skeleton yawned.

"They gained privileged membership in it."

Kennedy tried to play down the amount of countries the United States invaded.

"It was but a few islands in the Pacific Ocean."

"What about Cuba?"

"And Panama?"

"Cut it out, De Gaulle. You're just furious that it was the Americans and not the French who built the Panama Canal, thereby connecting the Pacific Ocean with the Atlantic Ocean."

"Don't forget that it was the French who sold it to you and piled up the rewards."

"Money does amazing things," the millionaire said confidently.

Abdel Hamid sighed.

"It appears our defeat in the war against Russia allowed the other Western empires to work up an appetite for the expansive lands that were under our control."

"You must have been weak," the skull said jeeringly.

"'The Old Man of Europe,' we used to call it," Churchill said, describing the state of the Ottoman Empire at the turn of the century.

"I was the Commander-in-Chief of the Ottoman Armed Forces, the Sovereign of the Empire, and the Supreme Authority of the Muslim religion."

"The Caliph of the Muslims!" added Abdel Nasser.

"That was before corruption spread in my army's ranks, as a result of my subordinating command's conspiracies and their treachery against me. My army was an ideological one: our wars were holy wars, dedicated to the Islamic conquest. Our aim was to spread the teachings of the Glorious Qur'an!"

"Let's be frank," Stalin said.

"Didn't you fight Russia to get your hands on our caviar?"

"A man who has 365 women in his harem could use some caviar," De Gaulle satirized.

The conversation had finally steered in the direction of medicine, which was something that Gandhi was interested in and in which he had much experience.

"Nutrition, particularly from proteins, is necessary for the Sultan to be able to fulfill his obligations towards the women of his harem."

"What interest did the Russians have in the Balkan peninsula, such that they would fight for their freedom?" the skeleton asked, directing his question to Stalin.

"After all, the Bulgarians and the Serbs are of Slavic Russian descent."

The millionaire peeked his nose in the discussion.

"Your Excellency, the Sultan, what is the nature of an 'ideological army'?"

"It is an army that goes into battle courageously, willing to die for the sake of its beliefs," Abdel Hamid said. He took a moment to take a panoramic view of the closed room while he refreshed his memory, and continued.

"The Turks had taught their children how honorable it is to fight without fear. We used to call the blood we drank in battle 'cherry drink.' For the Turkish soldier, to fall as a martyr in battle was a source of great esteem and pride for himself and for his family. All Muslim mothers wish for their sons to die as martyrs."

"When the soldier forgoes his fear of death, death takes flight from him," commented Hitler.

"Indeed," added Abdel Nasser.

"When a soldier believes in the cause he is fighting for, his strength grows tenfold."

"Religion was the essence of our Ottoman Islamic ideology," Abdel Hamid continued.

"If any Turkish soldier is asked who he is, he would always respond, 'I am a Muslim. A Muslim of Turkish descent.'"

"This is imperialism, just like any other," Stalin said.

"And what would you call Russia's invasion of Korea in 1945?" Abdel Hamid responded.

Kennedy was impressed by Abdel Hamid's question.

"They had no aggressive intentions," he said with a smirk.

"They just wanted to have a picnic near China's Great Wall."

Churchill couldn't help himself either.

"Indeed, they were so impressed with the area that they didn't allow our poor Japanese allies to picnic with them."

De Gaulle tried to strike a more serious tone.

"That is why the Japanese-Russian War broke out in Port Arthur."

Churchill became serious as well.

"The Japanese used electronic devices for the first time in the history of warfare. Japanese ships would observe the movements of the Russian Navy and pass the intelligence acquired back to Japanese Central Command."

"The Russians were finally defeated in Mukden in 1905," Hitler noted, overjoyed at the prospect of gloating Russian misfortune.

"I remember those wars," the skull said.

"I remember them well, in fact. A million Japanese soldiers had participated in those battles."

The skeleton began to sing and dance.

"Japan was victorious, and Tokyo was filled with people dancing."

"I bet you're Japanese!" said Stalin, angrily rebuking the skeleton.

"Stop with this dancing or else I'll crush whatever bones you have left."

"Why even get up, Mr. Stalin?" asked Abdel Nasser, aiming to calm Stalin down by stroking his ego.

"One huff and one puff and his bones would turn into ashes."

The skeleton ceased dancing, and rushed to sit next to Kennedy, who at this point had something to say himself.

"Afterwards, a treaty was struck with American mediation under the direction of President Theodore Roosevelt."

"How ugly war is," Gandhi said, grumbling.

"It was in the aftermath of that defeat that the Russian masses in tow with the liberal bourgeoisie moved to initiate its first revolt against the Czar."

Kennedy felt vindicated.

"The bourgeoisie does indeed have an important role to play in ending injustice, as demonstrated by its role in ending the Russian Czar's dictatorial rule."

"Only the bourgeoisie can overcome the social and ethnic barriers in society and unite the people into one nation," expounded Churchill.

"If anything, the bourgeoisie is key in the formation of a nation-state."

Abdel Nasser was sorrowed by the Arab bourgeoisie's failure to fulfill its historical mission.

"The European bourgeoisie took up the task of forming nationstates, it's true. But its motives were economic: it sought thereby to open up the entire continent for production and consumption. Our Arab bourgeoisie, on the other hand, were mere stooges for foreign powers."

"Why, imperialism and capitalism go hand in hand!" said the millionaire boastfully.

"The bourgeoisie is the legitimate child of capitalism. In the end, the interests of the Russian bourgeoisie clashed with the aspirations of the proletariat."

Abdel Nasser was well aware of what happened next.

"This led the Russian laborers to end their historic alliance with the bourgeoisie and to commence an alliance with the peasants instead."

"Well said, Mr. Abdel Nasser. I personally was a strong advocate for the bourgeoisie-laborer alliance, as the bourgeoisie at the time had called for the emergence of a bourgeoisie republic, which at the time was an understandable – nay, necessary – demand along the path of revolution in the face of Czarist tyranny. But after 1917 permitting the emergence of such a system would have been meaningless, even regressive and contrary to the demands of the revolution as compared to the Soviet republic. In the end, the laborers turned against the bourgeoisie and were victorious."

"Did Japan's victory over Russia change the balance of power worldwide?" asked the millionaire.

"Britain ended up allying itself with Japan," answered Abdel Hamid.

"That's correct," Churchill said.

"We did so in order to protect Britain's interests in the Far East."

Gandhi then raised his voice in protest.

"But then the Japanese became increasingly imperious and began invading their neighbors!"

"That's the nature of power!" shouted the skull.

Abdel Nasser thought it fit to draw a connection between power, haughtiness, and greed. "Imperial rivalries led to an arms race and the deterioration of relations between the great powers."

In De Gaulle's view, the result of this deterioration in relations was that the vying powers would strike alliances with certain nations to protect themselves from others.

"The first major alliance was struck between France, Britain and Russia."

"Against the Austro-Hungarian Empire!" shouted Hitler angrily.

The skeleton understood what that meant.

"That's how the balance of power shifted from complex to simple."

"'Simple balance of power?' What does that mean" the millionaire asked simplemindedly.

"That's when the power balance consists of two states in a state of antagonism and conflict with one another," replied Churchill.

"The beginning of war," said Hitler, concluding the discussion.

CHAPTER 7
Cherry Juice

The millionaire felt lost among the other greats. It was as if they were speaking a language that was difficult to understand or even to learn. After all, he had spent his life in the company of numbers, not letters, counting money and calculating prices. In life he had deemed all discussion about politics a waste of time, but now he was ashamed of how ignorant he must have seemed among his fellow peers, each of whom were seasoned in the art of politics.

He felt deep weariness and heavy exhaustion overwhelm his eyes, and he proceeded to make his way over to his cot for some much needed rest. All it got him was twisting and turning. His eyes refused to surrender to sleep's beckoning. His outer appearance was like that of a bird trapped in a burning oven: as much as he tried to clear his head and relent to sleep's all-embracing power, he simply couldn't hold back his thoughts, which continued to gush forth and collide with full force.

He decided to set sail deep into the oceans of his imagination, his mind preoccupied with the previous discussion about how the exercise of power necessitated alliance-building and the formations of balance of power. He was determined to organize and clarify his thoughts, hoping thereby to overcome that debilitating feeling one gets upon coming face to face with one's own ignorance. He was here to win, and to win he knew he needed to be powerful.

But that was the crux of the matter: in days prior he had amassed a large amount of wealth, but now he realized that wealth alone did not suffice. Power included a variety of capabilities, and the more one possessed of them the more secure one's hold on power would be.

He needed to understand what power was, and how to measure it. He had learned that from his physics teacher while he was a student in middle school. He laughed internally at the fact that death did not prevent him from remembering that day in physics class and what it taught him about power. The teacher was lecturing about the apple that fell from the tree onto the ground. He started to foam at the mouth, wishing that that apple had fallen in his hands – or, even better, directly into his mouth. At the time his family was struggling to make ends meet, and the only time he saw apples or bananas was in his school textbooks.

Then he remembered how, after he had acquired his first million, he would never have liked to see a dining table which didn't have an ample serving of that fruit which inspired Sir Isaac Newton to discover the law of gravity. Newton was also famous for defining force – which, after all is said and done, is merely a synonym for power –

This is precisely how universal stability is induced, and how balance is maintained. But how does balance between nations emerge, and how does it hold?

To make things easy for himself, he decided to anthropomorphize this concept with material indicators. The fastest thing he could think of was how the use of the traditional scale in old times would give both buyer and seller each their due, without being slighted in the least. After a moment's reflection, he pushed the thought out of his head.

Power wasn't about weighing cheese or potatoes. He had come face to face with the elusive interactions between politics and commerce, mighty armies and the deadly weapons they used. He then relented and went back to liking the analogy of the traditional scale, having remembered that heat is measurable and atomic rays have scales.

He visualized a scale that looked similar to the one that was engraved on a courtroom wall, situated just behind the judge. He then placed power in each pan, and as the pans fell out of equilibrium he would place more power in the lighter pan. This must be what the arms race looked like: states take recourse to relying on a second states' power, leading to the formation of an alliance between the two. When there is a constellation of states with roughly equal power, the balance of power is complex; when the various constellations of states morph into two competing powers – resembling the two pans of a scale – and reach an uneasy equilibrium, the balance of power becomes simple.

Dawn broke, and the millionaire continued to be immersed in his thoughts and conceptualizations. The skeleton approached him, noticing signs of worry on his countenance.

"It appears you haven't slept at all last night. You seem worried. What's with you?"

The millionaire explained the reasons for his sleeplessness and his preoccupation with the various questions about politics raised in the previous night's discussion which he still couldn't find an adequate answer to.

The skeleton smiled understandingly.

"Mr. De Gaulle and the rest of the greats will help you resolve all of the perplexing questions that you haven't found an answer to."

The two of them approached De Gaulle, who had been seated next to Gandhi. The skeleton took the initiative to begin the question and answer session.

"Why do wars happen, Mr. De Gaulle?"

"Because interests clash and ideologies collide," answered De Gaulle.

"Violence comes about as a result of avarice and the conceitedness of power," added Gandhi.

Hitler raised his voice, hoping to have his opinion considered. "The avarice of the Jews and their increased hold on wealth led them to crystallize their ideology at their First Zionist Congress in the Swiss city of Basel in 1897! It was there that they elected Herzl!"

"Is it true you used to know Herzl, Sultan Abdel Hamid?" inquired Abdel Nasser.

"Why, yes, I did. I met Hertzl after his numerous attempts to. . ."

"What did you think of him?!" the skeleton asked, overcome with curiosity.

"He was a fox: intelligent, with a smooth tongue. He offered me his services. . ."

"Just like that? Out of the goodness of his heart?" Abdel Nasser asked, aiming to stir doubt as to Herzl's motives.

"The Ottoman Empire had been overwhelmed with debt."

"What did he offer you, Sultan?"

"Imagine this, Mr. De Gaulle," Abdel Hamid replied.

"The nerve on that mind! He asked me to allow the Jews to immigrate to Palestine!"

"We Germans know these Jews very well. They know how to hit you where it hurts."

"And what is so grievous about a few thousand Jews immigrating to Palestine?" asked Kennedy.

"We in the United States of America have welcomed millions of immigrants!"

Abdel Hamid ignored Kennedy's question.

"He tried to inveigle me with his money. He offered me an enormous amount in golden liras, the equivalent of roughly three million pounds sterling, as well as annual tribute to the Ottoman state."

The millionaire began to foam at the mouth at the mention of money.

"And did you take the gold, Sultan?"

"He was trying to buy Palestine from me!"

The skeleton was confused.

"So, did you give it to him or no?"

"I had him thrown out! I told him that I would not sell him so much as an inch of that land – after all, it was not mine to sell. It belonged to the people. I told him that the Jews ought to hold on to their wealth and that they wouldn't be able to take Palestine away from the Muslims."

The millionaire tried to imagine himself in Abdel Hamid's place.

"Didn't you at least somewhat regret rejecting this rather generous offer?!"

"Nations can never be bought – or sold."

"Did he try again?" De Gaulle asked, though he already knew the answer.

"I'm sure he did," Kennedy replied.

"I know better than anyone how stubborn those Jews can be."

"As it so happens, he did try again. In 1902, he presented to me a formal request to permit the Jews to establish a Hebrew University in Palestine. I refused this request as well, since the university was just the starting point for the complete conquest of Palestine."

"Then they tried to ruin you, didn't they?" asked Hitler, sensing that a Jewish reaction against the Sultan was inevitable.

"They started backing the Committee of Union and Progress. The Jews offered them funding and other means of support for the Committee's revolt against my throne. I staved them off for an entire year – but, unfortunately, in the end they were successful in dethroning me and had me exiled to Thessaloniki in 1909."

Abdel Nasser sighed mournfully.

"The Palestinians had lost a strong ally in yourself, dear Sultan."

Churchill began to chuckle.

"We used to call him the 'Red Sultan'."

"That's right!" exclaimed Abdel Hamid.

"And why did you call me that?"

"Because of your famous love for. . .how did you put it, 'cherry drink?'" De Gaulle said with a snicker.

I don't like cherry drink at all. . ."

"Come on, Armenian cherries were your favorite," Kennedy remarked, winking at De Gaulle and Churchill.

Abdel Hamid pled his innocence, but to no avail.

"I had nothing to do with the deaths of those poor people!"

"Just like Pontius Pilate had nothing to do with what happened to Christ," said Gandhi, referencing Jesus's betrayal and subsequent crucifixion.

"Allow me to explain! First of all, the Russians were behind what happened to the Armenians, and after them the English and the French."

"Do I hear you correctly, Sultan?" shot back Churchill.

"Are you insinuating that we massacred the Armenians?!"

De Gaulle sought to set the record straight.

"The Armenians were persecuted in the Ottoman Empire solely because they demanded their national rights! France only stood in solidarity with them in this respect."

"But this was a blatant intervention in Ottoman internal affairs!"

"It's only natural that the oppressed would seek out someone who would sympathize with them and give them succor," said Gandhi, explaining the Armenians' conduct.

"We mentioned the Berlin treaty before – come to think of it, representatives from the Armenian community in Turkey were present. . ."

". . .in which the German Chancellor Bismarck demanded that religious minorities be granted their full rights and that the freedom of religious practice be guaranteed!" interrupted Hitler.

"The participation of the Armenians in that conference was equivalent to treason! All of the capitulations that the Ottomans were forced to make were specifically a result of their treasonous act!"

Kennedy cast a mocking glance at Abdel Hamid.

"And that is why you decided to punish them for their misdeeds by massacring them."

"I myself did not act against the Armenians. However, in my rage I turned a blind eye to whatever measures my governors and commanders decided to do with them."

"That's it?" Gandhi asked disapprovingly.

"That's it!"

The skeleton took up the narrative from there, describing the events the way a news presenter would:

"The Sultan's orders reached the governors and commanders on the ground. All protective measures had been lifted. It was open season on the Armenians and their property. Their homes were confiscated, their stores robbed of their contents, their crops burned to cinder, and their honor was violated. Their women – even those of minor age – were raped. The Armenians were left to fend for themselves, their property the target of every thief and highway robber and crook. They were dealt a cruel and merciless fate."

"Thus they did whatever they could to defend themselves, their dignity and their property!" exclaimed Hitler.

"They pleaded with the peoples of the world to come to their aid!" Stalin concurred, a tinge of anger in his voice.

"Their rebellion was put down mercilessly, and then they were exiled and banished from their homes," Churchill said reproachfully.

"Many massacres and horrors were visited on the Armenians in those days," the skeleton said, summing up the narrative.

"This is nonsense!" exclaimed Abdel Hamid indignantly.

"What about the Hamidi Brigades that you established in 1891?" asked De Gaulle.

"Those were Kurdish tribesmen!" Abdel Hamid replied.

"If there were any massacres carried out, take the Kurds to account for them!"

"But the Kurdish tribesmen were bound up with the Sublime Porte!" said the skeleton, having stumbled upon the import of Abdel Hamid's incriminating admission.

"I heard those tribesmen slaughtered a quarter of a million Armenians," said the skull.

". . .and destroyed tens of monasteries and churches!" said the skeleton, picking up from where the skull left off.

"Some churches were turned into mosques!"

"I never heard of any of this," replied Abdel Hamid angrily. He continued to deny any responsibility for what transpired.

"If you were aware of what was happening, then that is criminal," commented Abdel Nasser dispassionately.

"If you weren't aware, then that makes you an even greater criminal!"

Abdel Hamid felt he was being pushed into a corner.

"Whether I knew or not is immaterial. I'm pleased with what happened to them. Their malefactions could not have gone unpunished!"

Gandhi casted a mortifying look at the Sultan.

He then said to himself, "an entire nation subject to death and banishment, all because a Sultan couldn't keep his cool."

"What was the precipitating cause of the Adana Massacre, in which 100,000 Armenians lost their lives?" asked Kennedy.

"Because they had undertaken an alliance with the Young Turks to have me dethroned."

"Who were led by Enver Pasha along with his two colleagues, Djemal Pasha and Talaat Pasha."

"What those men did to the Armenians was worse than anything any of you have described thus far!" exclaimed Abdel Hamid, hoping to get some of the heat off himself.

"You're only gripe with Enver Pasha and his comrades was that they were successful in dethroning you!" noted De Gaulle.

"So they were the ones who ruled Turkey after you, Sultan?" asked the skull with a gloat.

"They ruled from behind the scenes, keeping Sultan Mehmet V at the helms as a front."

"It is quite unfortunate," began Gandhi, wringing one hand with the next, "that the twentieth century began with such a miserably bloody start."

The skeleton was interested in hearing more about Gandhi's beliefs.

"You are renowned, Mr. Gandhi, for championing the doctrine of nonviolence."

"Violence is necessary to protect ones interests," Churchill retorted defensively.

"It creates wars," Abdel Nasser added.

Gandhi wasn't impressed.

"The British need to 'defend' its interests in South Africa led to the Boer wars against the German and Dutch settlers. Mr. Churchill himself was present and took part in this war, even falling prisoner at some point. The violence I saw there — beginning with the apartheid regime and the mutual exchanges of violence that ended with horrific bloodshed was crucial in the development of my doctrine of 'Satyagraha (insistence on truth),' which I continued to hold fast to throughout my life."

"It appears everyone likes cherry drink," Abdel Hamid said, realizing he wasn't the only one accused of meting out violence.

"I may be a vegetarian, but I despise this 'cherry drink' of yours!" Gandhi shrieked.

"Cherries in South Africa," the skeleton wondered aloud, "in the Philippines, and in Turkey. When did this century take the plunge towards insanity?"

"In 1908, with the Austrian invasion of Serbia," replied Hitler.

"In 1910, Korea became a Japanese protectorate."

"And let's not forget Italy's invasion of Libya in 1912."

". . .or the Second Balkan War against the Ottomans in that same year."

"Turkey was defeated in that one as well," said Abdel Hamid sorrowfully.

"Your erroneous foreign and domestic policies were the key cause of your continuous defeats in battle," explained Hitler.

Abdel Hamid nodded his head knowingly.

"But I take no responsibility in those losses; in those days, I was in exile."

"What about the First Balkan War?"

"What could I have done, given the major support the Bulgarians and Serbs were receiving from Russia?"

"You could have formed alliances with other nations so that they can come to your aid," Hitler dictated.

"An alliance? With who?" asked Abdel Hamid. Then he sighed with regret. "How could a lamb ally with wolves?"

"A meek lamb," Abdel Nasser said with a bitter taste in his throat, "who suffocated the Arabs for four hundred years."

"The Arabs are our brothers in Islam," Abdel Hamid responded overweeningly, "We ruled with their consent."

"Well then you ought to have respected this brotherhood and treated the Arabs as peers with the Turks," commented Churchill, correcting Abdel Hamid's false notions.

"And what right does a non-Arab such as yourself have to peek your nose in our business?" Abdel Hamid replied angrily.

"Abdel Hamid! You are an enemy to the Arabs, an enemy to the Christians, and an enemy to the West!"

"Might you remember that Great Britain and France were the ones who initiated this enmity. The former colonized Egypt and Sudan provided support to the emirs of the Arabian Gulf to revolt against us, while the latter colonized Algeria and Tunisia and sparred with Spain and Germany over Morocco."

"Why did you not enter into an alliance with Germany?" Hitler wondered.

"We began entering into an understanding with the German Empire. The German Emperor Guillaume II had arranged his first warm visit to Anatolia in 1888, which resulted in a pact for mutual cooperation in military and economic affairs. The second visit occurred in 1898, which in addition to Istanbul included Damascus and Palestine."

Churchill was displeased.

"These visits had as their unstated goal the establishment of a foothold for Germany in the Near East."

"It was during that visit that the German Emperor visited the grave of Saladin in the Umayyad Mosque in Damascus," the skeleton explained.

"The Arabs loved him," Abdel Hamid said, remembering the visit warmly.

"They called him 'Haj Guillaume.'"

"You hear that, Hitler?" Churchill chuckled mockingly.

"'Haj Guillaume!'"

"Saladin was adorned with a golden crown," Hitler remarked, as if narrating the details from memory.

Abdel Nasser felt that Hitler's comments were demeaning to Arabs. "The Mighty Saladin does not need to be 'adorned' in a crown by anyone! He was crowned for time immemorial by history when he expelled the Crusaders from the Holy Land."

Abdel Hamid thought the conversation had taken a wrong turn. "Haj Guillaume was a friend of the Muslims, and for that reason we awarded him the rights to build the Baghdad-BasraKuwait railroad."

Churchill took a deep breath that indicated his relief.

"Had he completed that project it would have been a catastrophe for British interests in the region."

"And for French interests as well," De Gaulle followed.

"That is why you two stood in his way!" Abdel Nasser retorted, exposing the conflict of interest.

Abdel Nasser had opened the door for Hitler to wax philosophical.

"These two never wish well for Germany."

"Because Germany was stepping on our toes by trying to do business in our colonies!" responded Churchill in a rage.

"Your colonies?" Abdel Hamid retorted sardonically. "Yes, you must have inherited those from your ancestors!"

"Our army and our navy inherited them to us!" De Gaulle said with pride.

"Ah," Abdel Hamid sighed with regret.

"If only I had remained in power."

"We've seen your capabilities, Sultan," grumbled Abdel Nasser, "above ground and below ground."

Abdel Hamid needed to find a way out of this impasse.

"What about our domestic policies?"

"It would have behooved you to have ruled in accordance with the dictates of constitutional democratic governance," replied Kennedy with a tone as civil as it was unequivocal.

"We don't know about this constitutionalism or democracy of which you speak. They are foreign ideas to us."

De Gaulle moved in for the kill.

"That was your fatal mistake, Sultan. Instead of ruling in accordance with constitutional democratic governance, you chose to massacre the Armenians, persecute minorities and adopt a policy of Turkification."

Abdel Hamid's defense seemed ready-made.

"The policy of Turkification was not mine; in fact, it was adopted after I was gone by the Young Turks."

Abdel Nasser closed his eyes, as if to absorb the pain that the memory of such policies brought to his sense of Arab dignity. "Enver, Talaat and Djemal Pasha."

"You've seen one, you've seen them all," Kennedy remarked nonchalantly.

"If we were all on the same page, they wouldn't have fought to have me dethroned!" Abdel Hamid protested.

"That's true," concurred De Gaulle. But then he resolved to push Abdel Hamid into a corner. "But anyone who thoroughly studies their policies towards the Armenians, the Arabs and the Balkan states will find that they are a mere extension of your own policies."

"Your evaluation of my tenure has been quite unbalanced, General. Was it not Talaat Pasha – my sworn enemy – who said, 'I succeeded in a span of three months in achieving what Abdel Hamid was not able to do for thirty years?'

This is decisive proof that you are being partial towards me."

"The Turks conveyed to the world their ideology of violence," said Hitler, speaking from experience.

"What they did to the Armenians the Zionists subsequently did to the Palestinians."

"And your method of dealing with the Jews," asked Churchill, "who did you learn that from?"

"From them," responded Hitler irascibly.

"From us?!" Abdel Hamid howled.

"No, Sultan. I meant from the Jews. They were at once my teachers and my students."

Stalin jumped up from his seat in protest.

"This is a stark contradiction on your part! Either you learned from them, or you taught them! It can't be both!"

"Allow me to explain my point of view about this issue later. I'd like to hear how Abdel Hamid shall defend himself on this point."

"Most of the accusations that were hurled at me were unfounded rumors spread by the West to justify their conquest of Arab lands. The more despicable acts in war were committed by the secularists."

"It appears the Sultan is trying to deflect blame for the massacres and mass killings committed during his reign," said the skeleton with a desire to relay history accurately and dispassionately, "and instead to lay the blame completely at the doorstep of the secularists. All in all, it was he who ordered his governors to go into the areas where the Armenians resided in and to expel them from their homes and to march them into the Arabian Desert."

"The order to expel the Armenians from their homes and to confiscate their possessions ought to be considered a genocide," said Gandhi, his eyes welling up with sadness.

"People go and their possessions remain," said the millionaire, licking his lips.

"Looting and pillaging goes on uninhibited, and the enforcement of orders becomes a mix of obeying the Sultan's commands and paving the way to enjoy other people's property."

"To rob other people's property," Gandhi corrected the millionaire.

The skeleton began to narrate to those in attendance how the orders were carried out.

"They were made to leave their homes by force. The exiles made their way on foot through mountains and plains. In one of the more heinous crimes committed during the March, the soldiers forced the Armenians to cross through the rivers, hoping thereby to drown them and be rid of them once and for all. The elderly and the children marching at the very end of the column were subject to repeated beatings and lashings. Very few of them would survive. As for the women – especially the pregnant ones – their bellies were ripped open with knives and spears under the pretext that the women were being used to smuggle gold. Young girls were raped in front of their mothers and fathers.

Altoon – one of the survivors of the massacre – reported in her testimony:

"We were a new family. God gifted us with two beautiful baby girls. We lived among our people, having known only security and contentment. We gladly worked the fields and produced our own food.

"Then the Ottomans came and attacked us, armed to the teeth. They drove us out of our homes by force. They didn't allow us to take anything with us. They were screaming horrific obscenities at us. They gathered us in the town square. Everyone felt powerless. All you could hear was the sounds of weeping and wailing. When we were informed of the exile order, I began to weep. My husband stood by and calmed me, saying, 'Do not be afraid, dear. God is with us. He will not abandon us now.'

"It was winter time. The weather was freezing cold. We proceeded on foot for two days. The soldiers were growing crueler by the second, especially with those who protested or pleaded with the soldiers to give them food or blankets for their children. They beat my husband and tortured him until he fell to his death. They did not let me bury him, nor did they let the priest perform the funeral rites over him. We had to leave him out there in the open. Many others were abandoned in the same way, left for the crows and other birds of prey to feast on their flesh.

"Throughout this time I was forced to carry my baby girls through the long, arduous march. I was exhausted. The procession had passed by a swamp when suddenly my body and my soul gave out and I went plummeting to the ground. I unwittingly threw my girls into the water. I had no ability to move, but my heart couldn't stand to hear them screaming, 'Mother! Mother!' I threw myself to their aid. I was able to save one of them. The other had drowned. I placed one of them at the edge of the swamp and went back to pull my younger daughter out of the swamp. By then she was dead. The procession grew farther and farther away until it finally disappeared. I grabbed a small twig and used it to dig a grave besides a nearby tree. I then grew impatient with the twig and began to dig with my nails. In the distance I could hear Armenian women singing one of our folkloric songs:

She exited the garden

She drew the two of them to her chest with strength

Two fruits from the pomegranate tree

Two gleaming apples

She gave them to me, but I refused to take them

With her hand, she beat her chest

Three times, six times

Twelve times

She struck and struck until the bones of her chest were crushed.

CHAPTER 8
Playing with Fire

Gandhi reclused himself into a corner near the remnants of the millionaire's casket. With a sorrowful silence, he searched the recesses of his memory to bear witness to half a centuries' worth of war and catastrophe that blighted the record of human history. Human greed had been the root cause of all of this. It was greed which made it lawful for man to exploit his brethren in humanity by means of the most despicable methods and with a conceitedness that could brook no compromise with mercy, compassion or even the pangs of human conscience. All that had mattered was to achieve the goals dictated by man's insatiable desire for power and domination.

Images of South Africans being tortured, belittled at work and humiliated at train stations and other public places on account of the color of their skin passed before his eyes like scenes from a movie, as did the suffering of all colonized peoples who had born the brunt of colonialism's haughtiness, which manifested itself in the barbarity of its ruling class and the pompousness of the military forces charged with enforcing the former's commands with indescribable cruelty. The end result of the colonization legacy was staggering: billions of people the world over brought to ruin by poverty, hunger and indigence, their lives harvested by disease and plague and their societies bedeviled by ignorance, backwardness and illiteracy, all the while their countries' rich resources are stolen out from under them.

The skeleton was taking a stroll through the graveyard's courtyard. He had been on edge all morning, searching for someone to engage in dialogue or converse with. He passed by Gandhi and greeted him, but heard no response. Perhaps he was meditating or observing a vow of silence. Sultan Abdel Hamid II was fast asleep. President John F. Kennedy was aching with back pain, perhaps left by the bullet that tore through his body on the gruesome day that he was assassinated. Stalin was subsumed in a longwinded conversation with the skull, with each taking turns sharing stories about their prowess in leading their men into battle. De Gaulle was browsing through one of his books, while Winston Churchill was busy pondering over his latest painting. Hitler stood facing Churchill's back. He too had been painting that day, but his painting remained unfinished and he was clueless as to how to proceed.

Hitler cast a glance at Churchill. He noticed Churchill's cigar about to break loose from his fingers, and then heard the distinct sound of Churchill's snoring. He began to crawl on his hands and knees stealthily until he reached Churchill's color palette. He stole Churchill's red palette just as he had stolen Czechoslovakia before the eyes of his European adversaries during his life. He went back to working on his painting with a grin on his face.

Abdel Nasser was wrapped up in a song that Umm Kulthum, the premier songstress of the Arab world, had sang for him in life:

Our Leader. . .Dear, Beloved Leader

I have a rare request for you.

I have an urgent request for you.

From the blessed land of Egypt, On behalf of the millions who are madly in love with you, We – each and every one of us – is dying to see you.

Suddenly, the music got cut off. Tears welled up in Abdel Nasser's eyes. He had been touched by the songstress's entreats.

"My dearest Kulthum," Nasser whispered the way a lover confided in his beloved. "I too long for the Egyptian and Arab peoples, each of whom are as kindhearted as they are brave."

The skeleton, unhappy with the fact that everyone was engrossed with whatever they were doing, began to throw a tantrum. He then got a bright idea. He walked towards the General De Gaulle pretending to be afraid and hid behind him. De Gaulle saw him and put down his book.

"What is with you? You look frightened."

"It's the way Stalin glances at me. His eyes are seething with anger! He respects you and listens to you. Please, protect me from him!"

De Gaulle glanced at Stalin and saw him enveloped in conversation with the skull and laughing with each other.

"It doesn't look like Stalin even knows you're here. He's too busy with the skull."

"I know. Actually, I wanted to get your opinion on something."

"My opinion? About what?"

"About war."

De Gaulle laughed and cleared his throat. "War is an evil. Sometimes, a necessary evil."

"Death and destruction. . .tragedy and catastrophe. Famine, disease, and all sorts of unimaginable horrors. Isn't it possible for war to break out unnecessarily?"

"Are you perhaps referring to the assassination of the Archduke of Austria Franz Ferdinand in 1914 in Sarajevo?"

"Did that event – sorrowful as it may be – deserve to degenerate into the First World War?"

"I must say, Mr. Skeleton, I'm impressed with how wellversed you are in history."

"Why, of course," the skeleton said with pride, "this is my job. Thank you for your kind words."

"But you seem ignorant of how politics works."

The skeleton is astonished by the General's audacity, not to mention offended by his offhand remark. "How might I learn about politics, General?"

"There isn't one way. Some people have a sixth sense for these things. Others learn from experience. Others are inspired by their sheer sense of responsibility. You have to follow events in live time, read history, understand philosophy, and have a knack for inductive and deductive reasoning. You need to be able to weigh political events against the weight of global events. It also helps to understand economics and the current balance of power in the world. You can judge matters only after taking all of these matters into account."

"That's what I try to do, General."

"You need to eat, drink, and sleep politics."

"And what do political scientists believe are the main causes of the World War one?"

"At that point it was as if the world itself was on the verge of exploding. The events in Europe were the spark that led to this explosion. It was the epicenter of activity for all the great empires. Indeed, the First Moroccan Crisis in 1905 led to the worsening of relations between Germany and France. France proceeded to occupy some Moroccan lands in 1911, which led to Germany ordering its ships to move towards Agadir Port to prevent France from occupying further Moroccan territory."

"Why, then, did war not break out in 1911?"

"The issue was resolved temporarily when France agreed to relinquish control over parts of the Congo and to hand them over to German control. In the meantime, the deterioration of relations had led to an arms race and the formation of an intricate series of alliances. Austria allied with Germany, Russia with France and England. France was biding its time, waiting for an opportune moment to take back the Alsace-Lorraine region which Germany had annexed in the aftermath of the FrancoPrussian War of 1870."

"So, you're saying that France was responsible for the breaking out of the First World War?"

The question made De Gaulle feel uneasy.

"I think I may have misunderstood you this whole time."

"You see, General? I'm a quick learner!"

"Would that I knew you while I was President of the Republic of France. I would have appointed you Head Chef of the Elysee."

Mahatma Gandhi decided to join in on the conversation.

"I hear you guys are talking about the War. I was just thinking about it. Might I join your conversation?"

"Bienvenue, Mr. Gandhi. Have a seat, and enjoy listening to this Chef's take on politics."

Gandhi takes a seat.

"Go easy on him, General. He's learning, bit by bit."

"I changed my mind about him. I would not have hired him as a chef. Not even as a bellboy!"

"His political opinions must have been stark raving mad!"

The skeleton didn't like what he was hearing, and the Mahatma's presence gave him the strength to say as much.

"Didn't Napoleon Bonaparte march on Europe and the Middle East with his armies?"

"Indeed, it was Napoleon's invasions that led to the emergence of a sense of national spirit throughout Europe," Gandhi noted.

"And that's when the clashes between the nobility and the nationalists began to increase in intensity," remarked De Gaulle.

"The Renaissance came in tandem with the French Revolution."

"I really do admire the General, and I respect his views," the skeleton said to Gandhi. "But he's bewildering me with his fanaticism. First he says that Empire A is the arch-enemy of Empire B, and then he turns around and says that Empire B was an ally of Empire A?"

"Why, this is politics!" exclaimed De Gaulle. "There are no permanent enmities or everlasting friendships!"

The skeleton put two and two together.

"This must be the basis upon which alliances emerge between states and empires."

"It appears the skeleton is becoming adept at logical reasoning," Gandhi said to De Gaulle.

"Is that what you think, Mr. Gandhi? Why, Monsieur thinks that France is to blame for the breaking out of World War I!"

The skeleton felt it necessary to defend his opinion.

"Excuse me, General, but did you not tell me that France was intent on taking back the Alsace-Lorraine?"

"So I did. But I certainly did not say that France was responsible for the breaking out of World War I!"

"What was it then?"

"The rise nationalist fervor among the peoples of Europe! Is this clear enough, or do you need me to break it further down for you?!"

"No, it's clear enough. But it is my contention that this nationalist fervor had emerged in the aftermath of Napoleon's numerous wars!"

"Such is the nature of imperialist rivalry between the various regional empires," said Gandhi.

"Was Sarajevo the epicenter of this rivalry?"

The General grew agitated at what he felt were the skeleton's erroneous methods of analyzing history.

"Were it not out of graciousness to Mr. Gandhi," he said, raising his voice, "I would have thrown you out of this graveyard!"

Stalin and Sultan Abdel Hamid joined in the fray.

"What's with you, General?" Stalin asked.

"This skeleton is tampering with historical facts!"

"Would you like me to have him thrown out of the graveyard?"

"I was just thinking about that!"

Sultan Abdel Hamid tried to relieve the tense atmosphere.

"If you don't understand politics or history," he said, directing his speech towards the skeleton, "then you ought to remain silent and listen attentively. You have here a distinct opportunity to learn history from the very people who made it!"

"Yes, yes, I'll keep quiet. I want to learn. But may I ask a question?"

"Ask," Stalin said.

"The spark of World War I was lit in Sarajevo. But what does Sarajevo have to do with imperial rivalries?"

"Rivalries breed enmity," Gandhi retorted.

"Serbia was the arch-enemy of Austria in the Balkan peninsula," the Sultan confirmed.

"For this reason," continued Stalin, "Austria took the assassination of its Archduke as a pretext to attack Serbia. It was their aim to put an end to the desire of Slav nationalists in Bosnia to join Serbia, which, in turn, was intent on securing its independence. Russia supported the right of the Bosnian Slavs to join Serbia."

"Austria took the assassination as a pretext and declared war on Serbia," De Gaulle added.

"Immediately, its ally Germany jumped into battle at its side."

"Germany demanded that Russia remain aloof from the conflict," Stalin said, "but Russia refused."

De Gaulle believed a clarification of the French position was in order.

"France sided with Russia, and the German army advanced on France via Belgium and Holland."

Churchill – who had been listening attentively to the conversation – felt it necessary to come forth and express his opinion on the matter.

"We entered the war to defend Belgium's right to remain neutral, a right which we had undertaken to protect if need be."

Gandhi shook his head in disbelief.

"I hear you all talking about war as if it were some kind of festive get-together! This one brings his friend, that one his, and everyone comes and participates in the festivities and the fun!"

"That's quite a reading," Kennedy remarked amusingly.

"It goes to the heart of these gentlemen's motives, as it points to the reservoir of emotion that undergirds their decisionmaking. Whether it be love or hate, in the end it is our emotions that drive us, whether at a party or in the heat of battle."

"Yet love generates peace and stability, while hatred leads to violence and war," added Gandhi.

"Who were the main participants in this hate fest?" asked the skeleton.

Churchill replied:

"The Allies – Britain, Russia and France. . ."

"Versus the Axis – Germany, Austria and Hungary," said De Gaulle.

"Each of whom were playing with fire," Gandhi said with pain and sorrow in his voice.

CHAPTER 9

Who Might He Be?

On the morning of November 4, 1995, the Graveyard of the Greats witnessed what must have seemed at the time like a violent tremor. Teams of security forces backed by two battalions from the United Nations Protection Force armed to the teeth with advanced weaponry – had surged in to stand guard as multiple delegations made their way to the graveyard to attend the funeral oration of one of the greats. A long time had passed since the graveyard had welcomed a new resident. The commotion outside was so loud it brought the exchange inside the third wing to a screeching halt.

"I'll check up on what's happening," Gandhi volunteered, "and I'll get back to you guys when I know anything."

The skeleton offered to accompany Gandhi on his reconnaissance trip, whereupon Stalin suggested that the skull – owing to the greater ease of movement the latter enjoyed as well as his distinct ability to maneuver swiftly if an emergency situation were to occur – would be more suited for the task. The entire wing nodded in agreement, and Gandhi and the skull sauntered out stealthily to join the crowds gathered in the graveyard's courtyard.

The coffin, nearly buried under a mountain of floral wreaths, was being carried atop an artillery vehicle in the main square of the graveyard. Gandhi observed elegant black sedans accompanying the vehicle's movements, from which various world leaders stepped out to take part in this monumental event. He also observed that the participating delegations were composed of officials of the highest caliber: kings, emirs, prime ministers, ambassadors and consul generals took their assigned seats along the main podium which had been set up specifically for the occasion.

Gandhi and the skull proceeded to make their way back to the third wing without being able to deduce the identity of the man whose arrival had caused all this commotion. As part of the ceremony the artillery vehicle was made to fire twenty one artillery shells, a fitting testament to the majestic nature of the event and the lofty position of the man whose corpse was interred in the coffin that now stood amidst the main square of the Graveyard of the Greats.

Hitler had heard the sound of the mortar fire.

"This is rather reminiscent of how the Germans began their attack on the French following the invasion of Belgium."

"It's as if I could still hear the sound of that barbaric German bombardment. I feel now that I'm reliving those days of trial and tribulation which revealed the courageousness of the French forces who, in their efforts to repel the German attack, were fighting to defend France and her dignity."

The skeleton began to narrate the events in question.

"The Austrian Empire attacked Serbia with all it's might. . ."

Hitler jumped in: "in tandem with the German Empire, which proceeded to attack westward."

"Indeed," said Stalin, "the Czar had entered into the fray with fifteen million soldiers to boot."

"The French forces stayed the advance of the German armies towards Paris," De Gaulle said with the zeal of a National Guardsman.

"With British help," Churchill added sagaciously.

"Of course!" replied De Gaulle with a tender smile. "Great Britain was an ally of France."

"And the Ottoman Sultanate joined the war on the side of Austria and Germany in order to get even with Great Britain," noted Abdel Hamid, waving his hand.

"France as well, due to its unjust colonization of Arab lands in North Africa."

The skeleton glanced at De Gaulle and pondered for a bit, then said, "The war continued to expand, with China, Japan, Portugal and Italy joining on the side of the Allies."

"And Turkey had proceeded to bombard Russia's ports along the Black Sea with mortar fire," added Abdel Hamid.

"It's the historic enmity between the Ottomans and the Russians," Churchill said with a snicker.

"We served the Czar with distinction," Stalin said, striking a serious tone.

"But that did not stop him from employing arbitrary acts of barbarism against us for the most petty of wrongdoings. This led to an increase in the number of revolutionaries as the years passed during the First World War."

Gandhi let out a sigh.

"The Russian front had suffered heavy losses during the war," he said with sadness.

"The lack of arms or proper training debilitated our fighters' ability to withstand a German assault that made heavy use of advanced weaponry and artillery fire,"

Stalin shouted angrily.

"This only proves the strength of the German army," Hitler replied with a tinge of arrogance in his voice.

De Gaulle quickly interrupted him.

"On the Western front the battle had been transformed into trench warfare following the German armed forces' failed attempts to reach Paris."

"It is my impression that the performance of the British Navy was outstanding under your leadership, Mr. Churchill," said Kennedy.

Churchill was eager to explain.

"The British Navy had gained control over most of the oceans and lakes, allowing it to tighten the noose around the Germans and to take the war to their home court via the North Sea. We were able to prevent their navy from escaping to their colonies, and their men suffered shortages in ammunition and supplies."

Hitler refused to cede Churchill's interpretation.

"We must not forget the strength and pride of German engineering. Our submarines would pick off your ships one by one, causing them to drop like pigeons."

"But Mr. Churchill was also an inventor in his own right," said Gandhi, attempting to put Hitler in his proper place.

"He was instrumental in developing the British Navy."

Churchill found in Gandhi's words a means by which he could elaborate on his own innovations.

"In 1912 oil was offered as an alternative to coal. This was no mean feat."

"What good did this oil do for you?" asked Abdel Hamid.

"It was after the discovery of oil that I began to think seriously about using landships in order to break through the trenches and the barbed wire."

"A land ship?" the millionaire asked sardonically, "one whos engines run on fuel, able to plow through the sand instead of water? It's a rather tremendous invention!"

"Why don't you keep your mouth shut, mr. millionaire!" Stalin shouted at the millionaire in a rage.

"Landships are what later came to be called tanks."

The skull began to pack back and forth, seeking to attract everyone's attention toward him.

"Was this invention ready for use during the First World War?" he asked inquisitively.

"Of course!" De Gaulle exclaimed.

"It was an important innovation in the world of military affairs."

"How effective had tanks been in the First World War?" asking Abdel Hamid, listening attentively for an answer to his question.

Churchill went on to explain at length.

"In truth, the landship – or the tank, whichever – had entered into use for the first time during the First World War in the year 1915. At that time it hadn't yet become a very effective weapon, due to its inability to travel faster than thirteen kilometers an hour, a slow speed considering. It also had frequent mechanical failures as a result of the bumpy battle terrain."

The skeleton quickly posed another question.

"What is your second invention, Mr. Churchill?"

"It is not necessary for an invention to manifest itself in the form of a device," Mr. Churchill responded aptly.

"There are also innovations in terms of strategy – war tactics, if you will."

The skull was paying close attention at this point.

"Go on, Mr. Churchill. I am obsessed with learning about military tactics."

"The smartest ploy that Britain had in its arsenal was to strike at the enemy from within."

Abdel Nasser understood the import of Churchill's remark.

"You must be referring to Great Britain's secret correspondences with Sharif Hussein."

"Col. Lawrence, a member of our Arab Office in Cairo, was tasked with the mission of making contact with the Sharif, resulting in the Hussein-McMahon correspondences in 1915," Churchill replied.

"It was then that the British government gave the Arabs a written undertaking to grant them their independence and support them in their endeavors," noted Abdel Nasser dolefully.

"We needed to get the Arabs to join the side of the Allies against the Ottoman army," Churchill said, justifying his erstwhile practices in life.

Hitler wanted everyone to know what a snake the old Churchill was, but he didn't want to say so directly.

"That poor Hussein – he believed the British and declared himself the King of the Arabs, and heralded the announcement of the Great Arab Revolt against the Ottomans in 1916."

Abdel Hamid was stuck between feelings of anger and regret.

"The major mistake that the Young Turks leadership made can be reduced to Enver and Jamal Pasha's policy of Turkification and their depriving our Arab brothers breathing room for some level of independence. This in turn caused the Arabs to regret the day they joined with us in brotherhood and to seek independence from the Sultanate. In the end, they felt compelled to fight us."

Gandhi was in no mood for games.

"An injustice might lead to an explosive circumtance, ending with the overthrow of the standing regime."

Abdel Nasser strongly agreed with Abdel Hamid's words.

"The Arabs awaited their chance to be free of Ottoman rule, which had lasted some four hundred years. In the beginning all they had wanted from the authorities in Istanbul was to institute a limited set of reforms, such as the adoption of the Arabic language in the Ottoman parliament as an official language alongside Turkish, and that Arab males be allowed to serve their mandatory military service locally unless circumstances necessitated otherwise."

"It would have behooved them to offer the Arabs and the Armenians autonomy," De Gaulle said, criticizing official Turkish policy.

"This is consistent with what I was talking about before when I referred to the mistakes of Enver and Jamal Pasha."

"Abdel Hamid!" Kennedy interrupted.

"You always try to disassociate yourself from your misdeeds by putting all the blame on the men who took power after you were gone."

"But it was they who stuck to their Pan-Turanic program rather than accede to the Arabs' demands," answered Abdel Hamid.

The millionaire didn't understand what everyone meant by 'Pan-Turanism,' and so he asked the skeleton to explain what that meant.

"It was a nationalist political movement that arose among the Ottoman Turks towards the end of the nineteenth century. It asserted a kind of superiority, a right to rule for the Turks over all other races in the empire. It also justified the use of cruel and violent means to impose Turkification on the non-Turkish races,"

"Pan-Turanism was a creation of the Donmeh Jews, who considered the Turkish race the most superior of human races." He then added, "It seems they weren't aware of the Germans!"

Abdel Nasser struck a sorrowful tone as he explained what happened next.

"They confiscated our wheat crops in Syria, and forced young Arab men into exile in the year 1914 to fight in the Ottoman army. Were it not for their persistence in fighting the Ottomans the residents of Mount Lebanon would most certainly have starved to death."

De Gaulle was outraged at the mere thought of the prospect.

"It wouldn't have been the first time either. History records many instances of bloody religious warfare that ensued in the year 1860, and the Ottomans were slow to put a stop to it. They had sought to eradicate the Christians from Mount Lebanon, leading the French to send forth a peacekeeping expedition under the Emperor Napoleon III."

"That was nothing short of an outrage, a blatant interference in Ottoman affairs!" Abdel Hamid interjected violently. Kennedy lifted his head and looked Abdel Hamid right in the eye.

"This only goes to confirm that religious persecution was indeed practiced by Ottoman authorities against the Armenians and other Christians of the Middle East!"

"Were it not for the Great Arab Revolt and the entrance of the Allies into the area, the fate of the Arab Christians would have been worse than that of the Armenians!" added Churchill.

The skeleton wanted to have his opinion heard in all of this.

"But is it not also true that the Armenians refused to assimilate with the Pan-Turanic movement?"

"Such are the Armenians!" shouted Abdel Hamid in hatefilled rage.

"They live in Turkey and thumb their noses at its laws."

"And who could accept such unjust laws?!" Gandhi rushed to ask him.

"They are Armenian Turks. It would have been only natural for them to love Turkey as their homeland!"

Gandhi tried to respond to the Sultan's contentions calmly.

"I'm sure they loved Turkey. But I'm just as sure that they didn't love the Turks' oppressive policies towards them!"

"This is rubbish! We did not oppress anyone."

Kennedy shot a glance at Abdel Hamid, rage shooting from his eyes like sparks from a firework.

"Need I recount all of the massacres that occurred during your reign?"

"Do you understand what the terms 'ashmil' and 'tawriq' mean, dear Sultan? Or would you like me to explain what they mean to you?" asked Churchill with that famous English insouciance.

The skull rolled in to the center of the room.

"Would you mind explaining them to me, Mr. Churchill? I couldn't find a definition of those terms in any of the dictionaries in my possession."

Churchill lit his cigar and took a deep drag, then began his explanation.

"In the old days, when a Muslim passed by a Christian in the street he would say 'ashmil (Ar. 'go left!')!' that is, he would demand that the Christian turn to the left and walk away from the Muslims path, and the Christian would have to obey, no questions asked. If there were many people in the street coming and going in numbers too numerous to count, his misery would only be exacerbated, as he would simply not know which way to turn. He would then be asked to 'tawriq,' that is, to walk along the taruq, which is a decline in the middle of the road which ebbed about a foot beneath the road's surface. It was some four to six feet wide, and was used as a walkway for animals. In the winter time, it would be wet from all the rain, and in the summer time it would be filled with waste."

"This is hideous! Why, no one should accept to live like this."

De Gaulle pointed an accusing finger at Abdel Hamid.

"And His Excellency the Sultan claims not to have oppressed anyone."

Abdel Hamid was overstrained by the endless accusations and condemnations that were thrown at him.

"It is a Sultan's job to protect the integrity of his regime."

"Why didn't the Arabs rise up against the Turks in 1914, just as the war broke out?" the skeleton asked inquisitively.

"They held out hope that the Sultan would accede to their demands," replied Abdel Nasser, as if he had swallowed a bitter pill.

Gandhi took this as an opportunity to elaborate on his philosophy.

"But the policy of violence the authorities adopted to deal with their subjects' demands was the first nail in the coffin between the Arabs and the Armenians on one hand and the Turks on the other."

Kennedy fixed his seating position.

"In 1915 Enver Pasha accused the Armenians of spying for the Russians. He then issued a directive ordering their forced exile. They were made to leave their towns and villages, and tens of thousands perished as a result."

"In 1916 Jamal Pasha had 300 intellectuals and thinkers executed in Istanbul," added De Gaulle.

Abdel Nasser had long wished things had taken a different direction.

"In that same year he went after the Arab nationalist movement in Syria, and had ordered the most eminent Arab thinkers to hang at the gallows in Damascus and Beirut."

Churchill grinned slyfully.

"Jamal Pasha tightened the noose around the necks of the nationalists, thus further stirring Arab nationalist feelings against the Ottomans. This, as it were, helped us to conclude a swift pact with Sharif Hussein."

"Britain then promised the Arabs to help them in their quest for independence while stealthily agreeing with the French to slice up their lands among themselves," retorted Hitler, seeking to expose Britain's true aims in all of this.

"The Bolsheviks had uncovered this plot for themselves," said Stalin, gleaming with pride. "They knew about the pact as soon as it was agreed upon when they took power in 1917."

Abdel Nasser nodded his head in agreement.

"Indeed, it is the infamous Sykes-Picot Agreement of 1916, which placed the Northern Arabian Peninsula under the mandate of the French and the British."

Abdel Hamid caught hold of his breath and said with a gloat, "It would have been prudent for the Arabs to have learned a lesson from France's occupation of Algeria and England's occupation of Egypt and the Nile Valley."

"The Great Arab Revolt took place in 1916," Churchill remarked, pleased with the success of British intrigues in the region, "beginning with the bombing of the Hijaz railroad. Needless to say, British intelligence agent Lawrence had aided the Arabs in this operation, and in concert with one another they were successful in preventing the Turks from sending reinforcements to their armies in the Hijaz."

"The revolutionaries had taken control over Mecca and Medina," narrated Abdel Nasser, describing the victories of the Arab Forces.

"They continued to push northward towards Damascus via the cities of Aqaba and Ma'an."

"The Turks were finished in the Arab territories," Churchill said with glee, "and the balance of power during the First World War began to preponderate in favor of the Allies."

The skeleton proceeded to break down the costs of the war based on his perusal of the historical record.

"The newspapers and magazines at the time stated that the greatest number of lives lost were on Russia's Eastern Front."

"Everything has a price," Stalin said.

"It is true that we payed an exacting price, but our losses in the war helped usher forth the Communist Revolution in Russia and led to the dethroning of the Czar and the victory of the proletariat over tyranny and corruption."

"What happened to the Czar after he was defeated?" asked Abdel Hamid.

"The Czar and his family were imprisoned," Stalin answered.

"Kerensky took hold of government and ordered that Lenin be imprisoned."

"For having collaborated with the Germans," Hitler said with a chuckle.

"Did they arrest him?" asked the skull.

"Lenin disguised himself as a railroad worker and managed to evade Kerensky's police and make his way to St. Petersburg," Stalin said.

"Once the Communists came to power, Russia retreated from the war," De Gaulle said rebukingly.

"This was only to protect our revolution. We had no choice but to retreat," Stalin retorted.

Churchill decided to be more precise in his choice of words.

"Russia betrayed their alliance with the British and the French!"

Stalin was unmoved.

"That was how Lenin saw fit to act. He thought it of greater importance to act to solidify the gains of the revolution internally and to put an end to the senselessness of thousands of men losing their lives in order to satisfy your imperialist hunger games."

"Russia had secured their exit from the war by signing the Treaty of Brest-Litovsk in 1918," Hitler said.

"Russia lost much territory under that Treaty," Stalin interrupted.

De Gaulle was not impressed by Stalin's remarks.

"Germany stood to gain from the Treaty, as they were now able to move the 400,000 soldiers they had stationed on the Eastern Front and relocated them to fight the French and the British."

"Were it not for the fact that the United States decided to join the war on the side of the Allies, victory would have been Germany's," Hitler said with blind confidence.

"The world would have been a much different place even geographically speaking."

Hitler stopped to contemplate for a moment, and then he asked angrily, "Why did America enter into the War?"

"Germany was becoming a menace," Kennedy responded coolly, "it was refusing to abide by international law. German submarines were striking at commercial ships, and this greatly affected the United States's economic interests."

Churchill picked up where Kennedy left off.

"The Germans also tried to incite Mexico to declare war against the United States with the aim of seizing control of three American states."

The millionaire had a reason of his own to add. An important one at that.

"The United States feared that Britain and France would be forced to default on the enormous loans each of them took out from the U.S. in the event that they lost the war."

"The Allies benefited from the capabilities and supplies that the United States had to offer," Kennedy said, "which served to greatly weaken Germany."

"On the Arab front, the revolutionaries were making steady gains against the Ottomans," added Abdel Nasser with elation.

Gandhi wanted the others to hear how the Indians had contributed to the progress of the war.

"The British-Indian Army began an attack along the Mesopotamian river valley with the aim of conquering Baghdad first and then heading north to attack Turkey in the Anatolia region."

Abdel Hamid jumped to his feet.

"The attack was a complete failure, and we were able to inflict heavy losses in the ranks of the British Indian Army, who had either surrendered to the Ottomans or evacuated southwards."

"The plan was for the Russians to continue into Persia and meet the British at the meeting point of the Tigris and Euphrates rivers," Stalin noted, attempting to explain the failure of the British.

"But then the Ottomans got greedy!" Churchill remarked.

"Their determination to attain an all-out victory made them vulnerable to us and gave us the opportunity to send reinforcements to the evacuating forces. The latter then proceeded to initiate a new attack which led to the defeat of the Turkish Sixth Army in Mosul in 1917, pushing them back as far as Aleppo in Syria."

"In turn, the Greek forces in concert with the Allies laid siege to Turkish positions along the Aegean Sea," De Gaulle added.

"What about the course of the war in Asia China, Japan and others?" the skeleton asked inquiringly.

Churchill answered the skeleton's question with the confidence of a man who knew all too well what happened.

"Nationalist feeling grew with increasing fervor among the Japanese. The latter had taken to a form of ancestor worship which gave them the confidence to stroll through Asia as if it were a walk in the park."

"In those days Africa stood before the vying European imperial powers as if it were a piece of cake," Abdel Nasser said.

Hitler sighed deeply, and then uttered regretfully, "The German forces were on the brink of reaching Paris were it not for the Allies with newfound military support from the Americans initiating a counterattack at the same time that Bulgaria, Austria and Turkey fell in 1918."

The skeleton felt it appropriate to run up the numbers.

"The toll the war took in human lives amounted to some ten million killed and some twenty million injured."

"What good are any of these so-called 'victories' when the stark smell of death had pervaded every nook and cranny of the Earth," Gandhi wondered sorrowfully and regretfully.

"And what did it bring with it besides plagues and diseases and poverty, famine and hardship?!"

"Germany collapsed!" De Gaulle roared in ecstasy as victors are wont to do.

"The Axis Powers surrendered!"

"Smoke and fire everywhere," Gandhi thought to himself. He decided to undergo a fast as a form of protest against the consequences of war.

"Not to mention that the chests of the sparring nations were completely empty by the time the war was over. Enormous sums had been wasted!" the millionaire grumbled.

The skeleton felt it was time to wrap things up.

"A ceasefire was announced after four and a half years in which the world was poised on the precipice of disaster."

Just as the artillery vehicle had stopped firing after pushing out twenty one rounds of mortar fire, the First World War ended with the victory of the Allies over the Axis Powers.

Outside, the funeral orations had begun, with rabbis delivering prayers in Hebrew. Those in attendance gave sermons extolling the merits of the deceased, who was famous in life for having received the distinguished Nobel Prize for Peace. Sympathetic wishes were coming in from all over the world. In turn, the world over condemned Igal Amir, a right-wing Zionist fanatic who had carried out the assassination of the deceased man: Mr. Yitzhak Rabin, former Prime Minister of the State of Israel.

The funeral rites had come to an end, sorrow and sadness filling the air. The various delegations made their way out of the graveyard under the watchful eye of armed guards, who were on call to prevent any attempt by terrorists to infiltrate and attack the gathering.

The grave digger called four of his assistants to help him bury Mr. Rabin in the third wing. He made them carry weapons on their person, out of concern that another dastardly rat might choose to jump out of its hole and surprise them again.

Mr. Rabin's coffin was interred in the main hall of the graveyard. The grave digger's assistants came forth and carried the coffin, following the grave digger as he made his way to the third wing. He flung open both doors of the wing, and ordered them to precede him inside. The assistants proceeded to place the coffin in an empty corner and then made their way back out. The grave digger inspected the wing for a brief moment to make sure nothing was out of the ordinary. He then rushed to leave the wing, a smile spreading across his face. Nothing had taken him by surprise this time.

CHAPTER 10
The Murder Weapon

The investigator looked out of his office window, staring contemplatively at the long river as it pierced through the peaks and valleys that lay before him with the same force as the nail that he had extracted from the murdered general's skull. He knew at the outset that it was a crime of passion. That it had been carried out with such disturbing skill could only mean that the crime must have been committed with hatred and malice aforethought. He began to stuff his pipe with that scented tobacco which was his refuge at times such as this, when the facts of the case seemed too twisted and the questions grew more and more perverse. Much time had elapsed with no resolution in sight. He was particularly confounded by the murderer's odd choice of a murder weapon: what could a nail do that poison or a bullet couldn't?

Could it be that the general's head looked too much like a wall? Was the wall armored, or was it simply made up of earth and straw? How was the nail lodged into the cranium?

It was indeed a mighty mystery, but if anyone was capable of breaking the case wide open it was the investigator. It occurred to him that the best place to start was the murder weapon: how long was the nail? What features did it have? How thick was it? How was it extracted? What metal was it made of? Where was it made?

The investigator took a deep drag on his pipe, and blew the smoke far away. He asked himself what possible connection there might be between the nail and the wall, and he came to the hypothesis that the murderer had been working in some kind of workshop. This was a crime of terrorism as the preliminary reports coming out of the Central Intelligence Agency had indicated and when we are faced with an adversary who operates with such skill then it is only prudent that we take the necessary precautions. We must plant eyes and ears in every public place where it is possible such criminals might be found. Modern advanced technology, thankfully, will make our job much easier, and we will be able to go about installing hidden cameras and covert listening devices in every major city: in trains, subway stations, the roads, the sidewalks, the bridges, border crossings, airports, ports in every phone booth and private residence.

This is all the president of INTERPOL had been thinking about. The work ahead would be long and arduous, in need of continuous scrutiny and review. It was incumbent for him to work in complete secrecy, far from the prying eyes of the media cameras, so as to protect the investigation from being unduly influenced by outside forces. It was also prudent that the citizenry not know about his plan to wiretap everyone illegally not only would that result in protests about the need to respect human rights and needless headache, but it might also cause people to eschew speaking on the telephone, thereby nullifying the plan's very purpose. We need to find an intelligent way to be able to spy on people and procure the most intimate details about them. The difficulty of the operation is of no consequence to me if need be, I want to know what lies under the shadow of a black ant as it walks in the middle of the night, what people whisper to each other in the comfort of their own homes, whatever! I want to get access to everyone's home, without exceptions. I want to know everything that goes on behind closed doors.

The plan might need some six months to a year to be successful. I will work with the television manufacturers to force consumers to abandon their old equipment by blocking broadcast transmissions from reaching them, thus rendering them obsolete. Under the guise of technological advancement they will be made to purchase new TVs plasmas, maybe even LCDs. The picture will now be much clearer and much more crisp. The new technology might even include 3D imaging! Besides, people are always after the newer, hotter product. The trick will work on them hook, line and sinker. This way, we'll be able to monitor everyone's movements with precision using 'digital' technology, which will relay both audio and video to us twenty four hours a day.

The news outlets continued to follow up on the latest developments in the graveyard, broadcasting news and analysis about the radical terrorists and whatever updates it could muster about their activities and suspicious movements. Cain Goldstreak had taken notice of this, putting in numerous calls to his partners in the petroleum and financial industries in addition to other multinational mega corporations whose budgets individually beat out that of many nations in the developing world. Upon coming across a solid lead from one of his sources he made an effort to immediately inform the head of INTERPOL via telephone:

"I have new information from the United State that indicates that terrorist groups backed by the Axis of Evil had surreptitiously placed the rat in the general's skull. And that's not all: it was discovered via satellite imagery that thousands of rats are being raised and trained to occupy the skulls of other deceased members. For the first time in history the rat trade has made its way into the stock market, and the prices of its shares are on the increase."

"I happen to believe that these rumors are true, the lack of solid evidence to back them notwithstanding," replied the head of INTERPOL.

"Have you managed to come across any circumstantial evidence?" asked the grave digger.

"All I can say is that we have a mysterious crime that was well-planned and carried out in complete secrecy. We have many important steps to take before we can uncover the truth."

The grave digger was eager to help in any way he can.

"What about the international intelligence agencies? Are they being cooperative?" The investigator's response was a positive one.

"The Federal Bureau of Investigation (FBI) has taken the murder weapon into custody for further inspection."

"They get anything yet?"

"They found that the nail that was found in the general's skull was made in North Korea. It contains nuclear material and it is on record as having been sold to Islamist terrorists. It appears the terrorists used the nail to tear the general's head into pieces. He couldn't have survived such an impact for more than a few seconds. Based on this, the United States of America considers it its right to take measurs to put an end to North Korea's nuclear program. After all, securing the heads of generals is considered a top priority in U.S. National Security."

The grave digger switched the phone and held it to his other ear.

"The other Western nations are in full agreement with the United States about this matter. In consortium, they demand that the oil-rich nations who furtively back these terrorists pay billionsof dollars in compensation for the victims who were harmed in the Graveyard of the Greats."

The head of INTERPOL also had information about Israel's position on the crisis.

"Israel holds Hezbollah and Hamas responsible for what happened as well. It also accuses Syria of involvement in the conspiracy with Iranian backing."

"The United States has announced that it will implement further economic sanctions on Syria," the grave digger said, confirming America's support for the Israeli position.

The head of INTERPOL was impressed with the statement released by the Palestinian Authority.

"Yasser Arafat rushed to condemn Hamas and Islamic Jihad's indiscriminate attacks on civilians in the Graveyard of the Greats. In addition, he directed a medley of kisses to the leaders of the free world. Rumor has it that he specifically pleaded that Bill Clinton be the recipient of one of those kisses."

The grave digger felt it was time to bring the phone call to an end. He ended on a grim note:

"I feel like I can smell the scent of blood looming in the horizon. We shall keep in touch. I have many things to get done here. Death is calling my name. I have more graves to dig."

CHAPTER 11
A Democratic Solution

The skeleton sticks his nose in everything, whether it be big or small. His incessant desire to know drove him to think nonstop about who the new arrival might be. Meanwhile, the millionaire gawked admiringly at the new arrival's casket. He decided to take it by force if need be, or maybe to purchase it for a price - any price - to make up for the loss of his own beloved casket, which had been ripped to pieces by Stalin. He immediately stood up to get a better look at it, and the skeleton followed after him.

"Who do you think the new arrival is going to be?" he asked.

"He obviously must be one of the greats of the twentieth century," muttered the millionaire.

"Now, help me tear this fabric."

The millionaire rushed to tear the fabric that had been fastened around the casket. He removed the fabric to unveil a golden-plated Star of David, embossed and shining. The skeleton read aloud the line written beneath the six-sided star.

Yitzhak Rabin – Prime Minister of Israel.

Everyone heard the name of the new arrival. Hitler jumped out from his seat, and Gamal Abdel Nasser followed him, aware of Nazis' hatred of Jews.

"He's my enemy too, Hitler," he said.

"I cannot accept the presence of this Jew among us," replied Hitler with a mark of decisiveness in his voice.

"Me and the Jews have a vendetta that goes back generations!"

"Beware of him, Hitler. We must expel him from this wing."

John Kennedy heard Abdel Nasser and Hitler's exchange, and he approached the two of them and said:

"Calm down, gentlemen. As of now, he's just another dead person, like us."

"The Jews robbed our eyes of sleep in life!" replied Abdel Nasser, anger still seething in his eyes.

"I will not permit them to do so in death as well!"

Hitler added in a loud voice:

"They stole Germany's resources, and led to our defeat in the first world war."

Churchill and Gandhi joined in the fray.

"It's only polite that we welcome our new guest. We are now in a world that's very different from that of the living."

"It's a world of reckoning," said Gandhi, hoping to relieve tensions.

Gandhi's words only made things worse. Indeed, Hitler took them as a linchpin around which he formed his own diatribe.

"Let's give him his reckoning, then!" he said, anger returning to his voice.

"Meaning we should not accept him in our presence!" said Abdel Nasser zealously.

Kennedy took a deep breath, and then said serenely:

"You are all great men, even if politeness isn't your thing. Let's resolve this matter democratically."

Hitler looked with a strange glance at him and responded:

"Democratically?"

"How?" Abdel Nasser asked inquisitively.

"We'll take a vote," responded Churchill.

"After all, you two aren't the only ones in this wing."

Hitler took a glance at everyone in the room and said, "I agree to a vote. It must be that everyone hates Jews. Let's resolve this democratically."

"I'm fine with Mr. Rabin staying with us," Kennedy announced unhesitatingly.

"I'm not!" Abdel Nasser shouted protestingly.

"Neither am I," Hitler followed suit.

Churchill and De Gaulle voted in favor of Rabin staying, and Abdel Hamid decided to abstain. Stalin decided to vote in favor of Rabin's staying, but only after much hesitation. The millionaire, on the other hand, voted in favor of Rabin's staying without batting an eye.

It was settled, then. The overwhelming majority of more than two thirds of the wing's residents were in favor of Yitzhak Rabin staying. They all proceeded towards the coffin to help Rabin out of it, with both Hitler and Abdel Nasser looking on indignantly yet helplessly at the scene as it unfolded before them.

Kennedy rushed to be the first to greet Rabin.

"Welcome, Mr. Rabin! Consider yourself at home."

"Thank you, sir, for your continued support."

Churchill extended his hands to greet him.

"It's what friends do."

Rabin caught a glimpse of Abdel Nasser and recognized him.

"Why look who's here! It's the son of my uncle," referencing the common descent of Arabs and Jews to Abraham via his sons Ishmael and Isaac respectively.

"How are you?!"

Abdel Nasser refused to reply. Stalin approached Rabin and shook his hand.

"I see your face is as red as roses. What's that about?" he asked, hoping to ease the palpable sense of tension tht overwhelmed the room.

"Oh, it's my beloved people. Why, they have such abhorrent customs! At my funeral, a majority of them heaped up on my grave to give me a farewell kiss. They damn near tore the skin of my face off! I can still feel the beard's rabbis prickling my cheeks like needles!"

Kennedy chuckled.

"They really do love you."

"Yes. . . so much so that they had me killed. And now here I am, with you all."

"I hope you have a pleasant stay with us," Churchill remarked, as if to renew his greeting.

"L'Chaim," Kennedy added.

"I thank you all very much," Rabin said in a voice that mixed gratitude with sorrow. And don't you worry about whether or not I'll feel at home here. We're used to being exiles."

"It's imperative," Gandhi began politely, "that we reconcile Mr. Rabin with Mrs. Hitler and Abdel Nasser."

"Forget it!" shouted Hitler.

"I'll never make peace with him!"

Abdel Nasser was a bit more lenient on this question.

"There can be no reconciliation with Israel or the Jews until they return the lands they occupied in 1967."

"Why is it that you don't like Jews, Hitler?" asked Kennedy.

"They are corrupt, and vile, oh Kennedy! If you don't believe me, then ask Abdel Nasser, or Stalin for that matter. They know them just as well as I do."

"They tried to ruin our Communist Revolution," Stalin said, volunteering his opinion without Kennedy having to ask.

"When we tried to put them in their place, they fled to Europe."

"A leftist-Communist uprising took place in Germany, resulting in the formation of a socialist government that altered Germany's political system and turned it into a republic. This was a direct result of Jewish intervention. In the end, the government's weakened political stance led to its surrender during the First World War, and ever since Germany began to tear apart at the seems, overwhelmed by debt and an assortment of political, economic and social crises."

"How could Emperor Guillaume II allow them to do this to Germany?" asked Abdel Hamid.

"Why, they forced him to relinquish the throne! He ended up taking refuge in Holland."

Abdel Hamid felt great sorrow for the misfortune of an old friend.

"I am sorry to hear of this tremendous loss for the Emperor Guillaume II. He did immense good for Germany, a country he loved and for which he sacrificed much in order to secure its interests."

"Damn the Jews! Damn them to hell!" said Hitler. The more he spoke of his hatred for the Jews, the more infuriated he became. "They ruined Europe!"

Rabin wasn't going to stand for this.

He was going to set the record straight – but he wasn't going to give Hitler the dignity of responding to him directly.

"Why don't you tell him that the reason Germany collapsed following World War I was because of the Versailles Agreement of 1919!" he scolded Kennedy.

"What did we have to do with that?!"

De Gaulle was of the same mind as Rabin.

"Indeed, the Germans were delt a rather severe hand in Versailles. It was inequitable in the extreme."

"Germany was eliminated from its rightful place among the bloc of great powers," Hitler continued.

Kennedy proffered insights fit for an expert.

"Clemenceau's sole concern was in securing advantages for France."

"In turn, David Lloyd George was determined to penalize and crush Germany." With that, Rabin concluded the list of key players.

Hitler jumped to his feet and began to pace around the room. Sitting had done nothing but exacerbate his anger.

"They thought it fit to limit the size of Germany's army to one hundred thousand men!" he berated.

Churchill was enjoying the sight of an enraged Hitler.

"Britain and France proceeded to divide Germany's colonies between themselves," he said, a smile breaking across his face.

Gandhi raised his voice for all to hear.

"These are the repercussions of imperial greed."

Kennedy intervened to wash America's hands of any responsibility for Germany's plight.

"No one can deny that Britain and France were blinded by the thrill of victory and that serious blunders were made. Then American President Wilson had been preoccupied at the time with finalizing his Fourteen Points and left the Europeans to handle their matters internally."

Hitler went back to blaming the Jews.

"We must not forget that the Jews had a hand in formulating this humiliating treaty."

Rabin wanted to beat his head against the wall until he fainted.

He then presented his argument in the form of a question:

"Was it the Jews who dictated the terms of the treaty on the victors of that war?"

Hitler scoffed derisively at the absurdity of the question.

"They demanded the leftist government accede to the terms of the treaty. Jews were pulling the world by the strings by means of their wealth."

"Money makes the world go round," exclaimed the millionaire, obviously flattered by Hitler's last remark.

"Whatever wealth the Jewish people managed to acquire was simply and solely a result of their acumen and determination," said Rabin, pulling out all the stops, "we worked hard and reaped the rewards!"

Hitler jumped on Rabin's remark and used it to attack the Europeans.

"The Jews seized control of all the major financial centers in Europe and tightened their grip!"

His earlier warm embrace of Rabin notwithstanding, De Gaulle appeared to pick up where Hitler left off.

"Chaos began to spread throughout Europe.

We needed to find a swift resolution of the matter."

Even Churchill got caught in Hitler's trap.

"And we did find a resolution: British issued the Balfour Declaration in 1917, which promised the Jews the establishment of a national homeland for them in Palestine."

"If a calamity befalls the Arabs, "Abdel Nasser murmured, "Britain is usually the reason why."

Hitler rejoiced, seeing as he was successful in exposing the rifts between Europe and the Jews.

"And don't you think for a minute that England gave the Jews such a promise out of concern or friendship. The Jews were nothing but a pawn in England's imperial game, a way to keep the Arab world ablaze in turmoil and conflict, thereby giving England an ongoing pretext for them to intervene whenever it liked."

"They had their eyes on the Suez Canal from the moment they planted the Zionist Entity in our midst!" exclaimed Abdel Nasser, having found bitter truth in Hitler's claims.

Gandhi saw parallels in his own experience of British colonialism.

"They had their eyes on the Cape of Good Hope when they established the Union of South Africa in 1909 as a colonial settlement."

Rabin was alert to Hitler's tactic and thought it pertinent to snatch the rug from underneath his feet.

"The Jewish people will forever remain indebted and grateful to Her Majesty's government for issuing the Balfour Declaration and for paving the way to Jewish statehood."

The millionaire, in turn, sought to remind those in attendance of the relevance of commerce to their discussion.

"Maritime trade boomed in the aftermath of Jewish immigration to Palestine."

Stalin had been absorbing attentively the attendant discussion about Jewish hegemony over Europe's financial markets and let out with pride, "The Bolshevik Revolution was successful in nationalizing the major institutions of finance, trade and transport in the country. All means of production rested firmly in the hands of the people as a whole."

The millionaire was not impressed. He saw in the measures taken by the Communists in Russia a kind of attack on the freedom of commerce and the movement of capital that could only suffocate the dynamism of the marketplace.

"But these acts stifled global capitalism."

"The Allies were concerned about them as well," the skeleton added, cautious so as not to draw the ire of Stalin.

No amount of reason could sway Stalin. The ideology of communism retained a prominent place in his heart and mind.

"The capitalists did everything they could to bring about the downfall of the Communist Revolution and to curb its gains. In turn, the Soviet Red Army defended our revolution with ironclad resolve. Under the leadership of Trotsky our armed forces rapidly swept through until they reached the gates of Warsaw, before the French advisory team could make it. In 1920, the Soviets defeated the anti-communist alliance in

Poland, and the pegs of the world's first Communist state had been tightly fastened."

"The leftist epidemic was spreading fast through Europe, "Churchill blurted out. "It was imperative to stand in its way."

"The German people made a terrible mistake," Hitler said with remorse in his voice. "It would have behooved them to decimate the Left and their allies rather than surrender power to them. It was the left-wing government that acceded to the humiliating terms of the 1919 Versailles Agreement."

Whatever its flaws, for Churchill the agreement was a boon for Great Britain.

"Germany was stripped of its colonies," he said with a grin.

De Gaulle agreed.

"France re-acquired the twin districts of Alsace and Lorraine."

"Germany was made to pay 56 billion dollars in compensation," the millionaire added. He closed his eyes, astounded by the enormity of the amount.

"The First World War came to an end, and a new balance of power was struck," De Gaulle said, his words marking the beginning of the end of the discussion. The tension on his face had relaxed noticeably.

"Empires had fallen, and other empires proceeded to take their place," Churchill said.

"New nation-states appeared," the skeleton said, building on Churchill's expression, "such as Poland and Finland."

"The Austrian Empire came to an end," uttered Hitler sorrowfully, "precluded from forming an alliance with Germany."

Abdel Hamid was holding back tears.

"The Treaty of Sevres stripped Turkey of Armenia and the Arab countries."

"The stage was set," said Hitler angrily, "for Britain and France, who proceeded to gobble up the world between themselves."

Gandhi let out a sorrowful sigh, and then said, "The number of those killed in the war came out to some ten million people. The injured and incapacitated came out to twice that number."

The skeleton brought to mind the headlines in those days.

"The world began to heal from the wounds of war and to come up with ways of preparing for reconstruction and to make death and destruction things of the past."

The skull had been a witness to the developments on the battlefield.

"The Ottoman Empire capitulated when the British forces captured the city of Aleppo. A treaty was signed in Moudros in 1918."

Abdel Nasser's face gleamed with glee.

"The Arabs exulted in the defeat of the Ottoman occupation that had oppressed them for four hundred years."

"We had found the increased strength of the Japanese and their incursions into Chinese territory a worrisome development," Stalin said, his tone indicating that the developments in question disquieted him still.

"The Allies were not content with the Treaty of Sevres,"

Abdel Hamid said, concerned for the fate of his empire.

"They and the Greeks constituted an imminent danger to Turkey, intent on carrying off with whatever territories remained out of their possession."

Kennedy saw things from a different light.

"The United States of America came out of the war stronger, economically and militarily. President Wilson acted to prevent the outbreak of new wars and to secure peace and stability in the world by advocating the adoption of his Fourteen Points. In fact, its stipulations were the nucleus for the nascent League of Nations, which was formed in 1920."

"Congress refused to ratify the League's charter or to permit the U.S.'s entry into it," Rabin noted, as if to hint that the U.S.'s intransigence with the world body had quite the early precedent.

"But Her Majesty's government didn't let matters stand as they were," noted Churchill, hoping to encourage the idea of international cooperation. "We sent Sir Edward Grey to the United States with the task of pushing the latter into joining the League."

CHAPTER 12

An Ice Storm Hits the Graveyard

The millionaire took a seat next to Gandhi. Distracted and desolate, he began to ruminate about the vast amounts of wealth which were spent during the First World War. He sighed despairingly, wishing that the money had fallen in his pockets rather than being wasted on armies and ammunition. He imagined what he would do had he been a ruler. Why, he would have enjoyed ordering Stalin to the gallows, his just due for breaking his flashy coffin and stripping him of his eminence over the other residents.

The skeleton drew close to the two of them, quivering from the cold that was piercing his bones.

"Winter this year is much colder than last year," Abdel Hamid said, he too convulsing from the fierceness of the cold.

Gandhi cast a glance at the skeleton.

"The First World War not only left us with ten million dead and some twenty million paralyzed. It seems it has also robbed us of the heat that would have kept this poor skeleton warm."

Stalin approached the group, rubbing his fingers and blowing on his hands to keep warm.

"Look at you all, shivering from the cold! Where do you guys think you are, Siberia? Hah! Why don't you guys step up and do something useful?"

Gandhi was bewildered.

"What do you suggest we do? Look at the skeleton! He's breaking my heart!"

Stalin skimmed the room, and then pointed at the scattered pieces of wood that had once been the millionaire's coffin.

"Come on, let's gather these into a pile and light a fire."

"Damn him!" the millionaire muttered under his breath.

"Damn him to hell! He wasn't satisfied with ruining my coffin, now he wants to burn it for his pleasure!"

All the same, Gandhi rose to join Stalin, and the millionaire followed along hesitantly. They moved some of the wood to the middle of the wing and tried to figure out ways of getting a fire going.

Rabin stared on as the men continued to gather pieces of wood left behind from the smashed coffin. He cast a despondent glance at his own coffin, as if to bid it farewell: after all, it's fate had been sealed, and it's turn would inevitably come.

The millionaire hurled the final piece of wood into the pile.

"Now, how do we light a fire?" the skeleton asked bemusedly.

"Ask Hitler," Stalin replied indignantly.

"He made a career out of keeping the world ablaze."

Hitler overheard their tete-a-tete. He took whatever was left of Churchill's cigar and threw it into the hearth. A fire started, its warmth spreading and rapidly encompassing the four corners of the catacomb. Soon, everyone was thanking Stalin for his efforts.

Abdel Hamid sat in contemplation, thinking about the Allies and the victories they attained in battle by virtue of their brawn and the manner in which they wreaked vengeance on their subjugated adversaries. He thought about how vindictive they were in exacting humiliation and how they vied in slicing up the lands they conquered into colonies, whose resources they purloined all the while the colonized – condemned to live a life of ignorance and backwardness – were powerless to stop them.

Abdel Hamid sighed frustration at the downfall of the Ottoman Empire and its losses in battle after having thrown in their lot with the Axis Powers during the war. He looked back on how the Allies dismissed a vast amount of commissioned officers in the Ottoman army, precluding the latter the chance to rise from the ashes. He gritted his teeth and clenched his fist as he bristled with rage at how the Allies aided the Greeks in their battle to break Turkey's resilience. If only he could have his revenge.

Abdel Hamid's solitude caught the eye of the skull.

"What's on your mind, Sultan?" the skull asked.

"I'm thinking about the consequences of the First World War."

"Power! Might! Force!" the skull retorted.

Gandhi inched toward the two of them.

"I'm a firm advocate of power," Abdel Hamid said, "I understand it through and through. I know what its effects are, particularly when combined with wealth and authority."

"They wielded it without any sense of compassion," Gandhi riposted.

The skull was furious at Gandhi's remark.

"Compassion has no place in the calculus of power. It can only serve to weaken it, blunt its force and alter its very nature and meaning."

Abdel Nasser decided to join in the fray.

"There is always the possibility of being forgiving whenever feasible, a time-honored Arab tradition."

"That's the thing with you Orientals," the skull quipped.

"It's your idealism. Your minds are overcome by fantasy. Inventing excuses is your only skill. That's why you'll forever remain weak."

The skull had more to say.

"In the academy we learned that once central command pinpoints a confirmed target that we are to advance on it without hesitation."

The circle was getting wider, and Rabin decided to toss his hat in on the side of the skull.

"Compassion is the language of the weak," he said.

Kennedy was slowly beginning to enjoy the wing's newfound warmth.

"Wilson, Lloyd George and Clemenceau looked after international affairs following the end of World War I," he waxed energetically.

"But if the victors were operating on the logic of power, then isn't it fair to say that the principles of human rights that President Wilson advocated became obsolete?" the skeleton asked.

"It's interesting," De Gaulle rejoined.

"The League of Nations was established to uphold those very principles. Yet the United States decided not to join."

"Congress refused to approve such a move," Kennedy let out with a sigh.

"Unfortunately, British Secretary of State Edward Grey failed to dissuade Congress from making this decision," Churchill said, his head lowered and his eyes stuck to the floor.

Kennedy's words had a tone of consolation to them.

"Even the President of the United States couldn't stop Congress from refusing his request."

The skeleton scratched the back of his head, and then asked slyfully, "And what became of Russia in the aftermath of the War?"

Stalin replied, "Leave Russia alone. It was preoccupied with consolidating the gains of the revolution and confronting its enemies. It was not pleased with the plans the British and French had for the Old Man's former belongings. In fact, it was instrumental in exposing their plot to distribute the lands of the Middle East as war booty."

"Mr. Stalin," Churchill interjected, intent on trapping Stalin, "might you explain how those documents reached the hands of the Russian government?"

Rabin caught the hint.

"You're referring to the Skyes-Picot Agreement?"

"Actually, it's the Sykes-Picot-Sazonov agreement," De Gaulle said, his elbow leaning against his tower of books.

The skeleton gasped and nearly lost his ability to speak when he realized the import of De Gaulle's remark.

"In that case, Russia was part of the plot to split the former Ottoman territories in the wake of the war."

"A junior partner," Rabin said derisively.

"It only managed to stake its claim to a piece of territory in northern Iran."

Stalin didn't bat an eye.

"That was prior to the October Revolution, during the days of the Tsar. Lenin rejected France and Britain's conniving ways and opted to expose them and inform the concerned parties of their intentions."

Hitler had been listening quietly to the ongoing discussion. As he placed his hands above the warm blaze that arose out of the smashed pieces of wood that had once been the millionaire's coffin his heart seared with rage at the mention of Britain and France. Italy too drew his ire, as they had betrayed the Axis and joined the Allies in order to preserve their control over the north African colony of Libya. The loss of the German colonies in the Pacific Islands and Africa saddened him.

"Let's not forget the Allies' rapacity for the German colonies," he said, as if reminiscing.

"To the victors go the spoils," replied the skeleton coolly.

"Survival of the fittest," Abdel Hamid interposed with sadness.

"The law of the jungle!" Gandhi added.

Abdel Nasser was infuriated.

"I believe Clemenceau, France's Prime Minister, fancied himself in a hospital. After all, he began his life studying medicine, even if he didn't complete his studies. It appears he developed a taste for surgery and surgical procedures. Thus, when the map of the Middle East was presented to him during the Sikes-Picot meeting he wielded his red marker as adeptly as a surgeon with his scalp, tearing the Arab body apart and drawing borders, using (A) to indicate territories that would be placed under French control and (B) to indicate territories to be placed under British control."

"Was the agreement kept as is, without any adjustment or improvement of any kind?" the skeleton asked.

"Monsieur Sykes ended up regretting the decision to share the spoils with France," De Gaulle replied resentfully.

"He ended up doing everything in his power to take France out of the picture and replace it with the United States."

"In the accursed Versailles Agreement, France relinquished its claim to Mosul in favor of Britain," Hitler said, seeking to further enrage De Gaulle.

Rabin couldn't be more thrilled.

"The second compromise was even better: France relinquished its claim to Palestine in favor of Britain as well."

"And that delights you, doesn't it?!" shot back Abdel Nasser reproachfully.

The millionaire took a moment to think and then said, "Why, how else could they guarantee the fulfillment of the promise they made in the Balfour Declaration to establish a national homeland for the Jews?"

"Well, why did France agree to repudiate their claims to these territories?" asked Abdel Hamid.

"It was merely a ploy in France's sneaky little game," Hitler replied.

"That's correct," the skull added, "a political tactic whereby they relinquish their claims to some things in order to attain control over others."

Hitler agonized in knowing that what the skull said was true. "They sought guarantees for their ruses against Germany in Europe."

"It's a game of gains and acquisitions," noted the millionaire. "A game that can only keep the world once again at the brink of impending disaster," the skeleton muttered underneath his breath.

"Perhaps Congress made a mistake in refusing to ratify the United States' accession to the League of Nations," Kennedy said, changing his seating style into an upright position. "It's headquarters then became situated in Geneva, quite distant from the United States. The League allocated four permanent seats for each of Britain, France, Italy and Japan, the four of whom would resolve all matters of global concern in a manner that best suited their interests. They neglected to establish the International Court of Justice which the League's charter had provided for, and the League's mission ended up becoming diluted in the absence of a major political player such as the United States of America."

Abdel Nasser concurred with Kennedy's analysis.

"The League issued a series of Mandate Acts at the San Remo Conference in 1920: France was given a mandate over Syria and Lebanon, Britain over Iraq and Palestine. This, of course, meant a failure to go through on their promises to Sharif Hussein."

"Power, like love, is blind," the skull waxed lyrically.

"Mr. Gandhi?" the skeleton asked. "Didn't the British imprison you around that time, in 1922? Why did they do that?"

"Why, it was a repayment of kindnesses! India had fought side by side with Great Britain in World War I, and were instrumental in securing a victory for the Allies. It was only natural that they would offer us imprisonment in return."

"I hear that!" Abdel Nasser jeered.

Churchill was not amused.

"You know, we did let you off easy. . ."

"Indeed!" Gandhi exclaimed. "I was sentenced to prison without hard labor, as the colonial administration had feared the outbreak of popular riots. Given my nonviolent leanings, I can't help but sympathize."

"Seriously, why didn't you grant them their independence?" Kennedy asked, whispering in Churchill's ear.

"It wasn't the right time!" Churchill exclaimed in a loud voice.

"We feared for the lives of our settler population. Who knew what these rabble were up to?"

Abdel Nasser exploded in his rage.

"Naturally! For the colonizer only understands the language of force. Otherwise, they exult in their arrogance, deeming it unnatural for 'rabble' like us to fight for our country's freedom and independence."

The skeleton had a good question in mind.

"What did the Ottoman Empire reap from its entry into the war?" he asked, his question cutting short Churchill and Abdel Nasser's violent back-and-forth.

"We lost the war," Abdel Hamid said sorrowfully.

"We lost control over the Arab territories, Armenia slipped from our grasp. Turkey was given defined borders."

"Why don't you be thankful?" Hitler said as if to mock Abdel Hamid.

"If it were up to Britain and France they would have divided Turkey into pieces as well."

"I suggest that Turkey's national holiday be set at the day the Treaty of Sevres was signed in 1920," Churchill said with the confidence of a champion. "After all, it was that agreement that preserved Turkey's territorial integrity."

"The agreement had also called for the establishment of a Kurdish state," Kennedy added.

"As fate would have it," the skeleton said with a snicker.

"The Kurds would end up divided between Iraq, Iranand Turkey."

Abdel Hamid was sick and tired of this constant belittling of Turkey.

"The day that treaty was signed was a catastrophic day for the Turks. It could never be a national holiday, for a national holiday is like a lofty tree, watered with the blood of patriots. It is the blood of these patriots – pure like the driven snow! – that will kindle the torch of freedom that will inspire future generations and keep our homeland free and independent."

"Fine," Churchill said jocularly. "What say we consider it a national holiday for Armenia and the Arab countries?"

"The national holiday for the Arab peoples shall be set on the day in which the Palestinian people will liberate their land and regain their freedom and independence," Abdel Nasser said with inimitable zeal.

Rabin, who had been seated comfortably between Kennedy and Churchill, thought it wise to drop in a word:

"We in Israel have a national holiday. You Arabs, on the other hand, have some twenty national holidays, and you know just as well as I do that they'll never be combined into one. Israel's continued existence is a fait accompli: it was created to last. Never will it lose a war to the Arabs; a loss in battle would be nothing short of a death sentence for us."

Churchill's eyes nodded at Rabin encouragingly.

"The West would never permit for its beloved child – a child it took pains in raising and looking after – to be killed off just so the Arabs can be happy."

In the deep recesses of Abdel Nasser's memory hope commingled with regret.

"Would that the Arabs could agree on a single national holiday. Then the so-called 'Israeli' national holiday would be so much more easier to stomach."

"As long as Israel remains strong and retains its military superiority over the Arabs," the skull admonished, directing his remarks to Abdel Nasser, "then it appears likely that these 'countries' will only disintegrate further and give rise to the creation of more countries. If anything, that means there are going to be more national holidays in that part of the world."

"Why not give peace a chance?" Gandhi asked in astonishment.

"Peace?" Abdel Hamid asked sardonically, his right hand smacking his forehead as if put off by the simplemindedness of Gandhi's question.

"Why, as we Muslims say, Assalamu 'alaykum (peace be upon you), Mr. Gandhi! Or as they might say in English, 'Rise and shine, silly!'"

He continued on.

"Peace is a good thing in theory. But it requires first and foremost that states operate on good intentions and, second, that they are willing to implement agreements formulated on the basis of said intentions."

"Were the stipulations of the San Remo agreement implemented?" the skeleton asked doubtfully.

"Most certainly!" De Gaulle replied.

"Despite the stubbornness of the British and their determination to retain control of certain territories that were slated to be under the French mandate, such as Aleppo and Beirut."

Churchill found De Gaulle's description of British intentions disagreeable.

"Yet Britain complied with the terms of its agreements and withdrew its armed forces from the areas that were to be rendered unto the French."

"This is a point on which the West has the right to be proud," Rabin said, eager to reap points for the Allies. "They keep to their agreements, and are true to their promises."

Rabin's remark aroused Stalin from his stupor.

"Duplicitousness is a strange thing to take pride in. If only the rooms in which these folks met behind closed doors could talk and tell us about the arbitrary borders that were drawn in order to feed the West's avarice for territory and resources."

The millionaire pursed his lips.

"It only makes sense that states would do anything to get their hands on those."

"What of the promises made on behalf of the great powers to grant independence to the colonies that participated in the war? After all, they didn't hesitate to offer up their best men for the great powers' benefit!" the skeleton asked dispassionately.

The skeleton's question enraged Abdel Nasser.

"Initially, they agreed to help the Arabs get their independence in exchange for the latters help during the war. In the end, however, they imposed 'mandates' that colonized their countries!"

"It's amazing how things change," De Gaulle proffered in a cool and collected manner.

"The Arabs were in need of the mandates, to help them along the path to civilization and to train them to be able to rule themselves."

Abdel Nasser was not convinced.

"Why did you divide Syria into four nations?"

"Come on, Abdel Nasser," Rabin shot back slyly.

"A multitude of national holidays isn't such a bad thing. In fact, the Arabs ought to thank the great powers for giving them such a nice array of national holidays."

Abdel Nasser shot a glance at Rabin that could only indicate revulsion, and then asked, "And whatever happened to President Wilson's Fourteen Points, Mr. Kennedy?"

"The United States established the King Crane commission on President Wilson's orders on a fact-gathering mission and to apprise itself of the residents and what they wanted for themselves," Kennedy replied.

"It was the commission that deemed it necessary for Syria and Iraq to be granted their independence," Gandhi added.

"It also noted that the Syrian people desired for Faysal to be the Sovereign over all of historical Syria, including Lebanon and Palestine, and to nullify the Sykes-Picot Agreement and the Balfour Declaration."

Rabin's eyes protruded out of their sockets.

"Great Britain's honor would have been mired in dirt had such recommendations been implemented."

"Of course, Britain and France rejected the recommendations of that commission," Churchill replied, his composure fully intact.

"As a result, President Wilson declared that he was withdrawing his support from the Allies," Kennedy continued.

De Gaulle was incensed.

"France and Britain rushed to inaugurate the San Remo Conference in response."

In a voice brimming with sorrow Abdel Nasser explained the repercussions of that conference.

"They partitioned Greater Syria and declared the establishment of a French mandate over Syria and Lebanon."

"Britain took Iraq and Jordan," Rabin interrupted, "and Palestine as well but only after reassuring us that Balfour would be implemented."

With an inflated sense of vanity and self-importance Churchill rejoined, "Britain came through on its pledges and agreements, and French troops landed on Beirut's shores."

"Equipped with the latest in military technology the French proceeded to march on and occupy Damascus," Abdel Nasser continued, only stopping to sigh petulantly. "Upon their entry they were confronted by the newly formed Syrian army headed by then Defense Minister Yusuf al-Azmeh. He was martyred in the battle of Maysaloun."

"The French entered Damascus and overthrew King Faysal, who was then exiled to Italy," De Gaulle added with a ring of confidence in his voice.

"What could a rifle do against tanks and canons?" the skull asked rhetorically, seeking to cut the French army's sense of greatness down to size.

"Determination is more powerful than weapons," replied a vehement Gandhi.

Kennedy adjusted his sitting again and said, "It's also important to note that some powers might take advantage of conditions in the international arena. For instance, after the United States withdrew its support from the Allies, Britain and France directed their attention to the Old Man's fallout. In accordance with a cease-fire treaty negotiated with Turkey the Allies' navies seized control of the Bosphorus, the Dardanelles, and the Port of the City of Istanbul."

"Furthermore," Stalin continued, "Armenia declared its independence from Turkey."

Abdel Hamid remembered those days with sorrow.

"The Greeks – in concert with the Allies - occupied the city of Izmir, from whence they intended to conquer the entire Anatolian plateau."

"What was the Turkish government's response?" the skeleton asked.

"The Turkish government acceded to the demands of the Allies, sending Mustafa Kemal – who had then been promoted to the rank of lieutenant general – to crush the resistance of their own people."

"But Mustafa Kemal disobeyed his orders and joined the resistance, taking the lead and instructing them to remain valiant," Abdel Nasser shouted gloatingly.

"The Turkish government was certainly not pleased,"

Abdel Hamid responded.

"It issued a royal decree that not only relieving him of his command but also expressly deeming him an agent provocateur."

Abdel Nasser wouldn't let up.

"But General Mustafa Kemal rebelled against the government decision and formed a rival transitional government."

"As a result," De Gaulle said, "the government feared that Mustafa Kemal – later known as Ataturk (father of the Turks) - popularity was on the rise, and promptly sentenced him to death for insubordination."

Abdel Hamid was no admirer of Mustafa Kemal, but that didn't stop him from being fair:

"General Mustafa Kemal gathered a large number of men and proceeded to train and arm them. The valiant Turks answered the call of jihad, and fulfilled their national duty of resisting the occupying force."

The Turkish governments' position had been favorable to the Allies, as Churchill confirmed:

"The Allies laid a brutal siege, barring food and equipment from reaching Mustafa Kemal's troops. The Greeks, in turn, landed in southern Anatolia, and their forces proceeded in the direction of Ankara."

"The Turks under the leadership of Mustafa Kemal clashed with the Greeks and after three days of fierce battle – during which they inflicted heavy losses on the enemy and even captured their leadership – the Turks had triumphed, and Mustafa Kemal emerged as a national hero."

Kennedy proceeded to describe the other repercussions of the battle:

"The Turks imposed a suffocating blockade on the Armenians, as they suspected that the latter were covertly supporting the Greeks. This led to the mass exodus of Armenians from Cilicia who were fleeing for their very lives."

Abdel Hamid concealed his indignation about the matter of the Armenians and tried to take the conversation in a different direction.

"Mustafa Ataturk became a national savior; his victories in battle led the great powers to adopt the Lausanne Treaty of 1923 in which Turkey was recognized as an independent state that ceded control of Armenia and the Arab territories."

"But that 'independence' came with preconditions," Stalin said in his distinctive revolutionary spirit.

"Yes, the Four Crouzon Conditions," Churchill clarified while trying to conceal a mischievous grin.

Stalin proceeded to list the stipulations of the agreement.

"It secured free navigation through Turkish waters. . ."

"It declared the end of the Sultanate and Caliphate and transformed Turkey into a secular state,"

Abdel Hamid said, interrupting Stalin. He was too irate to delay mention of what he felt was the most far-reaching and consequential of the stipulations.

"Mustafa Kemal was elected president to lead the newly announced Turkish republic," Kennedy added, emphasizing the democratic character of the new regime.

With a heavy heart and a sigh Abdel Hamid commented, "He was offered the position of a sultan but he preferred to abolish the sultanate altogether."

"The 'Father of the Turks' didn't stop there," the skeleton added, "he also abolished the Islamic caliphate in 1924, breaking the long-held bond between religion and state."

"Mustafa Kemal replaced the Arabic script in which the Turkish language was written with the Latin script,"

Abdel Nasser added.

"This was followed by a ban on the hijab, and the fez was replaced with the European-style top hat. It was thus that Turkey cast off its Islamic heritage at the behest of the West."

Abdel Hamid was wringing his hands in distress.

"What a miserable loss! Four centuries of empire was erased with the stroke of a pen."

The skeleton sought to stir Abdel Hamid's anger while keeping the pretense of narrating events dispassionately:

"It was said that one of General Mustafa Ataturk's advisors relayed to him the desire of many of the Turkish people to perform the ritual pilgrimage to Mecca, to which he responded:

'Anyone who would like to go is welcome to go, but they must pay one hundred golden liras for a plane ticket. Travelling by land will not be permitted.'

"Those concerned were informed of the decision. Believing men and women dashed to register for the pilgrimage and to pay the desired fee. When hajj season arrived, no one was permitted to leave and protests broke out. It was then ordered that a painter should be hired to paint on the doors of all who paid the required fee: 'It's the intention that counts. May you be rewarded for your efforts.'

CHAPTER 13
The Yearning of a Whale

The skeleton crept into the gravedigger's office and thought it wise to remain alone for a while. He took a seat on the firm black leather chair. It was quite comfortable.

He found a few newspapers on the desk in front of him. He decided to skim through them for a bit, the headlines catching his attention. He then decided that sticking around by himself was a bad idea, and he rose from his place, gathered the newspapers under his arm and rushed back to the third wing.

The skeleton was pacing so fast that he lost his balance as he opened the door to the wing and almost fell, but then quickly regained his balance. The skull caught a glimpse of him as he stumbled in.

"Why are you running so fast? Is someone after you?" the skull asked.

"Maybe I'm just running away from the latest news," the skeleton replied, lifting the hand in which he held the newspapers which he brought with him from the gravedigger's office. He flung one in the direction of Winston Churchill and another at De Gaulle.

"Is it World War III yet?" Hitler asked.

The skeleton begins reading off the headlines in a loud voice:

"Love is forbidden! Love is outlawed!"

"This is nonsense!" Gandhi shouted.

"Mere tabloid fodder! Love is central to the progress of the human race!"

Stalin snatched the newspaper from the skeleton's hands and read the headline for himself:

"Princess Diana and her lover Dodi Fayed dead."

Abdel Nasser had been listening carefully.

"It seems the victim is Arab."

Stalin flicked through the paper.

"It says that he's the son of the Egyptian billionaire Mohamed Al-Fayed, owner of the Harrod's department store chain."

"Kindly read to us the details of the story in full, Mr. Stalin," Abdel Nasser said firmly but decorously.

"World news agencies report that on the 31st night of August 1997 Princess Diana passed away along with her lover Dodi Fayed in a gruesome car accident in a tunnel underneath the Alma Bridge in the French capital of Paris."

Abdel Hamid felt moved by the harrowing nature of the report.

"I suspect foul play led to their deaths," he asserted.

"But why Paris?" asked De Gaulle, his voice emitting a mixed tone of sorrow and rebuke.

"It's a city of romantic love.

Has the world really changed so much?

Has Paris changed such that love is seen as something condemnable?"

"If anyone committed a crime here, it must have been someone from the East," Kennedy observed.

"Why do you believe the criminal must be from the East?" the skeleton asked.

"Rumors had been spreading of a romantic relationship between Princess Diana and an Arab millionaire,"

Rabin said, seeming to back Kennedy's observations with the necessary evidence.

Kennedy scratched the back of his head.

"I heard of many stories coming from the East of couples being murdered for no crime but that they had loved one another sincerely and deeply, their lives cut short after having experienced but a few moments of passion, under the pretext of defending a family's honor. In those societies, it is forbidden for men and women to fall in love."

Gandhi, himself a man of the East, sought to correct Kennedy's misperceptions:

"Love between a man and a woman is a virtuous and honorable thing."

Abdel Hamid too understood the Eastern mindset.

"Love between a man and a woman is something that is encouraged in the East. But our inherited customs and traditions lay down a set of rules to keep a romantic relationship from spiraling out of control, most importantly that love can only happen within the confines of marriage and the family. And any trespasses. . ."

"And they are many," Hitler interrupted, "but they happen secretly, away from the glares of society."

"Illegitimate love relationships are considered an infringement on the requirements of honor and dignity," Abdel

Nasser shot back, ostensibly biased for the mores and values that he is familiar with.

"It's an attack on virtue that necessitates death,"

Abdel Hamid added.

"In the best case the matter might be dealt with by swiftly marrying the two perpetrators to each other in order to conceal the scandal."

"The most beautiful love is the kind that comes without an appointment, suddenly and unexpectedly, like a gentle breeze on a sunny day," the millionaire said. "Diana could have been that gentle breeze."

Rabin closed his days in an endeavor to remember.

"Prince Charles' popularity was on the rise when he married Princess Diana."

De Gaulle recalled a similar incident from his own time.

"Just as President Kennedy's popularity rose in France when word got out that he was marrying Jacqueline Kennedy.

"I saw this with my own eyes when he visited me at the Elysee Palace."

"I take all the credit for that," Kennedy responded. "After all, I'm the one who brought Jackie with me to France."

Rabin began to recount things he had heard about the incident.

"Apparently there was great friction between Prince Charles and Princess Diana that led to their divorce.

Diana must have been a stupid girl – that's probably why Charles' mistress Camilla Parker Bowles was able to replace her so quickly."

"On a lighter note,"

De Gaulle said, "the marriage had borne fruit: two boys, one William and the other Harry."

Hitler shot a glance at De Gaulle from the corner of his eye.

"You're a sneaky fellow, De Gaulle! Do you mean to say that jealousy had been the motive behind Princess Diana's death?"

Churchill folded the newspaper and said, "Love could never be forbidden in a country such as Great Britain which gave the world Shakespeare and his chef d'oeuvre, 'Romeo and Juliet.'"

"You seem to forget that Shakespeare had Romeo killed,"

Hitler replied glibly.

Churchill maintained a calm exterior.

"Well, the events of the play occur in Italy, not in Britain. Furthermore, Romeo drank the poison of his own volition as a testament to the momentousness of love after having realized that he couldn't live another moment without Juliet."

Kennedy was impressed by Romeo's sincerity.

"When Juliet awoke from her induced trance, she found her love lying beside her, lifeless."

"She saw the vial of poison in his hand and realized what happened,"

Churchill continued.

"As soon as she did, she decided to drink whatever poison was left. Finding it empty, she cast it aside and edged closer to Romeo and cupped his cheeks with her hands. Then she planted a long, passionate kiss on his lips, hoping to suck the poison from his lips. When that failed, she took his dagger and stabbed herself in the heart. She, too, chose to die with him of her own volition."

"Yet Princess Diana and her lover Fayed died in a tragedy that was not of their own choosing," noted Hitler, finding a contrast between the two stories.

Abdel Nasser was convinced that racial prejudice lay behind the murder of Diana and Fayed.

"Theirs was a forbidden love.

They had crossed a red line. For she is a princess, a holder of the noble bloodline. She had no right to love a young Arab boy.

Not only that, but she had no right to give in to her heart's desires in the first place."

Gandhi squeezed Abdel Nasser's hand.

He saw in love a means to attain transcendence.

"Love knows no racial prejudices! It cares not for color, or gender, or race! It's blissfully ignorant, not understanding or seeking to understand history or geography. It doesn't recognize borders!"

Abdel Nasser was unmoved.

"Why, how could this 'terrorist!' manage to infiltrate the borders of Great Britain, climb past the menacing walls of that intimidating palace and steal the heart of the princess! That was the nail in his coffin. This is forbidden, The skeleton proceeded to sketch the broad strokes of the conspiracy.

"If the deaths of Princess Diana and her lover Fayed had been engineered rather than come about as a result of a car accident, then it must have been that their love had been sentenced to death without the possibility of remand. It must have been that they planned for the murder with an eye for precision. The princess's heart and its desires had become a blight on the family's honor, and there was simply no alternative to executing the sentence."

"Prejudice is blind,"

Gandhi said disdainfully.

"It grows in the fertile soil of malevolence and hatred for the other. Oh, how many an innocent soul has been the victim of prejudice!"

"You should ask Hitler,"

Kennedy said with a childlike innocence.

"He's an expert in persecution and mass murder."

Hitler decided to play ball.

"If Diana's love meant the pollution of the noble bloodline, then it was not enough that she be killed. It would have been imperative for the killer to wipe out any trace of her in this world, even if that meant feeding her tender body to the sharks."

The skull contemplated what it would do in the killer's place.

"There are those who kill for money.

They tend to ensure that the deed is carried out successfully."

The skeleton went back to considering the aftermath of the crime.

"I imagine there were four contracted killers, on standby waiting to put the clandestine operation into motion. When the hand of the clock hit three in the morning, and before dawn had the chance to crack, they will head in the direction of Princess Diana's grave, a place filled with many emotions – love and sympathy blending with sorrow, anger, even rejection of the tragic death – left by her well-wishers in their many visits to the gravesite, during which they envelop her tomb with flowers and roses of different shapes and sizes, in addition to lilies, jasmine flowers and cloves, depicting a beautiful array of colors ranging from red to yellow. The flowers emit the distinct sense of perfume that can be smelled from hundreds of meters away."

Gandhi listened closely to the skeleton's description and sighed deeply.

He had found himself immersed in the scenario depicted by his words, and found himself impelled to add more:

"The white leaves of the jasmine flower, sensing the impending danger and fearing for the fate of the martyr of love, that princess who rests peacefully, and send an urgent cable that is carried by means of ether waves. The cable reaches the roses in the area, which immediately cease to emit the pure perfume smell that indicates the location of the princess."

Hitler tried to imagine how such an operation might be brought to fruition.

"The four hired killers scale the walls of the graveyard and trample the flowers underfoot," he said, causing Gandhi's romantic scene to combust into flames. But Gandhi wouldn't let up:

"In the midst of which they would kiss their boots and beg and plead for them to leave the princess be."

"But the promise of great financial reward had turned their hearts to stone," the millionaire said self-assuredly.

Abdel Nasser felt as if he were caught in a cobweb, stuck between feelings of sorrow and anger.

"They proceeded on their mission, broke through the door of the gravesite and stole the coffin with the poor princess trapped inside," he said with noted agitation in his voice.

"They then carry it away on a truck that would take them in the direction of the city port, leaving in their tracks the flowers and roses who weep mournfully at the loss of the princess."

"They board a ship that had been waiting for them,"

De Gaulle continued, "carrying the casket under their watchful eye.

The ship heads north at a speed of fifty nautical miles an hour."

Stalin yawned, and then continued, "It must be that they were in a rush to get to the part of the ocean where all the sharks are. Most likely they couldn't wait to be rid of the casket."

"So they can get their mighty reward," the millionaire continued, his hands scratching his belly. "The man who hired them must have gotten rather impatient in the meantime."

"The English are a rather cruel people," Hitler said in disgust.

"Look who's talking!" Churchill chastised.

"Well, the British are known for their cold-bloodedness," the skeleton said snidefully.

Gandhi was intent on steering the conversation back on topic.

"By doing so they've only gone and made their crime even more reprehensible!"

"It is a reprehensible crime,"

Abdel Nasser said.

"Whatever its motives might be, the crime remains a despicable act."

"It's textbook arrogance and revenge," the skeleton declared resolutely.

"Why not let justice run its course?" a moved Kennedy asked.

"Exactly, Mr. Kennedy,"

De Gaulle said in a forthright manner.

"And that's precisely what happened. Everyone knows that whales are aquatic mammals that live family lives: a female whale gives birth, nurses her young, falls in love, and is jealous of rival females."

"Just like humans,"

Abdel Hamid concluded after a short pause.

"From the emotional standpoint, yes."

"Actually, they are more loyal than humans," Kennedy remarked curtly.

"A whale who loses his female mate never goes for another."

"Such devotion!" Hitler replied satirically.

De Gaulle decided to tell a story of his own.

"In the depths of the ocean in which the mercenaries set sail there lived a white whale. It was six meters in length and weighed 1500 kilograms. He lived a lonely and sad life, having recently lost his wife, with whom he was madly in love. . ."

Abdel Nasser was not impressed.

"Perhaps he spent his time composing poetry for her."

"And stand by the ruins of his beloved and weep,"

Abdel Hamid said, referencing a recurrent theme in Arabic poetry.

De Gaulle ignored the peanut gallery.

"His sadness was accompanied with rage. He rose to the surface of the water to take a deep breath of fresh air and noticed the ship carrying the casket of the late princess. He dipped deeper into the water to keep a safe distance from the ship, and then – in a feat of uncontrollable rage - turned around and edged towards the surface of the water with the aim of destroying the ship. He picked up his speed and crashed into the ship with the back of his head, tearing it into many pieces. The four men drowned in the ocean water, and the wooden frame of the casket broke. As the whale sat and observed the outcome of his attack he observed the princess drowning. The scene of the princess drifting further underwater sent a shudder deep to his core. He shot through the ocean in the direction of the princess, swallowing her whole and carrying her off to a far away place, leaving behind the four hired killers, who continued to knock into one another in the ocean depths until they finally became easy prey for the white sharks that lay in wait."

Hitler would not let up.

"So she survived the sharks. . .only to be swallowed by a whale."

"Who would gnaw on her bones," the skull said with a fertile imagination.

"No," De Gaulle replied after calm deliberation. "When he reached the ocean's seabed – where he lived – he spit her out. He stared at her admiringly, and felt tenderness towards her. Her body emitted a pure fragrance that, in tandem with the intoxicating aroma of amber that emerged from the ocean, left the whale feeling rejuvenated. Her appearance had been something of a consolation, a means by which he could forget the sadness and loneliness that came with the feeling of being abandoned and deserted in his own habitat. Life rushed through his veins anew, and the whale decided to return her to her final resting place. And that's how the princess' body survived."

Kennedy was overcome with joy.

"Long live justice!"

Stalin was skeptical.

"I thought dolphins were mans' friends, not whales."

"It's the same species."

Abdel Hamid was on De Gaulle's side.

"Everyone knows how a whale saved the prophet Jonah, peace and blessings be upon him."

The skeleton thought a eulogy was in order.

"The princess was famous for her philanthropic activities, particularly her efforts to help cure AIDS and promote demining in previous war zones."

Gandhi smiled at the skeleton.

"That is why the whale saved her and left the four mercenaries to meet their fate."

De Gaulle concluded on a happy note.

"The salt in the ocean waters had returned the princess's body to the state that it had known in life, and the ocean's amber fragrance infused her with new life. She now spends her days with delight, swimming and playing with the whale. The end!"

CHAPTER 14
Blue Smoke

The smoke rising from Mr. Churchill's cigar coalesced into what appeared to be a cloud that hovered near the ceiling of the grave's corridor.

"Mr. Churchill!" Hitler said, with insults and saliva flying from his mouth as he screamed and shouted. "Would you please have mercy on my respiratory system and put out your cigar!"

Churchill shot a glance at his cigar, amused at the sight of the rings of blue smoke that shot out successively from the mouth of the cigar. "It appears you are ignorant of cigar etiquette, Adolf Hitler," he said with derision.

The voice of an annoyed Hitler was music to Stalin's ears.

"I'm a great admirer of etiquette," he told Churchill.

"Might you say more on the subject?"

"Well, there's a big difference between a cigarette and a cigar."

"It's true," Hitler said mockingly.

"They differ in size and in the quality of tobacco."

"No, I mean in terms of method, esteem, and etiquette."

"That's true," Stalin noted, clearly interested in the topic at hand. "What more?"

Hitler huffed and fumed, keeping up an uncomfortable silence.

"The common folk smoke cigarettes, while the elite smoke cigars." Sultan Abdel Hamid decided to join in the conversation and took a seat next to Hitler.

"A cigar has its own utensils and implements.

It is placed in an expensive wooden box.

It has its own cutter, and no seasoned cigar smoker would dare to tap away the excess ash no matter how long it gets."

"What happens if the ash ends up on a high-priced carpet?" Abdel Hamid asked.

"That is the underlying principle of cigar etiquette: the cigar is always more worthy than the carpet."

"From whence does a cigar derive its value?" Stalin asked with continued interest.

"From its distinct taste and its hand-made design. In addition, the more costly cigars are rolled on the thighs of young girls."

"I don't smoke, but I respect cigars, particularly high-priced ones," Abdel Hamid remarked.

Hitler goes off in a rage, a build-up of saliva interrupting his words as he says, "Costly or cheap, I don't care! It's poison! Your troops also used poison gas against our trenches during World War

I. I've had enough!"

The smoke grew particularly thick in the closed, unvented air of the wing. "Open the door, Mr. Gandhi," said Kennedy with slight drool emerging from his mouth.

"What if the gravedigger comes and finds the door open?" the skull asked anxiously.

"Don't worry," Abdel Nasser replied. "He'll probably think the wind threw it open."

"I promise to buy you a pricy wooden cigar box as a gift," the millionaire told Churchill.

"Thank you, Aristotle. Once again, I am reminded of the trips you and I took by sea."

"Don't you forget to get him a cigar cutter as well, Onassis," Hitler muttered angrily, obviously sarcastically yet in a tone that still sounded like an order.

"One that is both long and wide."

"Why wide?" Abdel Hamid asked naively.

"I want it wide enough to fit around this Jew's neck so that I can slice his head off," Hitler said, referring to Onassis.

Onassis cupped his neck with his hands and fell silent. Rabin took a seat next to Kennedy. He didn't stand for Jews being abused and insulted in life. He wasn't going to put up with it in death. "Onassis isn't even a Jew!"

"Anyone who hoards wealth is a despicable Jew, regardless of his ethnic origins," replied Hitler.

"He's nothing but an energetic and astute businessman!" Rabin exclaimed.

"Is there any truth to the idea that a capitalist Jew is inherently predisposed to exploiting the poor," Churchill said, directing his words to Rabin.

"A communist Jew is usually a conniver," Stalin added.

"A usurer of the first degree," Abdel Nasser joined in on the cacophony.

Abdel Hamid cracked his knuckles.

"They claim to be God's chosen people, and that heaven is theirs alone. Their record on Earth is filled with incidents of exploitation and connivance."

"Wealth accumulation is more important to a Jew than people's lives," Stalin continued.

"It's true! Jews even find war a means to accumulate wealth. To them it's just another windfall!" Hitler said, seething with the cumulative of decades of hate.

"The First World War harvested the lives of millions of innocent victims. It destroyed whole nations," Kennedy said bitterly.

"Enormous amounts of money were wasted needlessly," the millionaire said with pain, as if he himself had paid the costs of war from his own pockets.

"A plethora of newly invented weapons were utilized, including poison gas," the skeleton said, referencing a marked shift in the brutality of war.

"There is no escaping the conclusion that Jewish money was invested profitably in this war,"

Abdel Hamid said, as if speaking from experience.

"Like the Arabic expression goes, 'One person's calamity is another person's boon,'" the skeleton remarked haplessly.

"The Jews are the calamity!" Hitler told the skeleton rebukingly. "All of Germany's calamities in the war were due to them!"

"What a loss for Germany!"

Abdel Hamid said, wringing his hands.

"In the end they turned it into a national home for themselves!"

"We can thank Britain for that," Abdel Nasser responded swiftly, without catching Abdel Hamid's meaning. "After all, it was the British who helped them establish their national homeland."

"And in the heart of Europe!" Abdel Hamid exclaimed.

Abdel Nasser finally caught Abdel Hamid's meaning.

"No, Sultan, I mean in the heart of the Arab world."

Abdel Hamid was confused.

"Germany became an Arab country?"

Hitler was incensed.

"Germany is Germany! It always has been and it always will be!"

"I mean Palestine, Sultan!" Abdel Nasser urged with broken spirits, "Palestine, which Balfour promised to them in 1917."

"It is the land of Israel, Your Excellency!" Rabin screamed with pride. "The land that God promised to the Jews."

Abdel Hamid's mouth fell to the floor in astonishment.

"How were the Jews able to accomplish their goal?

I still remember when Herzl met with me.

I told him that he could have Palestine only over my dead body! In my life Palestine would have never come under their control. But after my death, I don't know. . .perhaps in their guile and craft they succeeded in bribing that Westernized officer Mustafa Ataturk.

He must have offered it to them on a silver platter. My heart aches for the loss of Palestine." He stopped for a moment to sigh dejectedly. "A loss indeed, for all Arabs and Muslims."

Kennedy rushed to defend Ataturk.

"It wasn't him who transferred Palestine to Jewish control, Sultan. It was the English."

The millionaire foamed at the mouth.

"A successful transaction it was for the British and the Jews."

Hitler put the blame on Churchill.

"Mr. Churchill was eager to come through on that promise during his tenure as an administrator of the colonies in 1922."

"I tried to come to an understanding with the Arabs about this matter," Churchill replied diplomatically.

"I clarified in my White Paper that we were determined to help the Jews establish a national homeland in a part of Palestine."

"I said it once, and I'll say it again,"

Abdel Nasser quipped, "Britain is responsible for most of the calamities that befell the Arabs."

"How could you make promises to give away a land that was not yours to give away?"

Abdel Hamid asked Churchill.

"That's business," replied Kennedy.

"They did it for financial compensation," the millionaire added.

"And for the Jews' service to Britain," Rabin said with pride.

"To secure the interests of Great Britain," Churchill said with his customary selfishness.

Abdel Hamid was restless. He thought for a moment and then asked Hitler, "If the Jews got Palestine, what then did Germany lose?"

"It lost the war,"

Hitler replied, "and lost even more in the Versailles treaty of 1919, which stifled Germany's growth and hindered its natural abilities by imposing humiliating military and financial constraints that no patriotic German worth his name could accept."

"You must be referring to yourself," Stalin said scornfully.

"I admire a patriot when I see one," Abdel Nasser said, casting an approving look at Hitler.

Churchill was outraged.

"Don't admire him just yet!" He shouted reproachfully. "Ask him how he became this 'patriotic!'"

Gandhi threw the ball back into Churchill's court.

"Perhaps it was the avarice of the Allies who emerged victorious in World War I."

"Love of one's country is not something that is taught. It flows through the blood – nay, it is at the core of one's being," Hitler said as he held his hand tightly to his chest.

Abdel Hamid's questioning continued unabated.

"You were once but a corporal in the German army.

How did you rise to become the head of state of Germany, at once peerless and invincible?"

"By virtue of my rhetorical skills and the strength of the ruling Nazi Party's ideology."

"A racist party through and through," Stalin said with contempt and scorn.

"Akin to the Fascist Party in Italy," De Gaulle said concurrently.

The skeleton's opportunity to participate in the discussion had come.

"In 1919 Benito Mussolini inaugurated the Fascist Party in Italy. Racism was central to the party's doctrine, as the party had emphasized the notion that nations were formed along ethnic lines."

"The party also spouted a totalitarian stance, one that deemed the authority of the state to be preeminent over individual rights and freedoms," Kennedy added.

"Their shared enthusiasm for dictatorial politics made Mussolini and Hitler natural allies," Churchill said with ostentatious loathing.

"Mussolini had marched on Rome in 1922 with a paramilitary wing known as the Black Shirts and succeeded in taking over the executive functions of government," De Gaulle recounted, intimately aware of the Fascist Party's road to power.

With the composure reminiscent of a dispassionate researcher in history the skeleton said, "The Fascists brainwashed children at schools and planted the idea that fascism and nationalism were synonymous in the minds of the Italian people."

"What was it that you admired about the Duce?" Abdel Nasser asked Hitler.

"It was his intelligence," Hitler replied.

"He managed to gather the Italian people around his platform, which took the form of a concordat which he signed together with the Pope in 1929."

Stalin attacked what he saw as the sinister nature of the Pope's motives.

"The Pope was awarded a city-state in the Vatican. The church had finally gotten everything it wanted and more."

"You might even say the Pope was compensated for years past," the skeleton said with an eye to pleasing Stalin.

And pleased he was. "And that's why the Pope put his support behind Fascism."

"To protect Italy from the threat posed by Communism," Hitler said, alluding to the historical enmity between communism and the church.

"Religion is the opiate of the masses," Stalin said, echoing Karl Marx's famous declaration.

"What were the similarities between Mussolini and Hitler?" Abdel Hamid asked in the spirit of inquiry.

"They both consecrated the personality of the ruler," Churchill said, rushing to answer before anyone else could, "as a man who had taken power from on high, with God's direct supervision and approval, to lead the nation – or, more aptly, to save the nation – and to ready it economically for impending war."

Gandhi grumbled with displeasure.

"War is such a detestable, horrid thing. These rulers determine when and where it is waged and pay for it out of the sacrifices of colonized peoples."

"Nothing is for free," the millionaire said without reservation.

The skeleton nodded his head in agreement.

"It might be an unfair equation, but the results are most certainly fair."

Abdel Nasser chuckled at the audacity of the skeleton's comment. "At first they patronize the colonized with the promise of good things to come when the former are in need of the latter's assistance, and then cast them aside when the threat to their rule subsides. And the skeleton is talking about 'fair results.'"

Gandhi with a tone of despondence.

"That's precisely what happened when the British refused to grant India its independence."

"Need I remind everyone about how Britain and France snatched Germany's colonies away from it?" Hitler asked with pronounced hostility.

"What of the Arab territories?" Abdel Hamid asked with concern.

"Did they attain their independence?"

"France continued to occupy Syria pursuant to the dictates of the San Remo Conference," De Gaulle said with the tone of a lawyer who knew his law all too well.

"Britain stationed its troops in Iraq, Palestine and Transjordan," Churchill continued.

Rabin had nothing but praise for British policy in the region.

"Great Britain is owed nothing but our most choicest thanks for its role in facilitating Jewish immigration to the Promised Land."

"Don't forget to thank France as well, Rabin," Abdel Nasser said, concealing his anger.

"After all, France partitioned Greater Syria. It carved Mount Lebanon out from its Syrian source and – after adding four other Ottoman districts to it – called it 'Greater Lebanon.'"

Rabin was indifferent. "What does that have to do with me? Let the Lebanese thank France for that themselves."

The course of the conversation did not sit well with Abdel Hamid, who cast a blameful look at Abdel Nasser.

"Britain and France had their sights set on acquiring the Arab territories since time immemorial. We informed our governors of this fact. But I suppose it's true what the Arabic aphorism says, 'You don't know how kind I've been to you until you try others.'

"They divided Greater Syria into four separate states. France did not suffice with that; rather, it went further and overthrew the King of Syria who had been part of the French-backed revolution to repel Ottoman control of the area. In the end, they threw him out and exiled him abroad."

Churchill thought this a prime opportunity to contrast France's treachery with Britain's dutiful fulfillment of its promises.

"But Britain had not only returned him to the throne as king of Iraq, it also crowned his brother Abdullah as the emir of Transjordan."

De Gaulle still believed France's decision to divide Syria was wise.

"It was imperative that we establish Greater Lebanon as a Christian state."

Abdel Nasser could not contain his rage.

"It's a prime example of 'Divide and conquer!'"

He exclaimed.

"This is the motto of colonial powers, which manifests in their establishment of states on the basis of ethnic or religious belonging. The state will rule in the name of one ethnic or religious group and exclude the plethora of other ethno-religious groups that fall under its control, thereby leaving each of these states on the precipice of a raging volcano and vulnerable to renewed intervention on the part of Western powers in its internal affairs."

The millionaire saw the logic of imperialism, for right or wrong:

"The nations that emerged victorious in the War needed a way to recuperate its financial losses in the war. The colonies seemed to them a natural solution to their problem."

Gandhi interrupted with an objection.

"Does war bring anything but calamity and destruction?"

"The gross debt of the warring nations shot up to staggering proportions," the millionaire continued.

Kennedy thought that the matter had been poorly thought out.

"The governments continued to print paper currency that was not backed by a gold standard."

"This led to an excess of currency that only served to complicate matters further," De Gaulle continued.

The millionaire slapped his forehead with his palm.

"Paper currency lost all its value and the world rushed headlong into the Great Depression."

Hitler remembered the lean years, as they were called:

"When I was released from prison I looked around to find people walking around as if they were dead. They lived under the yoke of an unemployment that did not befit the ebullient vitality of the German people, who were left impoverished and forced to beg in the streets. Factory closures and a steep rise in prices was the order of the day, a concomitant of the sharp fall in the value of local currency.

The government couldn't do anything as a result of the enormous deficit it had incurred. Funds were redirected to help pay the indemnity that was imposed on it after the war. The German mark had lost all its value and whatever buying power it had. A piece of bread was worth bags upon bags of paper currency. The conditions were miserable.

Something needed to be done and quickly, there being no more time for delay."

"The Germans had grown tired of the lousy conditions in which they lived," De Gaulle testified with the force of a man who knows his neighbors' suffering all too well.

"Matters were getting desperate, and the people were on the brink of losing all hope. Then Hitler came along with his oratory gifts and his astuteness and managed to foster in his people a renewed sense of hope. The masses gathered around him, and people began to join the Nazi Party in droves."

Stalin had a slightly different take.

"The Germans were of the belief that it was communism that had left them in such dire straits. It's understandable, however, as misery and despair can make it difficult for the heart to see clearly."

Needless to say, Hitler rejected the content of Stalin's testimony thoroughly and completely. "It was the Germans' commitment to Nazi ideology that drove them to elect me as president, I being the only candidate who could rescue them from the morass in which they found themselves."

Churchill found Hitler's self-aggrandizing portrayal hysterical.

"Why, yes! You rescued them from the morass and threw them into the mud!"

Hitler was not pleased.

"I know that you hate me, Churchill!" he said, screaming with barely a sliver separating their two faces.

"I know that's why you torment me with your snide remarks and your cigar that never seems to go out."

Kennedy was fair enough to acknowledge that Hitler was the German people's choice:

"It was democracy that brought Hitler to power."

"The suffocating financial crisis made the Germans eager to find a national savior, and the only one who seemed to fit the bill was Hitler," the millionaire explained, his analysis indicating that he was intimately familiar with the painful conditions in those days.

Kennedy was next to voice an opinion.

"The Great Depression had began in Germany, then spread throughout Europe and Asia until it hit the continental United States. As night turned to day five thousand banks had shut their doors for good. The crisis had gone international, shaking the pillars of the world economy. The crisis lasted from 1929 to 1933, and were it not for the wise decisions of President Franklin Roosevelt I fear World War II would have happened much sooner than it did."

Hitler found in President Roosevelt a mirror image of himself and a means by which to deflect the accusation that he was a dictator.

"Great nations need great leaders; it is for this reason that the American people elected him to the presidency three times, despite the fact that such a move is not countenanced by the U.S. Constitution."

"The people's will is the constitution," Kennedy replied.

"The people are the authors of the constitution and its protectors. Were it not for the people, there would have been no constitution."

The millionaire brought the conversation back to the Great Depression.

"The larger banks began to buy out the smaller banks."

Stalin sought to expose capitalism for its short-sightedness.

"The major corporations would buy everything out and seize control of the market. But then that would lead to smaller companies leaving the market tout court! In the end, unemployment would go up, and bankruptcy would increase."

Rabin saw eye to eye with the millionaire.

"The stock markets crashed," he said.

"Had the Federal Reserve not intervened and supplied the banks with money the global financial system would have collapsed as well," Kennedy said, his confidence in the American economy boundless.

Stalin couldn't disagree more.

"The Soviet Union experienced no such financial crisis, as the state had all of the banks under its control."

Kennedy was indignant, but he couldn't find anything to say.

"You Communists see capitalists as your traditional opponents and will do anything to drag us through the mud! You'll blame everything and anything on capitalism!"

Stalin was defiant.

"You Americans are a covetous people! You seek to Americanize the world – 'to carry a big stick,' to quote your revered president Franklin Roosevelt, and to get involved even in the most minute matters in countries far, far away. It is this penchant for sticking your noses where they don't belong that has wreaked havoc on humanity! But worry not, for I'm here to tell you the good news: one day, capitalism will fall. It will self-combust, and the world economy will continue to collapse again and again as a result of the exploitation and monopolization that are concomitants of standard capitalist practice. It is self-aggrandizement mixed with a desire to negate the other half led you to drown in a smorgasbord of greed and avarice. In fact, this 'institution-based state apparatus' that you take so much pride in is nothing but a vehicle that helps you satisfy your insatiable greed, a means by which you consolidate the foundations of the capitalist order and keep poorer nations ripe for future exploitation!"

CHAPTER 15
For Love of Metal and Fire

Once the Serbs were finished massacring their Bosnian brethren, the gravedigger decided to throw an extravagant ball. He invited the CEO's of the major seven corporations, heads of state of the G20 nations, and, last but not least, his friend, the head of INTERPOL.

The party was arranged to be held in one of the best tourist cities in the world, in a sprawling hotel that had been built atop a lush green hill underneath which flowed a gentle lake whose waters radiated beneath the warm rays of the sun.

At night the lake was a sight to be seen, like a princess in love obsessed with maintaining her good looks and slim physique. Its surface tinged with a gorgeous orange hue during sunset. The night shrouded the lake like a flowy black dress, and the like grew all the more comely when the silver moon appeared and shined on its forehead. It attracted the eyes of every lover of beauty in its splendor.

The invitees' motorcades had been arriving one after the other. The city was overflowing with security personnel and police officers who had earlier in the day broken up a demonstration that was staged to protest the meeting of these officials, whose decisions therein it was feared would serve to increase the misery of the local populace. Some of the protesters had tried to infiltrate the hotel and were caught by security guards. Clashes ensued, and the security personnel were successful in turning them away, but only after bloodying up a few of them.

The soiree began with flowery speeches that called for world peace and the need to assist poorer nations develop programs that would eliminate poverty and disease and distribute medication to those in need. The speakers' white chiclet teeth concealed sharp fangs that could tear their victims to pieces. This was a get-together of all the gravediggers in the world, each of whom had his own method for gravedigging. Cain's job was but to implement their suggestions and to adhere faithfully to the strict guidelines that they layed out before him, guidelines which in many a case strayed considerably from the dictates of morality and social justice. During one of the night's many intermissions the gravedigger accompanied the head of INTERPOL to the balcony that overlooked the lake. The two men had been brought together by the discovery of what had then been an unknown crime, and in the meantime their relationship developed into a full-fledged friendship. Each of the men had a glass of whiskey and the head of INTERPOL listened attentively as the gravedigger proceeded to pour his heart out to him. "Death rates are at an all-time high, and so is my workload. I know, this means business is booming and I should be excited. But this also means I have no time to take a vacation. And God forbid that I get sick – who could take my place?

I mean, as we speak thousands of people have lost their lives in civil wars, and their bodies lay abandoned at the side of the rode and they desperately need someone to bury them."

"You're an old man now, Cain," the head of INTERPOL said.

The gravedigger let out a hearty laugh.

"Don't you worry about me, my friend. I'm never going to die. If I die, then death will cease to exist! It'll have no flavor, no complexion, no smell! Ironically, only then will my life have no meaning."

"We all fear death, and we all try to push it out of our minds and try to forget about it. But it's coming – sometime in the future, in the darkness of the night, it'll carry its polished dagger and rip through the strings of your heart."

The gravedigger took a sip from his glass and savored the flavor in his mouth for a moment.

"I don't care when or where I die. What matters is that the revolutionaries remain alert and at arms, spreading commotion on the Earth. The world must never know peace or security."

The gravedigger glanced at the pure night sky, as if to count the stars.

"I love ideologies. I relish the moment when they clash. I adore the gun powder, the metal and fire that are chief ingredients of warmaking. I'm astounded by how easily they can blind people's hearts. I love the revolutionaries, and why wouldn't I? Every revolution is a boon for my business."

The gravedigger fell silent, thinking about how much had accrued to him as a result of all the warfare and conflicts going on. He then broke out in song:

The revolutionaries are increasing. . .

They fall like the rain, In the name of perseverance and dignity

Out of love, and a duty to sacrifice for one's homeland.

They fight it out for martyrdom . . . and they keep my heart at rest;

I'll dig all of their graves, and heap soil and dust over their heads!

He chuckled on the inside, knowing that life is the prerogative of the strong and that he will always be the victor, now and forevermore. He laughed out loud and then turned to the head of INTERPOL.

"Have you discovered who the killer is yet?"

The head of INTERPOL took a deep sigh.

"There were moments when I felt debilitated and embarrassed for not being able to solve this mysterious crime. In spite of my many years of experience and the thousands of times I was successful in finding the criminal, I must say this mystery has me stumped. I'm on the verge of losing confidence in my intellectual powers. In days past, I was skilled in analyzing data and making inferences; upon arriving at the truth, I used to see it as clearly as one sees the peaks of lofty mountains on a clear sunny day."

He stopped to take a deep breath and then continued.

"The mysterious circumstances of the general's murder have baffled INTERPOL offices worldwide. We've picked up our efforts in hopes of uncovering a lead that would help us identify the perpetrator of the crime. But our efforts have been complicated by the fact that much time has passed since the commission of the crime. In most crimes, one typically finds that the killer leaves behind traces of evidence that might point us to him. But here everything appears to be missing: the only thing we have is the long, rusty screw that we found nailed through the back of the general's head. Every time we reach a point in which we finally feel that we're on solid ground, it ends up being a house of cards. The iris in one's eye most certainly will have an image of the killer – but where are the general's eyes? Where is the body? Does it contain signs of blunt force or trauma? Nothing remains of the body save for the bones – but by your account those have mixed in with the bones of others buried in the graveyard and so we can't pinpoint with precision which bones are his.

The gravedigger nodded his head silently and twisted his face in bewilderment.

"Why did the murderer use a screw? Why didn't he use a gun, or a dagger?"

"The murderer undoubtedly had his reasons for choosing the implement in question," replied the head of INTERPOL.

"He did not want to leave a trace of evidence that could be used to reveal his identity or otherwise lead to his arrest."

The gravedigger sympathized with his friend's plight.

"You have quite a heavy burden on your shoulders," he said.

He then asked:

"What of the numerous security agencies in the world that you have a working relationship with? Have any of their activities helped you at all? I don't have to tell you, this is a crime of global proportions. Everyone must pick up the tab and help determine who the killer is. And I'd appreciate it if you hand him over to me once you're finished with him."

The head of INTERPOL guzzled down whatever was left in his glass and said:

"No worries, my friend. We'll find this criminal, and I'm confident we'll bring him to justice soon. The international security agencies have attached much importance to the case. Indeed, the CIA went above and beyond the call of duty. They requested that I send them the murder weapon and anything associated with it for testing. It also sent two samples of the skull's cranium to the most advanced laboratories in the world in order to conduct a DNA test. As it awaited the results of the testing to come out the Agency also took a pledge to protect generals, particularly since the latest intelligence indicates that they are direct targets for assassination. It sent them messages urging them to follow certain directives – such as implementing a change in daily routines, increasing the amount of personnel in ones security entourage and to avoid using the same routes in their daily travels more than two consecutive times - that will help save their lives and prevent these criminals from reaching them."

"This is important progress," the gravedigger remarked.

The head of INTERPOL carried on with his debriefing.

"The next step we took was to study the movements of certain personalities of note and try to find out who if anyone was keeping tabs on them. The hope is that the murderer belongs to a team of assassins that we uncover in the process."

The gravedigger set aside his empty glass on the balcony rails.

"What if these criminal cells are operating outside of U.S. territory?"

"I thought about that," the head of INTERPOL replied, "and I am in contact with security agencies in the developing world, who have been cooperating with us and have been of immense help in our work. Everyday I receive dozens of reports from these countries, and the measures taken by these agencies appear to be similar in their broad outlines: thousands of suspects are apprehended and anyone who even thinks about harming the general is sentenced to prison. Photographs taken via satellite indicate that dozens of security checkpoints have been set up in every city throughout the world, and they have orders to apprehend anyone who has a hammer or a screw in his possession."

"Sounds like the kinds of measures my own men would do," the gravedigger said with the utmost delight.

The head of INTERPOL continued:

"Not a single hammer or screw is left in those countries. The very mention of these two have been lifted from the educational curriculums. The downside to all this is that the lack of screws and hammers has led to something of a housing crisis in those places, and yet the Housing Ministries in various world countries have issued stringent orders to contractors and builders not to work with the aforementioned implements until further notice. Instead, builders are to make use of premade walls and to tie the walls together with metal wiring, with the added stipulation that construction will be brought to a complete halt in the event that a general turns up dead from asphyxiation or is found dead with a metal wire wrapped around his neck."

CHAPTER 16
Provocation

It is in the skeleton's nature to be provocative. It's a character trait that was instilled in him during the course of his work. He's a storyteller, and it is not out of the ordinary for storytellers to add or subtract to their stories if and when needed to secure a purpose. But recently he felt like his game was off, and that he was no longer the center attention.

He had been unable to sleep the entire night. He was engrossed in thought, working on a scheme to get him back in the center of attention – atleast within the confines of the graveyard – and recapitulate his sense of energy and dynamism.

He decided to start with President Kennedy, and approached him early that morning. He skimmed the room. The atmosphere was ripe. The time had come to put his plan into action. He bent over and, pointing his finger at the millionaire, whispered in the President's ear:

"I never liked that millionaire. He's a pompous idiot. He thinks he's more powerful than all of us because of how wealthy he is. He lived a life filled with intrigues and subterfuge. Why, he even had the gall to insult your Excellency personally! And this was after you were assassinated in 1963!"

President Kennedy was visibly worried.

"What did he do? Did he try to smear my good name before the American public?"

"No, he couldn't do that anyway. The American people love you, and remember you till this day. The Democratic Party throws your name around, knowing it's their ace in the hole to get wavering party members to get off the sidelines and vote."

"Thank God," Kennedy said with relief.

"You know he died in a five star hotel?"

"Was he maligning me in that hotel?"

"Why, no. . .but he did die from intestinal indigestion that he suffered after having had a very oily meal."

"Yes, I recall that being printed on his tombstone."

"They put together a team of around a dozen of the most renowned specialists in the medical profession. They succeeded in purifying his intestines of toxins and had him on a respiratory machine in hopes of keeping him alive. . .but in the end, death is death: no one has authority to stop it. It's more powerful than the most menacing of authorities."

"You said he badmouthed me. . .but you didn't tell me what he said?"

The skeleton hesitated in his response.

"He was in love with the First Lady. . .your wife, Jacqueline Kennedy."

Kennedy found the skeleton's remark puzzling.

"What's wrong with that? Everybody loved Jackie."

"Indeed, so did I! But he. . ."

"He what?" Kennedy replied angrily.

"He loved her in a way that was different from everybody else." He paused for a moment and then said, "He married her."

Kennedy was astonished.

"You must be delirious! Are you out of your mind?! You're not making any sense!" he shouted hysterically.

"I'm not making this up. It happened. All the news agencies reported on it."

President Kennedy was dumbfounded by the news. His blood started to boil.

"My Jackie loved me. . .she wouldn't forget me so quick. . ."

"He must have seduced her with his wealth, sir."

Stalin recognized irritability and anger in Kennedy's facial expression, and proceeded to walk towards him.

"You seem upset, Mr. Kennedy. Has anything upset you?"

"It's that filthy millionaire."

"But I made sure that I destroyed the casket that was causing all the problems. He doesn't own a thing anymore!"

"He does too," Kennedy said, his eyes shot downwards in grief.

"Indeed, sir, he gave her the gift of a pear-shaped diamond pendant weighing 2.34 carats, with a special bracelet that was worth in the ballpark of seven million dollars."

The more Kennedy heard, the more disheartened he got.

"Women. They're sick in the head, I tell you. And this is their sickness!"

"Please don't upset yourself, your beloved wife loved you more than him – in fact, she kept your name until she died, and she was buried next to you upon her death in 1994."

Kennedy relaxed a bit, but he remained annoyed at Onassis.

"I'd be careful listening to what that skeleton says," Stalin told Kennedy, hoping to relieve whatever tension was left.

"After all, its his fault for getting you all riled up like this with his big mouth. Be patient. It won't be too long before I cut off his tongue and feed it to the cats."

The skeleton became frightened and took cover behind President Kennedy.

"I have nothing but the utmost respect for President Kennedy!" he pleaded.

"I'm not mad at him, Stalin!" Kennedy said, hoping to dissuade Stalin from harming the skeleton.

"It's that millionaire."

"Onassis! Onassis!" Stalin called out with a roar that pierced through the graveyard and could be heard by all its inhabitants.

The skull began running around aimlessly through the wing's corridor, startled by the raw, coarse voice that he thought resembled that of the gravedigger. The millionaire trembled in fear, recalling Stalin's iron grip and how it shattered his casket into pieces. He remembered how the casket had kept him warm and cozy and regretted ever having his knocking and pleading for his neighbors to help him out of it.

Gandhi stood by him to relieve him of his fears, and walked with him to face Stalin, who had raised his fist menacingly as if threatening to strike the millionaire.

"Who gave you permission to enter into this graveyard, you enemy of the proletariat?!"

"Death must have given me permission, sir," he replied with his eyes downcast.

Stalin lowered his first.

"But you were not one of the greats to deserve the honor of being one of our number," he said with contempt.

"He must have been placed here by mistake," Hitler said derisively.

Rabin was on the verge of raising his voice to defend the millionaire, but then feared that Hitler would team up with Nasser to have him ejected from the graveyard and decided to remain silent and spare himself the trouble.

The millionaire was not ashamed of his wealth.

"I requested my agents to purchase the best place for me to be buried in!"

"You and your wealth can go to hell!" Stalin replied scornfully.

"At ease, gentlemen," Churchill said, rushing to the millionaire's aid.

"Mr. Onassis was instrumental in helping us to prosecute our wars. He offered us financial assistance, and for this reason alone he deserves to be among us."

Rabin now summoned up the courage to speak himself.

"His ships were of immense service to us in helping to transport poor Jewish immigrants to the land of Israel."

Kennedy recognized flexibility in Stalin's demeanor.

"Are you prepared to vouch for him, Mr. Churchill?"

Churchill shot a glance at the millionaire. He'd never seen him so timid and meek. He remembered how gracious and hospitable he was when he hosted him in his own private island of Skorpios off the coast of Greece.

"Yes, I vouch for him," he replied confidently.

Gandhi came forward and stood between the two opposing sides.

"I vouch for him as well. After all, reconciliation is a king among virtues."

The millionaire began to breathe normally again.

"I thank you all, and my sincerest apologies to you, Mr. President, if I've done anything to hurt you. It was only my love and admiration for you that drove me to remain close to your family, in order to protect them after you were gone. What's past is past."

"You need not worry," Kennedy replied graciously.

"As long as these gentlemen vouch for you, you're alright by me. At any rate, I'll get the full story from Jackie herself when I go to see her."

De Gaulle tapped Kennedy's shoulder encouragingly.

"I'll join you in paying a visit to your beautiful Jackie."

"Sure," Kennedy replied, but only to be polite.

"Jackie was a great admirer of you and your works."

Abdel Hamid studied the face of the millionaire.

"It seems to me, our dear millionaire, that you have facial features characteristic of people from the East. Your olive complexion and inflection resemble that of the people of our region. Where are you from?"

"Why yes, Sultan, I was born in the Turkish city of Izmir in 1906. I immigrated to Greece and from there to Argentina in 1922."

"How did you gather your wealth?" the skull asked inquisitively.

The millionaire took a deep breath and then responded:

"It's a long story, filled with dashed hopes followed by renewed ambition and an ironclad desire to accomplish my goals. When I arrived in Argentina I had only sixty three dollars in my pocket."

Abdel Hamid was impressed by Onassis's story.

"You're a Turk, after all. Hard work and determination are in your blood."

"When did you gather your first million?" Abdel Nasser asked.

"At first, I was a telephone operator in Argentina. I soon realized that one can make real money by working in ship transport along the high seas. I quit working for the telephone company and began working with transport ships."

"You still didn't tell us how you gathered your first million," the skeleton asked impatiently.

"I was twenty five years old. I began to acquire my fortune while dealing in tobacco in the city of Buenos Aires. That's when I bought my first ship, which I used to hunt whales."

"With credit to the United States for selling you military ships that had gone out of service following World War II," Kennedy said.

"I don't deny that, sir. America had been like a mother to me."

"And what about Turkey?" Abdel Hamid asked resentfully.

"Turkey is like a father to me, your Excellency," the millionaire answered.

CHAPTER 17

An Apology

Hitler was distressed beyond measure. His chest was constricted, and his heart weighed heavily on him. He needed to say something - anything - to keep it from bursting. He remembered the speeches he used to give to his people. Many a time he had succeeded not only in walking away with their hearts and minds but also in instilling in them a renewed sense of zeal and unbounded enthusiasm.

He yearned to put this priceless gift - buried deep beneath the embers that enveloped his heart - to use once more. He made up his mind to give a speech, one that would ease his mind and soothe his bitter grief. His living mates had spent their lives fighting his ideology and distorting its principles; it had become imperative to finally lay all doubts pertaining to it to rest.

He looked around for a podium or a dais from which he might give his speech, but all he could find was Mr. Rabin's coffin, sitting unassumingly in the corner of the wing. Not a bad idea, he thought to himself as he walked towards the coffin intent on ascending it.

Rabin didn't like what he was seeing. He turned to Churchill and Kennedy and stated his grievances in hopes that they might protect his coffin from Hitler's callous disregard:

"Please, do something! This man is trespassing against my property!"

Churchill was sympathetic to Rabin's concerns.

"Come down from there, Hitler! Leave Mr. Rabin's coffin alone at once! You are aggressing on other people's property!"

Gamal Abdel Nasser jumped to Hitler's defense.

"Rabin voraciously defends his property while seeming to forget that he took the Palestinians' lands by force!"

Kennedy sought to come to Rabin's aid without angering Nasser.

"What has passed has passed; there's a reality on the ground, and negotiations are the way forward. But this is neither here nor there - in this place we will not permit anyone to transgress against the property of others."

"We should not get so up in arms over a coffin," Stalin intervened. "After all, in the end we're just going to break it apart and store it as firewood for next winter."

The millionaire was consoled by the fact that he wouldn't be the only one to have suffered at Stalin's hands. Hitler took the opportunity to begin his speech on a sardonic note.

"Oh greats of the twentieth century! Esteemed gentlemen! I would like today to say a few words informing you of my true nature - and you of yours."

Laughter broke out in the audience.

"Laugh if you like, but all of you are Hitler, all things considered. You all here hide behind a facade - were it not for the fact that I lost the war I would have been the most noble and esteemed person in this room. The most humane, too!

"Everyone knows that the press and assorted propaganda machines play a role in obscuring truth from falsehood. Why, how many a leader has been responsible for the deaths of thousands, only to appear virtuous and unimpeachable, a hero even! He knows in his innermost, however, that he is a liar!"

"As the Near Eastern proverb goes, 'when a cow falls to the ground, everyone pulls out their knife!' When Hitler fell, Germany fell, and each of you pulled out their knife to tear her apart!"

Hitler paused to take a sip of water.

"If I was a wolf, then you all are no sheep! Take a look, see for yourselves what you have become! You've turned into ferocious beasts. Sheep don't consume the flesh of other animals; you folks didn't even leave the bones.

"You all emerged from the war reborn as patriotic leaders - yet no one can be blamed for lighting the flames of war but you. Then again, you all had in Hitler a scapegoat onto whom you could displace all the blame. You lied to your peoples, and they believed you - they believed you, not because of your integrity, but in hopes that you would save them from the calamities of the war to which you had recruited them. They had hitherto been innocent of any disposition to warfare[, and now you've turned them into killers]. Then you washed your hands of the whole affair after the war was over, purifying yourself in the lakes of victory. Why, victory is a strange thing - it changes things, turns them on their head! It erases the most heinous crimes and pardons the most unforgivable of sins.

"Defeat is a cruel. . .cruel thing. . .

"All of you are Hitler, disguised as something else. Why do you all persist in this masquerade? Cast off your masks! Reveal your true selves!

"Hitlers with different names, you hit the Japanese cities of Hiroshima and Nagasaki with atomic weapons, and yet you persist in shedding crocodile tears and putting all the blame on Hitler. You are more 'Hitlerian' than Hitler! We Germans took the lands occupied by our armies and united them under one flag, the flag of the Reich. As for you, you planted the seeds of war in the world: you established a Zionist-colonial state that took zionism as its state religion. Then you established a national homeland for the Muslims in Pakistan, and left Kashmir as a flash point for destabilizing the relations between the Indians and their Pakistani brethren. The fuse is in your hands, and you light it up whenever you deem it convenient. You planted an apartheid state in South Africa, your hearts having refused to reject slavery in their innermost. Yet you claim you are the victims - nay, saints, whose job it is to protect humanity! Why, if you would but spare humanity from your rotten designs, from your endless greed, the world would be a much better place!"

Hitler pointed his finger at Stalin.

"Your history is a distortion, and you refuse to see who the real monster is! This man sacrificed twenty million Russians on the altar of personal aggrandizement, and to appear as a strong, courageous leader."

Then he pointed his finger at Churchill angrily. "Churchill humbled himself before Roosevelt and begged for his protection. As for the poor De Gaulle, you treated him like a golf ball: on occasion, you'd call him to join you in your meetings, on others you'd keep him away. Sometimes you acknowledged his existence, and at other times you ignored him. I respect this man - even though he was my nemesis on the battlefield. I respect him for his determination and his resolve, and for all his efforts in keeping France free. Everything he did was to keep the French a dignified, strong people. He is the Hitler of France, a France that was in dire need of a Hitler who would be able to expel the occupying armies, just as Germany was in need of a Hitler to restore its dignity and self-confidence, to remove the injustice and humiliation your limitless greed inflicted upon it. I sought to save my people from famine, poverty, from the Great Depression that followed the First

World War. Your short-sighted desire to destroy Germany came about because you couldn't attain our greatness or the purity of our Aryan blood. So you colluded with one another against her, and sometimes numbers can defeat courage. In fact, Germany hadn't been defeated in World War I - I'm a German fighter, I know! But the left and the Jews tore the country apart from within and made your objectives easier to accomplish. I recorded all of this in 'Mein Kampf.' It was thus imperative that the Jews and Communists be punished for bringing about our downfall. It is well known that a soldier who betrays his duties and flees from the battlefield is executed by firing squad. Traitors ought to be torn to shreds and their parts thrown along the side of the road. It is only the just due of those who bring about the downfall of a nation that they be cut down and exterminated. We lost the war because of the Jews and the left. They got what they deserved! Perhaps some innocent people were caught up in the ordeal - but this is war, and the military machine is incapable of distinguishing guilty from innocent. Did not the number of victims during World War II reach sixty million? Why is it such a big issue that some ten percent of them happened to be Jews?"

Stalin stared at Hitler in horror.

"Six million Jews! [Is that but a number to you,] You tyrant!"

Hitler was unmoved.

"Who are you to speak to me of tyranny! This monster who swallowed twenty million Russians whole now sits here and pontificates about tyranny!"

"Killing is an irredeemable evil the moment the first victim loses his life," Stalin said, rushing to his own defense without taking a moment to think matters through. "Every additional victim is just a number."

"The Germans are an honorable people. They made reparations to the Jews. Tell me, do the Russians have a sense of honor?" Hitler shot back.

Stalin felt the sting left by the disparaging question.

"Russia's greatest honor lies in the triumph attained by Communism when it blotted out and eradicated Nazism and Fascism."

"The reparations the Germans paid were not nearly enough," Rabin said intemperately.

The millionaire began to drool.

"The reparations were quite generous - gargantuan even, if I might say."

Gandhi took pity on the way the two men's minds worked.

"All the money in the world could not compensate for the death of an innocent child."

Hitler's chastisement was unsparing.

"Why don't you take your nonviolence and ascend to the heavens! Those of us who live on planet Earth know that violence begets violence, and that the price ideologies pay to triumph must be paid in blood. Your strategy of nonviolence cost India half its territory. First you lost western Pakistan, then you lost eastern Pakistan."

"Had the Indians persisted in that strategy they would have lost the other half of their territory as well," Rabin said with a smirk.

Kennedy was taken aback by Rabin's demeanor.

"You don't seem to be resentful or even disturbed by Hitler, though he is responsible for the deaths of over six million Jews?"

"It is true that the Jewish people - God's chosen people - lost a few million of their number in Hitler's ovens. The world will never forget. . ."

". . .but it got the Jews empathy and support!" the millionaire interrupted.

"The Jewish people will never forget the Holocaust," Rabin continued.

"They will continue to remember it one generation after the other. It will remain in our collective memory. Mothers will impart knowledge of it to their feeding infants, and we will teach it to our sons and daughters in our schools."

"And it is for this reason that I am surprised by the fact that you are not resentful of Hitler?"

"Because the service Hitler rendered to the cause of the Jewish people was greater than the collective efforts of thousands of Jews combined."

The skeleton didn't catch Rabin's meaning.

"How could this be so when he annihilated half of the Jewish people?"

"Hitler's barbaric deeds against the Jews united them into a people, a people who were oppressed, deprived, constantly on the run, strangers in the world. He instilled fear in their hearts, but he gave them the will to set their sights on Israel and to accept it as their national home."

"Had I known my services were so appreciated, I would have exterminated the other half as well!" Hitler declared from atop the coffin.

"I am Hitler, the Ubermensch, the man with the helping hand, the man who defeated you all! The man who was elected by the German people. I put Germany on its feet from top to bottom, and prepared it to rebuild and develop its infrastructure! I sought to lift the burden of injustice from the shoulders of my distinguished people. As it is their wont to do, the German people put their creativity and ingenuity to work, taking mediocre factories and transforming them into production lines for the manufacture of weapons. When Germany needed them, they were there, pushing their collective abilities and energies to their outermost limits. We were at war, not just with our enemies but with time itself. The laws were harsh, but the German people endured all hardships in order to restore Germany's acclaim and hard-won reputation. The vanguards were at the schools, and university students were accepted on condition that they undergo military training and pledge to help rebuild Germany. We knew we were heading for war, and we began manufacturing armored vehicles, tanks, warships, submarines, warplanes, heavy artillery guns, automatic weapons and other modern weaponry, not to mention ammunition."

De Gaulle was crestfallen and glum.

"I but wish the people of France had done the same, but they had been too distracted by their victory in the First World War. I had apprised the officials of my government then of the need to further improve our weapons arsenal and to improve our army's capabilities, but my warnings were not taken seriously. They simply assumed that Germany would not rise again."

"Our uncompromising and ironclad determination made it inevitable that Germany would rise again," Hitler said boastfully.

"Do you wish us to applaud you, Oh Supreme Leader?" Stalin responded spitefully. "You are nothing but a stubborn idiot who refused to listen to reason."

"You were quite the fearsome man, Hitler," Kennedy added.

"You fell victim to delusions of grandeur and you set about crushing Europe from east to west."

"That is what I call grandeur!" Hitler said, correcting Kennedy's false notions.

"You say they are delusions. Why, I consider your words a testament to the greatness of my leadership and its many accomplishments. After all, a great man must clear the path to grandeur from all impediments that might stand in his way."

"I acknowledge your many accomplishments, Hitler," Abdel Hamid said with approbation.

"You represent the Germany I know. You remind me of the glorious Ottoman Empire as it spread through East and West."

Churchill was disturbed by Abdel Hammid's commendations.

"It appears the Red Sultan is no less of a Hitler than Hitler himself!"

"Red Sultan, Yellow Sultan - none of this matters. What matters is that Hitler defeated your armies, and this demonstrates the strength of his army and the wisdom of his leadership."

Abdel Hamid's praise was like music to Hitler's ears.

"Do you all hear what the Sultan is saying? Were it not for the fact that it does not befit a Sultan to repeat himself, I would have asked him to say his words again! He is more bold and fearless than all of you combined! Come on, admit it! Why have you all fallen silent? Or are you all still terrified of the Jews and the Communists?"

Stalin was on the verge of losing his temper.

"No one ought to fear the Communists."

"Ask the capitalists about them! If you could but open their hearts and see how much they love you!"

"We are the people who have cause to be afraid, particularly of the anti-Semitic nations. But we feel safe so long as the

West remains by our side," Rabin said, defending his Western compatriots.

"Why, of course! Do fathers ever abandon their sons?" Abdel Nasser said, pointing everyone's attention to the fact that Israel is the spoiled child of the West.

"You are all from one and the same family!"

Rabin sought to distinguish the Jews.

"We are a Semitic people."

"So are we. But our family is different from yours."

"You could have had your greatness, Hitler, were it not for your highhandedness, the cruelty of your disposition, and the sheer amount of death you dealt during the Holocaust," Gandhi said in a rebuke to Hitler, Hitler was obstinate.

"History is witness to a plethora of massacres and genocides.

What makes the Holocaust so unique?

"The smell of burned flesh," Gandhi replied unguardedly. Now it was Rabin's turn to rebuke Gandhi. "I see that, while you held your hand from consuming the flesh of animals your entire life, your appetite has opened up to the flesh of those Jews who were burned in the ovens!"

"You misunderstand. Don't think that I treat Jewish meat as if it were venison. I'm merely commenting on the subject at hand."

"I demand that Hitler make an official apology to the Jews," Churchill castigated. "There is no excuse or justification for the crimes of the Holocaust."

"The Holocaust is a despicable and inhuman act. It was an act of genocide against an unarmed, defenseless people, among whom were the elderly, women and children. I'm perturbed by the sheer numbers of those killed, the numbers going to show the existence of a deep-seated sense of malice for the Jews as a people. That certainly explains the downright gruesome manner in which they were slaughtered, with gas and fire!" De Gaulle proffered.

"We, too, are against every kind of massacre, whether it occurs against individuals or groups. We are intent on taking those who are responsible for them to account, regardless of whether their victims were Jews. . .or Palestinians," Abdel Nasse said.

Rabin was agitated. Signs of agitation could clearly be read on his face, as if he were trying to conceal a dirty secret.

Gandhi caught a glimpse of Rabin taking cover behind Kennedy and said :

"I see you're trying to hide behind your finger, Rabin.

What is it? Did a thorn prick you?" "Indeed, thorns do prick fingers."

"There seems to be a lot of thorns in this catacomb," Abdel Nasser said, cautioning Rabin. "Mr. Rabin, you ought to learn to pull the thorns that prick your fingers yourself. It would be nice to give Mr. Kennedy some rest for a change."

Rabin was embarrassed. "It is the most basic human right that one be allowed to live with dignity, peace, security and freedom!" Kennedy exclaimed.

"What say you, Abdel Hamid?" The skeleton asked with smug. "Do you think Mr. Hitler ought to apologize to the Jews?"

"Contrition is a moral virtue," Abdel Hamid replied.

"Is this your way of issuing an official apology for your massacres against the Armenians, Sultan?" De Gaulle asked deviously.

Abdel Hamid went into a fit of rage.

"What do I have to do with the Jews? They came to me, and I refused their request. I have nothing else to say!" He shouted.

Rabin extended his hand to Hitler.

"We accept your apology, Mr. Hitler."

Hitler turned his face away scornfully, rejecting Rabin's extended hand.

"I will make matters easier for you, Sultan. Rabin, read my lips and I'll make you understand: I will never apologize for what I've done. I have no regrets. If history were to repeat itself, I would have done it all over again. That's who Hitler is. Hitler doesn't go back on the decisions he makes."

CHAPTER 18
A Stay in the Ocean

Diana looked back on her stay in the ocean. The whale had been a true friend and a gracious host. The whale had held a most delightful reception in her honor, and he had gone above and beyond to make her feel at home. She remembered he let out a thundrous bellow, which she saw on his face but couldn't hear herself, as the sound waves of the whale's voice operated on frequencies higher than can be heard by a human being. The bellow turned out to be a royal summon. Swiftly and surely two mermaids appeared before the whale. The mermaids were twin sisters, exactly alike in comportment, height and grace. They had chestnut-colored hair, with eyes between green and blue, beneath which was a soft, well-proportioned nose that gave way to a small, unpretentious mouth with sleepy, cherry-colored lips which spoke of naught but love and beauty. The whale charged them to serve as minders for her, and Diana was given a large sea turtle to transport her through the ocean on its back. Its shell was as comfortable to sit on as can be.

The reception began with a stroll amidst the subjects of the ocean kingdom, and the parade took off. Much preparation had gone into organizing the event. The convoy in itself was quite extraordinary - the whale marched ahead in majesty with Diana to his side, followed by their two stunning minders -

one on their right, the other to their left - each of whom swam behind them in perfect symmetry to one other.

Groups of sea creatures assembled along both sides of the procession, greeting the whale and his esteemed guest.

"The dolphins put on a splendid dance performance, rocking upwards and downwards and bopping in delightful choreographed movements that celebrated the arrival of our spectacular procession. We passed by a group of golden seahorses, next to whom stood hundreds of mullet fishes surrounded by a band of shrimps. The big fishes would come and swallow them whole, the same way strong countries do to weak countries above dry land."

The princess remembered how much she laughed when the whale asked her if she was hungry and how she shook her head in the negative as she watched and enjoyed the procession. The convoy continued on its way, passing the tiger trouts and atlantic salmon who swarmed to greet them. Suddenly a cowfish with long horns approached the convoy, but was forced to turn back by the two mermaids. She then saw a batfish spread its wings as it swam alongside them. It was truly a sight to see, one that would certainly not happen twice.

The memory of those mesmerizing scenes enchanted her imagination – fishes of every hue, even silver and gold; there were striped catfish, squirrelfish, pigfish and swarms of sardines. The convoy finally landed on the ocean floor, where they were met by a dazzling and colorful array of coral reefs of varying shapes and sizes.

"After a short rest the two mermaids disappeared into a cave and came out with a wreath of roses. They proceeded in the direction of the whale, who ordered that the wreath be crowned over my head. As the mermaids fitted the wreath over my head, I heard the whale moan mournfully. He appeared to be reminiscing about days past. He shot a glance at me with the rose crown above my head and said: 'Charming princess, allow me to thank you for bringing me back sweet memories.'

"I was struck by shyness at his words. He then continued:

'You remind me now of that phenomenal statue that overlooks the coast of New York City. 'The Statue of Liberty,' which the French people gave to their American counterparts as a gift. Me and my late wife used to gaze upon it with admiration every time we ascended to the ocean's surface to catch a breath of fresh air.'

"I was moved by his words, and even more so when tears began flowing from his tender, despondent eyes. He tried to conceal them from me as I drew near to him and kissed him on his forehead. I took my hand and began to stroke his enormous body ever so compassionately and affectionately. I moved back a little so that he can catch a glimpse of how happy I was with the rose crown he gave me. Nothing, not even the Crown of Wales, had ever given me such happiness.

'Am I missing anything?' I asked with a smile. He closed his eyes in contemplation, and then opened them again. 'Yes,' he said, nodding his head. 'The torch.'

'No freedom is lost from the lack of a torch,' he continued. 'For all intents and purposes, your presence eliminates the need for a torch and a flame.'

"It was you who defended the dignity of beleaguered women the world over," he said as he serenated her. "It was you who confronted the despots and tyrants in their highhandedness. You are freedom. Your name will live on as a dagger in the heart of tyranny. The awfulness of the crime that was done to you will remain a blot in the face of justice."

He then drew close to me to bid me farewell. His last words were:

'I hate goodbyes, but it is time for you to return to where you truly belong. The mermaids will accompany you as the sea turtle takes you there.' I bid him farewell. I left a piece of my heart with him.

We swam upwards. Two days into our trip we ran into a turbulent river. The turtle swam with all its might against the river current, and we managed to turn into a creek with water so pure and fresh. I could see the creek's floor clearly with my bare eyes, and I became distracted by the lovely sight of small river fish as they came and went. They made way for us to cross through and continue on our journey. Finally, the turtle stopped at the banks of the creek.

"Here we are, Your Highness," the first mermaid said. "It is here where you belong."

"We are loathe to part with you," the second mermaid said.

"But our mission has been completed."

I thanked the two minders for their grace and kindness and bid them the most touching farewell. I took off the rose crown and entrusted them to return it to that tender whale as a token of my appreciation, an everlasting reminder of my affection, and a tribute to his late wife, whom he loved so much.

I left the banks of the rivulet behind me, and I walked under the tree branches and into the main square of the cemetery. I stood for a moment under the sun's rays as they dried my wet body and restored warmth to my inner spirit.

CHAPTER 19
A Call to Arms

Following the conclusion of Hitler's now all-too-familiar speech, the third wing went back to business as usual, and the routine swell of noise and commotion returned in full force. The skull seized the moment to express to Hitler his profound admiration for the latter's strength. Behind them De Gaulle was relaxing on a rocking chair, and Abdel Hamid was engaging Abdel Nasser in a game of backgammon, the clamor of their voices rising with every throw of the dice. Gandhi, who was seated next to them, followed the game with great interest. Rabin had taken the millionaire aside as they began to discuss the details of a recent Israeli weapons sale in Africa. Stalin appeared preoccupied, his eyes fixed on Rabin's coffin. Churchill was showing Kennedy his latest painting.

The skeleton approached De Gaulle and said, "The weather is nice today."

"You can talk about the weather all you like, but don't you dare bring up politics."

"You're always unfair to me, General."

"And you give me migraines with your inability to comprehend the simplest things."

"Try me again this time! If I fail, I promise I won't ever ask you about politics again!"

"I sure hope so. Nothing enrages me more than having to abide the whimsies of dimwits."

"Thanks, General."

"If you prove yourself this time, then my previous comment need not be understood as an insult to you. I'm going to give you another chance."

"We have a deal," the skeleton replied, accepting the challenge.

"Boxcars!" shouted Abdel Hamid as he threw the dice. He then proceeded to congratulate himself in Turkish. "Aferin, Sultan! Aferin!"

"Aferin, Sultan! Aferin!" Gandhi said in loving imitation.

The skeleton diverted his attention to the source of the clamor and said, "It's a Middle Eastern game. It seems Abdel Nasser is forming a new alliance with the Ottomans, and that Gandhi will be a witness to this alliance."

De Gaulle adjusted his seating position and said, "This is interesting. France will be in a position to know how to deal with any and all developments that may arise."

"Are you saying, then, that alliances play an important role in the sphere of international relations as they play out on the world stage?" the skeleton asked, pretending to betray some familiarity with political matters.

"Why, of course. Prior to the break out of the Second World War, Hitler strengthened his alliances with other nations, beginning with Duce Mussolini."

"Mussolini dreamed to restore the glories of the Roman Empire, and to seize control of the Mediterranean Basin and convert it into Italian waters."

Stalin invited Hitler to defend Mussolini.

"They're talking about the dreams of your friend, Mussolini," he said, pointing at De Gaulle and the skeleton.

"This skeleton never ceases to ask questions about complex political matters of which he understands nothing," replied Hitler with an air of superiority in his voice.

"But De Gaulle is a seasoned politician and an intelligent man," Stalin said, loathing the chip on Hitler's shoulder.

Sultan Abdel Hamid roared with triumphant laughter as Nasser proceeded to slam the backgammon board shut.

"You were lucky this time!" Nasser protested.

"But I won't let you beat me the next time we play, or any other time after that!"

Gandhi joins Hitler and Stalin as they sit near De Gaulle.

"And what did Mussolini do to achieve his goals?" The skeleton asked.

"In 1935, the Italian army marched on Ethiopia via Eritrea," De Gaulle replied, drawing on the deep recesses of his vivid memory. "They employed poison gas in the course of their advance, violating the Geneva Protocols of 1925."

"And who amongst you hasn't violated protocols and assorted international agreements in the pursuit of their objectives?" Gandhi asked, defying everyone present to answer.

Hitler dodged the question by offering platitudes for his friend:

"The Duce was quite the ambitious and courageous leader."

Abdel Nasser had a different opinion.

"Mussolini crushed the revolution of Omar Mukhtar with unparalleled cruelty. He executed him despite the fact that he was a decrepit old man well advanced in his years. I find it outrageous that Hitler could find common cause with such a man and refer to him fondly as 'Duce.'"

"The Duce was Hitler's ally during the Pact of Steel that was signed between the Fascists and the Nazis in 1939*," De Gaulle replied with a collected demeanor.

"Allies ought to understand one another, to be true to one another - even to love one another," Hitler said, extolling his alliance-building strategy.

"It appears this alliance increased Germany's strength manifold," the skeleton commented.

"That alliance was the first attempt to circumvent the restrictions of the Versailles Agreement," De Gaulle continued.

"What strengthened Germany was the determination of the German people and their resolve to rebuild their country and to frustrate the restrictions imposed upon them," Hitler said with pride and esteem.

"They proceeded to accomplish this by toiling with perseverance in the way of construction and maintaining excellence in the training of employees and the manufacturing of products. After all was said and done, not a single person in Germany was left unemployed."

Abdel Hamid found the productive employment of German resources appealing.

"This must be how Germany became well-armed and strong."

"Pooling one's resources gives one added strength," the skeleton added.

"Well said, skeleton," De Gaule said, extolling the skeleton's analysis.

"It appears your knowledge of political matters has improved substantially."

All the talk of strength caught Rabin's attention.

"Maintaining one's strength entails expanding one's sphere of influence."

"That's what I had in mind," Hitler said, confirming Rabin's judgment.

"You are quite the exemplary model for Rabin," Abdel Nasser taxed Hitler.

"Might I consider this remark a personal insult?" Rabin asked, bewildered.

Abdel Nasser's response was lukewarm.

"It's not an insult. It's the truth."

Gandhi rearranged Rabin's words so as to extract newfound insight.

"When the end-goal of achieving strength is to expand one's territory, then the attainment of said goal can only come at another's expense."

"At the expense of one's neighbors," De Gaulle said, hoping to identify the 'other' in Gandhi's remark more clearly.

"And what did France do to prevent its neighbor Germany from expanding at it's expense?" the skeleton asked.

"In 1929 France began constructing the famed 'Maginot Line,' which gave some French officials the deluded feeling that they were safe from German attack. As a result, they neglected to re-arm their forces. This ended up being a fatal mistake, one that the Germans caught on to and took advantage of."

"Who was Hitler's other ally, aside from the Duce?" Abdel Hamid asked with great interest.

"Hitler always searched for allies who were tenacious and strong-minded," said Kennedy, who had decided to join in on the conversation.

"To gain in strength with their help!" The skull exclaimed with exhilaration and confidence.

"Or perhaps to shield himself from their evil plots and designs," Gandhi said, alerting the skull that Hitler might have had other considerations in mind.

"Hitler had aspirations that went far beyond the borders of Europe alone," Churchill said, backing Gandhi's hunch.

"He decided to form an alliance with Japan as well," Kennedy added. "He bestowed upon the Japanese the honor of being Aryans as he went about forming the Berlin-Rome-Tokyo axis."

"Japan had been the strongest power in the Far East," De Gaulle said, providing further context.

Based on information he had from what the news agencies were reporting at the time, the skeleton began to narrate:

"Japan did not make do with occupying Manchuria and Korea and most of the Pacific Islands. In 1937 it waged a war against China itself, aiming to occupy and colonize it."

Abdel Nasser then offered his own take on Hitler's military strategy.

"Hitler was setting up focal points for himself throughout the four corners of the globe. Once he fortified one such point and solidified his control over it, he would move on to another part of the world and set up a new focal point there."

"Exactly like cancer cells," Rabin said.

"They begin with one organ and then spread out to the rest of the body."

"I was no cancer, Rabin!" Hitler shot back, clearly infuriated.

"I had been the best surgical doctor humanity has ever known. The world is like the human body, replete with both good and bad. My plan was to excise all that was disfigured and repellent about it and leave behind a perfectly beautiful world, one in which the Aryan race – superior in its purity and intelligence - would dominate."

"Hitler chose Japan as his ally in the Far East, and took advantage of the Spanish Civil War that had broken out in 1936 between the nationalists and the republicans," the skeleton said, summarizing the gist of Hitler's movements prior to the outbreak of World War II.

"Hitler in concert with his Italian allies backed the Nationalists, who were headed by Franco," De Gaulle explained.

"This support was interpreted as an outright insurrection against the Versailles Agreement."

"Who supported the Republicans?" Abdel Hamid asked.

"The Soviet Union backed them due to their leftist leanings," Stalin replied.

"Spain was a good choice, and an excellent focal point in southwestern Europe," the skull said, sharing his approval with Hitler. "It has quite the strategic position, as it overlooks both the Atlantic Ocean and the Mediterranean Sea."

"What about Africa?" the millionaire asked with a bluster, feeling that there were some weaknesses in Hitler's strategy in the choosing of focal points.

"Hitler had an indirect presence there, as his Italian allies had occupied Libya and Ethiopia," Abdel Nasser replied.

"Just see the world through my lens, how tiny it was!," Hitler said, snobbishly putting his cleverness and strength on display.

"My support for General Franco was perceived as a threat to France, and my treaty with Japan put pressure on the Russians, as the former were known for their anti-Communist policies."

"It was France and Britain's being lax with you when you broke, even defied, the terms of the Versailles Agreement that was the true threat!" De Gaulle said, howling Hitler down.

Churchill's point of view diverged from De Gaulle's. He thought there had been adequately good reasons for France and Britain to go softly with Hitler. "The more imminent threat to us had been from Stalin and the Communists. At first, we thought that Germany could act as a fortified barrier that might prevent the spread of Communism from the East."

Stalin thought there was some hyperbole in Churchill's description of the events in question.

"The West overestimated the strength of Soviet power. Russia was behind the more advanced nations by a time span of some fifty to one hundred years."

Kennedy tried to explain the extent to which the West would go to hinder the spread of communism.

"The fear wasn't of the Soviet Union alone. Rather, we were also afraid of the nations that had been struck by the Marxist fever."

Gandhi found the mass movements in favor of communism understandable.

"It is not uncommon for oppressed peoples to adopt ideologies that are equipped with the means to help them cast off their shackles."

Kennedy felt sorrow at how easily nations can be deceived.

"An ornate lie can blind people from seeing the truth. In the name of communism dictatorial governments went about crushing their peoples and fighting the voice of democracy. Protests for freedom and greater rights were broken up violently, and dissidents were actively pursued and dragged to prison. Detainees were subject to torture in retribution for their anti-government activities, and some even died under torture."

The skeleton picked up where Kennedy left off.

"The masses were manipulated by the government, which forced them to swallow its ideological vision by utilizing an ironfirst approach to rule as well as a sustained propaganda campaign that made ample use of endearing slogans designed to seduce the masses by taking advantage of their noble patriotic sentiments."

Abdel Nasser had first-hand experience with these kinds of tactics.

"Governments ought to adopt a platform of reform in order to ensure that they'll have the backing of the masses."

Abdel Hamid agreed with Nasser, but he had his reservations.

"Reform is a good thing, necessary even. But it ought not be pursued the way that Europeanized general, Mustafa Ataturk, did. He ended up granting greater freedoms to women, outlawing polygamy and, even worse, in 1934 he granted them the right to vote!"

"No wonder his enemies plotted to have him killed!" Churchill responded sneeringly.

"The Islamic religious activists were right to do so!" Abdel Hamid replied in all seriousness, not seeming to catch the sarcasm in Churchill's voice.

"He turned everything upside down! Rome wasn't built in a day. . ."

Gandhi wasn't pleased by Abdel Hamid's response.

"Religion is God's and God's alone! Politics, on the other hand, is a wholly human endeavor. When religion creeps into politics, it loses its lofty character and its exalted ideals," he exclaimed.

"Politics and religion are two sides of the same coin," Abdel Hamid responded calmly.

"There's no separating one from the other."

The skeleton was on Gandhi's side.

"But when religion buts into politics, it loses its spiritual character and turns into a political party. Religion ought to be more open, more accepting than a political party."

"'Render to Caesar the things that are Caesar's, and to God the things that are God's.'" the millionaire said, citing a verse from the Gospels.

"Thus saith our Lord, Jesus Christ."

Gandhi proceeded with his explanation.

"When religion becomes ideology, it becomes an easy instrument in the politicians' toolbox, which they can brandish like a weapon whenever and however they choose."

"Why don't any of you learn from history?" Stalin rebuked.

"When religion reigned supreme, Europe and Russia drowned in the gloom of the Dark Ages. And that's how we ended up with that sordid religious feudalism."

He knew why Stalin was attacking religion.

"His Holiness Pope Saint John Paul II considered communism one of the great evils of the twentieth century."

"And Nazism as well," Rabin added.

"But he also considered European secularism a catastrophe in it's own right," Kennedy said.

"He deemed it contrary to the teachings of Christ, and that Europe would not be healed until it returned to the religion of the Gospels."

Stalin was not convinced.

"The Pope issued his edicts against these ideologies by means of his Church and its teachings. He condemned these ideologies as 'evils,' and this is what led to the rise of secularism which had been the impetus for the European enlightenment.

Of these various secular ideologies, communism was the most fair-minded and equitable of them."

Kennedy was insistent.

"But he also said that enlightenment need not entail the eradication of religion. It simply meant that religion ought to be kept out of the public sphere and firmly within the realm of private belief."

Hegel's dialectic flowed through Stalin's veins, and he had no problem alluding to it in his response. "Individuals are the building blocks of society. When the Pope relegated enlightenment to individual choice he covertly intended to excommunicate and punish all those whose choices went against his preferences. In this way, he desired to keep religion and the teachings of the Church as shackles that may continue to keep humanity in check and prevent them from evolving and prospering."

"But religion is simply an expression of ethics," Gandhi said with innocuous faith.

"Religion is the opiate of the masses, just as Marx had said!" Stalin insisted in a spirit of obstinacy and confrontation.

He then gestured to De Gaulle.

"This is why the French Revolution separated religion from the state. Indeed, it goes without mentioning that Italy had stood by Franco during the Spanish Civil War because the leftist Republicans had confiscated the properties of the Church and the landed gentry and redistributed them among the peasants."

Kennedy simply couldn't sit idly by as his Church was being attacked.

"Why, of course, it was no different from your policy of eradication against the Kulaks in 1930, whence you took their lands and converted them to common use."

The skull sympathized with Kennedy.

"Didn't Lenin himself say you were too severe?" it asked Stalin.

"The Soviet Union was going through a difficult period. The West conspired against us, and the enormous weight left by Tsarist rule had left the Russian people whimpering from poverty and famine. Then Lenin died from a gunshot wound he had sustained during one of the many assassination attempts against him, and it was my job to get the wheel back on the cart and keep things moving again."

"Forget about wheels and carts!" Abdel Nasser said as he sunk into despair. "In the Arab world things moved only at the behest and in the direction of the colonists' pockets."

"As for us Jews, since time immemorial we longed for the state of Israel, the dream home of every Jewish man and woman," Rabin said, "and so we dug the foundations on which to build our homeland with our nails and fingers."

The skeleton took a deep breath and then asked, "Behind every ideology is a fearsome dictator. But can dictatorship lead the way to democracy?"

Stalin nodded his head affirmingly.

"Of course. It is by virtue of Communism that Russia was able to become strong and independent."

The skull felt reinvigorated by all the talk about strength.

"The Fascists sought to establish an expansive empire," it said, giving an example of the kinds of aspirations Mussolini entertained when he became strong.

"It had been imperative for the Third Reich to become the strongest power in Europe, and to unite the Germanophone countries into one superpower," Hitler intervened.

"I began in 1938 with the Czech region of Sudetenland, and then I followed it up by taking Austria."

"It seems the West was overly lax with Hitler," the skeleton said, referencing Churchill's earlier defense of his initial approach to Hitler's expansionism.

"Britain and France were in no rush to war," Churchill clarified. "And hence we pursued a policy of appeasement. In 1938 a conference was held in Munich in which Britain, France, Germany and Italy participated with an eye to keeping the peace in Europe."

"What was the outcome of the conference?" Abdel Hamid asked.

"Czechoslovakia ceded control over Sudetenland," Hitler said in a reply that was at once hard-nosed and conceited.

Hitler's conceitedness drew De Gaulle's ire.

"But you were not content with Sudetenland, so you went ahead and wiped Czechoslovakia off the map!" he charged.

Rabin proceeded to narrate the next stage of events.

"Poland was locked between Russia and Germany, each of whom had territorial ambitions in the area."

For Churchill, Hitler's excesses would not go unchecked.

"Britain and France reassured the Poles and concluded a mutual defense pact with them."

For once, Kennedy was understanding of Stalin.

"The Soviet Union was hemmed in between Germany and Italy to the west and their Japanese allies to the east. It would have only been natural for you to have formed an alliance with their enemies."

"'The enemy of my enemy is my friend'," Gandhi proffered. Stalin shot an angry glance at Churchill and said, "The British Prime Minister Chamberlain damned any possibility of that happening. His fiery rhetoric against the Soviet Union and against Communism were severe indeed, and this pulled us away from Britain and her allies. Hitler was in need of international support for its annexation of Czechoslovakia, so instead in 1939 we decided to conclude a non-aggression pact with him."

Abdel Hamid shook his head disapprovingly.

"He annexes Czechoslovakia and Austria by force, and you give him a non-aggression pact."

"What did you gain from this agreement?" the millionaire asked.

"We split Poland between ourselves," Stalin replied with glee.

". . .and the Baltic states," Kennedy added.

The armies of the world were on full alert. "The world broke up into Axis and Allies," the skeleton said. "Severe enmity reigned between the two."

Some countries, on the other hand, decided to bide their time. Abdel Hamid wished that Turkey had not gotten involved.

"For a while Turkey held off on joining either of the two sides."

"The Allies worked hard to tempt Turkey to join its side," Abdel Nasser said.

"In 1939 France - which was occupying Syria at the time - gave Turkey the Iskenderun region in northern Syria in contravention of the very mandate provisions which dictated that France preserve its control over every inch of mandated territory. They did this in order to ensure Turkey's support in the upcoming World War."

Gandhi was seized by emotion.

"They buy and sell territory as they please, and the subdued, impoverished, impotent peoples of the world end up paying the price."

Rabin felt that war on many an occasion was necessary.

"The ends justify the means," he said. "It is not important who pays, who goes hungry, and who dies. Ideological warfare is not in the slightest concerned for prices or for who pays them. It will proceed to achieve its goals without once batting an eye."

The skeleton had been listening carefully.

"I think I hear the sound of warplanes roaring overhead."

"I can smell the gun powder!" the skull shrieked.

"And that's when the German armed forces conducted an aerial bombardment on the city of Warsaw," Hitler said coldly.

CHAPTER 20
Heart Ache

The politicians and statesmen had made their decision, and the world was poised to go to war. Armies were ready and prepared to carry out any and all commands that might come their way. Fear and anxiety pervaded the hearts of people whose good sense and experience made them painfully aware of the horrors that wars bring in their wake. Various news agencies went to work broadcasting and airing impassioned speeches directed at the citizenry replete with ideological undertones. There was mass mobilization along the frontlines, and iron helmets atop the heads of soldiers, who vied against time from within their barracks. Their sturdy shoes hit the ground with force as they moved swiftly and seamlessly and without much thought. The roaring of warplane engines and the clattering of tank tracks can be heard from every quarter. Assembly lines picked up the pace, hurrying to produce the supplies and provisions their armies sorely needed.

The lengths man will go to crush his enemy. Cain killed his brother Abel. Man is an enemy to his follow man. The bulbul birds abruptly ceased their twittering and fled to escape the madness of mankind. Rodents and reptiles retreated into their burrows, leaving humanity's sons to settle their affairs between themselves.

The skeleton began to narrate how the war began:

"German warplanes conducted an aerial bombardment on the city of Warsaw. France and Britain had each vowed to protect and defend Poland in the event of an attack."

Churchill had thought it necessary to stop Hitler.

"We declared war on Germany in 1939, and the Second World War was in full swing."

De Gaulle decried Poland's pitiful fate.

"British and French forces never reached Poland. There was no one to defend her, no one to put the Germans in their place."

Hitler was huffish and overweening.

"Because the German. . ."

". . .and Russian armies occupied Poland very quickly," Stalin interrupted.

Hitler wasn't pleased with having to go halves on victory with Stalin.

"And then our army headed west to surprise the French and the English.

To Abdel Hamid launching a surprise attack against the French and the British was quite the onerous affair.

"How was it able to overcome the Maginot Line?" he asked.

The millionaire reflected for a moment, and it dawned on him how arduous it must have been to penetrate a line that had been so thoroughly fortified in order to drive away any such attacks. "It must have taken many years and cost exorbitant amounts of money to construct the Maginot Line," he said, adding weight to Abdel Hamid's question.

"The German armies were well-trained and well-equipped," Hitler replied confidently and vigorously.

"They strongly believed in their own abilities and were confident that victory was theirs. Our best, brightest and most seasoned officers had planned the attack, and I was most impressed with the plan that they had put together. I ordered my armies to launch a full-scale attack, with every battalion and legion participating in the effort: the Air Force, the tank battalions and the armored regiments would go to work first, followed by the infantrymen. I wanted the attack to hit them with the force of a massive flood."

The skull was impressed with Hitler's confidence.

"Were you able to cross that heavily secured line?" he asked with fascination.

Hitler felt the skull was luring him into a trap.

"Of course not."

The skeleton was confused. He tried to remain silent, but his curiosity got the better of him.

"Then how did the German armies manage to penetrate into the heart of France?" he asked.

The skeleton's foolishness made Hitler laugh.

"We used torrential waters"*

Everyone was astounded by Hitler's answer.

"You fought with water?"

"I've been to war many times," the skull said, "but I've never heard of such a move."

"That's because you only fought with catapults," Abdel Hamid said jokingly.

Rabin had enough of jokes.

"We in Israel came to know later on the importance of water in war," he said in a serious tone.

Rabin's seriousness paved the way for Hitler to explain his plan.

"As water gushes forth relentlessly and smashes into a strong barrier in its way - such as a tall rock, for instance - the water will not be able to penetrate it. But it can maneuver around it and continue flowing. That's what oour armies did: we maneuvered around the line, crossing into Holland, Belgium and Luxembourg, and finally advancing into the Ardennes, and surprised the French, who weren't expecting to meet us there."

The skull listened attentively to the details of the plan. He wanted to hear more.

"How long did your occupation of these countries last?" he asked.

"The German armies' attacks were swift and severe," Hitler replied boastfully.

"They coined the term 'blitzkrieg (lightning war)' to describe the fierceness of our advance. Denmark and Norway had fallen like leaves during autumn season. The German armies continued their advance over Belgian territory until they reached Dunkerque Port in northern France. That's where they met British forces and engaged them in battle."

Churchill had no qualms admitting his surprise.

"The German attack was as fierce as it was unexpected. We were forced to pull back our forces and to send ships to save them."

"The German army attacked the ships that came to carry away the soldiers with unprecedented brutality," De Gaulle said angrily.

"Hitler's forces must have had a field day with the British," Abdel Hamid sneered.

"I ordered a series of yachts and small row boats be dispatched to them," Churchill said with a voice at once sorrowful and stately. "Within a month we were able to save 200,000 soldiers."

"They left behind their weapons and equipment, which became ours for the taking," Hitler gloated.

"We handed them a humiliating defeat, and we were able to subdue France within a time span of six weeks. We seized control of Paris and raised the flag of the German Reich above the Eiffel Tower."

De Gaulle had enough rage in his heart to kill him, but he decided to keep silent. Churchill took up the task of cutting Hitler's arrogance down to size.

"And yet Great Britain remained a thorn in your eye."

"Were you able to pull the thorn out?" Abdel Hamid asked Hitler, clearly trying to provoke him.

"Britain is lucky to be surrounded by a protective ocean," Hitler replied grudgingly.

"So you surrender to the ocean?" Abdel Hamid asked, again seeking to provoke Hitler.

"We had no alternative. We needed a meticulous plan to obliterate Britain and the ocean that surrounded it."

"At the time we were much delighted by the force of our ally's advances," Stalin said in the spirit of friendship. "After all, we did have a non-aggression pact in place with him."

"We were much disappointed by the statement made by Soviet Prime Minister Monsieur Molotov in which he bragged that the tanks that attacked France had been filled with Soviet fuel," De Gaulle responded.

Churchill was equally outraged.

"Molotov seemed thrilled when he said that the bullets that killed our soldiers were of Soviet origin."

De Gaulle took a deep breath.

"As if that wasn't enough, the Soviet Union also established diplomatic relations with the Vichy regime," he said rebukingly.

Abdel Hamid was rather amused at the direction the conversation had taken.

"Was the German naval fleet capable of invading the British peninsula?"

"The German naval fleet did precisely that."

"German warplanes conducted a sustained bombardment campaign against British airports and runways," Kennedy said, his sympathies clearly with the British.

Churchill shook his head cheerlessly.

"For 57 days straight."

"London was bombarded by air, as were its industrial centers with the aim of pummeling its economy and forcing it to surrender," De Gaulle said, clarifying Hitler's goals.

It wasn't only the sheer amount of destruction loss that saddened Gandhi, but also the wanton disregard for human life.

"Some 25,000 civilians lost their lives during the campaign."

"But they failed to break our resolve, "Churchill announced with pride. "Great Britain persevered."

Hitler cursed the snow and ocean in his heart as he explained the reasons for the failure.

"The ocean was like an ally to Britain. It helped them persevere, as did the long distance which forced the German warplanes to fly at a considerable distance from their bases. On the other hand, British warplanes were able to conduct their sorties and return to battle on the same day."

Churchill gleamed with pride and joy.

"The British people and their pilots were determined to resist. It was their tenacity and will to resist that foiled the German attack."

Rabin was impressed with British military capabilities and their ability to repel a surprise attack on the British peninsula. "English radar systems that were invented in 1936 detected the impending German attack and identified the location of the enemy warplanes."

Stalin's stubborn mentality gave way to an opinion that differed markedly from that of Rabin.

"Had Hitler persisted in his bombing campaign but a few more days he would have brought about Britain's downfall and the war would have been his."

"What did Italy do during the war?" the skeleton asked, seeking clarification about the role Hitler's European allies played.

Abdel Nasser had been listening attentively to the course of the discussion.

"After it annexed Albania, it declared war on Greece, attacking it from the east."

Abdel Hamid didn't know what happened next, but he was hoping the Italians triumphed.

"Was Mussolini able to occupy Greece?"

The skeleton spelled out the results of the battle.

"The Italian attack failed to produce the desired results, despite its numerous attempts."

Abdel Nasser testified to the courage of his neighbors to the north.

"The Greeks resisted the Italian attack with audacity."

Rabin hadn't expected that the Greeks would hold on for long.

"The Greek resistance may well-nigh have changed the course of the war."

"Hitler knew what the consequences would be if his Italian allies were to be defeated in Greece, so he rushed to their aid," Stalin said, drawing on his military expertise.

Power took hold in Hitler's voice as he said, "German regiments advanced on Greece and were able to occupy it within a month."

Abdel Hamid was overjoyed.

"How heroic! You've done well, Hitler. The Greeks had been arch-nemeses to the Ottoman Empire."

Hitler continued to expand on his many victories.

"We carried out a parachute landing on the Crete Islands and succeeded in seizing control of them in a matter of ten days. German forces took some 1,200 British soldiers prisoner."

Churchill felt Hitler had overstated his case. The British did not stand idly as the Germans proceeded with their invasion. "The British naval fleet was quite successful in its operations against the Italians and the Axis-allied Vichy government in the Mediterranean Sea Basin."

The skeleton took it upon himself to announce the results of the battle.

"Germany in concert with its allies had seized control of sizable amounts of territory."

"Perhaps at that time the German leadership had had enough," Gandhi said with firm conviction.

Hitler demurred at Gandhi's hopes and proceeded to correct the latter's false notions with much conceitedness.

"We wanted to take over the world. And this was no mere delusion: after all, our armies had reached the Dardanelles and the Bosphorus Strait in record time."

The skull had some military expertise of his own, and so he asked, "What were the biggest obstacles you encountered during the war?"

"Gas shortages were like an Achilles Heel to us. It was our major point of weakness. It was for this reason that we set about developing chemical petroleum. By 1940 we were able to use it to supply our armies with roughly half of its energy needs."

Stalin knew all too well about Hitler's petroleum problems.

"The Germans were heavily dependent on tanks to secure swift victories - and tanks need fuel to run."

Hitler needed a solution, and fast.

"But chemical petroleum alone would not solve our problems. We were greatly seduced by the glamors of Soviet petrol, and Soviet deposits were well within our armies' reach. So I ordered my generals to seize control of them so that they might be available for immediate use."

"I trusted Hitler," Stalin said, betaken by feelings of astonishment and overwhelming rage.

"I couldn't believe he would order his armies to overrun our positions."

"The world isn't big enough for the both of us, Stalin," Hitler said with audacity.

"You're a double-crosser, Hitler," Stalin shot back.

"Why, I feared that you would double cross me," Hitler said with a collected demeanor.

"After all, you're half giant and half beast."

Stalin was crestfallen.

"Had we remained united we would have been a power that could not be stopped," he rebuked.

"There are real differences between the Soviet Union's communist ideology and Nazism," Hitler responded heartfeltedly.

"Hatred for the Left is at the very core of Nazism. Though our interests coincided at certain points, there was no escaping a showdown between Nazism and Communism."

Stalin's response betrayed his dashed hopes.

"I truly believed in our friendship."

Hitler was unmoved.

"Even if I took your hand in friendship now I would have no scruples about fighting you tomorrow."

De Gaulle looked at the two of them and smiled.

"Indeed, it was the ideological similarity between Fascism and Nazism that preserved the relationship between Hitler and Mussolini."

Hitler folded his hands behind his head.

"As the German regiments invaded the Soviet Union, I felt a renewed sense of relief. I told Mussolini at the time that my friendship with the Soviet Union had taken me away from my roots."

"I'm sure you all know the story of the scorpion and the frog," Stalin said, stammering in his speech. "The scorpion stung the frog, and when the frog asked him why he said that this was his nature. So it is with Hitler: at the first opportunity he stung me as a scorpion does."

Abdel Nasser had a different ruling on the matter.

"The fault lies solely on the one who carried the scorpion on his back and helped him cross the river."

"Please, Hitler," Stalin pleaded sorrowfully.

"Don't say anything more. Don't tell them what you did to me."

"That is your right, Mr. Stalin," Gandhi said to him encouragingly.

Hitler found the request strange.

"Why do you ask this of me?"

"So that humanity does not lose its trust in one another," Gandhi replied on Stalin's behalf.

"In the event that happens states could never form alliances, and friendships between individuals could never develop."

Rabin, unlike the other two men, saw Hitler's move as quite unremarkable.

"This is the nature of politics. Japan had been a member of the Allies in World War I, and then moved to the Axis in World War II."

Churchill clarified the reasons behind Japan's shift.

"Britain and the U.S. had imposed economic sanctions on Japan in hopes of putting an end to the latter's repeated incursions into Chinese territory and to put a limit to its ambitions in the Pacific."

Abdel Hamid contemplated for a moment and said, "Japan must have took advantage of Britain and France's engrossment in the war against Hitler to build itself up as the main superpower in the Far East."

Churchill deemed Abdel Hamid's opinion sound.

"The Americans had something of an isolationist policy that prevented them from entering into the war."

Gandhi was hysterical.

"It seems the powerful think with their muscles and not with their brains."

Kennedy adjusted his chair and said, "The Japanese may have been short, but boy did they have muscles."

Abdel Nasser empathized with Kennedy.

"The Japanese took advantage of the American giants' state of inadvertence. The latter had been enjoying a lovely vacation along the warm Azure-colored waters of the Pacific Coast."

"In 1941, 353 Japanese fighter planes attacked the American military base in Hawaii's Pearl Harbor. The attack resulted in the deaths of some 2,400 Americans, and the destruction of some 188 warplanes and the drowning of 19 warships," the skeleton said as he read off an old report.

"It was like a stab in the back, considering that the United States had concluded a peace treaty with them," Kennedy exclaimed, his tone evidently despondent.

Rabin held the Japanese responsible for the abrupt turn in the course of the war and the attendant change in the balance of power. "The Japanese attack on Pearl Harbor pushed the United States to enter the war on the side of the Allies."

Churchill shot a glance at Hitler and made a victory sign with his hands.

"Hitler had not expected the U.S to enter into the war on our side."

Hitler's response came rashly.

"All of the reports from the Gestapo indicate that Jews with ties to the major weapons and petroleum lobby groups pressured President Roosevelt to enter the war."

Churchill's face betrayed an unmistakable sense of serenity.

"As soon as the United States entered the war my heart was at rest and I began to sleep peacefully."

Kennedy was stoked.

"The United States responded to the attack on Pearl Harbor by destroying four Japanese aircraft carriers."

"The respective actors in Asia and Europe were now part of the same global fray," the skeleton said.

Stalin proceeded to clarify the Soviet Union's impending military strategy.

"We adopted a scorched-earth policy that left Germany unable to benefit from its supply storages and weapons stockpiles."

Hitler was noticeably outraged.

"Winter fell before our forces were able to reach Moscow," he said in a spirit of provocation and haughtiness. "I hate that damn snow! It caused the deaths of thousands of my men, and prevented us from getting needed supplies to them."

"How did the Germans react to the Russians' scorched-earth policy?" The skull asked inquisitively.

"We laid siege to Leningrad, and I ordered my men to wipe the city off the face of the Earth," Hitler said in an attempt to save face.

Gandhi found both sides worthy of contempt.

"A million people died in that city as a result of famine."

Hitler's heart was as cold as the snow he hated.

"German forced occupied 90% of the city, and were it not for the recurrent problem of gas shortages we would have rid the world of Communism."

Stalin's eyes jumped out of their sockets.

"It was the perseverance of the Soviet Red Army backed by the strong will and unbounded conviction of the heroic Russian people that enabled us to fight off the German advance with valiance and might. The city of Leningrad pressed on for a year and a half. Though the Germans cut water and supplies to the city, Red Army brigades using light weaponry clashed with the invading armies and, though they paid a heavy price, in the end they were victorious over the enemy."

Gandhi weeped for the innocent victims of the war. His heart ached as he brought to mind the causes of conflict.

"The various parties fought one another with bayonets, knives, sticks and stones, even with nails and teeth. They had no option but to either kill or be killed. Peoples' blood flowed through the streets, while their leaders smoked cigars and edged the soldiers on as if they were spectators watching a football game."

CHAPTER 21
A Hornets Nest

O the second day after Japan's surprise attack, Congress unanimously voted to approve the United States' entry into the war. The behemoth's vacation was over, and with ample amounts of economic and military resources at his disposal he went about his work. In the aftermath of the humiliating blow the Americans had been dealt in Pearl Harbor President Franklin D. Roosevelt was entrusted with the task of avenging America's honor, restoring her deterrence and establishing once and for all that the U.S. was a force to be reckoned with. The United States joined the war on the side of the Allies. In turn, Germany and Italy stood by Japan and proceeded to declare war on the United States. As a result, the Pentagon immediately went to work on a new military strategy with particular focus on conducting operations in Europe and Indo-China. Experts prepared war plans to strike Japan in the heart of the Pacific Ocean. What had previously been two separate wars, each with their own trajectories - one in Europe, the other in Asia - was then consolidated into one war - a world war.

Kennedy took pride in America's ability to restore its sense of honor.

"America's first attempt to put on a show of force came during the Battle of Midway, in which American forces destroyed four aircraft carriers belonging to Japan."

Churchill was well aware of the course of events as they transpired in real time.

"We were preoccupied with fighting the Germans, and that gave the Japanese the opportunity to attack Burma, Indonesia and Malaysia."

The millionaire ruminated about the economic incentives of the war.

"The Japanese must have been drooling at the prospect of gaining control over Indonesian petrol reserves."

Churchill was pained by Britain's losses in the Far East.

"A Japanese military victory there was the most humiliating setback we were made to suffer since the war began."

"The Americans under General Douglas MacArthur proved themselves a worthy fighting force," Kennedy said so as to reassure Churchill.

"The Pacific Isles were falling to American armed forces one after the other."

Skeleton felt De Gaulle had played an important role during that critical phase.

"Your passionate speeches restored the vigor of the French people, who tuned in to BBC radio to hear them."

De Gaulle was not consoled.

"It was a very difficult moment for France. Our brave nation was under German occupation, and our resistance forces were in need of funding and weapons."

"But the United States' entry into the war on the side of the Allies must have been a boon for you?" Abdel Hamid asked comfortingly.

De Gaulle didn't budge.

"It wasn't all it was cracked up to be at first."

Kennedy was astounded.

"Did not the United States of America supply the Allies with weapons and equipment by way of the lend-lease program?"

"And monetary support in the form of loans, too," the millionaire added.

There was no inveigling De Gaulle.

"The United States had preferred to deal with recognized governments, and so it refused to work with us. The least that can be said is that President Roosevelt didn't offer me the same courtesy he did Churchill and Stalin."

"You mean they kept you in the dark about their meetings in Casablanca and Tehran," Hitler said, playing on De Gaulle's insecurities.

Churchill felt De Gaulle was owed an explanation.

"At the time, De Gaulle, you only represented the French resistance. There were others in France that we had to play ball with as well."

"I was fighting in the name of France, and every movement I made in the political arena was in the name of France - all of France. I resisted the Nazis side-by-side with the English, but it wasn't in England's interest that I represent France, or for that matter that anyone represent France aside from them."

De Gaulle's nationalist spirit seemed to be getting out of hand and that made Churchill uncomfortable.

"I sincerely hoped that you and I would be on the same side here. I find your words disappointing. You seem ready to pick a bone with anyone, not only the Germans, Italians and the Japanese but also your American and English friends as well."

De Gaulle was beside himself.

"You must be joking!" He shouted, throwing his hands hysterically.

"You can't be serious! I would be very upset with you if you were. If there was anyone on the face of this Earth who had been sincerely loyal to England, then it was me."

Churchill bit on his cigar and shook his head in disdain. De Gaulle continued ranting.

"I told Roosevelt that I was too proud to bow my head in humiliation before the Americans."

Kennedy defended America's position with impressive zeal.

"America was - and is - the most powerful country the world had ever known. We lead the world economically, politically, militarily - even cinematically and culturally. It isn't in France's interest to go toe to toe with us."

"We are the people of France! We take pride in our Frenchness. Our rich history and beautiful language know no superior."

"We are the people of manifest destiny, De Gaulle. We gave the world the gift of democracy, economic prosperity, and religious freedom. We have and always will be the land of the free and home of the brave."

"Do you know who I am?! I'm from France! France, whose revolution changed not only Europe but the entire world."

Kennedy was stung by De Gaulle's jibe against the United States.

"And don't you forget that the American Revolution too left its mark on Europe and the world."

De Gaulle took a deep breath.

"France was a major empire in the nineteenth century," he said, singing his nation's praises.

"It certainly was right up until its defeat and occupation at the hands of Hitler during World War II," Churchill said, his insult-wrapped-in-a-compliment designed to bring De Gaulle down to size.

"No matter - I am the man who restored to France its freedom," De Gaulle said, clearly proud of himself.

Churchill respected De Gaulle's tenacity.

"This is true," he said with an air of unabashed admiration in his voice. "You are a stubborn man, De Gaulle. Though I find such a trait intolerable, I must say I respected your resoluteness towards Germany."

"You might like to know that I have two brothers, one crazy, the other sane," he replied vivaciously.

"I think of myself as being somewhere between them."

"I'm a great admirer of you, General," Kennedy said, soothing De Gaulle's nerves.

"Both your crazy side and your sane side."

De Gaulle finally relented.

"I too admire America - though I have my reservations about its policies."

All this talk about love had gotten to Churchill. He decided to share some feelings of his own - though in a direction opposite that in which the conversation was heading.

"I wasn't a big admirer of your father, Kennedy." Kennedy was caught off guard.

"Why is that?"

Apparently an offhand remark of Kennedy's father, Joseph Kennedy, had gotten under Churchill's skin. "Your father had predicted that the British would lose the war. He actually thought that Hitler was going to win!"

Hitler felt giddy.

"Your father, Mr. Kennedy, was a man of piercing insight. That's why Churchill resents him."

Churchill seemed incapable of remembering that statement.

"All I know is that Joe Kennedy left Britain and returned to the United States in 1940, just after German armed forces began its bombardment campaign against London."

"Britain again! Oh how I wish that I could have ripped that thorn out by the roots," Hitler said, dejected and disappointed.

"Perhaps it was a mistake to forge East before finishing off the job to the West," Abdel Hamid said, reproaching Hitler.

Sultan Abdel Hamid's words disturbed Churchill.

"What argument do you have with Britain, Abdel Hamid?"

Abdel Hamid took the stand in his defense.

"I don't mean to offend you, Churchill. I'm speaking objectively here. Hitler had a plan in place for waging war against Britain, but then he attacks Greece thousands of miles away, not to mention his other diversion in the Crete islands."

"There was no choice but to attack and occupy Greece," Hitler explained. "We needed to save the Duce."

Rabin looked at Churchill and said, "Hitler's support for the Fascists is what kept them standing after the string of losses they suffered in Greece."

"The British army launched a successful attack on the Italians in the north African territory of Libya," Hitler said, though his face still beamed with optimism.

"They reached as far as Tobruk."

"Was it then that the tide turned for Great Britain?" Abdel Hamid deduced.

"Their happiness didn't last long, Sultan!" Hitler pounced.

"I sent them Rommel along with some of our best tanks. He succeeded in utterly routing them and even hounded them down as they retreated hastily over the desert sands. That's how he got the name 'Desert Fox.'"

"It would have behooved the English to seek the aid of the Free French Forces stationed in Chad, just south of them in the Sahara," De Gaulle said, his words hitting Churchill like a rock.

Hitler concurred with De Gaulle's opinion.

"The British lost a golden opportunity to paint Rommel into a corner. The English were in control of the entire Libyan coast to the north. All they needed to do was join forces With De Gaulle's men to the south and they could have laid siege to our armies in the Sahara. We would have been stuck between the two tongues of a plier, and it would have been impossible to send in reinforcements."

"You might be our enemy, Hitler," De Gaulle said with a tone of indirect gratitude.

"But I was thinking precisely the same thing."

"Why is it that the English abstained from taking advantage of this opportunity, gentlemen?" the skeleton asked slyly.

"The British and their egocentrism," Abdel Nasser shot back immediately. "They wanted victory to be theirs alone."

"And what did you do to bring matter to a close, Hitler?" Abdel Hamid asked cautiously.

Hitler took a moment to think.

"We needed to retake Tobruk," he replied.

"So I ordered an immediate strike by the German Air Force on the English forces, who were forced back by the sheer amount of firepower, and during the withdrawal our forces were able to take 35,000 English soldiers prisoner."

"Romel planted landmines in the surrounding area, which came to be called 'The Devil's Garden,'" Abdel Nasser said, describing the measures taken by Rommel to impede potential reprise attacks by Allies forces.

Gandhi wanted to draw attention to humanitarian concerns with his next comment.

"It is unfortunate that even after the war had ended the warring parties decided to leave the landmines behind to lie in wait for the civilian population."

To Stalin the paramount concern was to inflict maximum damage on the enemy.

"After we emerged triumphant in the Battle of Stalingrad I ordered that 400,000 landmines be planted and 5,000 kilometers of trenches be dug in order to keep us insulated."

Churchill wasn't about to lose hope.

"We marshalled our forces in Egypt and sent them reinforcements, supplies and armaments - anything they needed to force a defeat on the Axis, whatever the cost."

"In that year a famine broke out in Egypt," Abdel Nasser said, describing the repercussions of the Allies' new military strategy.

"Afterwards there were demonstrations all over in which people openly called for a German victory."

Gandhi knew well how a colonizing power dealt with resistance in its colonies.

"The British soldiers responded by heaving live fire at the unarmed protesters."

For Churchill, the ends justified the means.

"The Egyptian protests came at the absolute worst time. We were being routed by Rommel in the Sahara, and to stick it in our eye the Egyptians chanted slogans in praise of him. We had stop them using whatever means were necessary. The goal of the British leadership was to put all efforts to stopping Rommel in his tracks in the quickest time possible."

The skull saw the reason in Churchill's argument. He understood where the latter was coming from. "It was perhaps for this reason that you switched the commanders in Africa, moving General Auchinleck to Syria while appointing General Montgomery in his stead."

Churchill nodded his head affirmatively as he heaped praises on his new commander.

"General 'Monty' as we used to call him had been one of the most important military leaders in British history."

Hitler's esteem for his General echoed that of Churchill for Montgomery.

"Field Marshall Rommel may be perhaps the most important military commander in the history of man."

Hitler's homage for his General rubbed Churchill the wrong way.

"In the end, General Monty handed Rommel a sound defeat, and the Allies were able to expel the Germans from Libya and from Africa and chased them back as far as Malta!" he objected.

Abdel Hamid had been a great admirer of Germany's strength, and so the astounding news of Germany's loss required explanation.

"A commander of Rommel's stature could not have been defeated without a cause," he said.

Stalin took it upon himself to explain.

"A key reason is that the Russians were beginning to register victories against the Germans along the eastern front, which prevented Hitler from aiding Rommel with reinforcements and weapons."

"Fuel shortages were also a major problem," Hitler added.

"They prevented Rommel from putting his tanks to full use in his larger military scheme."

The skeleton read aloud a report that was relevant to the discussion at hand.

"The Allies destroyed some twenty ships carrying fuel to the besieged Axis troops."

Kennedy took pride in the role the United States played during the war.

"The American armies fought the Japanese in the Pacific while simultaneously maintaining a presence in Europe and North Africa."

"We occupied Europe, and we were on the verge of taking Moscow as well," Hitler said as he described the extent of his force's strength.

"We maintained a presence in the north African territory of Libya - whence our Italian allies also maintained a presence - as well as Tunisia, Morocco, and Algeria by means of the French forces allied to the Vichy government. The same goes for Syria and Lebanon."

Opposite the strength of Hitler's forces was a firm conviction on the part of the Allies that they were going to win. The Americans in particular stood at the head of the High Command which oversaw the Allies' joint military efforts.

"Eisenhower took the reins as Chief Commander of the Allied Forces, he led an attack in North Africa in which direct clashes occurred with the French forces allied to the Vichy regime," Kennedy said.

Despite all of this Hitler insisted that his forces retained the upper hand.

"The Germans handed the Americans a sound defeat in Tunisia."

No one bothered to mention the role De Gaulle had played in all of this, and so he thought it proper to remind them:

"The French commander Jean Lannes* was taken captive in Algeria. He managed to convince his men to surrender to the Allies, and the majority of them ended up joining the Free French forces."

"But the Free French forces opened fire on the Americans who came to liberate France and the rest of Europe!" Kennedy said in angry protest.

De Gaulle's response had a hint of contrite sadness to it, which eased Kennedy's anger.

"Don't get so sore, Mr. Kennedy. What is truly unfortunate in all of this is how battles ensued between the French forces allied to the Germans against the Free French Army, in which many lives were lost on both sides. Brothers were killing each other, and for what?"

Abdel Nasser empathized with De Gaulle.

"I understand you well, Monsieur De Gaulle," he said in a consolatory tone.

"When brothers fight one another, the one who loses the most is the nation to which they belong."

"The Germans and the rest of the Axis Powers were finally expelled from North Africa," Rabin said with deep tranquility.

"'This is not the end nor the beginning of the end, it is the end of the beginning,'" Churchill said, recapitulating a famous statement he had made during that critical moment.

The skeleton redirected the discussion to the eastern front.

"The war between the Russians and the Germans was one that pit one giant against the other, each of whom were intent on achieving victory."

Kennedy felt that the United States had played an important role in how the course of the war along the eastern front played out.

"American support to the Russians was instrumental in tilting the balance firmly in the latters' favor."

"The American economy was able to pull itself together by supplying the Allies with whatever they needed to conduct the war," the millionaire said with glee.

"Factories were operating day and night," Kennedy added.

"Unemployment nearly vanished, and the American people worked strenuously to make sure what needed to be done got done."

"Indeed! In turn, the Americans' pockets got fatter, and Wall Street went to work. The value of stocks reached record highs."

"More importantly, the brave men of our armed forces showed the enemy what was what on the battlefield. They sang our national anthem as they engaged the enemy with courage."

Abdel Hamid interrupted the conversation and directed his remarks to the Allies' leadership:

"Had Hitler enjoyed the support of an ally like the United States victory would have been but a distant dream for you all."

Hitler was downcast.

"I never expected the United States to join the war so soon into the war."

"The fault was none but your own, Hitler," Stalin rebuked.

"Had we remained allies we would have been unstoppable."

"No one was a match for Hitler," Abdel Hamid said, recapitulating his earlier praise for Hitler's strength.

"Otherwise he wouldn't have been able to pile up the victories on the ground with such speed."

Churchill scowled at Abdel Hamid and replied, "And yet we defeated him in Al Alamein, in northern Africa."

Abdel Hamid adjusted his seating position and cleared his throat. In his right hand was a rosary made of pearls.

"Listen, Churchill. Everyone knows that occasionally courage on the battlefield must give way to superior numbers. You defeated him only because of your numbers."

Hitler swayed his head as if his favorite song was on.

"I thank you for your kind words, Sultan."

Kennedy tried to steer the conversation back to the factors which caused the the balance of power to shift in favor of the Allies.

"A million and a half American soldiers reached the coast of England in 1943. . ."

"The French forces stationed in north Africa, Syria and Lebanon all switched sides and joined the ranks of the Free French resistance," De Gaulle added.

Speaking as if he were reporting live from the scene of the story, Churchill said:

"The Allies decided to move on Italy, with the attack proceeding from the direction of north Africa."

The German military strategy required the commanders to make a difficult decision.

"The leaders of the Third Reich were forced to pull some forces from the Russian front to stave off the attack of the Allies in Italy."

Rabin related the consequences of that decision.

"The German forces were weakened along the eastern front and were made to suffer a series of harrowing defeats."

As Stalin said, the time had come for the Red Army to pursue an alternative course of action.

"The Russians went from being on the defensive to going on the offensive, and they moved towards Berlin."

It appeared that a German defeat was inevitable.

"It was then I knew that if Germany were to be defeated then only two great powers would remain in the world: the United States and the Soviet Union," Hitler said.

"They will be able to offset one another, and the rules of history and geography will impose themselves and force the two great powers to test one another's resolve, whether militarily or economically."

"Communism will spread and defeat the capitalist order, and the global proletariat will reign supreme," Stalin said, revealing the political strategy he intended to pursue after securing a solid victory.

The United States was the leader of the capitalist bloc, and Kennedy took it upon himself to respond to Stalin's provocations.

"The free world is bound to win: it is only right that the markets be free from state intervention and be allowed to help transform this big world into one small village through commercial exchange."

Abdel Nasser let out a sigh that betrayed the weakness of his position in the ensuing balance of power.

"It doesn't seem we in the Arab world will be able to do anything but remain on the sidelines."

The skeleton paid close attention to the heated differences of opinion and said, "It's shaping up to be a war of ideas and a clash of ideologies."

"The developing world shall pay the price of this war with increased poverty and suffering," Gandhi predicted.

"The ideology of Nazism was frighteningly close to wiping out all of world Jewry," Rabin said, hoping to take Gandhi's statement as a base to draw sympathy for his people's plight.

"A great deal of them survived," Hitler interjected discourteously. "We just didn't have enough damn time."

"There is no such thing as war without calamity," Kennedy moralized.

"This is true," Gandhi concurred in a low voice.

The skeleton raised his voice to draw attention to himself.

"That famine that Gandhi spoke about - the people of China experienced such a famine at the hands of the Japanese colonists, who fed them nothing but humiliation and disgrace."

Kennedy heard the skeleton and said, "America responded forcefully to the barbaric practices of the Japanese, and taught them a lesson that they'll never forget. It established a precedent for benign interventionism in world history."

Gandhi rose in protest of the notion that violence ought to be countered with further violence. He had wished that America's 'lesson' to Japan been less cruel in its own right.

The skeleton, in turn, was acquainted with the demands of military expediency.

"The American General Curtis LeMay, notorious for his hardline views on war, is famous for once suggesting that in war, 'you've got to kill people and when you kill enough of them, they stop fighting.'"

The mention of LeMay piqued Abdel Hamid's curiosity.

"And what did that General do?" He asked.

"He invented a way to light up Tokyo without electricity," Abdel Nasser replied tongue-in-cheek.

"The city looked quite different when he got through with it."

Stalin laughed and picked up the punchline:

"While he was at it, he ended up warming up the water in Tokyo's canals."

The skeleton explained what Stalin and Abdel Nasser's little joke was about. "334 B-29 bombers conducted air raids over Tokyo on the 9th of March 1945. They unloaded their burdens along a radius of some six square kilometers, and all the beautiful homes built in the traditional Japanese manner of wood and fabric were reduced to what looked to the naked eye like gardens of fire."

"Tens of thousands of people lost their lives on that night," Gandhi shouted beratingly.

"Neighborhoods that were unfortunate enough to have been a target of the air raids were reduced to rubble."

Kennedy felt sorrow for the innocent victims of the American campaign, but then said, "The Japanese's overweening ways left the Americans no choice but to act in the manner in which they did."

"Following the Allies' victory in Italy, I knew that the hour of France's liberation had arrived, and all that was left was for me to wait patiently," De Gaulle said dreamily, like a revolutionary just beginning to see his efforts bear fruit.

Churchill was just as excited as De Gaulle was.

"Normandy had been chosen as the point of landing for the operation. We monitored the weather conditions to know when the right moment was to proceed."

"Prior to landing on the French coast, the Allies undertook a sustained bombing campaign on Germany by day and by night," Kennedy said. "Over one thousand air raids were being conducted a day."

"The Allied Combined Bomber Offensive hit German cities with relentless force," Abdel Nasser related.

"The German city of Dresden was laid to ruins in the aftermath of the Allies' attack," Gandhi said, saddened by the results of the campaign. It's houses fell to the ground, one after the other, and poisonous black smoke enshrouded the sky."

De Gaulle's moment had come.

"The Allies' landing operation was a success, and the French resistance moved on the Germans from within French territory."

As victory loomed in sight, Churchill was ecstatic.

"German fortresses began to fall one by one to the advancing forces."

Stalin wanted to remind everyone about the role the Soviet Union played.

"By East and by West," he said as a rejoinder to Churchill's remarks.

Kennedy attributed the lion's share of the positive outcome to American intervention. "General Eisenhower had given the order to occupy Berlin."

Hitler swallowed, his throat suddenly dry.

"The Germans resisted the advance with courage and bravery – until the very end."

To Stalin Hitler's words sounded like an admission of defeat.

"You are a reckless scoundrel, Hitler," he said aggressively.

"How I wished that you had not committed suicide! I had hoped that I could have payed you back your insolence myself."

Hitler pulled himself together, his haughtiness did not waver even now.

"When an honorable leader loses a war, he must either relinquish power or, better yet, commit suicide. I chose the latter option."

Stalin gritted his teeth in rage.

"I wish I can kill you right now. If only a man can die twice."

With a mix of relief and revengeful satisfaction Rabin said, "The Allies were triumphant over the Nazis, and Germany surrendered shortly after word that Hitler had committed suicide got out."

The skeleton remained on edge.

"Despite the fall of Fascism and Nazism, the Second World War had not come to an end quite just yet. The Japanese were stubborn, and with unbending resolve refused to surrender to the Allies. They would not yield to the Allies despite the latter's attempts to persuade them otherwise."

"It was left to the United States to end the war and force a capitulation from Japan," Kennedy said reassuringly.

"Then U.S. President Harry Truman didn't want to prolong the inevitable, and so he ordered U.S. forces to put a new weapon into play."

"The 'Atomic weapon,'" Gandhi said, forming air quotes with his fingers as he said the words.

Everyone lowered their heads in shame. The skeleton read out the report:

"The first atomic bomb was dropped on Hiroshima."

With the determination needed to end a war Kennedy continued, "And yet the Japanese still refused to surrender, and this forced the Americans to drop the second bomb, this time on the city of Nagasaki."

"It is with great pleasure that I congratulate everyone on the end of World War II," Gandhi said derisively.

"With best wishes to the United States and to humanity at large – after all, the two atomic attacks only ended the lives of some 120,000 people."

"Not to mention the harm caused by nuclear radiation," added Abdel Nasser.

Churchill's only concern was that victory belonged to the Allies.

"Japan then surrendered unconditionally."

The skeleton concluded by saying, "Given the insane things man has wrought on himself – what good is regret now? The Japanese Emperor's rule had collapsed. His throat ached painfully and his heart knew only the bitterness of defeat and surrender. Tears poured from his eyes, and the hair of his eyebrows fell out from the effects of the radiation. He said rebukingly:

'I advised my commanders not to awaken the American behemoth, but they attacked him anyway. They entered a hornet's nest and took Japan along with them. In the end we were stung by fire, gun powder, discharges of flames. . .and atomic bombs."

Rabin put all the blame on Hitler.

"Hitler is responsible for all of the calamities of that war."

Hitler denied the charge, but his energy was spent and his strength grew weary.

"Truman was the one who hit Hiroshima and Nagasaki with atomic weapons – not Hitler."

All the talk about World War II brought warmth to the graveyard. President Kennedy felt the catacomb getting stuffy, and headed out to the cemetery garden outside to catch a breath of fresh air, whence he might find a gentle breeze caressing the tree branches. Sultan Abdel Hamid II decided to follow along.

CHAPTER 22
The Heart of a Janissary

Droplets of water adorned her silk-smooth body like fresh raindrops left behind by the early morning dew resting atop the leaves of blooming roses. Abdel Hamid caught a glimpse of her pulling herself up along the banks of the rivulet as she exited the water with nothing to conceal her naked form. He rubbed his eyes to make sure he was seeing clearly, and then pinched himself repeatedly to make sure that this was no dream. He realized that what he was seeing was no make-believe fantasy - it was real! Kennedy was close by admiring the geese and ducks as they swam and played in the water. He felt revitalized by the waterfall's drizzle.

Abdel Hamid ran to Kennedy's side.

"You seeing what I'm seeing?" he asked Kennedy.

"I certainly do!" Kennedy replied, his eyes fixed on the waterfall. "It's a rather lovely duck, isn't it? The way it moves reminds me of battleships as they traverse the ocean's swells."

"No, I mean the tsunami that's coming from the direction of the spring!" he said as he pointed in the direction of Princess Diana. President Kennedy took a good look at her as she stood in the center of the cemetery. The rays of the sun covered her body, adding a splendid glow to her magnificent presence. They drew closer to her, and yet she was not frightened: the serenity of the place seemed to give her some sense of safety and security.

Sultan Abdel Hamid gawked in amazement as his eyes studied the well-proportioned figure that stood before him. He gazed upon her with an insatiable rapaciousness; his eyes watched her from top to bottom, pausing in every moment to close in on and give every part of her body its due. His desires were pulling him apart; his eyes wanted to take in her naked body in its fullest while simultaneously giving every part of her body its share of attention. Oh how he wished that he had four spacious eyes suited to the task of capturing the radiance of her gracious form and searing it into his memory for permanent safekeeping: her wet blonde hair, draped to her long, pearl-white neck her lofty chest that yearned to break down all barriers, and the nipples of her maroon-colored breasts as they chanted for freedom.

Her bosom, round and cylindrical and wrapped like a ball of yarn, appeared as if sculpted by the fingers of an inspired and refined artist who, when finished completing his masterpiece, stared at his work in awe, unable to comprehend how he could have put this magnificent piece together. It was a sight that no man can be satiated from looking at: her legs were like two marble columns that met at the top, a hilltop that calls all those who lay eyes on it to scale its peaks – and yet Abdel Hamid did not move a muscle, having yet to tire of the pleasure he was in.

Kennedy was aghast upon seeing her. They exchanged glances: Kennedy was betaken with the sadness in her eyes, the while she was impressed by how handsome he was. Her heart beat rapidly the way young girls do when they fall in love for the first time. Her eyes lit up with delight. To Kennedy her eyes were like a lighthouse, shining brightly upon a ship lost at sea, exhausted from recurrent confrontations with the violent motion of the ocean waves. Their eyes conversed with one another, and yet not a word was spoken. Her eyes said:

"Where have you been? I've waited an awfully long time for you. I searched for you in the fields, in the forests, on the bridges and roads, and in every house, coffee shop, bar and restaurant – even in the world of literature, in both poetry and prose. All I ever got was a blank page. They killed me before I could find you."

Kennedy's dreamy eyes had a response of their own: "I've known many women in my life – but I feel like your image was imprinted in my mind before I ever laid eyes on you."

Her eyes hit back with that blunt coquettishness women were known for: "I would be sorely mistaken if I were to say that I truly knew love before knowing you, or that I could love anyone else after having met you. A consort of princes and kings: you are my prince, my king, my angel and my heart. My final place of refuge – had I known that death would bring us together I would have sought after it along time ago."

The message was heard loud and clear – it circulated through their bodies and lit up their hearts like a lightning bolt that strikes in the midst of a dark sky overcast by black clouds, accompanied by the sharp sound of thunder that blesses this most unexpected of unions.

Kennedy walked towards Diana and covered her with the coat that he was wearing. He put his hands on her cheeks and drew her close to him, their lips meeting in a kiss that kept them tethered together for quite a while.

Abdel Hamid II remained astonished by what he had seen. He closed his eyes, hoping to conjure back the image of the princess's naked body. His inability to do so left him caught between the pleasure of memory and the anger of being incapable of retrieving it, as the moments in which he caught a clear glimpse of her did not last for long. Women in the Sultan's eyes were nothing but concubines, whose sole job was to satisfy his insatiable urges and to leave him happy and satisfied enough to be able to rule his domain and to subdue his subjects. The women of the sultan's harem were plentiful and abundant. They all shared a common dormitory in one of Istanbul's famous palaces. The one who was responsible for looking after the affairs of the palace was a man close to the sultan who enjoyed a position of prominence in the bureaucracy of government. In exchange, the man in question would be made to undergo castration, so that there would be no issue of being tempted to betray the sultan. The castration operation was carried out rather primitively: with a searing iron rod, in much the same way that farmers and peasants brand their donkeys and mules in the many villages and far-away towns of the empire.

As Kennedy went off into the distance in the company of Princess Diana, Sultan Abdel Hamid began to ponder about the secrets of the creation of the woman's body – sublime on the one hand, yet mysterious and enigmatic on the other. Despite the many torrid nights he spent in their company, he could not decipher their myriad ways, particularly as concerns their ability to enchant many men with just a single glance of an eye. It dawned on him then that throughout his long life he never met a woman special enough for him to love.

Gandhi had gone out to look for him and Kennedy, worried when the latter two failed to return to the catacomb at their usual time. The sun was well-nigh on the verge of setting, and Gandhi had an answer to Abdel Hamid's riddle:

"Your heart was coarse, like the janissaries that served in your militaries. You left no fertile ground for it to blossom and flourish."

"What you say is true to an extent, Mr. Gandhi. But you still haven't answered me – what is the key to this riddle?"

"You must fall in love," Gandhi replied, placing his hands on Abdel Hamid's chest.

CHAPTER 23
An Eye for an Eye

The Second World War came to an end in Europe following the twin suicides of Hitler and his wife Eva Braun. Germany surrendered to the Allies as Berlin fell to the twin armies of the Soviets who invaded from the east and the Allied Forces - comprised of Britain, the U.S. and France - who invaded from the west. Germany was then divided into East and West, and each invading army began to fortify its positions in the areas under its control. The German people tasted the bitterness of defeat once more; once again they were made to taste humiliation and disgrace at the hands of a foreign army.

Springtime in Europe is famous for its beautiful fields and gardens. Its parks - teeming with the most splendid array of roses and flowers - emit an enchanting blend of fragrances and scents. But the spring of 1945 was quite different: in that year the air reeked of the asphyxiating smell of fire and gunpowder. Death was everywhere: severed heads, torn boots, human remains strewn left and right, scattered corpses of soldiers, old men, children, pregnant women giving birth prematurely, roads riddled with potholes, buildings levelled to the ground, and endless fields of smoke and fire.

The spectacle was quite frightening: killings went on and on, mercilessly and without an end in sight. The shelters teemed with people who possessed nary a piece of bread to assuage their hunger.

Hitler committed suicide upon realizing that defeat and surrender were inevitable. By committing suicide he meant to take responsibility for the way the war had gone. He was a great man, and the crown of his achievements was this act of suicide. It had been no small feat for him to see his glorious people on their knees surrendering in humiliation and scorn. He had been confident that victory was his until the very last moment.

After having successfully subdued Europe in both its eastern and western flanks, Germany itself was now under occupation. He was the ubermensch, a superman – and superman was now dead.

That Hitler had committed suicide angered Stalin.

"You needed a way out, you scoundrel!" He rebuked Hitler.

"Death is a thousand times more honorable to a German than allowing his neck to bend before a barbaric occupier such as yourself – or, alternatively, an obese and foolish one such as Churchill," Hitler shot back haughtily.

"Had it not been for the United States rushing to your aid, you two wouldn't have been smiling right now."

Churchill just couldn't bide the insult.

"I never despised anyone more than I despise you," he told Hitler.

"I could care less if you like me," Hitler riposted. "A desire for your admiration was one that I never had."

Kennedy intervened, hoping to ease tensions.

"The war has ended, and what's past is now past. There is no need for this exchange of insults – and, more than that, it does not befit leaders of your caliber to descend into such low depths."

But Rabin was enjoying the back and forth that arose between the two.

"It's Hitler's fault – he's the one who called Stalin a barbarian and Churchill fat and stupid," he said, hoping to get the barbs going again.

Hitler exploded in rage and shouted in Rabin's face:

"You know, Rabin, I regret. . ."

". . .that's terrific, Hitler!" Gandhi interrupted. "To regret is to express remorse for one's misdeeds!"

"Damn you and your incessant interruptions, Gandhi! What I meant to say is that I regret having killed only a few million Jews."

"Gandhi has good intentions," Abdel Hamid said, coming to Gandhi's defense.

"All he ever wanted was to drive away evil."

"I'm not one to empathize with the weak. Not ever," Hitler told Gandhi. "And if there ever was a weakling in life, it was you, Gandhi."

"I am not weak! Quite the contrary, I have a will of iron, and a strength to forbear that is quite powerful in its own right. An 'eye for an eye' leaves everyone blind. Nonviolence is the greatest power that humanity has at its disposal. It is more efficacious than any destructive weapon designed by the ingenuity of man."

Hitler looked at Churchill, and then responded to Gandhi:

"You, Gandhi, are a direct descendant of British liberalism. You were powerless to preserve India's territorial integrity – rather, the British fooled you to go with their plan for the sake of Muhammad Jinnah, the father of the Pakistani people."

"A people desired their independence. How could we stop them?" Churchill coldly observed.

"Britain's history is replete with its gracious help to peoples who seek after their freedom," Rabin said, coaxing Churchill.

"Because the world needed an Islamic state in Pakistan to go with the Jewish state in Palestine," Stalin interrupted as he shot Rabin a grimace. Rabin fell silent.

"Excuse me, but why did the Americans agree to the establishment of a state for the Muslims in Pakistan?" the skeleton asked without hesitation.

"To act as a stalwart against the spread of communism," Kennedy replied.

The skeleton had a follow up question.

"And the Jewish state?"

"The Jews were a people scattered throughout the four corners of the globe, and there was no denying the need – as Herzl aptly pointed out – for them to choose a land without a people for a people without a land," Rabin replied confidently.

"Which land are you referring to?" Abdel Hamid asked in a daze.

"Why, the Promised Land," Rabin responded with glee.

"The land of Palestine, which God had promised us."

"But Palestine was populated by the Palestinians," Gandhi argued, wrapping his loose garment more tightly around himself. "It certainly was no empty land."

Rabin let out a laugh.

"No worries, my friend. The words of our ancestors shall come true, and the land will be left without a people," he said as he patted Gandhi's thigh reassuringly.

Abdel Hamid had found a linchpin which he could use to defend his empire's performance under his reign.

"You all accuse the Ottomans of annihilating the Armenians. Is not the choice of Palestine a means by which to exterminate an existing people?"

"What extermination, dear Sultan?" Rabin replied sternly.

"I'm merely talking about transfer."

"That's chutzpah of a particularly Zionist flavor," Abdel Nasser contended.

"A Zionist lie," Abdel Hamid added, "meant to make truth look false and the false look true."

Abdel Nasser felt his throat get parched. He took a sip of water in a cup he had nearby and said, "The Palestinian people were forced out of their homes by the Zionist strategy of transfer and exile. It's only natural that they have a right to return to their lands."

Abdel Nasser's views resonated with Gandhi.

"It's ethnic cleansing, plain and simple," he insisted.

"What do you have to complain about, Gandhi?" Rabin remonstrated.

"Do you think you know better than the U.S., Russia and Great Britain?"

"What do these countries have to do with what I said?"

"Did not Mr. Stalin himself – in coordination with Messrs. Roosevelt and Churchill – agree to allow twelve million Germans to return to their original homeland from the countries in which they were residing in?" Rabin said, clarifying his viewpoint.

Abdel Nasser knew the direction in which Rabin was heading, and he couldn't disagree more.

"But the Zionist Jews took the lands of the Palestinians by force and strong-armed them into leaving their original homelands."

Rabin was angered by Abdel Nasser's words.

"We did not take anyone's land – we simply returned to the land of our ancestors!" he shouted scornfully.

"It is the Palestinians who had been squatting on our land – not the other way around. All we did was force the squatters off and return the land to its rightful owners."

"Oh, it's as simple as that?" Abdel Nasser asked contemptuously and reproachfully.

"We had but two options," Rabin went on.

"To kill them off, or to transfer them out. The lofty values of our people would not permit us the first option, so we chose the second."

"Values!" Abdel Nasser exclaimed derisively.

"Why, how lovely! The violence the Zionist gangs perpetrated against the Palestinian people had planted fear in their hearts, which had hitherto only known safety and stability. So they went with what they knew: they fled for their lives under the cover of night. They were left terrified by the crimes committed in Deir Yassin and other villages, and they fled in fright, leaving behind their fields, their homes – whose keys they kept with them. They managed to escape by the skin of their teeth along with their children, many of whom died from cold and disease and famine. After all was said and done they were placed in refugee camps which provided them no protection from winter's cold or summer's heat."

Abdel Nasser's words impacted Rabin, whose facial expression betrayed sorrow and sympathy. But he gathered up his strength and said, "It is true that our mission was difficult – but there was no possibility of backing down. The survival of the state of Israel requires us to make difficult decisions, decisions which the Palestinians will simply have to put up with."

Churchill attempted to resolve the dispute with a single sentence.

"Israel was created to survive. It is now a reality – debating its existence is futile."

Abdel Nasser peered entreatingly at everyone in the room.

"What about the rights of the Palestinians?" he implored.

"Well done, gentlemen," Gandhi replied, seemingly sincerely.

"Justice and fairness are done for."

"It was within my ability to eliminate all of the world's Jews," Hitler said, directing his words at Abdel Nasser.

"But I kept a few of them alive so the world would know why I set out to annihilate them."

"This is what you say to justify the systematic murder of all these weak, defenseless people during the Holocaust?" Kennedy asked resolutely.

"I pity you, Kennedy," Hitler replied. "History will prove that what I have said was correct." Hitler then fell silent, wanting to keep to himself.

The spirits of the victims of Qana, Deir Yassin, Sabra and Shatila burst into the room, singing in an angelic chorus:

A victim once, now an oppressor

Sheep who pull out their teeth and put fangs in their place

The places have changed, the names have been replaced

The world had once condemned the tyrant, and fought for the oppressed

But now dust has been cast in their eyes

"I found that death by poison gas is a very compassionate way to end someone's life," Hitler whispered, stoically and reservedly.

His voice was nevertheless heard loud and clear.

Rabin insisted that the Zionist cause was just.

"We did not haul the Palestinians into the gas chambers."

"No, but you did kill them with bullets and napalm," Abdel Nasser retorted.

"There are various ways to kill, but there's only one way to victimize," Abdel Hamid said pleadingly.

"We did not crush the bones of the Palestinians so as to wipe out any trace of their existence!" Rabin averred.

"But you did cast them into mass graves," Abdel Nasser stated.

Nevertheless, Rabin still felt there was no comparison to be made between the suffering of the Jews and the Palestinians.

"The Gestapo forced the Jews to wear a yellow badge in the form of the star of David to identify them as Jews. Did we do that to the Palestinians?"

Despite all disagreements, Abdel Nasser acknowledged the right of the Jews to resist.

"The Jews did not remain silent in the face of increased oppression. They resisted in the Warsaw ghetto, and held out against the Nazi military for three weeks."

Rabin was proud of the Jewish resistance.

"This rebellion was a symbol of Jewish resistance to the Nazis."

"And yet the Israelis refer to the Palestinians as terrorists, and the Fedayeen as fanatics?" Abdel Nasser said, hoping to take Rabin's pride in the Jewish resistance as a means of comparison.

The souls of Israel's victims returned to the catacomb and cried:

They traded in the barbed wire for iron and steel

They sought vengeance against the Nazis

But they followed in their footsteps

They waged wars, and expanded.

The dead greats did not want to listen to the cries of these spirits. There is no blame on them – it is only the living who must hear and see.

The screams of these persecuted spirits were hoarse, weak, scattered. The winds suffocated their echoes. The mountains drowned in the midst of the valleys – crushed and vanquished, they had nothing left but to whimper and sob.

CHAPTER 24
The Skull's Scenario

The skeleton knew that he was getting on in years. What he knew – or, more precisely, what he remembered – could make a young boy go grey-haired. During his life he had witnessed two world wars, in the course of which humanity reaped pain and sorrow for the destruction it had sewn all over the globe. Diseases spread as a result of the unburied corpses that were left to rot in the streets. Women and bereaved mothers were left to fend for themselves, alone to mourn their plight. Children shielded themselves with the walls that the aerial bombardment campaigns of the various armies had not gotten around to levelling yet. Bitter cold enwrapped their fragile bodies, which were wincing from starvation. The economies of many world countries had collapsed. War is a rapacious beast; it devours everything in its path and yet keeps demanding more.

The skeleton looked around him, and saw Hitler, Stalin, De Gaulle, Churchill, Kennedy, Rabin, Abdel Nasser and Abdel Hamid engaged in a debate about the conditions of the world following the end of World War II. Gandhi, on the other hand, was alone, grimacing and in mourning. He was ruminating on how to market his angelic concept of nonviolence in a universe in which half of the world's residents are devils, ideologues of different shapes and hues, all residing in one and the same place, all holding the other responsible for the miserable state the world is in all the while refusing to acknowledge the innate sense that they too had contributed to the present crisis in their own right. The skeleton then wondered aloud: what is the fate of the world – what is the end game?

His thoughts were interrupted by the sounds of chuckling and giggling coming from the skull and the millionaire. The answer to the skeleton's question had come rather swiftly:

"Terrific! Strength has chosen to ally with money. . .these giggles shall be a source of great calamity for the peoples of the world."

His inner thoughts were interrupted once again, this time by De Gaulle as he offered his analysis on the repercussions of the Second World War.

"Truman, Stalin and Attlee were successful in monopolizing the administration of world affairs, and yet they were made to acknowledge France's esteemed position among the great powers."

Kennedy apprised everyone as to the role the United States played in the war.

"France owes a great debt of gratitude to the Allies – and, most particularly, the United States – for their help in liberating it from Nazi occupation."

De Gaulle's response was firm yet polite:

"The People of France have been thankful to the United States for its efforts and for standing by their side as they fought for their freedom. But you must not forget, Monsieur Kennedy, the stiff resistance the French people put up and the many sacrifices they made to expel the German occupier and to restore its sense of dignity."

Rabin proffered his own opinion about the repercussions of the war.

"The victors in the war are inevitably those who are able to enforce their will on others; in turn, the defeated can do naught but acquiesce and relent."

Gandhi suggested a way for nations to resolve their differences without having to resort to armed confrontation.

"As His Holiness Confucius once said, 'The best victory is to win a war without going to war at all.'"

The skull was unpersuaded by Gandhi's argument.

"Power is what makes a victory a victory – there is no sense to calling a victory 'a victory' unless one party manages to make a show of force that forces the other party into submission," he vociferated.

"True power comes from the mind, not from the use of weapons," replied Gandhi.

"At the end of the day wealth is itself commensurate with power," the millionaire said poisedly.

"Is the intellect alone sufficient to create a lasting peace between nations?" the skeleton wondered.

"The intellect and power go hand in hand," Kennedy replied.

"The mind deliberates, and power enforces the mind's decisions."

Gandhi insisted that brute force was a method that ought never be resorted to.

"Force blinds the heart and the mind. Its volition can only be brought about by means of an artillery shell or the barrel of a rifle. Force can never be a friend to the intellect – one bullet can lay even the most formidable mind in the world to waste."

Kennedy found the use of force to be a necessity in certain circumstances.

"There are many occasions in which a bullet and a rifle can be used to keep the peace and save thousands of lives."

"Indeed, the rule of law requires forces to consolidate and protect itself," the skull pronounced in a vindicated tone.

"That is precisely what I mean," Kennedy retorted.

De Gaulle too supported the disciplined use of force.

"Had the League of Nations possessed a sufficient amount of power to impose its dictates on others no country would have been brazen enough to ignore its decisions – the Second World War and its dreadful calamities might well have been avoided."

Abdel Hamid was growing sick and tired of constantly hearing about the repercussions of war.

"What did the victors in World War II do to avoid the breakout of war in the future?"

The skull had an unwavering belief in power – to the extent that he deemed all other methods antiquated and obsolete.

"It was this very weakness of the League of Nations that led to its disbandment in 1943."

Plans were already in motion to establish an international body that did not suffer from the same weaknesses as the League of Nations.

"At the conference of the Big Three – Roosevelt, Stalin and Churchill – in Tehran we conferred about the weak standing of the League of Nations and decided to establish a body to take its place."

"The United Nations was established in 1945 in the city of San Francisco, California," Kennedy added.

"It was encouraging that membership in the United Nations was not restricted to those nations that emerged victorious in World War II," Abdel Nasser said with just a hint of hope in his voice.

"Rather, all peace-loving nations willing to abide by the stipulations of the United Nation's charter and resultant decisions were welcome to join."

Churchill, in turn, had been one of the founders of the nascent United Nations.

"Our main goal was to achieve stability and world peace, as well as socioeconomic cooperation at an international level, and the protection of human rights."

This time, Kennedy had good news to share about the United States' relationship with the United Nations.

"The Senate approved the adoption of the U.N. Charter, and New York City became the site of the United Nation's permanent headquarters."

Once the establishment of the United Nations became a fait accompli, the new body would need to allocate certain responsibilities to various councils which were beginning to take shape. The most important council, as the skeleton noted, would be under the control of the great powers of the day:

"The International Security Council had emerged as a way for the United Nations to deliberate on world affairs, and to this effect it chose that the council ought to have five permanent members, they being. . ."

"France," De Gaulle interjected, wishing his country to take the spotlight.

"The United States, Britain, the Soviet Union, and China."

Abdel Hamid welcomed the newfound agreement among the world's nations.

"The establishment of such a body is certainly good news."

Gandhi remained skeptical. He took a moment to contemplate and then said, "The question that arises here is whether this body will be able to remain neutral in terms of ideological affiliation."

"It is in the nature of ideology to mire itself in everything," Rabin said, confirming Gandhi's worst suspicions.

The millionaire concurred with Rabin's opinion.

"If it seems inevitable that ideology will play a role in the way the United Nations operates, then it's because the U.N. will need the wealthy nations to contribute financially to help carry out its mission."

The skeleton sympathized with Gandhi's misgivings.

"You, Mr. Millionaire, are a disgrace," he rebuked. "All you ever talk about is money! Haven't you had enough of numbers? Hasn't the piling up of cash in your bank accounts and mansion vaults grown tedious? Enough of your greed! For God's sake, man, you now reside in the world of the dead!"

The millionaire was silent, opting not to respond. Kennedy chuckled and then proceeded to steer the conversation away from the skeleton's berating the millionaire and back to the United Nations. "A number of organizations grew out of the United Nations. . ."

"The International Trade Organization, for one," De Gaulle said.

The millionaire shot a quick glance at the skeleton and rattled off, "The World Bank and the International Monetary Fund."

Gandhi took a deep breath.

"I but wish that this new organization would help alleviate the world's problems transparently and ethically."

"What do you mean 'ethically?!'" Hitler demanded.

"We already know that the great powers would divide up the world as they saw fit! Russia invaded all of Eastern Europe – Bulgaria, Albania, Poland, Romania, Hungary and Czechoslovakia – and imposed its Communist ideology on each of them. It also divided Germany into East and West."

"We did not impose our ideology on anyone!" Stalin pleaded. "We merely assisted the Communist parties in these nations to take power."

"I am certain that the Communists could not have taken power in Germany without your help."

As for the Soviet Union's intervening in the Eastern European countries, Churchill noted that "following the expulsion of the Fascist and Nazi armies Greece fell under English control. In 1946 the Allies organized a referendum for the Greeks to choose their system of government and to put a lid on rising tensions between the monarchists and the communists. We kept the Soviet Union at arm's length from Greece, and nevertheless civil war broke out between the two sides."

Stalin found the Allies' exclusive hold in managing Greek affairs to be an affront to the Soviet Union and the role it thought it ought to play in Eastern Europe.

"The Soviet Union supported the communists in Greece because of our shared ideology."

"And the United States supported the monarchists due to their support for free market capitalism," Kennedy said.

Civil war had broken out in Greece at the behest of foreign powers. De Gaulle, however, seemed relaxed.

"The war lasted three years, and ended in a sound defeat for the communists."

The Allies' ideology too dictated their moves on the ground.

"The Allies established democratic governments in the countries under their control," Churchill said.

"And the Soviets established communist governments in the areas under the control of its armed forces," Stalin retorted.

"That includes most of the Eastern European countries."

"Wars broke out between the colonizers and the colonized, with the latter hoping to break free from under the yoke of the former," Gandhi said, his heart not at rest.

Hitler guffawed in the loudest voice he could muster and said, "And was India compensated by Britain for its help in the war? Did the latter grant you your independence?" Hitler asked derisively.

"Indeed!" Gandhi replied sarcastically.

"By dividing India into two states!"

"Freedom and independence are not a gift that one state grants another," Abdel Nasser declared.

"They are human rights, and when a colonizing power refuses to yield to the demands of the people, it is only natural that the latter respond with revolution, resisting and sacrificing their own lives in order to take what is owed to them."

De Gaulle concurred with Abdel Nasser's view.

"With determination and resilience the Free France resistance forces were able to secure their independence from Germany."

"As the colonized grew more conscious of their situation, they set out to secure their independence through peaceful protests in some circumstances and through armed struggle in others."

Stalin had a good example of this:

"The guerilla warfare waged by the Koreans under Kim Il-Sung led to the independence of Korea from Japan in 1945."

Churchill had an example of his own.

"The Vietnamese similarly fought against the Japanese under the leadership of Ho Chi Minh and General Giap and in the end they too were able to expel the Japanese."

The leaders of the capitalist world were wringing their hands, and the skeleton proceeded to explain to everyone else why:

"In 1948 a Communist Revolution ensued in China led by Mao Zedong against the government of Chiang Kai-shek."

Stalin was excited, even proud, to claim a victory for Communism:

"With the help of the Soviet Union they emerged victorious in 1949."

Abdel Hamid shared his assessment on these series of developments:

"I see that many changes took place in the world after I left it."

Stalin wanted to bring his ambitions into sharp relief.

"The Soviet Union had been eager for Finland to join the Union of Soviet Socialist Republics, but their participation in the war meant they had secured the right to establish their own independent state."

Though the Balkan states had attained their independence from the Ottoman Empire, Sultan Abdel Hamid remained interested in their fate, wondering what had happened to them.

"The military commander Josip Broz Tito fought on the side of the Allies against the Germans, and so we guaranteed him independence and he went ahead and established the Republic of Yugoslavia."

The skeleton seemed thrilled.

"They flipped a new page after the war was over, and left the past in the dust bin of history."

De Gaulle wrote the first sentence in this new page.

"France granted Lebanon its independence in 1943."

Churchill read the next line:

"Syria declared its independence in 1946, as did Jordan."

"India achieved its independence in 1947," Gandhi said. To Gandhi, India's independence was bittersweet.

"I did not celebrate on independence day, as I was in mourning over the secession of Pakistan."

Abdel Nasser thought the Allies' generosity needed explaining.

"To keep their colonies from switching allegiances to Germany and Italy – particularly in 1941 when the latter two had taken the war directly to England and France – Britain and the Free French promised them their independence after the war was over."

Churchill found something askew in Abdel Nasser's interpretation of these events.

"Mr. Eden – our Foreign Minister at the time - had explicitly told the British House of Commons that the government looked upon all independence movements in the Arab world that aimed for economic, cultural and political unity with the utmost sympathy."

Abdel Nasser acknowledged Britain's role in supporting the establishment of the Arab League.

"Egyptian Prime Minister Mustafa el-Nahhas hastened to invite Syrian Prime Minister Jamil Mardam Bey and Mr. Bechara El Khoury of the nationalist bloc in Lebanon to discuss and plan for the creation of an Arab League that would unite the Arab countries after the war."

The Jews, as Rabin noted, were worried.

"When they issued their press release, the Jews were very frightened that the Balfour Declaration would be nullified and, along with it, the dream of a national home for the Jewish people. The unity of the Arabs into a single political entity would be a key obstacle in achieving that dream."

Churchill drew strength from Rabin's remarks. He jumped out of his chair and told Abdel Nasser, "You see, Mr. Nasser? Britain has been most sympathetic to the aspirations of the Arab people!"

Hitler felt that Churchill was beginning to influence Abdel Nasser's thinking.

"Don't trust this old fox!" he warned him.

"Does a hungry fox pass let a chicken pass him by without pouncing on him?!"

Abdel Nasser lit up a cigarette and took a deep drag.

"It appears you know Mr. Churchill well."

Churchill tried to ignore Hitler's warning and continued his plea.

"The Arabs indeed established the Arab League in 1945, and its Charter was signed by all concerned parties in the Zaafarana Palace in Cairo."

Abdel Nasser paid heed to Hitler's warning, asked, "Had the British and the French been honest in their promises, they should have kept to them and granted the Arab countries their independence as soon as the war was over."

De Gaulle was vexed by Abdel Nasser's remarks.

"No one forced us to come through on those promises, but we did anyway!"

"Why, you promised these broken, colonized people the sun and the moon in order to buy their apathy during the war, in fear that they would cause disturbances that might tip the balance in favor of the Axis Powers!"

"It is permitted during war to use any and all means necessary - psychological or otherwise," Kennedy said.

Gandhi sighed ruefully.

"What is it about these despicable wars that they allow warring parties to tamper with moral precepts and to forget about the toll that these wars take in victims and in the destruction which they wreck upon the world?"

"It is in the nature of war that concepts take on new meanings, or even change completely," the skull said in response to Gandhi's indignation.

"The weak must fall prey to the strong, and that is why the strong need to be able to control how the rules are understood."

Gandhi fastened his garment around his body. The skull's response had struck him as odd in its callousness.

"And the victims?"

"Every war has its price," the millionaire replied coldly.

"Homes collapse, residences go up in flames," the skeleton said, describing the effects of war.

"Bridges are destroyed, as are factories and plants. Whole cities lay in ruin where lawlessness and chaos reign supreme. Store fronts are vandalized, and its doors are left to the mercy of rioters."

The millionaire contemplated the image the skeleton was trying to paint and said, "material losses that simply cannot be measured or calculated."

Gandhi could care less about the kinds of calculations that run through the millionaire's head – he had calculations of his own that occupied him: anything that could be purchased with money was of little value; but the millions of innocent lives that were taken in the war were of limitless value – the crimes done to them could not be forgiven, much less forgotten.

The skull was a man of experience, and he wanted his grave mates to treat him as such.

"Ask me whatever you might want to know about war. War was my profession. I am a general notorious for my power and force – even if nothing remains of my worldly possessions but my skull. Each of you, my dear friends, know me well: I served you all and helped you to attain supremacy for your ideological positions. War is no picnic, nor a barbecue, nor a night out on the town, nor a calming stroll by the beach. It is nothing short of fiery eruptions, evil volcanoes that explode and wipe out humankind and every other living being, even the rocks."

Abdel Hamid had his own experience to share.

"Not everyone experiences the vagaries of war – some people lose out more than others."

Gandhi felt pained that none of the greats were taking his concerns seriously.

"A human being is a human being, regardless of the color of his skin, the language that he speaks, where he lives or the ethnic group which he belongs to."

"Most of your victims happened to be Jews – isn't that right, Hitler?" Stalin asked.

"There is no love lost between me and the Jews," Hitler said without batting an eye.

"They are the cause of every calamity in this universe. Miserly people, monopolists, usurers – they have all the wealth in the world and they use it to plot their stratagems and schemes. They are wolves in sheep's clothing. You say millions of Jews died – it had been my utmost desire to see not a single one of them survive."

Rabin was furious.

"These genocidal machinations that you wrecked upon the poor Jews of Europe!"

"You may be a Jew, Rabin, but you don't know them like I do," Hitler said in all seriousness.

Hitler then directed his remarks to Stalin.

"And you – did you not leave millions of dead in your wake?" he asked pointedly.

Stalin laughed as if to show Hitler that he could care less for the latter's opinion of him.

"That's true – and there are quite possibly many more than we know about. But I didn't target the Jews specifically."

De Gaulle eyed the two of them carefully and said, "That's true. Your victims were Russians, your own people. More than twenty million of them in fact."

"Most of Stalin's victims were killed because they posed a threat to him," Kennedy clarified.

Churchill was eager to reveal the painful truths he knew about communism.

"Mao Zedong's victims numbered some 23 million people."

Abdel Nasser wanted to be fair to the communists – and to find fault with Churchill.

"Most of the victims you refer to were not killed but rather died of famine."

Abdel Hamid felt the conversation was far from over.

"What did the victors do after the war was over?" he asked contemptuously.

"They piled up the spoils and divided it up between themselves," Hitler sneered.

"Unfortunately the Soviet Union did not allow for democratic governments to emerge in the countries that had been occupied by the Red Army," Kennedy observed.

"Stalin propped up communist puppet regimes that were loyal to him," De Gaulle added.

"That's how he became the second strongest power in the world."

Stalin set out to clarify the Soviet Union's intentions with the self-confidence that he was known for.

"Leninist-Marxist ideology aims to establish a worldwide communist regime."

"It seems we killed off the wrong pig," Churchill said, whispering in Kennedy's ear.

"It would have behooved you to know Stalin's true intentions before deciding to trust him."

"I tried to tell Roosevelt this myself. It doesn't seem he was as distrusting of Stalin as I was."

"The United States invaded Japan and occupied the Pacific Isles," Stalin said, interrupting Kennedy and Churchill's mutual whisperings.

"Britain took Australia and Hong Kong, and France remained in possession of Vietnam."

"The British did not leave Egypt or Sudan," Abdel Nasser said, seeking to steer the conversation in the direction of North Africa.

"The French kept their presence in Tunisia, Algeria and Marrakech, and they shared custody over Libya."

"India, too, remained a British colony after the conclusion of the war," Gandhi said, "reneging on their promise to grant India her independence as soon as the war was over."

Rabin found the colonizers' conduct understandable.

"Perhaps conditions in the international arena were not conducive to an immediate implementation of these promises. But I know the British – they came through on their promise to us in 1947. They set a five month deadline to end their mandate over Palestine and they went through with it."

Abdel Nasser clapped his hands derisively.

"The British truly are an honorable people! The five month waiting period was the equivalent of an indirect announcement that the Balfour Declaration had begun to be implemented."

"That's correct!" Rabin shot back.

"And here you were accusing good old Britain of failing to keep true to her promises. The five month period was time we needed to acquire weapons and train our men in the Haganah and the Palmach to make adequate use of them."

Rabin had fallen in Abdel Nasser's trap.

"The same gangs that later perpetrated the Deir Yassin massacre among a myriad of other such horrors."

Churchill absolved himself of any responsibility for the massacre, saying, "We came through and ended the mandate after the five month period was up. After that what happened in Palestine became the responsibility of you two."

"Zion had been reborn," Rabin said vaingloriously.

"We officially declared the establishment of the state of Israel in 1948. Later on I was given the honor of being the Israel Chief of Staff."

Abdel Hamid could not believe his ears.

"And what did the United Nations do in response to this?"

"It continued to stand firmly by Resolution 181 which it had put out a year earlier in which it had set aside some 55% of historical Palestine for the establishment of a Jewish homeland," Kennedy replied.

Abdel Hamid's worst fears had become a reality.

"And how did the Arabs react to the establishment of this alien state?"

"Five Arab armies – Palestine's neighbors, Jordan, Syria and Egypt, as well as Iraq and the native Arabs of Palestine – joined forces and waged war against the Jews," Abdel Nasser replied.

"I myself fought and was stationed in the Palestinian village of Faluja – we had been fighting with obsolete weaponry, the while the Zionist gangs were fighting with the latest military technology that they had at their disposal."

Churchill confessed to the implementation of the Balfour Declaration, but he absolved himself of any responsibility for the Arab loss of Palestine, saying, "It is true that Her Majesty's Government granted the Balfour Declaration to the Jews, but the real blame for consolidating Zionist rule over Palestine falls on the Arabs and their governments. They ought to take the historical responsibility for that – it's a historical and national obligation to do so."

Rabin was glowing with pride.

"The Arabs were defeated and Israel securely held some 75% of historical Palestine to its name."

Abdel Nasser proceeded to clarify what the new situation was shaping up to look like.

"The Palestinians were expelled from their lands and homes," he said, obviously downcast.

"They were made to reside in refugee camps in the nearby countries. The Nakba has been a complete success, and the Palestinian cause became the Arabs' number one cause celebre.

The skeleton wrapped up:

"A new nation planted smack in the middle of the heart of Arab territory. Destruction abounded, as did an economic depression in Japan and Europe. Eastern Europe was indoctrinated with communist patterns of thinking, and the western world under the leadership of the United States attempted to work through the new situation and find solutions to very pressing issues."

"Money solves all problems," the millionaire interjected, feeling as if he had just pulled a rabbit out of a hat.

Kennedy was in agreement with the millionaire.

"The millionaire is right. The solution to the crisis had been set with the emergence of a program of economic recovery in Western Europe. This program was developed in 1948 and adhered in its broad strokes to Marshall's Plan, which called for congress to invest seventeen billion dollars in Western Europe."

Churchill was openly grateful to the Americans.

"Mr. George Marshall was not only the architect of our military victories, but he also personally supervised the implementation of the American plan. His generosity knows no bounds."

Stalin himself acknowledged the power that money could engender and said, "The United States got all its ducks in a row and went to work implementing its plan to rebuild Europe. I must admit that the plan was a remarkable success. Quite honestly, it was a slap in the face to us, and was crucial in preventing the spread of socialism, as the Americans had stipulated that any government that wanted to receive aid must make all necessary efforts to fire communist ministers and to fight leftist political groups tooth and nail.

Their tactics may seem ruthless, but Kennedy was nothing short of proud of what the Americans had done:

"Marshall's Plan was directed against economic breakdown, against hunger, against poverty, against chaos. It aimed to revive the world economy."

Stalin saw Marshall's Plan in a different light from Kennedy.

"They struck at the roots of all revolutionary movements in Europe in fear that they would end up joining the communist revolution."

Abdel Nasser thought of the Marshall Plan as resembling a business transaction.

"The goal of the Marshall Plan was to Americanize Europe."

"And from there, to Americanize the world," Abdel Hamid added.

The millionaire had put in good money to help support Marshall's program.

"American money began to swarm Europe's markets."

Given that newly-liberated France was in desperate need of funds, De Gaulle was forced to concede to the preconditions of the program.

"The debtors stipulated that repayment must be given in American dollars, relying thereby on the Bretton-Woods agreement of 1944 in which the American dollar was made to take the place of gold."

The millionaire caught De Gaulle's meaning.

"The American dollar became the only viable currency left in the world, and the United States of America took its position on the throne as the new empire that would lead and defend the old capitalist order."

"Did the victors go roughshod on their enemy's leadership as they did during the first world war?" Abdel Hamid asked cunningly.

Churchill's answer resembled that of a seasoned judge.

"Why, of course. The Nurermberg Trials were set up in 1945 just after the war had ended to put the Nazi leadership on trial."

Though he had lost the war, Hitler did not give up hope.

"It is my expectation that the German people will pick themselves up by their bootstraps just as they always have: by means of their strength, determination and ingenuity, just as it had done in the aftermath of the first world war. The German people are like a phoenix, rising from the ashes. This is what you fear – this is what you always feared! Only a coward fears those who are strong: for the strong and intelligent come to each others aid, join ranks and increase each other's natural abilities."

"It must be, then, that the leadership of Germany and Japan and the other nations that allied themselves with these two got the severe punishment that is their just due," Abdel Hamid concluded.

Abdel Nasser scratched his head and thought about what Abdel Hamid had said for a moment.

"That is certainly what happened," he answered.

"But what would have happened had the Axis Powers emerged victorious in that war?"

Hitler's face shot up with a smile, as if he had somehow managed to convince himself that he in fact did emerge victorious in that war.

"I like how you think, Mr. Nasser."

Nasser's ideas were perturbing to Rabin.

"What a flight of fantasy," he remarked derisively.

"Look at how worried Rabin is over the fate of Israel and the Jewish people!" the skull said, directing his remarks at Rabin nonchalantly.

"And yet had this scenario obtained, we would have been atleast fifty years ahead of you all. Communism would have fallen as early as World War II."

Stalin was curious.

"What would have happened to the United States?"

"It would have turned out to be that same strong, behemoth-like empire that you know now," Kennedy shot back with confidence.

"Or maybe it would have thought twice about intervening in world affairs, perhaps limiting its sphere of influence to the two Americas," Abdel Nasser proposed.

"Perhaps ideas and beliefs would have shifted drastically in a very different direction than we now know," Gandhi added.

The skull had set up the plot in his scenario with precision, and now he began to imagine his ideas come to life. In the skull's mind, the war tribunal was no longer in Nuremberg, but in Paris and London.

The skeleton helped to flesh out the scene that the skull had in mind.

"A different coterie of leaders – some even in this room – would have stood trial instead: Churchill, Stalin, De Gaulle, Eisenhower, Montgomery."

Stalin glanced at him in contempt but the skeleton continued on.

"Mr. Winston Churchill would have been sentenced to death by hanging, a thick rope wrapped around his neck.

Perhaps his body would be left to dangle over a metal girder in a service station – just like Mussolini in Italy."

Churchill began to run his hands over his neck.

"Mr. Charles De Gaulle too would meet a miserable fate," the skeleton continued, "a violent death would await him – but not by hanging like in Mr. Churchill's case. No, it would only be befitting that he be put to death in the traditional French way – beheaded by means of the sharp and heavy blade of a guillotine."

Gandhi covered his eyes and said, "Death is such a horrendous thing, isn't it?"

Hitler imagined himself standing behind a judge's chambers.

"I would have ordered Mr. De Gaulle's punishment mitigated, as I respected his determination and the hardships he suffered in order to liberate France."

"If only the German army had been as compassionate with us," De Gaulle replied caustically.

"They wanted to take their revenge for what Napoleon Bonaparte had done," Hitler replied cold-heartedly.

The skeleton went back to flesh out the skull's scenario.

"As for Eisenhower, he would be sentenced to death by being cast into the Atlantic Ocean. I'd also throw in his British chauffeur – the one he fell in love with – so that they could keep each other company on the one hand and provide a sufficiently ample feast for the sharks of the Altantic on the other."

"A hero like Eisenhower does not deserve an ending such as you describe!" Kennedy objected.

The skeleton chuckled on the inside.

"Finally, the most fantastic death sentence I reserve for Mr. Stalin."

"You got quite the imagination on you, I must say," Stalin replied disparagingly.

The skeleton opened his eyes wide and continued to flesh out the images as they played out in his head.

"You'll get the Siberian special – first, the guards will have you beaten mercilessly, to within an inch of your life. Then they'll tie you up in chains and throw you to the ground. Every now and then they'd flip your face so that both sides get frostbite. Heavy metal weights would be placed on your back to prevent you from adjusting your position. Lastly, your feet will be tied to ropes and dragged by dogs all over the snowy Siberian landscape."

"Why, you son of a bitch!" Stalin screamed, his eyes seething with rage.

The skeleton laughed again internally and said, "If this manner of dying isn't to your lying, perhaps I might suggest another way, one that the Ottomans used quite often."

Abdel Hamid shot a glance at Stalin, smiled and then asked the skeleton, "Are you referring to the khazuq, the unique Ottoman method of impalement?"

"Yes! You tell me, doesn't it suit him well?"

CHAPTER 25
A Red Spot

Fierce winds coming from Germany blew through Europe, carrying with them the spark that would ignite the flames of World War I. It was from Germany that World War II began as well. As for the Cold War that erupted between the United States and the Soviet Union, it was precipitated by a series of crises that hit the German capital of Berlin, which had been under military occupation by the four armies that emerged victorious in World War II.

"It was my singular pleasure to see disagreements explode between the Allies themselves. I thought, who knows, maybe they'd just kill off one another," Hitler said, commenting on the aforementioned crises in Berlin.

By now Abdel Hamid had grown tired of war.

"It would have behooved the powers that emerged triumphant in the war to have learned its brutal lessons and to crown its victories by fostering a spirit of cooperation and working to achieve peace."

Gandhi's hopes were dashed.

"We wanted a world that was safe and stable, where no one got rich at the expense of the poor, no gluttony for some and extreme hunger for others. We wanted a world in which everyone was equal, where social justice was a reality, and to be able to secure the kind of economic conditions by which we would be able to guarantee a dignified life for all of humanity."

"Well said, Gandhi," Stalin said encouragingly.

"What you said constitutes the basic building blocks of socialism."

"Gandhi, a communist!"the millionaire exclaimed sardonically.

"Quick, somebody get a doctor!"

Stalin pounced with the ferocity of a sustained aerial campaign.

"You're the one who is sick, millionaire! Perhaps he could find a solution for your swollen, hanging belly!"

The millionaire patted his belly snobbishly.

"A potbelly is necessary to exhude confidence and respect."

Gandhi ignored the millionaire's sarcasm and directed his words at Stalin.

"Leave him be, Stalin. It is useless to debate someone who thinks with his stomach."

Abdel Hamid steered the conversation back in the direction of the war, and the reasons why disagreements broke out between the Allies.

"Who started the trouble in your midst?" he asked them.

"It's all their fault," Stalin retorted, pointing at his Western counterparts.

Churchill objected, and proceeded to a spirited defense of the conduct of the Western countries.

"Obviously I find this false accusation unacceptable. Rather, it's the Soviet Union's fault, they were the ones who let victory go to their head. They forgot that were it not for the fact that we provided them with equipment and weaponry Hitler would be taking a shvitz in the Kremlin."

Stalin insisted that it was the West's fault.

"I don't deny that our alliance was mutually beneficial in wartime. But it was the 6-Power Conference in London in 1948 – from whose proceedings you intentionally excluded the Soviet Union – and your establishing of a capitalist, democratic regime in Bonn that made us nervous."

"Our issues could have been resolved diplomatically," Kennedy said in a rebuking tone.

"But the Soviet Union thought it wise to lay siege to all the roads that led into Berlin."

The skull made a case for the Soviet's show of force.

"Force is always capable of proving itself in matters of conflict resolution."

Hitler was outraged by the Allies' behavior.

"Oh, how miserable is fate, which allowed Germany to be used as a playground for you all to run around in and take at your leisure."

"What became of that crisis?" Abdel Hamid asked concernedly.

"Each side held on tight to the area under its control and established rival governments therein," Hitler said in a fit.

The skeleton attempted a dispassionate assessment of the repercussions of the German crisis:

"The ideological fray between the communists and the capitalists turned out to be a major one, eventually leading to a 'cold war' in which all means, methods and tactics were seen as legitimate to use – except force."

Abdel Hamid feared that this state of affairs would lead to renewed hostilities.

"As I understand it, the United States emerged the strongest of the parties that participated in the war, particularly in its possession of that disastrous weapon with which they administered the coup de grace that led to the war's conclusion."

"You mean the nuclear bomb?" he asked, barely able to conceal his admiration.

"We ourselves had an increased sense of confidence in our strength when we were able to successfully test our first nuclear weapon in 1949," Stalin responded forcefully.

"We then topped off the victory of the communist revolution in China by concluding a friendship and cooperation treaty with her in 1950, in which we promised to help one another against our common enemies."

Abdel Nasser found the prospect of the crisis worsening between the two parties unlikely.

"The communist-capitalist alliance led to the defeat of Fascism and Nazism. The two sides had engaged in battle on the same side; each side knew the others capabilities."

The skeleton agreed with Abdel Nasser's opinion.

"The two ideologies – though mutually exclusive from one another – went through a clean divorce after the end of the war. The Allies divided into two camps, each of whom were in possession of a nuclear weapons capability."

The United States needed to move fast.

"The U.S. responded to the spread of communism by taking measured steps, primary among them the establishment of the North Atlantic Treaty Organization (NATO) in 1949," Kennedy said.

"This was in Europe," Gandhi said.

"But what about Asia?"

"The French hastened to solidify their presence in the international arena, in particular by sending additional battalions as reinforcements to Vietnam."

Stalin then spoke about the role Russia played in that area.

"Korea was similar to Berlin in those times. The Russian army halted their advance at the 38th parallel north line pursuant to a side agreement between us and the Americans."

Kennedy nodded his head in agreement.

"We agreed to divide Korea between ourselves, with the American military maintaining a sphere of influence south of the aforementioned line," he said pointedly.

"To the victor goes the spoils," Hitler said cynically.

"Each army propped up a puppet regime in the areas that lied under its control," the skeleton said, alluding to the similarities Korea had with Germany in this respect.

Stalin had intended to push further, dissatisfied with the line's position in dividing north and south Korea.

"I conferred with Kim Il-Sung about the possibility of rooting out the seeds of capitalist rule in the American-supported south and uniting the two Koreas into one communist government. He appeared eager to do so."

In Abdel Nasser's view, the repercussions were disastrous for the Korean people.

"Each camp doubled down, leading to the outbreak of civil war in which a man was willing to kill his own brother to serve a foreign agenda."

Churchill held Stalin responsible for the deterioration in conditions.

"It was the communists who went on the attack first."

"North Korean forces – mustering some seven infantry divisions – launched an invasion across the border dividing north from south," Stalin said coarsely.

"Within weeks they managed to secure crushing victories, culminating in the occupation of the southern capital of Seoul."

"A lightning fast victory it was," the skull said, following up on Stalin's remarks.

De Gaulle felt other reasons were at play in the swiftness of the North's victory.

"The North had a fighting force of about 135,000 soldiers, whereas the South could barely summon more than 65,000."

Stalin indirectly alluded to Russia's support for the North Koreans.

"The North Koreans had some 150 fighter aircrafts of the MiG-15 variety at their disposal, in addition to 15 T-34 tanks."

Abdel Hamid was left suspicious by the swiftness of the South's defeat.

"Did the West watch idly as its allies went into retreat?"

"The West does not make it a habit to abandon its allies," Rabin replied reassuringly.

Kennedy confirmed that Rabin's hunch was a valid one.

"The United States took it upon itself to liberate Korea from the communists. It brought the matter before the Security Council and secured its approval for an international force made up of some fifteen countries to intervene."

Hitler felt securing the council's approval to be a tall order.

"How did the Americans manage to secure the security council's approval given the Soviet's veto power?"

"The Soviet Union abstained from attending in protest of the council's refusal to transfer China's seat in the Council to the People's Republic of China," Stalin replied.

Gandhi wringed his hands in disappointment.

"This is exactly what I had feared!" he warned everyone.

"That some nations would commandeer the U.N. in a way that would give preeminence to their interests."

Stalin clarified what the facts on the ground looked like.

"Kim Il-Sung's forces managed to take control over the entire Korean peninsula."

Kennedy noted that the American response was prompt.

"General MacArthur, commander of the American armed forces in East Asia and NATO's Supreme Commander of Allied Forces, plotted to expel the communists from Korea by means of a landing mission near the Port of Incheon in Korea's south."

"Was the operation successful?" the skull asked.

"The Americans – backed by air cover and an influx of weapons and reinforcements from American bases in Japan – were able to make the landing," Kennedy answered.

Churchill was impressed by the success of the operation.

"With determination – and massive amounts of firepower – anything is possible."

"And how many civilians were killed in these battles?" Gandhi asked in response to Churchill's excitement.

Kennedy ignored Gandhi's question. He was too preoccupied with the success of the operation.

"The United States was able to achieve the operation's goal by liberating the capital of Seoul, and from there our men were able to proceed with liberating vast amounts of territory in the south."

Churchill confirmed the remarkable shift in fortunes.

"The North Koreans pulled back even farther than the 38th parallel north line!"

Stalin explained the reasons behind the withdrawal.

"The weakness of the North's logistics system and shortage of food and ammunition were key causes behind the withdrawal."

Kennedy's main concern was to reinforce America's gains in the war.

"The Americans continued their advance north until they reached Pyongyang, the capital of the North. Following a sustained bombardment campaign Pyongyang fell to American hands."

Abdel Nasser apprised those in attendance of the North's response.

"The North switched to guerilla warfare, carrying out numerous operations against international forces."

The skull sensed that a direct Soviet intervention was inevitable.

"I bet the Soviets pulverized them in response."

"Actually," Churchill corrected the skull, "the Chinese were much more excited about the prospect of jumping into war than the Soviets were."

To Abdel Nasser, the Chinese had apt reasons for doing so.

"China entered the fray in order to protect its national security interests, as Mao was convinced that the Americans forces would not hesitate to continue their advance into China if North Korea fell completely to them."

Stalin agreed with Abdel Nasser's analysis.

"Kim Il-Sung requested my assistance, and I decided to help him covertly until China took up the task of openly joining the fray on the side of the North. After all, China had a better claim to intervening than I did."

"The Soviets had armed the Chinese," Rabin charged, as if intent on exposing the Soviet's dirty little secret and leaving it out in the open.

"The Chinese took care of the rest."

Abdel Hamid accused the Soviets of abandonment.

"Were you afraid of confrontation with the Americans?"

"Had we been afraid of such a prospect, we would not have intervened in Korea from the outset. Our role in aiding the Chinese was no small one: not only did we arm seven Chinese divisions, we also helped them to cross the Yalu river that traverses the Korean-Chinese border by providing them air cover. Our MiG-15's clashed head on with American fighter jets during that precarious moment."

De Gaulle exposed other ways in which the Soviets managed to conceal their participation in the battle.

"Soviet pilots wore civilian clothes so as to give the Soviets plausible deniability in the event one of them happened to be captured by the Americans."

The skull wanted to cut to the chase.

"Who emerged victorious in these battles?"

"The Chinese proved themselves on the battlefield, fighting bravely and courageously and inflicting heavy losses on the America's 10th Division," Stalin asserted self-confidently.

Churchill found Stalin's assertiveness laughable.

"The Soviets showed themselves willing to fight to the last Chinese soldier. Despite their best efforts not to get involved directly they still managed to lose 300 fighter jets."

The skeleton informed those in attendance about the U.S.'s response to the Chinese advance.

"In the face of the heavy losses the Chinese inflicted on the international forces the Americans began to seriously consider the prospect of using atomic weapons."

Gandhi was mortified.

"It appears Korea met the same fate as Japan," Abdel Hamid observed.

Gandhi was beginning to grow pale, and so De Gaulle hastened to reassure him.

"The Europeans strongly objected to the use of atomic weapons – most particularly British Prime Minister Clement Attlee – in fear of a Soviet response-in-kind which would lead to the outbreak of a new world war."

Gandhi began to unwind a bit.

"That was a wise, reasonable decision."

"Europe benefited much from its experiences in the two world wars," Abdel Nasser said, building off of Gandhi's remark.

"It had become the wisest, most collected party in this respect."

"The Soviet propaganda machine went to work instilling fear of the Americans in the communist countries by broadcasting harrowing accounts of the Hiroshima and Nagasaki attacks," the skeleton said, drawing on the recesses of his memory.

"The war lasted for three years," Rabin said.

"The Korean War came to an end after complicated and difficult negotiations, and a truce was signed in 1953 between the Americans and the North Koreans," Kennedy said. "Alas, the South Koreans refused to sign off on the truce."

Gandhi was appalled by the toll the war had taken on the innocent.

"The civil war was nothing short of psychotic, where one and the same people turned their rifles against themselves. Millions were killed, each side's economy was in shatters, and the North was no closer to achieving its dream of uniting the peninsula. Quite the opposite, the war consecrated the division between a communist north and a capitalist south.

The victory of the communists in the north came much to Kennedy's chagrin.

"North Korea became a jungle, hemmed in from all sides by barbed wire. It was now closed off to the world, no one knows what goes on there. Even those who have managed to escape over the years have only been able to share limited insight as to its inner workings."

"Because of fear," Churchill retorted. "Day and night, they are afraid."

"Although a few North Koreans have managed to escape from that jungle, they continue to be haunted by bouts of fear and trepidation, a consequence of the brutality of the ruling regime, which takes pride in ruling by an iron fist." De Gaulle said.

"Aristotle once said that virtue is a mean between two vices," Gandhi remarked, hoping to bridge the gap between Communism and capitalism.

Rabin was exasperated by Gandhi's attempt to play peacemaker To him, Aristotle's remark was ludicrous.

"Centrism weakens an ideology's power and strength," he said.

Through it all, Stalin remained a spirited communist.

"The strength of one's principles renders centrism a moot point," he said.

To Kennedy, Stalin's obstinacy brought the position of the communists in North Korea into sharp relief.

"There is no sense of centrism or pragmatism in North Korea; they are principled, yes, but principled in an unyielding, inflexible, rigid, like a Basalt rock. It can brook no compromise with any competitor.

'You're either with us, or against us," is their motto. The people there are cast into two categories, and their loyalty to the ruling regime is measured on a scale running from 60 to 100."

The skeleton found the scope of the scale odd.

"What happened to the rest of the numbers?" he asked.

"Everyone else is deemed a subversive," Kennedy replied.

"Their names are inscribed in invisible ink, no one bothers to read their names unless they are an intelligence officer or an executioner."

The millionaire was led by his curiosity to ask, "And how does the ruling regime treat its loyalists?"

"Allow me, Mr. Kennedy," Churchill interjected.

"Go right ahead."

Churchill continued, "I am certain, Mr. Millionaire, that if you were in North Korea you would get nothing short of a 95 or above. After all, it is this group that shares in the wealth and the power of the regime – you would be just as flabby and stout as you were in life."

Churchill's description moved Gandhi to remember the poor and penniless in his native India.

"How do the rest of the Korean people live?" he asked.

"They are all laborers and soldiers, made to wear a single uniform," Kennedy replied with contempt.

"The poor are given meals commensurate to their loyalty to the regime," the millionaire scoffed.

"He who is not loyal – or worse, protests his plight – is stripped of the small batch of rice that the ruling elite is so kind to provide for him."

Abdel Hamid found the whole affair odd.

"Is this what communism is?"

"No, it is not," Stalin replied angrily.

"Actually, you might say that it is the epitome of communism!" Hitler said scornfully.

"What of the non-loyalists. . .or, better yet, the opposition?" the skull asked.

Now more than ever Kennedy was proud of the accomplishments of American democracy.

"According to U.S. intelligence, anyone found to harbor enmity towards the regime is deported."

Abdel Hamid let out a sigh of relief.

"That's not so bad," he said. "It's a big world, after all."

"With plenty of mass graves for everyone," Rabin shot back.

"Those in power go after everyone suspected of being at odds with the regime," Kennedy said, basing his remarks on U.S. intelligence reports.

"And their families – as far back as an uncle of the eighth degree."

As Churchill spoke, it was obvious that he bore especial enmity to Communist regimes.

"In this kind of atmosphere, the family goes about sifting out the disloyalists in their ranks – informing on them or even killing them themselves in order to protect the rest of the family."

The skeleton recalled an interview he had conducted with a Korean man in the course of one of his investigative reports.

"I conducted an interview with an American businessman of Korean origins named Mr. Chang. He spoke bitterly of the ordeal he had underwent: 'My father was married to another woman before he met my mother, with whom he had two sons. They were pretty well off, but he took a stand against the Korean Civil War, objecting to the fact that fellow countrymen were turning their guns against each other. He was accused of being a bourgeois liberal. Upon learning that he was wanted by the regime, he fled for South Korea, in hopes that his wife and children would follow him. They were never able to make it passed the barbed wire. How I wish that I could learn the fate of my two siblings. I always wonder whether I could help them in some way – somehow manage to free them of the open air prison in which they live."

"Tell this businessman that he should be grateful to Uncle Sam," Rabin advised the skeleton.

"Had he remained in Korea he would have never known his siblings – or anyone for that matter, considering the 'uncle of the eighth degree' policy."

"Oh, how blessed is he who manages to escape injustice," Gandhi exclaimed.

The skeleton shared some pleasing news with Gandhi.

"The Japanese occupation of Indo-China came to an end following their surrender in World War II."

Abdel Nasser was impressed with the resistance put up by the peoples of Indo-China.

"The determination and resolve of these peoples to struggle for freedom and independence became a symbol and a model for all colonized peoples."

Stalin condemned France for not allowing the Vietnamese to enjoy their independence.

"The Japanese withdrew from Vietnam, and the Socialist Republic of Vietnam attained its independence," he told De Gaulle.

"But the French refused to let the Vietnamese decide their own affairs – instead, they occupied Vietnam and took Japan's place as colonialist ruler."

"That was only a natural step for France to take," De Gaulle charged.

"After all, they were in Vietnam before the Japanese."

Abel Nasser supported the Vietnamese decision to resist the new occupiers.

"It was unreasonable to expect the Vietnamese to expect the French occupation of their land."

Gandhi called for peaceful resistance, considering the balance of power was not in Vietnam's favor.

"What can you do with one arm tied behind your back?" he asked rhetorically.

"All of the weapons in the world are no match for belief in one's cause and the strength of one's convictions," Stalin replied with unbounded revolutionary spirit.

"I agree with you, Mr. Stalin," Abdel Nasser said as he began to describe his admiration for the Vietnamese.

"When a nation has heroes like Giap and Ho Chi Minh to defend it, it would be wise for any occupier to just pack up their things and go!"

"Giap and Ho Chi Minh learned guerilla war tactics from the Chinese," Stalin said, extolling the methods of the Vietnamese resistance.

To Kennedy, the situation was ripe with danger.

"I must say, however, that I admire the determination of these two men."

Abdel Nasser was enthused about the rapid force these two men managed to muster.

"They left Hanoi for the jungles to resist the French."

De Gaulle was livid.

"Actually French armed forces clashed with Giap's men in 1950 and handed them a crushing defeat, forcing them back into the jungle."

"The French were able to withstand the resistance," Abdel Hamid said, summarizing the consequences of that battle.

To Stalin, the affair had only just begun, De Gaulle's views notwithstanding.

"The brave have a saying among themselves: 'If a bullet doesn't kill me, then it can only make me stronger.'"

De Gaulle took pride in his country's military strategy in Vietnam.

"In 1953 the French laid a trap for the guerillas by opening a series of outposts in the Dien Bien Phu valley."

"It was a wise military plan indeed," the skull vehemently observed.

"It's in the nature of prey that they fall for traps," Churchill added, speaking from years of experience.

"But a leader like Giap proved himself smart as a fox," Stalin said, rebutting Churchill's remarks.

"He discovered the trap, and amassed a fighting force of some 75,000 men at the head of two hundred heavy artillery pieces, which he had moved to the mountains to be taken apart and put back together again, and led his men in a battle against some 15,000 French troops."

"Fierce clashes broke out between the two sides," Hitler said, relishing the failure of the French military plan.

"The French were forced to surrender. 5,000 French troops lost their lives, whereas the communists lost some 15,000 on their end."

"Why didn't the Americans provide their French allies with weapons and equipment?" the skull asked.

Kennedy felt the conditions on the ground prevented America from coming to France's aid.

"The guerilla's artillery guns prevented our attempts to send aid."

De Gaulle hung his head in shame.

"The loss was rather painful to the French. It was only a matter of time before we withdrew from Vietnam, which, at the time of our departure, was divided into north and south."

"And then the Americans took the place of the French," the skeleton remarked snidefully.

Stalin fleshed out the skeleton's remark more fully.

"With the United States locked in fierce competition with the European states over colonies, the Americans felt that the French withdrawal was a golden opportunity to take Vietnam under their wing."

"Just ask me," the skull said, hoping to ease De Gaulle's sense of shame.

"I know better than anyone how vexing guerilla resistance movements can be!"

Kennedy knew that the Americans had made a mistake by going into Vietnam.

"The Americans remained stuck in the swamp that is Vietnam for many years. It was a boneheaded mistake that we paid for dearly before we were able to make it out of there."

Rabin saw the American predicament in Vietnam in a more positive light.

"That the Americans refused to bend was more important than whether or not they were able to subdue Vietnam," he said.

Abdel Hamid took Rabin's remark as a base upon which to pull Rabin into a conversation about the Palestinians.

"Is this your way of indirectly assuring me that you weren't able to hold on to your victories in 1948?"

"Your celebrations are premature, Sultan," Rabin said self-conceitedly.

"Our victory in 1948 was decisive. We established the state of Israel. Our motto then was that Israel's borders in the future shall extend from the Nile to the Euphrates – although, to be sure, we remained on guard from Arab reprisals for quite some time afterwards."

"What was it that made you so apprehensive, Rabin?" the millionaire asked inquisitively.

"Gamal Abdel Nasser," Rabin groaned.

The skull found Rabin's response rather odd.

"Apprehensiveness is typically followed by fear and vigilance," he said.

"I've never heard of a strong army that fears an army that is weaker than it is – how was Abdel Nasser able to ruffle your feathers?"

"It began with the Revolution of July 1952," Rabin replied.

"After our defeat in the 1948 War and the attendant loss of Palestine," Abdel Nasser said, explaining the precipitating causes that led to the 1952 revolution.

"A few of us officers – we had dubbed ourselves then 'The Free Officers' felt it was imperative that our army restore its sense of dignity and acclaim following the fiasco of 1948. We held numerous meetings in which we plotted our come back. Everything was planned with precision, down to the last detail. And it worked: our coup was a success, the army managed to take the reigns of power, and forced then King Farouk to abdicate in favor of his son Ahmad Fuad."

"Did you really retain the state's monarchical character?" the millionaire asked, seeking clarification.

"Yes, until 1953, in which the members of the Egyptian Revolutionary Command Council to abolish the monarchy and establish an Arab Republic in Egypt. General Muhammad Naguib was declared president."

"Oh, how I hate military coups!" Abdel Hamid cried out, remembering the calamity that befell him and his rule.

"Why must everyone be so power hungry?"

Abdel Nasser denied Abdel Hamid's charge, saying, "We were not power hungry at all! We would have rather things happened differently, but the revolution's platform for reform necessitated that we take power for a while."

"You do little to show your respect for democratic ideals by taking power by force," De Gaulle said, as if to set a trap for Abdel Nasser.

But in actuality Abdel Nasser was prepared for that remark.

"A democratic mode of government was the principal plank in the revolution's platform. The revolution had sought to establish a regime of social justice, form a strong national army, wrest the economy from bourgeois hegemony, crack down on what remained of the old feudalistic order and do away with the vestiges of colonialism."

Churchill took De Gaulle's side of the debate.

"But Great Britain had granted Egypt her independence by means of the Anglo-Egyptian treaty of 1936."

Abdel Nasser rose to defend Egypt's dignity.

"This is true, but the grant of independence was cosmetic in nature until the British pulled its military forces out of Egypt pursuant to the Anglo-Egyptian Agreement of 1954."

Abdel Hamid added his voice to that of Churchill and De Gaulle.

"It seems to me, Nasser, that you were simply hungry for power."

"Me?!" Abdel Nasser asked with astonishment, his finger pointed at his chest.

"Yes you!" Churchill responded, "as proven by the fact that you conspired along with the other members of the revolutionary council against President Muhammad Naguib and forced him into house arrest."

Abdel Nasser sighed, feeling himself cornered. Nevertheless, he decided to reason with them.

"It was Muhammad Naguib who conspired with the Muslim Brotherhood to have me assassinated as I was giving a speech in Alexandria to a large crowd of people who had gathered to celebrate Britain's military withdrawal. As I was preparing to give my remarks in al-Manshiyya square, the assassin began to make his move. No more than three minutes had passed since the commencement of my speech when suddenly the assassin moved in within seven meters of where I was standing, pulled out his weapon and started firing at me. I just stood there and stared at him – I couldn't believe what I was seeing. But I stood still. I didn't flinch. I knew that this was the manifestation of a conspiracy against Egypt and the desire for change in Egypt. The assassin discharged a total of eight bullets. The crowds rushed for cover, scared for their lives. Chaos spread through their ranks. And yet I continued to give my speech, even as the bullets were flying. 'Let everyone remain in his place!' I demanded. 'I gladly give my blood for you, my very life for you! I gladly give my blood for the sake of Egypt!'"

"You are a courageous man, Nasser," the skull interrupted.

"I am no coward," Abdel Nasser continued.

"I gladly accept death for the sake of freedom, dignity and glory for my people."

Gandhi felt heartburn in his chest. After all, he had been the victim of an assassin's bullet himself.

"Did they manage to apprehend the perpetrator?" he asked.

"And what were the repercussions of the assassination attempt for Egypt?" Abdel Hamid asked.

The skeleton took it upon himself to answer in the form of a news presentation.

"The event in Alexandria flamed the revolutionary zeal of the people, stirred not only by hatred for the perpetrators but also by a desire for freedom and independence. The flames of revolution had fanned, and what sparked them was that red spot that smudged Abdel Nasser's shirt.

CHAPTER 26
Two Roses to Look At

The most delightful rendezvous is one that happens spontaneously, without prior appointment. The thick fog passes through the forest like a handsome knight. The knight descends furtively from the mountain's peak, decked out in a white cape and riding atop a wind horse that neighs with pride. The wet leaves of the forest grazed his shoulders playfully, and the branches extended their hands to greet him as he continued to push forward. He had long promised to return to this mountainous region close to the sea, and this time he was here to stay. The earth, though wet and moist, latched tightly on to the edge of his soles, fearing that letting go meant never seeing the knight again.

He continued to make his way through the forest as if pulled by a magnet, driven by the enticing fragrance and natural aroma emitted by his beloved's perfume. She had been taking a stroll among the roses, stopping every now and then to pick a flower and smell it to her heart's delight.

Diana's soft, heaving bosom, white as ivory and polished around the edges, had been carefully shrouded by an elegant black coat, which had once belonged to a noble man who had left it to dry the droplets of morning dew that adorned her body like the beads of a well-made pearl necklace, the two strands of which attach to reveal nipples as rebellious as twin gazels.

He wrapped the sleeve of his long coat around her. Her heart quivered and began to beat rapidly, fluttering with frenzy between her ribs. Having taken note of his alluring charm she proceeded to reciprocate with a heartwarming smile and, once she had his attention, proceeded to kiss the flower in her hand and present it to him as a gift. The flower turned into a carnation in his hands. He paused to take in a whiff and then planted it in her hair. Now, he had two roses to look at.

Such was Kennedy and Diana's rendezvous. It began with childlike innocence, with a dove's gentleness and an olive branch's harmoniousness.

He extended his hand to meet hers and their hands formed a knot. Her fingers pressed forcefully on his, and he requited with soft pressure. They were as if joined at the hip, walking side by side, crossing through the garden with the rivulet from which Diana had first emerged running parallel to them. The experience had been hallowed in their memory as one that buried the pains of the past. They climbed up the graduated terrace, passing through the trees and stopping to sit as lovers do under an old evergreen oak tree. Overwhelmed by emotion, Kennedy rushed to give her a long, passionate kiss. A soft breeze blew through the garden, and an almond tree rose to the sky. The sun bid farewell to the horizon, and a silver moon – lodged behind the mountains far, far away - rose to take its place, keeping them company and watching over them. The sky was pure, its stars glimmering, sending down its smiles and providing romantic lightning as a way to celebrate this joyous love.

Kennedy again pressed his lips on the princesses, taking her in a long kiss. Their saliva mixed together, the two lovers were taken in intoxicating bliss. Their lips could barely muster a word, but their embrace spoke a thousand and one lines, like a prosaic song, honest, warm and tender. As far as he was concerned existence evaporated away, and only she remained.

She was now the only reality. The world with all its wonders ceased to be the center of attention – it was now but a spectator, calling on the trees and the stones to speak and testify to what they were seeing.

The two lovers' bodies had been cold, nearly frozen. Their embrace dispersed warmth and life. Blood flowed through their veins once more. The marks they had left on each others lips could be read more clearly and precisely than fingerprints. The moon hid bashfully, recusing to its place of rest, and a grey cloud shrouded its radiant face.

Love had forced away the depressing loneliness of night. They were now in a comfortable, welcoming place. Kennedy was always certain that he had never been defeated – save for the day he died, when he was assassinated by a treacherous man's bullet. But today the magic in Diana's eyes furnished him with renewed strength. As she wrapped her hands around his waist and placed her head on his chest, he recalled the conversations Abdel Nasser and Abdel Hamid II had about the houris of paradise in the Muslim tradition. They had been right all along. Here she was, his first houri, and, because he had no desire for any houris after her, his last as well.

Why did they meet? How did their love spark so suddenly?

That's how fate works: it rears its head at the right moment, by appointment – and the best appointments are those in which the intimacies of love are unleashed.

CHAPTER 27

A Place under the Sun

The security detail of Mr. Gamal Abdel Nasser - who at the time was Egypt's Prime Minister - feared that he had been shot in the chest. In reality, he had survived the assassination attempt. The red spot on the President's shirt was nothing but a smudge of red ink from a ballpoint pen that broke during the attempt by the detail to pull him back for his protection when the rain of bullets came at him as he stood behind the podium.

The detail apprehended the perpetrator and, after interrogating him, found out that he was a member of the Muslim Brotherhood. The Brotherhood had conspired with the President of the Republic Muhammad Naguib to assassinate the leading members of the revolutionary command council. The skeleton said:

"Public anger simmered like a volcano ready to burst, raining down rocks and hot ash upon the Muslim Brotherhood organization that the perpetrator had belonged to. It started with Muhammad Naguib, who was forced to abdicate his position as president and placed in house arrest under close watch. The revolution had gained overwhelming public support for its designs, through which the Egyptian masses were able to take revenge on the Muslim Brotherhood by burning down their meeting places."Churchill listened carefully and then said, "You're a lucky man, Nasser. Not only did you survive an attempt on your life, but you also managed to secure the support of your people."Rabin was noticeably envious of the attention Nasser was getting.

"You should thank your red ballpoint pen for helping you to paint yourself as this great hero."Abdel Nasser wasn't pleased with Rabin's remark.

"You all actively seek the death of all those who speak in favor of independence and freedom. I extended my hand to all. I made it clear that I was going to respond to others in kind: to be convivial with those who were convivial to me, and hostile to those who were hostile to me."Churchill edged close to Nasser and said in a diplomatic tone, "But we offered to enter into an alliance with you, but you refused."

"An alliance between two nations in an unequal power relationship with one another is no alliance - it's dependency," Abdel Nasser replied. "This was not an acceptable option for us. The residue of colonialism - with its attendant poverty and ingrained humiliation - had already been too much for us to bear."Gandhi empathized subjectively with Abdel Nasser.

"Mr. Nasser, what did you do to do away with the bane of colonialism?"

"We began with agricultural reform. We confiscated land from the landowners and gave it back to the peasants, who had toiled on the fields for centuries yet lived in abject poverty."

"Finally, the meek have found someone who shall stand by their side!" Gandhi replied with the highest admiration and respect.

"Why, certainly. After all, we fought the revolution for their sake – for Egypt's sake."

Stalin remarked naughtily, "It is imperative to crack down on all enemies of the revolution in order to protect it."

"The revolution needed to clean house first," Abdel Nasser added, "before it could direct its attention to foreign enemies."

Rabin was furtively spiteful of the value of Abdel Nasser's revolution.

"The revolution spoke in big, shiny, glamorous slogans – but in reality it cracked down on the very freedoms it claimed to be fighting for."

"You threw all of your political opposition into prisons," Churchill added.

"Whatever happened to freedom of opinion?"Abdel Nasser defended his position with determination and anger.

"The revolution protected the right to free opinion – but it was under no obligation to protect those who advocate for destructive opinions."The skull offered an opinion.

"That's a facile argument. Everyone sees an opinion contrary to their own as being destructive. It is only power that determines what is and what is not a constructive opinion."

"But this is dictatorship!" Gandhi protested. Hitler seconded Abdel Nasser's opinion.

"Good for you, Nasser! Welcome to the Strongmens Club. There ought to be nothing that may stand in the way of a successful leader who seeks to lead his nation."

Kennedy objected to Hitler's opinion.

"Democracy and the will of the majority are the only help a strong leader may count on in the pursuance of his aims."Abdel Nasser found in Kennedy's words a means by which to hti back.

"In 1956 we administered a democratic popular referendum in which I was named the President of the Arab Republic of Egypt."

Sultan Abdel Hamid was impressed with Abdel Nasser's counterargument.

"You accuse Nasser of dictatorship, and yet here he proved to you that he took power by democratic means."

Kennedy responded to Abdel Hamid:

"The United States of America carried the torch of freedom and democracy to the world, which began to take new shapes and forms in the second half of the twentieth century."

"There is no escaping the fact that brute force is necessary to carry this torch and raise it high without the risk of having someone else put out the torch's flame," the skull said.

Kennedy continued, "The requisite force was there – and we formed alliances to make sure it stayed there." Stalin said, "The NATO treaty was the beginning of the mission to confront Soviet power in Europe."

Churchill hailed the NATO alliance:

"The alliance constituted a successful deterrence to Soviet aggression – but the Soviet moves in the East led to the formation of a new alliance, this time in southeast Asia, comprised of the U.S., Britain, France, Australia, Pakistan, and the Philippines. It was designed to besiege the communist countries there." Stalin said, "The communist countries posed a threat to them, so they went about forming alliances, the last of which was the Baghdad Pact – the signatories of which were: Britain, Turkey, and Iraq – in order to build a base for the West near the Soviet positions in the Middle East."

Abdel Hamid directed a question to Stalin.

"What was the Soviet response to these alliances?"

Stalin replied, "In 1955 the Soviet Union entered into the Warsaw Pact along with the Eastern European countries."

Hitler was optimistic.

"I always knew that the Allied Forces would splinter due to ideological differences – in the end, each of them wanted a bigger piece of the pie for themselves."

"You see, Stalin?" Churchill rebuked.

"You see how Hitler gloats at us?"

"You have only yourselves to blame, you capitalists! It was you, after all, who sought to install regimes loyal to you in territories that were liberated by the Red Army."

"This is the nature of democracy, Stalin," Kennedy shot back.

"Every people has a right to choose whichever system of government it prefers – through elections, not by imposition."

"What if the people make the wrong choice?"

"There is nothing wrong with the people making the wrong choice once or twice – because the third time around the people will hold their elected leadership to account. That was our objective – to ingrain the principle of democracy in the world."

"How could the West claim to have democratic rule in any substantive sense when it continues to allow the owners of capital the ability to buy off votes? In the communist countries, however, the cadres are the ones who elect their leaders. You harbored within yourselves a deep-seated enmity towards us, and formed alliances to counter our activities. We only responded in kind."

Hitler pondered the state of the world after his fall.

"Western alliances, eastern alliances – each one competing with the other to increase their power and ability to attain hegemony. What about you, Nasser? Which camp did you belong to?" "I chose to stand with neither East nor West – rather, I along with Jawaharlal Nehru, Tito, and Ahmad Sukarno chose to form the Non-Aligned movement, the highlight of our activities being the 1955 Bandung conference in which 29 other nations participated."

Hitler was puzzled.

"But Tito was a fierce revolutionary communist who undertook many campaigns to unite Yugoslavians against the Germans," he replied. "After he overcame the challenge posed by the monarchists he declared himself Chairman of the Presidium of all of Yugoslavia. He formed four military battalions that directly threatened the German presence in Yugoslavia."

Churchill said, "That is why we supplied him with weapons and ammunition."

"He was a committed Marxist," Stalin gloated. "He was dazzled by the revolution in Russia, joining the Red Army at whose hands he learned the arts of war."

"Did he go to Russia specifically to train at the hands of the Red Army?" Sultan Abdel Hamid asked inquisitively.

The reply came, "During the First World War, he fell prisoner to the Russians. He was incarcerated when the revolution broke out and proceeded to join its ranks."

"I ordered ten German military battalions – backed up by six Italian battalions - to pull his power out from under him. They succeeded in besieging him but he still managed to escape our grasp, withdrawing into the mountains along with the members of his four battalions. The clashes had left more than four thousand people injured."

"How could you let him escape, Hitler?" the skull asked provocatively.

"After a year I ordered my paratroopers to land near his headquarters – and yet he was able to escape once again."

"Tito was a good friend to me," Abdel Nasser said.

"He believed in the right of the people to self-determination, and supported liberation movements around the world. We worked together closely in the framework of the Non-Aligned Movement." The skeleton said, "Tito was as patriotic a Yugoslavian as De Gaulle was to France. With the end of the Second World War, he declared his independence from the Soviet Union and the Western nations."

Stalin clarified the reasons why Tito declared his independence from the Soviet Union.

"Though he was a committed Communist, his nationalistic stance led him to swerve from the principles of the Socialist International."

"Nationalism is a receptacle for the nation, required to keep the latter safe and to protect its interests," De Gaulle said.

"It is for this reason that I distanced myself from Britain and the United States and I worked to serve France first and foremost."

Stalin empathized with De Gaulle.

"I understand you well, Mr. De Gaulle. Your visit to Moscow helped me form a good impression of you."

"I must say, you received me well, but in the end you offered me little in the way of substantive help."

"Your aspirations seemed too far-fetched, given France's state at the time."

"Everyone knows that De Gaulle is a man of will and resolve," Hitler remarked.

"His skillful employment of both helped restore to France her dignity and returned her to her proper place among the great nations."

"Power produces greatness," the skull said matter-of-factly.

"And wealth fortifies power," the millionaire added.

"The primary goal of capitalism is to acquire wealth and horde it in the way of investments that require state protection," Stalin said with a hostile tone.

"How did America manage to establish military bases for itself in each of Turkey, Iran, South Korea and the Philippines?" the skull asked with intense admiration.

Kennedy responded coolly and collectedly, "That was rather simple: all we had to was alert these nations to Stalin's ghoulish menace."

Stalin remonstrated against Kennedy's charge, and proceeded to wage a full-fledged counter-attack against the latter.

"How dare you call me a ghoul you capitalist. . .imperialist. . . self-defeatist. . ."

Hitler said, "Easy, Stalin! Let him continue what he was saying."

"I don't mean you personally, Mr. Stalin, but the Soviet Union as a whole, in terms of its communist ideology and its weapons arsenal, and in particular its nuclear weapons capabilities."

"This is our belief system. All of the nations of the world shall become Communist – including the United States of America."

The skeleton declared, "The Western world received the news of Stalin's death in 1953 with great relief. The giant had died – that same giant who had solidified communism's power and helped to make the Soviet Union the second most powerful nation in the world. At this time the decorated military officer Zhukov – who was instrumental in defeating the Germans in each of Moscow and Leningrad as well as securing the latters' surrender in Berlin – returned to Moscow and regained his stripes. This put him in a position of authority within the military, which pulled considerable weight in calibrating the scales of political power and helped to determine the makeup of the leadership in the Kremlin. A council comprising three of Stalin's closest confidantes was formed to rule after the latter's passing. At its head was Khrushchev, the General-Secretary of the Soviet Communist Party. Voroshilov was given the chairmanship of the Presidium, and Bulganin was named Prime Minister. Zhukov worked behind the scenes to hand Khrushchev the big seat in 1957."

Hitler shared his hopes with Stalin.

"You must have died by poison as well, Mr. Stalin?"

Before Stalin had an opportunity to respond Abdel Nasser said, "Seven Jewish doctors mixed poison in your food."

Rabin felt shut in between Hitler and Abdel Nasser, but he sprung to make his case:

"This is utter nonsense, and a slur against the Jewish people!"

He took a deep breath and continued, "It's true that the media outlets at the time hinted at this, but the doctors in question were most certainly innocent."

"Poor gents," the skeleton noted sarcastically.

"It was for this reason that the Soviet Union cut diplomatic ties with Israel."

"So the doubts raised by the supposed Jewish connection to Stalin's death caused a break in relations between the two countries," Abdel Hamid said in what seemed like an indirect accusation of guilt.

Stalin could care less.

"Let it be known to you all that Lenin and Stalin never died – they shall live forever."

"True indeed," Kennedy said mockingly.

"Your sitting here today is proof enough of this."

Stalin retained his sense of vigor.

"At least in the minds of the Soviet peoples."

De Gaulle said, "That is because the rest of the world's nations were looking for its place under the sun, particularly after a war whose black smoke had haunted the skies for so long."

Churchill was intent on protecting his nation's rights.

"Britain intended to retain control of its colonies."

"As did France. But the consciousness of the colonized peoples and their will to be free and independent made this matter rather difficult for us. This is what we found in our confrontations with the Algerians."

Stalin came out in full revolutionary zeal.

"The success of the national liberation movements yanked the rug from underneath the feet of the British and the French."

The skeleton had his doubts.

"Yet are these nations capable of running their affairs without sufficient experience?"

Abdel Nasser forcefully replied, "The colonial powers could not accept the thought of losing their colonies. In Egypt, following the success of the revolution it was left to us to move in the direction of building our army first so as to protect our nation. Then we set about building our economic structure."

"Don't you forget that it was the Soviet Union who supplied you with weapons," Stalin reminded Abdel Nasser.

Kennedy said, "The United States offered you funding to build the Aswan Dam."

Abdel Nasser replied, "But America tied its funding of the Aswan Dam to the fulfillment of two preconditions: first, that we cease purchasing weapons from the Soviet Union, and second that we reconcile with Israel. We rejected both of these preconditions at the time, and the Americans responded by pulling its funding from the project."

Abdel Hamid asked, "How did you proceed after that?"

"We nationalized the Suez Canal, and directed the revenues we acquired thereby to fund the building of the Dam."

Rabin rose in a fit of anger:

"The nationalization of the canal was an act of piracy, and an unjust appropriation of French and British rights to maritime passage. It posed a threat, in turn, to the state of Israel."

Stalin supported the measures Abdel Nasser had taken.

"Silence, Rabin! It was Egypt's right to nationalize the canal, for Egypt has a right to full control over its means of production, and the canal was its most important means of production."

Churchill reacted furiously to Stalin's remark.

"The nationalization of the canal came as a slap in the face to both Britain and France!"

Rabin continued on, clearly agitated:

"In 1956 representatives of France, Britain and Israel met and agreed to invade Egypt via the Sevres Protocols. The goal had been to occupy the Suez Canal, yet the three parties failed to take into account the positions of either the United States or the Soviet Union."

"The three nations launched an attack against Egypt, and our armed forces – in concert with the Egyptian people – stood bravely to counter this unwarranted aggression," Abdel Nasser said, beaming with faith and conviction.

As Churchill noted, the expectations of the political apparatus in England clashed rather severely with reality.

"Mr. Eden had expected that the Egyptian people would fall apart following the dual French-British warning – that it would surrender, run into the streets, burning and looting at will, and demanding a new leadership take the place of Nasser."

De Gaulle, in turn, had only wished that the Arab peoples didn't rise in solidarity with Egypt.

"The Arab peoples did not abandon Egypt to fight its battle alone. They held mass demonstrations to protest what they called the Tripartite Aggression against Egypt, during which they attacked our embassies and set them on fire."

The millionaire was apprehensive.

"A group of Syrian officers engineered the destruction of oil pipelines that passed through Syrian territory, causing a near complete halt of oil flowing from the Middle East. This, in turn, led the value of the sterling pound in the international markets to plummet at once."

Kennedy added further reasons for why the aggression failed to accomplish its objectives:

"The United States stood against the Tripartite Aggression. Eisenhower was furious with British Prime Minister Anthony Eden for failing to consult with him about the Suez operation and for unleashing it just days before the American elections were due to take place. The whole fiasco brought Eisenhower dangerously close to losing the election."

Stalin, however, was insistent that it was the Soviet Union that foiled the attack:

"The Soviet Union directed a fierce warning to the countries that invaded Egypt, threatening to launch a nuclear attack against London and Paris if they failed to pull back."

Rabin responded by playing down the effect the threat had on France and Britain's actions.

"That the Soviet Union was serious in its threat to use nuclear force was rather doubtful."

"Yet even doubts necessitate caution," De Gaulle said, eager to protect Paris from harm and in a manner befitting a wise military leader such as himself.

Kennedy concurred with De Gaulle's assessment.

"Who could risk a confrontation? The disastrous consequences of Soviet nuclear missiles falling over their heads weighed heavily against any other potentialities."

Gandhi was delighted by the stance the United Nations had taken in the whole affair.

"The United States demanded an end to the attack and an immediate withdrawal. The resolution gave expression to an outraged world's conscience."

"How could you dare nationalize the canal?" Churchill asked Abdel Nasser antagonistically.

"Did you not learn from Dr. Mohammad Mosaddegh's experience in Iran?"

Abdel Nasser confidently replied, "Dr. Mosaddegh was successful in nationalizing Iranian petroleum reserves, but the United States sacrificed him on the altar and brought the Shah back to power. In return, the United States was promised 40% of Britain's share in Iranian petroleum."

"Are you saying that the United States also sacrificed its own allies elsewhere to secure gains in the Arab world?" De Gaulle asked, pushing his fishing expedition into rather murky waters.

Kennedy sought a life line, and he found one.

"The Eisenhower Doctrine was in full effect in the United States' stance against the aggression."

"Abdel Nasser's victory in successfully nationalizing the canal came as a painful blow to the two old empires of Britain and France," the millionaire said with intense disenchantment.

"It broke the stranglehold both countries had in terms of financial investments in the region, and constituted a direct challenge to foreign hegemony over the third world. It encouraged many such countries to carry out their own liberation movements, the bloodiest of which were the Algerian Revolution and the Guerilla War in Vietnam. Later, with the communist revolution in Cuba the revolutionary spirit had spread even further, crossing the Atlantic and becoming a thorn in the side of the United States."

CHAPTER 28

Appearances can be deceiving

Fierce winds whipped through Egypt, bringing in their midst the Tripartite Aggression that sought to bring about Abdel Nasser's downfall and to retake the Suez Canal. But the will of the Egyptian people to persevere in tandem with the support of the Arab peoples and American and Soviet calculations regarding the Middle East all converged to render the aggression a complete failure. The aggression's impact on Egypt was severe: British and French warplanes and battleships took turns laying entire neighborhoods in the city of Port Said to waste, leaving more than a thousand innocent civilians dead.

"The winds died down, and the aggressors withdrew," the skeleton said.

Churchill found the United States' stance against the joint British-Israeli-French operation to retake the Suez Canal by force quite strange.

"The United States of America abandoned its allies and failed to come to their aid."

"It is you who failed us! You didn't even bother to consult with us about your military operation."

"British Prime Minister Anthony Eden had no viable option but to undertake military action to overthrow Abdel

Nasser, whom he used to call the 'Hitler of the Nile,' and to seize control of the canal."

"That's a new one!" Abdel Nasser said in a sarcastic tone.

"I never heard that one before. These Europeans! It was a political ploy which Eden used to justify the aggression. Thankfully, ended up blowing up in his face and destroying his political career."

The skeleton confirmed:

"Eden resigned after the tripartite campaign failed to produce results."

The skull felt sorry for the fate that befell Eden, yet couldn't help gloating at his misfortune.

"Every battle has its winners and losers, and shattered hopes and ruination are the just due of the losers."

Rabin felt the skull's observation deserved correction.

"Cleverness is to know how to turn a loss into a victory."

"Don't wax philosophical on us, Mr. Smarty Pants!" Hitler grumbled as he interrupted Rabin's ruminations.

"To lose is to be weak, to be defeated. To win is to attain victory."

Gandhi saw things differently.

"Killing civilians is no victory. Rather, it's the greatest loss imaginable."

Rabin insisted on his opinion, drawing on his years of experience on the battlefield.

"We in Israel also went through difficult times. We wanted to benefit the lessons taught by painful defeat. Ben Gurion moved quickly, paying a visit to Paris during which he conducted highlevel negotiations with intelligence and astuteness. Despite the setback in Egypt, Israel used this visit to secure an excellent deal in which the French promised to arm

Israel with the latest and most developed military technology, chief among which was the nuclear reactor in Dimona."

Churchill justified his cooperation with and support for Israel by saying, "The aim of Britain along with France and Israel in mounting the three-way attack on Egypt was to restore their hegemony over the affairs of the Middle East, first by handing Abdel Nasser – and, ipso facto, Egypt – a sound defeat and then by crushing the other liberation movements in the Arab world."

Stalin evaluated the repercussions of the aggression.

"Abdel Nasser emerged triumphant and resilient after the tripartite aggression on Egypt failed to accomplish its aims. In turn, the United States of America succeeded in evicting Britain and France from the region so as to take their place."

Hitler wanted to counter Stalin's analysis by pontificating on what the Soviet Union's intentions might have been in the whole affair.

"The Soviet threat to bomb London and Paris and its stance against the tripartite aggression was a linchpin by which it sought to pave the way for its entry into the Middle East."

"The United States could not allow the Soviets to flaunt their ambitions and go unchecked," Kennedy shot back, "and so it rushed to proclaim the now-famous Eisenhower Doctrine."

Stalin cried out, "It's an imperialistic doctrine par excellence. Congress gave it to Eisenhower on a silver platter in order to give the U.S. a pretext to reign over the Middle East in the name of protecting the latter from the Soviet threat."

Abdel Nasser said, "Both Egypt and Syria rejected the Eisenhower Doctrine because it was a furtive attempt to gain entry into the Middle East under the pretext of fighting communism, the while the U.S.'s real aim was to interfere in the internal affairs of those countries that did not wish to bend to American power. But Lebanon accepted it."

Churchill found an alternative solution.

"Britain moved to strengthen the Baghdad Pact with the aim of finding a chink in Syria's armor that might be used to counter the spread of Arab nationalism."

"Iraq, along with Turkey and Israel, took direct action to paint Syria into a corner," a dazzled Rabin said.

Kennedy, in turn, took to praising Lebanon's stance vis-à-vis the Eisenhower Doctrine.

"The pro-western president of Lebanon Camille Chamoun relied on the Eisenhower Doctrine for support when he called for the United States Sixth Fleet stationed in the Mediterranean to edge closer to Lebanese shores."

"Did Turkey retake control of Syria?" Abdel Hamid asked inquisitively.

"I ordered my army to dispatch an Egyptian navy fleet carrying two entire armed battalions armed to the teeth with heavy weaponry to the port of Latakia," Abdel Nasser responded with great pride.

"This led to a shift in the balance of power in the Middle East." In turn, Churchill said, "I dispatched British armed forces to Jordan to reinforce the siege laid by the members of the Baghdad Pact on Syria."

"What did the Syrians do to break the siege?" the skull asked.

Abdel Nasser calmly responded, "They requested that Egypt agree to a merger that would unite the two countries immediately."

"Accepting unity is a way to increase one's strength."

"In the beginning, I rejected the idea of an immediate unity, and I told the Syrians that I was for unity, but that the matter required study, consultation, and a period of time in order for the idea to mature. In addition, a referendum needed to be held to ensure that both peoples approve. But the Syrians did not allow for the possibility of further delay. The unity government was established, and the two peoples merged to form the 'United Arab Republic.'"

Rabin heard their conversation and whispered loud enough for everyone to hear, "I wish that this never happened, because it placed Israel between a rock and a hard place."

Kennedy drew near unto Rabin to reassure him.

"And this is why the United States rushed to land its troops on Lebanese shores."

The millionaire hummed, "The divergence of interests between thevarious petroleum companies was the primary trigger that contributed to the rise of this United Republic."

The skeleton said from afar, "From what I know, any Arab unity is an obstacle to Western interests."

De Gaulle said reproachfully, "The millionaire seems to have it right, for the American ARAMCO company supported the coup of Husni al-Za'im in Syria in return for his promise that the new Syrian government would ratify the extension of the TAPLINE program. Likewise, the Iraq Petroleum Company based in London supported the coup of Sami al-Hinnawi in exchange for his agreement to extend the oil pipelines into Iraq."

Stalin acknowledged the wisdom of the Syrian decision.

"The Syrians were sick and tired of the endless series of coup attempts that unfolded in their country. These coup attempts were instrumental in throwing them into the lap of Abdel Nasser."

"The mouse fell in the cat's paws," Rabin remarked with caution.

Abdel Nasser heard him, and immediately responded, "Syria is no mouse! The Syrians sacrificed much for this unity!"

"Then the Eisenhower Doctrine must have been defeated, as was the Baghdad Pact!" Hitler cried out in delight.

Abdel Hamid explained the reasons why the Baghdad Pact failed to accomplish its aims:

"The Turks went to sleep one night and woke up the next day to find that their neighbor to the south – though under siege – had grown overnight from a population of six million to thirty six million."

As far as Churchill was concerned, the English knew nothing of despair.

"In response to the formation of the unity government between Egypt and Syria, Feisal II – then the king of Iraq – traveled and met with Hussein, the King of Jordan, and the two agreed to unite the two Arab kingdoms."

Abdel Nasser didn't break a sweat.

"The Hashemite Union fell through in the same year due to a military coup against the Iraqi monarch led by Abdul Salam Arif and Abd al-Karim Qasim."

Rabin spoke as if he were eulogizing at someone's funeral, "Feisal, the king of Iraq, was killed, along with his Prime Minister Nuri al-Sa'id at the hands of those responsible for the coup. The monarchy came to an end, and the Republic of Iraq took it place."

The millionaire smacked his hands with regret, "The oil fields are gone!"

Churchill was livid.

"The West was deeply concerned, fearing that the newfound Republic of Iraq would join the United Arab Republic."

"Abdel Nasser had stirred our anger by standing in solidarity with the Algerian Revolution," De Gaulle said furiously.

"Every cloud has a silver lining," Rabin said with cold nerves.

Abdel Nasser explained, "The Israelis took advantage of France's indignation at Egypt to secure an advanced weapons deal that included a nuclear weapons capacity."

Rabin staunchly replied, "It was our responsibility to increase our strength in order to confront this stalwart Arab resurgence that constituted a direct threat to our very existence."

"The United States's use of nuclear weapons during the Second World War was instrumental in helping to retard the spread of communism."

De Gaulle proceeded to reveal his cards one-by-one with the skill of a seasoned gambler.

"It's in the nature of great powers to create imaginary foes which they can use to cower weaker nations and peoples into submission."

Stalin was impressed with De Gaulle's candor.

"The United States of America painted a frightening picture of a communist menace – with the Soviet Union at its head – at the fringes of western Europe, prepared to wipe it off the map as soon as the opportunity presents itself."

De Gaulle threw down his second card.

"In order to make Europe bow to America's commands."

Hitler said with regret, "The Americans succeeded in sowing fear in the hearts of western Europeans, who willingly deferred to the U.S. as a result of their fears."

De Gaulle rushed to reveal his third card.

"France vigorously refused to give in to the Anglo-Saxons." De Gaulle's statement struck Hitler as peculiar.

"How did you have the gall to depart from the European consensus and stand against dependency to the U.S.?" He asked.

"By virtue of France's rich culture and her vast historical experience," De Gaulle replied.

"France had suffered greatly, more than any other nation, from the vagaries of war, particularly at the hands of the Germans. After Germany fell France saw to it that, in an atmosphere in which fearmongering about the outbreak of new war reigned rampant, that it was in France's interest to pursue peace – and so it worked to push the world in the direction of peace."

"For France to stand in the face of American policy meant risking losing its share in the spoils of World War II," the millionaire warned.

De Gaulle could care less.

"With the war over France has no appetite for other people's property, and it will continue to maintain and strengthen its old ties with the two great powers."

"Appearances can be deceiving," Abdel Nasser muttered to himself.

But then he thought it would be nice to paint De Gaulle into a corner.

"What about the third world countries, particularly the Tripartite Aggression against Egypt in which France participated? Is this your war of expressing your lack of desire for other people's property?

De Gaulle was unnerved.

"You have every right to raise doubts about what I say, Nasser. But I was out of office when the events you mention transpired. As for the push to peace of which I speak, then it was the official policy of the French Fifth Republic which took power after the tripartite aggression."

"What about France's colonies?" The skeleton asked.

"The Fifth Republic thought it proper to afford these nations the respect they deserve by dissolving the colonies and granting the natives their independence, which is what it did."

"Did you try to instigate your fellow Europeans to stand in the face of American hegemony?" Hitler asked, hoping to poison the atmosphere.

"Don't call it instigation. To advocate against war is not instigation. The French respect the American people, but to move in the direction of world peace is an ethical requirement that is in the best interests of all humanity, including the American and Soviet peoples. It was France's responsibility to take up its historic role and lead the way in this matter so as to earn its rightful place among the greats."

The skull said, "Even a plea for peace requires force in order to be heard."

"And money as well."

De Gaulle continued, "What good is all this talk of justice if we weren't able to enforce it? Force protects a nation's laws and freedoms; it is what makes an empire into an empire. Needless to say, all this talk of force is finance-dependent of course."

"What was taken by force cannot be retrieved except by force!" Abdel Nasser shouted angrily.

"Our message of peace was, first and foremost, a European one, for it was Europe that suffered the horrors of war. This was the starting point of an attempt to unite Europe around our message, and I moved to form an alliance of European nations."

Gandhi fied in irritation.

"For once I but wish the voice of reason was heard more loudly than the voice of war."

"Were you successful in your endeavors?" Abdel Hamid asked as he shot a glance of admiration and approval at De Gaulle.

"I, too, was always against war. It is a plague upon all nations, exhausting them and then obliterating them."

De Gaulle moved to reveal his second to last card:

"I succeeded in forming a European Common Market, whose initial six members were France, Italy, Germany, Belgium, Holland and Luxembourg."

Churchill censured and rebuked De Gaulle:

"The Common Market was an exercise in continental isolation, a prospect which Britain deemed unacceptable. The idea must be abandoned at once, as it will get Europe a war that, though initially of an economic nature, might go on and take on a rather ugly character in other facets of life."

"If the countries of western Europe continue to operate on an old-world mindset, then they will never adapt to present realities," De Gaulle said with evident vexation.

"Europe will never have the opportunity to be European."

"That's a wonderful thought – a Europe that is European," Hitler said in agreement.

"It would be even better for Europe to become German."

De Gaulle revealed his final card.

"It is not possible to exclude the German people from the fold of Europe, the many wrongs Germany inflicted on France notwithstanding."

"And the Jews as well," Rabin interrupted.

De Gaulle continued, "We are not against Germany, but we are against German expansionism. I realize that the German people are a mighty nation, ready to rise out of the ashes and to turn its weaknesses into strengths. It might also, if left to its own devices, turn into an outlaw that could cause major trouble for us. It was necessary, then, for us to renew our confidence in her and to welcome her back to the fold by guaranteeing her safety and securing the borders it shared with her neighbors."

Kennedy shot a glance at Churchill and said, "The close relationship between the U.S. and Britain shall remain a model for what true allies look like."

"This sounds like the first nail in your project's coffin," Hitler observed, aiming to provoke De Gaulle.

De Gaulle gloated, "Britain fought long and hard to bring about the demise of the Common Market, and when it failed to disrupt our work Britain requested to join it."

"But why did you not approve their request to join the Market?" Rabin asked, seeking clarification.

"Because it would be a greater threat to our success as an active member, given its designs to disrupt our activities."

Abdel Nasser understood the British strategy.

"You mean they'll try to destroy it from within?"

"That is what I feared, and so I refused with all the strength that I had to permit it to join. With fortitude and determination I resolved to destroy all obstacles that might impede the success of our mission."

The skull looked at De Gaulle and said, "Such a feat requires force as well."

"Force is the primary factor in any successful strategy. From the very beginning I worked to secure France's independence by building up her strength."

"You had no need for such a thing," Kennedy interrupted.

"After all, France was and continues to be a member of the NATO alliance."

Churchill took advantage of Kennedy's objection to say, "I told you that De Gaulle was a stubborn man that would never accept American patronage. That is why he left NATO and formed a close relationship with Germany."

"A wise decision indeed," Hitler said welcomingly.

Churchill objected and said, "How could it be a wise decision when our common enemy, the Soviet Union, sits on a slew of nuclear warheads?"

"That is why I ordered France to develop a nuclear weapons capability."

Stalin said, "Soviet interests intertwined with the American point of view that France be discouraged from producing nuclear weapons."

After counting, adding and subtracting, the millionaire concluded, "Producing nuclear weapons costs a fortune."

Kennedy remarked with astonishment, "The United States of America offered to sell France already made warheads in order to save it some money."

De Gaulle calmly replied, "We willingly accepted that offer, with the express condition that these warheads become France's property and their use being subject to no stipulations or restrictions. But America wanted to impose restrictions on their use."

Abdel Hamid asked De Gaulle, "You did not have enough experience to build the weapon alone. So how were you able to get the job done?"

De Gaulle answered, beaming with pride:

"We decided to move forward with building our nuclear weapons capacity with our own hands. It may be less effective than the Soviet's nuclear capabilities, but it is no matter that my enemy can kill me ten times over when all I need to have is the ability to kill him once. We might not be able to destroy him completely, but the bomb will be able to sever his arm."

"In 1960 France successfully conducted its first nuclear weapons test," the skeleton said with a radio-like voice. "France was now the fifth nation in the world to go nuclear."

De Gaulle breathed a sigh of relief.

"This way, the decision to defend France remained our own." Trapped between disgust and hope, Gandhi said, "I hope one day that the use of weapons becomes a thing of the past, and that international conflict and crises be resolved by means of reasoned dialogue."

Hitler said mockingly, "You dream more often than you should, Gandhi."

The skull was firm in its convictions.

"Power gives one confidence."

De Gaulle added, "France was able to make its mark in world affairs and to restore its dignity after its humiliating defeat by acquiring the bomb."

Gandhi insisted on searching for alternatives to violent conflict.

"Is it not the role of the United Nations to resolve conflict and to implement the principles of its charter?"

Abdel Nasser pointed to the tricks the great powers played in the world arena.

"The Allies, in practice, stood against the implementation of the U.N. Charter, especially as concerned their activities in their colonies. This state of affairs left the colonized peoples no choice but to initiate revolutions to secure their independence with their own hands."

Stalin expressed his support for these revolutionary movements, saying, "The liberation movements spread throughout the world – into Asia, Africa, and Latin America - as a result of increased political consciousness and the suffocating brutality of colonial power."

With unconcealed malice Kennedy said, "The nations of the third world attribute the causes of their decline to colonialism, the while they for hundreds of years sat atop an ocean of natural resources that they were unable to extract and put to use. Everyone knows that the West needed primary materials for its manufacturing facilities. Were it not for the fact that they went to the source where these materials could be found and extracted them there would be no way for the world to reach the developed state it finds itself in today. Cars need metal, planes need aluminum and other minerals, the missiles which pierce our skies need uranium, and every factory and workshop needs petroleum. The West is responsible for the development and leisure everyone the world over enjoys, and yet all anyone ever hears is about how colonialism is so bad!"

Stalin was infuriated.

"This is twisted, reprehensible logic! That the natives lacked the know-how to extract their resources for themselves does not justify their exploitation and torture. These nations rose to take back their rights and attain their freedom and independence, and for this reason the Soviet Union supported these revolutions."

"Yes, you supported these nations under the pretext of fighting for freedom and independence, but what you really aimed to do was to take them under your wing and impose your repressive mode of government on them," Churchill quipped.

"Just take a look at the Eastern European countries, for instance."

Stalin forcefully replied, "Not true at all! The Soviet Union backed liberation movements all over the world – we stood by the nations that fought for their freedom and contributed to helping them develop their economies. Many of the countries we helped were not necessarily ruled by a communist party: in Egypt, after the West tried to stall the construction of the Aswan Dam and tied their support for it to stipulations that undermined Egypt's independence, we helped the Egyptians build the Dam even though at the time Nasser was busy throwing members of the Egyptian Communist Party into his prisons. None of that prevented us from helping the Egyptian revolution."

Rabin fired back, "The West is not as awful as you picture it to be, Mr. Stalin. The West stood by the side of the Jewish people and the state of Israel with everything they had. The United States even allocates a portion of its budget to providing economic and military support to most of the nations of the third world, including Egypt."

"France did not bat an eye at standing by the peoples of its former colonies – the 'Francophone Nations' – and assisting them in their development," De Gaulle asserted.

"Pushed out the Door, Back in from the Window," Nasser scoffed.

Kennedy said, "Everything the communists put their hands on turns to ruins. Take, for instance, the enthusiastic coverage Castro's revolution got in the American news media in 1959. I remember very well how the American television networks extolled the guerillas led by Castro as they overran the city of Havana and took down the Batista dictatorship."

"Guerilla warfare always made me nervous. Tell me what you know about that war?" The skull asked intriguingly.

Abdel Nasser knew the leaders of that revolution well.

"The plot to undertake revolution began in Mexico in 1955. Che Guevara met Fidel Castro and his comrades while they were imprisoned there. Fidel Castro saw that the revolutionaries were in need of a leader, and that he had found his man in Che. They became close friends soon after, and following their release from prison they walked the path of revolution together. They made their way to the Cuban mountains where the revolutionaries set up their encampments. The mountains were a launching point for armed attacks against Batista's army and, in spite of a few setbacks, they continued their struggle with resilience, conviction and obstinacy until victory was theirs."

CHAPTER 29
A Shoe Flies at the U.N.

In the second half of 1960 the United States of America – both its government and its people – were preoccupied with the presidential elections, which are held every four years. A certain apathy towards foreign policy and international relations prevails during these times. Tensions were flaring between the Republican and Democratic parties, and the race became increasingly heated as the year started to unwind. Ample use was made of the twin weapons of money and media coverage, and the two candidates were actively campaigning for votes in every state, each of them trying to woo voters to their platform. It had always been Mr. Joseph Kennedy's dream that one of his sons attain high office, and when he lost his eldest son he put all his hopes in his next oldest son, Mr. John Kennedy, who entered into the presidential fray as a candidate for the Democratic Party opposite Mr. Richard Nixon, his opponent and the candidate of the Republican Party.

John Kennedy walked in the way of his predecessor, President Eisenhower, unlike Khrushchev who turned away from the legacy of Stalin and broke off from Stalin's path.

Stalin was rather upset about this, overtaken with rage by Khrushchev's behavior.

"That uncultured peasant! I helped him rise to the upper echelons of the political order. That ingrate!"

"It's a sin to do a good deed for someone who doesn't deserve it," Abdel Hamid said, condoling with Stalin.

"It was my mistake, which I now regret. I am convinced that everyone reaps what they show, except when it comes to helping people: if you give someone shoes to walk with they begin to step all over you."

Gandhi objected to Stalin's cynical outlook.

"A good tree bears good fruit."

De Gaulle remarked, "True, but the seeds of a good tree will fail to bear fruit if planted in concrete. It needs fertile soil, supervision, water, fertilizer, and great care."

Gandhi continued, "Such is the case with world peace as well: a good politician is similar to a successful farmer."

The skull was incensed.

"Begone with all this talk about farmers and their fields! Were diplomatic overtures sufficient to achieve peace and end the Cold War?"

De Gaulle responded optimistically, "We had much reason for hope in this respect, and that world peace was at hand by means of dialogue and understanding, especially after Khrushchev's two successful visits to the United States and France."

"This is delightful news!" Gandhi said, brimming with hope.

"I imagine that the entire world was happy to learn of the rapprochement between the Eastern and Western blocs."

The skeleton replied with sorrow, "The Chinese were not pleased with this rapprochement. Mao Tzedong condemned Khrushchev's visit to the West, calling him a capitalist and imperialist and accused him of betraying the principles of Leninism and Marxism which call for capitalism to be destroyed."

Stalin was furious with the Chinese.

"Khrushchev accused them of intellectual stagnation, leading to an impasse in relations between the two countries. The Chinese then moved in the direction of self-reliance."

"Perhaps the impasse might lead to internecine war between the two major powers of the Socialist camp," the skull surmised with glee.

"The world may be on the brink of a new world war!"

De Gaulle was irate with the skull's faulty logic.

"Take it easy, General. You seem too eager to go to war."

The skull took a spin around the gathered men and then said intently, "You gave us the Cold War, a war lacking in flavor and taste, dull and uneventful. I'm an action kind of guy – strategizing, warplanes pounding enemy positions, missiles and artillery shells everywhere!"

"Would that the rat remained stuck in your head so that we might be relieved from having to listen to this nonsense!" Gandhi interrupted angrily.

Abdel Nasser tapped his hand on Gandhi's thigh softly so as not to break him in two.

"Leave him be, Gandhi. It seems as if the nail that was rammed in the back of his head turned his mind into mush."

De Gaulle steered the conversation back to the diplomatic course.

"It was agreed that a Four Powers Summit would be convened at the Elysee Palace in Paris."

"The aforementioned summit was a disaster," the skeleton confirmed, drawing on official press releases.

"Khrushchev was the one who made it a disaster!" Kennedy objected.

"Further investigation will reveal that in actuality it was the United States who is responsible for the summit's failure," Stalin replied sternly.

Churchill was embarrassed.

"It's true, unfortunately. The Soviet Union had good reason to be upset this time."

De Gaulle opened the notebook containing his memoirs and read, "On the First of May, the curtains parted to reveal a skeevy plot that well-nigh shattered the summit's chances of succeeding. The Russians had shot down an American spy plane flying over the Soviet Union's airspace and captured the pilot. It was, without a doubt, an outrageous violation at a most inopportune moment."

"The fact of the matter is the plane had accidentally gone of course," Kennedy rejoined.

"The White House announced that it had taken the necessary steps to ensure that such missions shall not recur."

"The Americans are the kind of crowd to rob you and then send you a letter of apology," Hitler cracked.

"Was the summit held?" Abdel Hamid asked.

De Gaulle looked into his notebook.

"Khrushchev was the first to speak at the summit's opening day. He insisted that the United States take the initiative and admit responsibility for its belligerence, condemn the act in question, make the necessary apologies and hold the officials responsible for that violation to account, without which no further cooperation would be possible."

Hitler pursed his lips.

"These are incendiary preconditions designed to bring about the failure of the summit."

Stalin angrily replied, "This is a matter that touches on the Soviet Union's honor and dignity!"

Abdel Hamid wanted to speed things up a bit.

"How did the summit end?"

"Before day's end Khrushchev shouted out, 'What devil made the Americans do this despicable act?'" De Gaulle answered.

"You allow us to be insulted in your own home!" Kennedy told De Gaulle, reproaching him.

"I immediately noted that there are plenty of devils in the world who cause mischief."

Hitler sought to agitate things further.

"It's true what you say about devils and their temperaments. Why, how else might we explain the fiasco at the plenary meeting of the United Nations General Assembly, where Khrushchev flouted diplomatic convention with his shenanigans?"

Stalin defended his comrade, "Every action has a reaction. The head of Philippine's delegation to the United Nations, Lorenzo Sumulong, accused the Soviet Union of colonizing the Eastern European countries."

"What happened after that?" Hitler asked provocatively.

"You were there, Nasser. Why don't you tell us?"

"Khrushchev responded by accusing the Filipino delegate of being an American puppet."

Nasser fell silent, but Hitler liked to see things through to the end.

"Why did you pause? Go on, give us a good picture of what happened at this event – and what a splendid event it was!"

Continued silence. Nasser refuses to respond.

"Khrushchev took off his shoe and began waving it in the air," Hitler continued.

"Then he started slamming it on the desk in front of him. The President of the United Nations General Assembly broke his hammer after slamming it repeatedly while attempting to get Romania's Foreign Minister to quiet down. The delegates in attendance began to rush out of the room amidst the ensuing chaos."

"The next day Khrushchev's shoe was on the front pages of all the major newspapers," the skeleton continued.

Abdel Nasser sought to divert attention from the Khrushchev matter.

"The United Nations accepted 13 new nations as member states. . ."

"Indeed, the year 1960 was rightfully called 'the year of independence,' as more than twenty African nations attained their independence in that year," the skull said.

"Khrushchev indicted the Americans for their racism," Stalin gloated. "He said in his speech, 'They are here celebrating the entry of African nations in to the U.N., the while the delegates of these countries can't find a single hotel in New York willing to take them in."

Churchill exclaimed, "There was a time when we thought that Stalin was the only megalomaniac from Russia we'd have to put up with. Khrushchev proved himself even more insane than Stalin was!"

Stalin confidently replied, "How foolish the West is! Anyone who defends the freedom of the weaker nations and struggles against colonialism and exploitation with the aim of protecting his nation, ideology and belief system is dubbed by them as evil and insane, fit only for a mental institution, or, worse, assassination. Is there anything more repulsive, more insane than this?"

Kennedy said, "When I took the oath of office, there were many urgent matters that I needed to attend to on the homefront, as well as a string of thorny ongoing crises on the international agenda. I preferred to deal with matters swiftly and effectively, and despite the many obstacles I decided to work for justice, for freedom and for progress."

Gandhi empathized with Kennedy's sheer sense of responsibility.

"To lead a country of enormous weight, power and esteem like the United States requires a man who is wise, patient, and responsible."

"The United States' willingness to back the attempt of Cuban exiles to invade and seize control of Cuba ended up being a boost for the socialist countries."

"Are you referring to the Bay of Pigs operation?" the millionaire asked.

"Yes, that's right, the Bay of Pigs."

Gandhi had trouble believing what he was hearing.

"How could an attempt to bring down the revolution be a boost to the socialist countries?"

Stalin smiled.

"The failed attempt to take the island led Castro to declare Cuba a socialist state. The communists were now in power in the heart of the Americas."

"The enemy of my enemy is my friend," Abdel Hamid witticized.

Hitler explained the game the Soviets were playing.

"The U.S.'s backing of the Cuban exiles in their effort to invade the island forced Castro into the arms of the Soviet Union."

Abdel Nasser added, "The failure of the operation gave the Cuban revolutionaries renewed confidence in themselves. It became clear to Castro and his comrades that the United States was an enemy that sought to bring about the revolution's downfall, and they rained down hard on American companies and interests in the country."

Kennedy was in low spirits.

"Castro had the nerve to rip the mutual defense pact between Cuba and the United States to shreds. He even demanded we evacuate from Guantanamo Bay."

Stalin broke out in uproarious laughter, so much so that his eyes began to well with tears.

"What are you laughing at, Stalin?" Churchill asked with genuine curiosity.

Stalin continued laughing.

"Let us in on the joke."

"I'm laughing at the Americans' insolent behavior. They think they are so intelligent, more so than others," Stalin replied as he wiped the tears from his eyes.

"They move to overthrow Castro and then are outraged that he would rip the mutual defense treaty in response. Is this not laughable? Mutual defense against whom? Against whom, Mr. Kennedy?"

"Against our common enemies, of course."

Stalin was irate.

"Don't you mean your enemies? Those who stand against your interests?"

Abdel Nasser explained the Cuban position to those in attendance:

"The United States' participation in the attack is sufficient cause for immediate nullification of the pact."

"It is the right of every nation to defend and protect its interests," Kennedy asserted. "Did not the Soviet Union tear the city of Berlin in half and build the now infamous wall that stood between east and west?"

"The wall was necessary to halt the flight of East Germans to the western parts of the city," Stalin replied.

"They were fleeing the state of poverty, fear and repression that the communists had built. They yearned to finally enjoy the promise of freedom and democracy in the Western world," the millionaire said.

"The capitalist world, the world of exploitation, and of greed!" Stalin scoffed.

"I used to tell people, 'Anyone who thinks communism is so wonderful should go see Berlin,'" Kennedy rejoined.

"Every system has its faults," Gandhi said, drowning in his sorrows.

"The socialists claim their aim is to liberate the peasants and the workers from oppression, and yet their leaders were the most severe dictators. The capitalists speak of freedom, democracy and human rights, all the while they deprive the third world of their most basic rights. People in that part of the world have lost their humanity, becoming mere numbers, parts of a cog – not to mention the rampant racism against blacks. The long legacy of slavery is a sufficient indicator that something is wrong with that system."

Kennedy said, "The United States took a progressive step forward when, in 1862, President Abraham Lincoln officially declared the emancipation of all slaves in confederate territory."

"Some law," Stalin shot back hysterically.

"Mere ink on a page," Abdel Nasser added.

"Despite that law racial discrimination persisted against blacks, who continued to be deprived of their basic rights," Stalin continued.

"The front seats in passenger buses were white only, and blacks were prohibited from entering the bus from the front," Abdel Nasser added.

"Blacks were also required to give priority seating to whites when the bus was full. Any violation of these rules meant police involvement, which in turn meant imprisonment."

"Did the blacks respond violently to these measures?" the skull asked.

"Fortunately, nonviolence was the school of thought adopted by Mr. Martin Luther King, leader of the movement against racial discrimination in the U.S.," Gandhi replied proudly.

"The movement began in 1963. I am one of the great admirers of the tremendous historical speech he gave in front of the Lincoln Memorial, in which he said: 'I have a dream that my four little children will one day live in a nation where they will not be judged by the color of their skin but by the content of their character.'"

Kennedy said, "The United States supported the freedom and independence of the colonized nations, as well as their right to self-determination, including that of the African nations."

Hitler replied mockingly:

"It would be wise for the Americans to clean house first by granting freedom to the blacks in their midst before they go about supporting independence movements in Africa."

"But it is most certainly the right of all nations to determine their affairs for themselves," De Gaulle said.

"But many French restaurants posted signs that read 'No Dogs or Blacks,'" Gandhi replied, flustered.

"Is there anything more humiliating, more disgraceful for a human being than to be treated as such?"

De Gaulle agreed in principle with Gandhi.

"In the end, we righted our wrongs: France went about granting the African nations their independence, a first practical step in the path of affirming the right of all peoples to self-determination."

"Britain acted likewise, withdrawing from Cyprus and granting it independence," Churchill said.

Abdel Hamid sighed with relief.

"Finally, freedom's sun has risen, and the colonized nations can finally bathe in its warm rays. . ."

"Wait a minute, Sultan!" Abdel Nasser interrupted.

"France did not grant Algeria her independence as a token of friendship!"

De Gaulle objected to the tone of Abdel Nasser's remarks.

"I myself announced Algeria's independence live on television in 1962!"

"But first a million and a half Algerians had to sacrifice their lives as martyrs!" Abdel Nasser interrupted again.

"They fought for their independence for eight long years, with the help of their neighbors and their Arab brethren in Tunisia and Morocco, Egypt, Syria and Iraq. This is not to mention the support they received from the communist countries, and in particular the Soviet Union and Cuba, as well as other third-world nations."

"Algeria was a unique case," De Gaulle responded, "because of it's proximity to France and the fact that our citizens grew attached to it."

"Its rich gas and petroleum reserves were attractive as well," the millionaire added.

"Did Algeria end up joining the United Arab Republic after independence?" Abdel Hamid asked.

Abdel Nasser was downcast.

"Unfortunately, the enemies of Arab unity were successful in causing Syria to secede from the union with Egypt. And with that, the beautiful dream of Arab unity was lost."

Rabin chuckled on the inside. Israel was now rid of an imminent danger to its existence.

CHAPTER 30
Who Rules the World?

The repeated attempts to bring about Nasser's downfall and evict him from power continued unabated, in some instances by trying to prop up a substitute to lead the Arab world, in others by plotting coups against his rule. If all else failed, they were ready to have him physically removed by means of assassination.

He irritated France with his support for the Algerian revolution, and angered Britain when its attempt to seize control of the Suez Canal failed. Israel felt threatened by his attempts to secure weapons from the Eastern bloc and to build a strong national army. The Arab world was at a boiling point, and he was an obstinate believer in the Arab nation and their right to liberation. He was in dire need of international support, and so he strove to maintain strong ties with the socialist countries, and worked actively with the Non-Aligned movement of which he was an integral part. He was the voice of the Arabs on the world stage. He also strived for friendly relations with the United States in the form of an exchange of letters between himself and President John F. Kennedy, but his increased strength was perceived by the Americans as a threat to their ability to control the oilfields in the Arabian Gulf.

The secession of the Northern Region (Syria) from the United Arab Republic in 1961 was a smack in the forehead to Abdel Nasser. His face began to pour with sweat, and his temperature flared. Gandhi approached him with a piece of cloth that had been dampened with cold water in his hands.

"You look like you might have a fever," Gandhi said gently.

"Let me help you."

Gandhi placed the wet cloth on Abdel Nasser's forehead.

"The enemies of Arab unity are the real pain," he replied.

Gandhi dampened the cloth with water a second time as he made his best efforts to bring down Nasser's temperature.

"The Arabs are very good at blaming others for their mistakes," De Gaulle said.

Abdel Nasser threw the wet cloth off his forehead and sat up straight.

"And what mistakes did we blame you for?"

Churchill began to rant, "'Colonialism is the reason for our backwardness! Colonialism is the cause of ignorance, illiteracy, poverty, disease! Everything that ails the Arabs is colonialism's fault. If a barren woman is unable to bear child, then colonialism is to blame!"

Abdel Nasser rejoined, "Was colonialism not behind the breakup of the unity between Egypt and Syria?"

Kennedy replied, "The abandonment of democratic principles, poor administration, the forced dissolution of political parties, in addition to the neighboring countries' not taking kindly to the unity – all of this brought about the secession that seems to be the cause of your fever."

Abdel Hamid agreed with the import of Kennedy's assessment.

"That is why Saudi Arabia and Jordan backed the military coup against the unity government. Both deemed the united republic a major threat to their monarchical regimes."

The millionaire held in his hand a calculator which he made ample use of prior to expressing an opinion on any given issue.

"Threatening someone's source of livelihood is like playing with fire. Nasser's nationalization of the canal and agricultural reform policies stirred the landowners and factory owners to conspire against the united republic."

Stalin contemplated the relationship between capitalism and the means and tools of production.

"It's true. When the wealthy elite sense that their hold on capital is in peril they become ferocious beasts and start baring their fangs. The measures Castro took vis-à-vis the American capitalist enterprises as well as his demand that Guantanamo Bay be returned to Cuban sovereignty drew the ire of the United States."

"This Castro is a madman. . .I'm sure of it!" The skull scoffed.

"What leverage does a small island have against a major world power?"

Stalin replied, "He appealed for help from the Soviet Union, which rushed to his side."

"They must have had an ulterior motive in responding to Cuba's appeal for help," Hitler cynically observed.

De Gaulle knew what that motive was.

"The Soviet Union took Fidel Castro's invitation as a pretext to deploy Soviet military forces to Cuba."

Kennedy seemed to be upset.

"The purpose of this deployment was crystal clear: to harass the United States by situating their armed forces so close to America's doorstep. We immediately commenced military preparations in the Caribbean Sea pursuant to Operation Ortsac."

"That's 'Castro' spelled backwards," Churchill muttered.

De Gaulle added, "The Soviet Union was intent on posing a threat to the United States. That became eminently clear in 1962, when the Soviet Union installed 40 missiles containing nuclear warheads in Cuba."

Stalin said, "The Soviet Union denied the existence of such missiles in Cuba, and countered by accusing the United States of having belligerent intentions and engaging in unwarranted aggression against the southern and western cities of the Soviet Union by installing its ballistic missiles in the Turkish city of Izmir."

"Shame on the Turks! How could they allow foreign missiles on their soil?" Abdel Hamid said angrily.

"You ought to be grateful to the United States for installing those missiles in Turkey," Kennedy said reassuringly, "as they protected Turkey from a Soviet Communist invasion."

"Did the Soviet Union succeed in getting those missiles to Cuba?" the skull asked inquisitively.

De Gaulle replied, "American U2 spy planes were able to locate the missile bases on Cuban soil."

Rabin took the opportunity to sing the praises of the United States.

"But President Kennedy refused to tolerate the existence of these missiles or to back down in the face of Soviet threats to America's security."

"The faceoff between the United States and Cuba – or, more aptly, the Communist world – was predetermined by destiny," Kennedy opined calmly.

"Our destiny is to take these challenges head on, and so it was. I ordered the men of our armed forces to prepare to strike in the heart of the Soviet Union."

The skeleton had been pacing around in the main hall of the catacomb. Upon hearing Kennedy's observation he grinded to a halt and observed with cautious interest:

"The crisis between these two giants has reached a breaking point."

"Were you intent on going through with your threat, Kennedy?" Hitler asked with genuine curiosity.

Before answering the question Kennedy glanced at everyone's faces, and then called on the skull, who was busy imitating the swinging gait in the skeleton's walk.

"Come closer, skull, if you don't mind."

The skull nervously moved to the center of the hall.

"I simply wanted to get your advice on something," Kennedy reassured the skull.

"Please share your honest opinion with us."

The nervousness disappeared from the skull's face.

"Go on, then," he said with collectedness.

"I'm all ears."

"The Russians broke into my home under the cover of darkness without my permission. What should I do?"

The skull exulted in its own sense of importance. It stared into space and went back into the distant past, the days when it was a General, contemplating war tactics, planning for battle and leading his battalions and warships to in a bid to crush the enemy.

"You must lay siege to them, and take the war to their doorstep with whatever means are available to you, even declare a third world war if need be."

"And so I did," Kennedy said with conviction.

Abdel Hamid asked, "Did you ignite World War III, Mr. Kennedy?"

"Look at the ease with which you all throw around the word 'war!'" Gandhi said with sorrow.

"Wasn't the crisis resolved by means of diplomacy and reasoned dialogue?"

De Gaulle answered, "Khrushchev responded to Kennedy by saying, 'We and you ought not to pull on the ends of a rope with which you have tied the knots of war.'"

Abdel Hamid pursed his lips and nodded his head, saying, "I admire diplomacy and dialogue."

But Churchill was delighted at the Soviet Union's retreat.

"The Russians dismantled their missiles and withdrew from the Americas. The intruders had left Kennedy's 'home.'"

Stalin interrupted to defend the wisdom of the Soviet decision. "But the Soviets took the keys to the house with them, as they secured the American administration's promise not to attempt an overthrow of the Cuban regime."

The skull asked, "What was next for Cuba?"

Kennedy replied, "We imposed tight economic sanctions on Cuba in hopes of securing its surrender."

Gandhi whispered to himself, "They punish a million human beings because they have an issue with one man named Castro."

Hitler was not impressed with the United States's position in its negotiations with the Soviet Union about Cuba.

"Why did you agree not to overthrow Castro?" He asked Kennedy with disdain.

"Cuba is but a small child whose games annoy the neighbors," Kennedy said with a confidence befitting a strong man.

"Our biggest concern at the time was to solidify our control over East Asia and to stop the spread of communism to the countries that neighbored the Soviet Union and China."

The skeleton said, "Do you mean North Korea and Vietnam?"

De Gaulle expressed his disappointment in Kennedy.

"I advised Kennedy not to get involved in Vietnam, but he did not heed my warning. Instead, he doubled the number of military advisors he had in southern Vietnam."

"That's how it always begins," Abdel Nasser observed. "First, you bring in the advisors, and before you know it you have a fullfledged military presence."

Kennedy responded, "I took De Gaulle's concerns into account. But the United States' entry into Vietnam was an ineluctable necessity. We needed to protect those nations that aspire for freedom in Asia. The presence of the Soviet Union and China was more than we could tolerate."

"The Soviet Union shall remain a thorn in your side," Stalin cried out.

"In fact, you are in great need of us. You need us to cower other nations into submission and to justify your interventions in other nation's affairs."

"The thorn will pierce your hands only if you let it," Gandhi blurted out, piquing everyone's interest.

Abdel Nasser leaped with delight.

"That is precisely what ended up happening! Those nations that aspired for freedom rose with everything they had to foil intervention attempts by foreign powers. They grabbed their rifles and fought oppression and exploitation in Cuba, Nicaragua, Algeria and the African continent. . .and in Vietnam as well."

Rabin withdrew from the conversation, but first he said, "What I fear the most is that the Palestinians might read this novel."

Abdel Hamid reacted as if he were bitten by a snake.

"I too fear that the Armenians might read it."

Abdel Nasser was visibly upset.

"A novel simply encapsulates volition. A thorn can cause one's hands to bleed if one is not careful."

"Rather it is the heart that bleeds," Gandhi said, correcting Nasser's misconceptions, "and the nation licks its wounds."

The skull asked with intrigue, "Were the Vietnamese able to persevere in the face of advanced weaponry?"

"The Vietnamese made up their mind to create their own destiny," Abdel Nasser responded with verve.

"De Gaulle was right to advise Kennedy not to get involved in Vietnam. His advice is that of a wise, reasonable, thinking man. The United States paid the price of the invasion in blood."

"I understand the obstinacy of warriors," De Gaulle said, resting his back on his chair.

Kennedy's assessment was based on different criteria.

"The American soldier is a tenacious fighter, armed to the teeth with advanced weaponry. Resistance is futile."

Abdel Nasser continued, "A nation's resolve and her will to fight are more powerful than any weapon. When anyone tries to rob her of her dignity, she sheds tears that are heard loud and clear. The mountains roar, the stones turn into bombs, and the jungles summon the trees and plants to battle. Then comes the humans, who are at the forefront. All the nation's capabilities merge and become one whole intent on wiping away their nation's precious tears. Beware! Beware, oppressors of the world! When the national spirit awakens and resolves upon resistance, then you've already lost."

De Gaulle folded his fingers behind his head.

"The Americans got bogged down in the Vietnamese swamp," he said, relaxed.

Hitler roared with laughter.

"The French took a beating not too long ago, and now it's the Americans' turn."

"When waging an attack, the Vietcong would pop out of the ground like a mole animal with a knife or a spear in their hand," Stalin said, describing the courageousness of the Vietnamese resistance.

"They'd grab the American soldiers off guard, kill them and disappear without a trace into a series of elaborate tunnels set up throughout the jungle. The entrances were camouflaged with leaves and branches, making it difficult for the soldiers to locate the enemy after the attack was over."

Churchill was outraged by how highly Stalin held the Vietcong in his account.

"The Vietnamese relied upon deception, appearing unexpectedly out of nowhere. The American soldier, already bewildered by the death of his fellow soldier, would become paralyzed by the feeling that his turn was next. His morale would collapse, and his waking moments felt like a dream, or, better yet, a horrific nightmare. It was as if he were facing off against the ghosts he used to read about in his storybooks as a child or that his grandmother would tell stories about as he lay in his warm bed before bedtime."

Abdel Nasser picked up one of De Gaulle's books and started waiving it around.

"Novels are no longer mere fiction - they are a form of truth telling, in a sense. The resistance mounted by the Vietnamese became a model for all nations that yearned for liberation. The Vietcong were in high spirits. Their goal was clear: to expel the Americans, liberate their land, and re-unite the two Vietnams."

Rabin re-joined the conversation.

"Perhaps it might share the same fate as the unity between Egypt and Syria," he waxed sardonically.

"The failure of a first attempt by no means entails the abandonment of the objective," Nasser said, challenging Rabin's assertion to the contrary.

"Was there ever a repeat attempt to unite with Syria?" Abdel Hamid asked.

"I always knew that there is strength in unity. I received a request for help from Field Marshal Abdullah al-Sallal, leader of the Yemeni revolution in 1962 against Imam al-Badr. Intervention in Yemen offered the possibility of reviving the movement for Arab unity, and I saw in the liberation of Yemen a necessary step in the effort to defeat Zionism."

Rabin called out for help, "Do you hear what Nasser is saying? He still wants to drive us into the sea!"

"But that's not what he said," Stalin insisted.

Rabin was adamant in his response.

"This is what Nasser desires – this is what all Arabs desire! He sent the Egyptian army into Yemen and seized control of the Red Sea, including the Straits of Tiran, with the aim of closing in on us. He committed seventy thousand troops to the mission."

Abdel Nasser lit up a cigarette.

"The Zionist entity is an alien presence in our region," he said with agitation.

"They expelled a portion of the Palestinian people from their lands. It is racist and expansionist to the core – it's slogan is 'Your borders, dear Israel, extend from the Nile to the Euphrates.'"

Gandhi was outraged by how heated the exchange had gotten between the two men.

"You two say that you are cousins, but all I see is you two fighting like Indian roosters. Why don't you two just make up and spare us the heartache?"

Rabin rose to Israel's defense:

"Nasser's belligerent intentions towards Israel are manifest and deeply rooted. At the first meeting of the Arab League – which was convened in Cairo in 1964 – he called for the establishment of the Palestine Terror Organization."

"It's the Palestine Liberation Organization, an umbrella group for a variety of Palestinian factions, the most prominent of which was the 'Fatah' movement."

"Afarem!" Abdel Hamid said in Turkish.

"Well done, Nasser! You've done a heroic job in establishing this Fatah movement with the goal of expelling the Jews."

"Actually," Abdel Nasser replied, "I had nothing to do with it: it was Yasser Arafat who established this movement along with three of his colleagues in 1959, the year in which the Palestinian national liberation movement was born. They called their movement 'Fatah,' which was an abbreviation of the words 'Palestine Liberation Movement,' in Arabic, written backwards."

Rabin was furious.

"The official headquarters of the Palestine Liberation Organization was in Cairo, which demonstrates Nasser's belligerent intentions towards Israel."

De Gaulle asked Rabin, "How was Israel able to break free from this blockade?"

"We, of course, have France and the United States to thank for that," Rabin replied gratefully.

"The two of them approved our request to purchase weapons that Israel was in dire need of. We strategized long and hard. Our aim was to take our neighbors by surprise. When the opportunity for war presented itself in 1967, Israel launched a surprise attack against Egyptian military air bases by means of fighter jets that flew at low altitudes. We were able to completely destroy some 85% of the enemy's warplanes, which were just sitting out there in the open waiting for us. With 40% of his troops bogged down in Yemen, Israel taught Nasser a lesson he would not forget."

Churchill was elated.

"Israel's seizure of the Suez Canal helped Britain to regain some of its lost glory. I am certain that Mr. Eden was delighted to hear the news."

"What befell Israel's other neighbors?" the skull asked passionately.

"We occupied the Golan Heights and seized control of the Syrian part of Mount Hermon," Rabin said with a tone of self-congratulation.

"We took the West Bank from Jordan, including the city of Jerusalem."

"It was a pulverizing victory which drew the world's attention to how strong Israel was and how weak the Arabs were," Kennedy said.

Stalin decided to make an observation about Israel's victory, "Crucial to the attainment of this victory was the Western world's support for Israel. The United States, eager to protect its interests in the Middle East, transformed its friendship with Israel into an alliance, and began funneling large sums to it in the form of aid grants."

Kennedy responded, "The Soviet Union's expansion into Cuba and Africa, as well as its backing of the Vietcong, drove the Americans to form that alliance to halt the expansion of the Soviet Union into the Arab world."

"Congratulations, Stalin," De Gaulle said.

"The Soviet Union has become the scapegoat the Americans needed to justify their intervention in world affairs."

Kennedy expressed his displeasure with De Gaulle.

"This must be why you withdrew from the NATO alliance in 1966."

De Gaulle replied coolly, "I withdrew because the Soviet Union no longer posed a threat to Europe, and because Europe was no longer in need of American financial support."

Abdel Nasser held his head in shame.

"I accepted responsibility for our defeat in 1967. I tendered my resignation and abdicated whatever official positions I held."

Hitler clapped his hands and said, "I admire your sense of responsibility. It befits a noble leader who loses a battle or a war to either abandon power or commit suicide."

The skeleton approached Abdel Nasser and placed his hand on Nasser's shoulder comfortingly.

"But the Egyptian people did not accept their leader's resignation. Everyone - big or small, man or woman, peasant or laborer, even the elderly and children - went to the streets and chanted, 'Nasser! Nasser!'"

Rabin found the skeleton's words of dubious value.

"Why not say that the State Security Investigations Service and the deep state were the ones who went into the streets and chanted for Nasser's return in order to provide cover for his defeat? This is the game that dictators play, they dupe the world into believing that they have popular support and that their strangehold on power is in line with the dictates of democracy."

Abdel Nasser objected, "If all our adversaries are like you, Rabin, then the world shall never know peace and stability," he said in a sad tone.

"You are a greater danger to humanity than any earthquake or volcanic eruption."

Abdel Hamid was vexed from learning of the Arabs' defeat in a war that caught them off guard and led to a loss of even more of their territory.

"What did the Palestine Liberation Organization do, having now lost its homeland in its entirety?"

The skeleton answered, "Its main headquarters was relocated to Amman, where its forces deployed along the border with the West Bank."

Rabin found the whole matter quite puzzling.

"As the Arabs themselves say, 'God's Earth is vast!' They have a wide range of territory. They have enough territory for themselves! I don't understand why they are so mesmerized with this little strip of land on which the Jews decided to build their national homeland?"

Abdel Nasser rose to his feet and wagged his finger threateningly.

"It is true that the Arab is, by his nature, gracious and hospitable, but not when his guest attempts to steal his land from under him and force him out of it. You call this your homeland - no Arab who has a shred of dignity can accept this claim of yours!"

Abdel Hamid appeared nervous.

"Didn't the Arabs resist these usurpers?"

"I ordered the Egyptian army to withdraw from Yemen. The army was successful in carrying out brave and courageous attacks against the Zionist entity. The affair came to be known as the 'war of attrition.' The enemy made light of the Palestinian resistance factions, and the Israeli army in 1968 attempted to wipe them out at once. They were confronted by all of the Palestinian factions, side by side with the Arab Army of Jordan, whose artillery canons successfully halted a new Israeli advance from crossing the Jordan River."

The skeleton added, "The Arab Army of Jordan's military command issued its fifth communique, which read in part, 'Our forces continue to engage the enemy in fierce battle along the frontlines. The battle is currently being fought using light weaponry in the village of Karameh, where the enemy's losses in terms of lives and equipment have been severe.'"

Abdel Nasser cried ecstatically, "The Arabs were determined to wipe away the shame of defeat, and despite the differences between the fedayeen and the Jordanian authorities the two fought side by side under the battle cry, 'Every rifle shall be aimed at Israel.'"

Rabin said with a pout, "Israel lost that battle and for the first time since the beginning of the Arab-Israeli conflict we sustained heavy losses in terms of men. We were forced to leave many of our killed behind on the battlefield, along with a number of our military vehicles. But the cooperation between the Palestinian factions and the Jordanian government shall not last: each of them will want to take exclusive credit for the victory. It is worth mentioning here as well that Israel was very pleased with the numerous failed attempts the Palestinians made on Jordanian King Hussein ibn Talal's life."

"Why would you be pleased by the king's survival though he handed you a defeat in the Battle of Karameh?" the skeleton asked simplemindedly.

"That is how politics works, you dimwit!" Rabin replied.

"The king felt threatened by the PLO, and this pushed him to move to expel the PLO from Jordan in order to regain his sovereignty. And that is where our interests met."

Abdel Hamid was listening attentively.

"Unfortunately, what Rabin envisions is true," he said.

"Perhaps Israel is behind the attempts on the King's life, and the blame was pinned on the Palestinians in order to stir the flames of conflict between them."

Hitler agreed with Abdel Hamid's opinion.

"The Jews are a conniving people. They manipulate everything for their ends."

Churchill said, "I understand how King Hussein thinks. After all, he is a graduate of our academy in England. He could not tolerate slights to his sovereignty in his own kingdom. When the Palestinians staged an armed insurrection against his rule in 1970, he decided once and for all to put a limit to the Palestinians' misdoings. The Jordanian army commenced a sweeping military operation which involved bombarding the Palestinians' military bases and laying siege to the refugee camps where many armed Palestinians were stationed. In the end, the Palestinian factions were forced to evacuate the cities and disperse into the countryside. These events later came to be known as 'Black September,' in which more than five thousand Palestinians lost their lives.

With great vexation Abdel Hamid asked, "Where were you, Nasser? Why didn't you stop this bloodbath between fellow Muslims?"

"I held a joint meeting with King Hussein and Yasser Arafat in which the two of them pledged to cease all hostilities and take steps towards reconciliation," Nasser replied.

Rabin breathed a sigh of relief.

"Nothing stays the same for long. Though Nasser had gone toe to toe with the West, dedicating his life to turning the Arabs into a force to be reckoned with, he never learned what his life work amounted to, nor even what became of the reconciliation efforts between the Palestinians and Jordanians, because he died."

"He who owns the East and its petroleum reserves, rules the world," De Gaulle said, eulogizing Nasser. "Abdel Nasser was set to rule the world, but the West's telecommunications technology left him in a daze."

"Were you killed, Nasser?" the millionaire naively asked.

Abdel Nasser shot a spiteful glance at Rabin, and then answered the millionaire's question.

"You are a fool, Mr. Millionaire. Though you used your wealth to turn the world into your own personal playground, you left the world brainless and with your hands empty."

CHAPTER 31

An Unidentified Person of Interest

"THREE MILLION DOLLARS?"

With a particularly big question mark - so read the headlines on the front pages of all the major international and local newspapers. It was also prominently displayed in televised news broadcasts, transmitted on the Internet, and seen in LED news tickers hanging in every department store, building front, and major street where every shopper and passerby would have the opportunity to read it. In less developed nations where such technology was not available the headline was written on the walls with red and black graffiti.

The headline continued to be displayed as such for two straight weeks until every man and woman young or old had the opportunity to read it. It became the talk of the town: people were ranting about it everywhere, at coffee shops, street sidewalks, homes, work and school. It started to get on people's nerves as no one seemed able to penetrate its ambiguous and vague phrasing. Suddenly, the security apparatuses adjusted the headline, removing not only the question mark but all ambiguity as well: the headline was now clear and to the point. It read, "THREE MILLION DOLLARS AS A REWARD

371

FOR ANYONE WHO APPREHENDS OR ASSISTS IN THE IDENTIFICATION OF THE SUSPECT WHO RAMMED A NAIL INTO THE GENERAL'S HEAD."

And thus everyone who read the headline or heard about it came to learn of the General's importance and the menace posed by the perpetrator of the crime who has for decades defied the authorities' efforts to identify and apprehend him. Prize hunters, too, were in on the search efforts, though their efforts were of no avail, their greediness leading them to falsely accuse many innocent people who only won their release after being subjected to heavy questioning and, in many cases, torture.

When there is not enough evidence to crack the case and the clues that might possibly lead to the identification of the perpetrator fail to pan out, allowing the latter to slip from the investigator's grasp, doubts and suspicions sharply rise to the surface. So it was with the head of INTERPOL, who began suspecting the General's family of involvement, on the theory that the General was an affluent but miserly man, leading some members of his family to slip a sedative in his food or drink and murder him as he slept.

The head of INTERPOL could not sleep. He spent the night twisting and turning in bed, rising early the next day to make it to his office at first light. He intended on inspecting his mail in hopes of finding a solution to the insomnia that had become a rather unwelcome addition to his nightly routine in that it deprived him of needed rest. He took a sip of coffee as he flipped through the cables and photos that had just reached him from all over the world. He paused to get a closer look at a cable sent to him by the head of INTERPOL operations in Geneva, in which he confessed his inability to gain access to the murdered generals' bank accounts, as the Swiss Banks claimed to be bound by strict privacy laws that prevented access to anyone without the account holder's permission. He threw the report aside and began preparing a file to bring with him on his upcoming trip to the United States, where he hoped to learn of the results of the lab tests that were conducted on the skull's cranium as well as to discuss the various efforts being made to crack the case locally and abroad.

As he browsed through the documents that he needed for his trip the head of INTERPOL came across the gravedigger's written deposition. He took it in his hand and collapsed on the couch near his desk. Suspicions began to whirl in his mind and eat away at his brain cells. An important question presented itself: What precludes the possibility that the gravedigger himself rammed the nail through the General's head?

The head of INTERPOL requested another cup of coffee, and walked over to his desk and opened the drawer. He pulled out a smoking pipe and began stuffing it with perfumed tobacco as the questions continued to run through his mind in swift rushes unabated. What motive did the gravedigger have in killing the General, considering that he was nothing if not an honest servant of the deceased? He was never a suspect in this case – why would we deceive me?

The questions ceased briefly as his assistant entered with the cup of coffee that he had requested. He signaled his attendant to leave the cup on the table near the couch, and proceeded to light up his pipe. He felt revived by the perfumed scent of the tobacco which he had grown accustomed to for the past twenty years. He watched the steam as it continued to rise from his cup of coffee and upon taking his first sip he was able to dispel the doubts he had and convinced himself that his way of thinking was mere delusion. With the second sip of coffee a new theory had imposed itself on his thoughts which took him far back into the past. He now believed that the gravedigger had indeed rammed the nail into the General's head, but only after the latter had died, unintentionally and with no malice aforethought. In the past, coffins were mere slabs of wood pieced together using nails to form a box in which the corpse would be laid. Perhaps the gravedigger had found one of the sides become loose and sought to reinforce it so as to prevent the General's corpse from slipping through during the burial process, and that is how a long nail managed to find itself jammed into the General's skull, only to be discovered when the rat escaped and brought all the fuss in its wake.

The American intelligence agencies were certain that the General's death was a homicide. Many a time a murder investigation will go sour, and not too much time passes before the crime gets buried with the deceased. But since the case involved one of the greats there appeared to be no option but to rummage through the historical record and make an account of even the most intricate details that might help identify the real killer. The investigation began with an examination of the old archives, whose outdated and forgotten contents had been tossed in underground vaults, left to mold and rot. Computer programmers became increasingly charged with the responsibility of to store and process the data and files acquired – including photographs, reports, fingerprints – into an electronic format in a way that would facilitate investigators' quick retrieval and access to the files.

The United States of America offered full-tuition scholarships to students from the developing world who were interested in studying computer science, hoping to equip them with the skills needed to qualify them to deal with complicated computer matters in the quickest time possible. It got so that one of the development consultants wished that ten more greats would be found killed, which might cause the more advance nations to increase learning grants to the developing world and bridge the gap between the two in terms of quality of education.

The United States of America decided to convene an international conference in Las Vegas, the world capital for organized crime, for which it invited all personalities involved in investigating the General's case. Situated in the Nevadan desert, the city had achieved fame as an important destination for international tourism. The Venetian Casino and Hotel was chosen as the site for this conference. Visitors to the hotel are immediately struck by the feeling that they are walking through the streets of the Italian city of Venice. Perhaps the organizers of the conference chose a hotel that resembled the Italian city as a nod to the Mafia, the lynchpin of organized crime in the modern world, had come from the Italian island of Sicily. A slew of limousines had made their way to Las Vegas Airport, awaiting the arrival of the invitees and accompany them to the hotel. The head of each delegation was assigned a suite that had been prepared with all the amenities that they might ask for. The head of INTERPOL stood outside the Paris Las Vegas, admiring its unique architecture. It seemed as if the hotel owners had taken France's prized Eiffel Tower and relocated it in the heart of the Nevadan desert.

The invitees, especially those visiting the city for the first time, were mesmerized by the sight of dazzling lights and gushing cascades that poured into water fountains situated near the hotel entrances, surrounded by lush green gardens in the heart of the desert. It was a token of America's unique ingenuity, which managed to gather the world's civilizations into one city.

The proceedings were now underway. The conference hall seemed particularly suited for the event. The conference's host began with a welcoming address to the participating delegations, during which he announced that he was pleased to call on the head of INTERPOL to take the reigns and direct the conference's sessions. The head of INTERPOL took the stage, thanking everyone in attendance for their outstanding efforts in this case. The U.S. intelligence chief handed him an envelope which contained the results of the lab tests. It read in part:

TOP SECRET

Given the peculiarity of the results contained in the lab report, the tests were repeated three times. The results were identical each time.

1. DNA: The owner of the sample had an (XY) chromosome – in other words, he was a male.

2. Ethnic Background: 67 markers were tested and, after reviewing the genetic code in the nucleus, we found a perfect match with samples whose heritage is that of the blue-blooded nobility of the Middle Ages.

Height: The taller he is, the more dangerous he will be.

Age: As old as time itself.

Physical characteristics: He expands and contracts, depending on the political situation.

Distinguishing marks: Power, a will to dominate, and a lack of compassion.

The following was included in another report attached to the envelope:

"The use of pressure tactics during the questioning of detainees led thousands to admit direct participation in the General's murder, and millions more had the intent to do so.

"They succeeded in killing him in the Soviet Union in 1917; then again in Vietnam, in Algeria, India, and in South Africa. . .

"The crime took a more precarious route when Generals began to spar among themselves, resulting in a succession of assassinations and counter-assassinations the likes of which had been seen in the first two world wars. An abandonment of democratic principles increases the risk of assassination manifold, particularly in infighting over power due to military coups.

"We also find that taking measures to restrict the use and possession of nails, hammers and industrial wire will have no substantive effect in protecting generals from harm, as assassination teams discover new methods to carry out their objectives."

The conference came to an end, and the General's case was closed once and for all. Before the file was sent for storage, the lead investigator had written on it that "the suspect remains unknown, and the case shall be deemed final, pending the discovery of an unidentified person of interest." The gravedigger was infused with a renewed sense of energy in his work. He clenched his shovel with force, and treated every new corpse as if it were that unidentified person of interest.

CHAPTER 32
A Gold Lighter

The relationship between Churchill and Hitler was more than mere quibbling over ideology. It was a test of strengths, an existential battle, one in which the attainment of victory was an imperative. This state of affairs led to a strong dislike between the two men. And yet despite their distaste for one another the two men shared many things in common, including a love for painting, and the corroded walls of the catacomb provided each of them an opportunity to embellish them with all the paintings they had hoped they could paint that they couldn't get around to in life.

Everyone was enthusiastic about the idea. Gandhi went about repairing the walls and making them ideal for painting. Abdel Hamid didn't do much other than offer his encouragement, while the remainder worked to bring the idea to life - with the millionaire promising to pick up the tab for expenses. The skeleton was an industrious worker, happy to be rid of the many years of insipid inactivity. As for the skull, it saw in the enterprise a chance to relive his war days anew. This time around the battle was of a different kind, though the greats were still in charge they were now bound by the aesthetic standards of art.

Churchill lit up his cigar, his razor-sharp mind alerting him to the tremendous responsibility he now carried. He closed his eyes to see where his imagination would take him. Hitler hastened to grab his brush and went to work. He started by painting blue skies covered by thick clouds shaped like strange animals and interposing grids, beneath which he drew fields like silk brocade whose grass was darkish green, in the midst of which ran a gushing river. Near the river he put up a series of gargantuan buildings, the sight of which reawakened in him long-lost ambitions that, in a previous life, he waged insane wars to achieve, only to end with failure, rampant destruction in Germany, Europe and throughout the world, and, finally, his death by suicide.

Churchill took hold of his brush, gliding left and right all over the wall, leaving behind an array of zigzag lines that were meant to be a base for the mural he intended to paint. The wall was covered with a bluish hue that came together to reveal a ship sailing peacefully through a vast Azure-colored ocean. The sun was getting ready to set, reflecting its orange hue on the light clouds as they swam through the sky. The portrait was pleasing to the eye, just like Europe was in the post-war era.

In the Middle East, turmoil began to boil over, auguring a series of fateful events with long-term consequences for the region. A volcano was about to erupt, spewing its fiery lava to sear all of the states in the region. It all began with the death of Abdel Nasser, who was succeeded by Anwar Sadat. In Syria, regime change came at the hands of the Corrective Movement, led by Hafez al-Assad, a patriotic military man whose vision of uniting the Middle East under the banner of Arab nationalism was not looked kindly upon by Israel.

Tensions flared in Jordan during the events of Black September. The Palestine Liberation Organization was handed a sound defeat by the Jordanian authorities that ended their presence in that country, whereupon the Arab League issued a resolution which permitted the PLO to relocate to Lebanon, where they were able to regroup and resume military operations that struck deep in the occupied Palestinian territories. During this time Israel was exulting in its triumph in the 1967 war, believing that the Arabs no longer possessed the ability to bounce back from their defeat. But the setback, known in Arabic as the naksa, of 1967 led to increased cooperation among the Arabs that started to bear fruit on the ground. Preliminary efforts were made to support the Palestine Liberation Organization as well as the Arab countries that neighbored Israel, later giving way to a principled use of oil blockades as a weapon to counteract western support for Israel. The year 1971 witnessed a host of international developments that defined that decade.

The first comment on the murals was made by De Gaulle.

"I always wished that competition between sparring nations be kept to the realm of science and art rather than spilling over into war," he said.

"In any case, Europe has benefited much from its experience at war: if anything it is now the calmest, most reasoned continent in this respect."

The skull responded, "As long as there are power games to be played and factories capable of producing weapons, then the flames of war will never die down."

"I find the renewed outbreak of direct hostilities between the great powers improbable," De Gaulle said as he gazed at the colossal buildings in Hitler's painting.

The skull disagreed with De Gaulle's point of view, insisting on the misguided presumption that war is inevitable:

"Weapons stockpiles need to be emptied at some point, and all newly developed weapons needed to be tested and evaluated for effectiveness."

"Every time a disagreement ensued between the United States and the Soviet Union, the world would follow these developments with caution, fearing that at any moment it could be destroyed by nuclear war," the skeleton said apprehensively as he placed his hand on his heart. "Thus, to keep things under control the two great powers would fight their battles on other peoples' soil rather than risk direct confrontation."

"Have you never heard of proxy war?" the millionaire asked confrontationally.

"What do you mean, 'proxy war?'"

The millionaire was delighted. He finally felt knowledgeable enough to speak about politics. He adjusted his seating position and said, "The super powers' populations had grown weary of war, especially when those wars were fought at home. Therefore, their leaders took to waging war by proxy, which was designed to relocate the battle outside of its own borders. This was done primarily by means of stirring civil war within a single nation's borders or regional war between two neighboring countries."

The skeleton was persuaded by the millionaire's analysis.

"In this way, weapons can be disposed of profitably by selling them to the warring sides, and newly developed weapons can be put to the test."

"It is from this vantage point that the Soviet Union worked to conclude treaties of friendship with those nations that it sought to cooperate with," Stalin said, enthused by the prospect of political action designed to spread the Communists' school of thought.

"Indeed, in 1971 a treaty of friendship and cooperation was concluded between the Soviet Union and Egypt," Nasser said.

"Another such treaty was concluded in the same year with India," Gandhi said, folding his hands together.

"And another treaty with Iraq the year after that," Stalin added.

"What about the United States?" Abdel Hamid asked. "Who did they conclude treaties with?"

"Its alliance with Israel was all it needed," Rabin replied glowingly.

Abdel Nasser agreed.

"They turned Israel into a spoiled ally that gets anything that it asks for."

Stalin became so consumed by envy that he grew fatigued.

"And most of the Latin American countries as well."

Gandhi said as he pontificated on the prospect of war between neighboring countries, "In 1971 a third war broke out between India and Pakistan, in which the Soviet Union supplied India with advanced weapons."

The skeleton searched through the deep recesses of his memory and said, "The first war between the two nations broke out in 1947 as a result of their dispute over the Kashmir region, resulting in Kashmir being divided between India and Pakistan."

Abdel Hamid sought to make a point as he directed his remarks to everyone in attendance:

"The Indian usurpers carried out numerous massacres against the Muslims of Kashmir, resulting in the deaths of over 200,000 Muslims."

Gandhi ignored Abdel Hamid's remark, as did everyone else.

"The second war came in 1965, once again as a result of a dispute over territories. India secured a victory in the third war, allowing India to seize control over East Pakistan's airspace. In the aftermath of India's triumph Bengali nationalists formed the state of Bangladesh, seceding from the Pakistani motherland."

The skull briefly remarked, "These were rather important developments on the Asian front."

Kennedy found himself in agreement with the skull, but noted, "A more important development was Taiwan's expulsion from the United Nations Security Council, to be replaced by the People's Republic of China."

"What's right is right," the skeleton said, clearly pleased.

"It was a mistake for a great power like China to remain excluded from the Security Council."

Churchill, seated next to Abdel Nasser, asked to borrow his light. After lighting his cigar, Churchill took Nasser's lighter and put it in his pocket.

"The Chinese leadership had been conceited and egotistical even prior to their being accepted into the Security Council," he told the skeleton.

"You think they got any better afterwards?"

"China was expanding into nearby territories," Gandhi said with a noticeable tone of indignation in his voice. "It backed Pakistan in its wars against India."

Stalin was straightforward as to his annoyance with the Chinese.

"The Chinese moved to outshine the Soviet Union, publishing tracts that glorified Maoist thought and exaggerated the Chinese Communist Party's accomplishments and distributing them to the developing countries in its midst."

Kennedy too shared his displeasure with the Chinese, though his reasons differed from the others.

"The Chinese stood on the side of the Vietnamese in their war against the Americans."

The millionaire became increasingly concerned with the Chinese's rise in power, and he expressed his concerns, saying,

"The Chinese must have contemplated moving into Africa. It's an easy market for anyone to market their goods on."

Abdel Nasser suddenly remembered his lighter.

"Give me back my lighter, Churchill!" He demanded.

Churchill duly pulled the gold lighter out of his pocket, though he was slow in returning it. Abdel Nasser extended his arm and said, "Give it to me!"

Once he got it back, he relaxed and said, "Haven't you English had your fill of the Arab countries' riches?"

The skull approached the two of them, and spoke directly to Abdel Nasser saying, "Were the Arabs a strong people, they would not have permitted the English and others to take anything from them! It is in the nature of the strong to plunder, and the weak to remain silent."

Abdel Nasser was noticeably affected by the skull's remarks.

"It was my responsibility to restore my men's confidence in themselves and to rebuild our armed forces. This we accomplished during the war of attrition in which our armed forces scored a series of incredible victories against Israel, foremost among them was the destruction of an Israeli oil rig stationed in the Atlantic, and the success of the frogmen operation in Eilat."

Abdel Nasser's reclaiming of his lighter made Rabin anxious, in the same way a thief becomes anxious when a police officer approaches him. It's difficult to accept that the Arabs would forget their defeat in the 1967 war. But Rabin's anxiety dissipated when he called to the mind Israel's air superiority. His anxiety vanished entirely when he remembered how Israel built the Bar Lev line along the coast of the Suez Canal, made up of a string of sand walls raised some twenty meters high and inclined at an angle of 45 degrees from the western part of the canal. Observation posts were built to cover the entire line, designed to put observers in the position to warn the higher command of any impending attack. The line was equipped with napalm tubes that poured into the Suez Canal, ready to be lit at the earliest indication that a crossing attempt was underway.

Rabin stood up and fetched a container filled with cold water. He dipped his feet in the container and relaxed, sipping a hot cup of coffee that he held in his hands. His worries about Israel's security were put to rest, and his confidence boosted as the air-to-air battle between Israel and Syria over the Mediterranean Sea unfolded, during which Hafez al-Assad made the brilliant decision not to use missiles so as to preclude Israel from learning the full extent of his nation's military capabilities.

Stalin predicted a shift in fortunes between the Arabs and Israel.

"The Battle of Karameh was the first victory the Arabs were able to secure following their defeat in 1967. This victory led them to contemplate an even greater victory, and the Palestinian resistance began intensifying its armed attacks against Israel, the while Egypt and Syria were preparing for a new war, this time well-planned and designed to wipe away the shame of defeat."

"I expect the Palestinian attacks on Israeli interests to continue unabated," the skull observed.

Rabin had reason to be worried.

"Terrorist attacks were launched from Jordan and Lebanon. Israel deemed putting a halt to those attacks a priority, and it went about liquidating those responsible and harassing the governments of Jordan and Lebanon, in hopes of ending the armed Palestinian presence in those two countries."

De Gaulle understood the logic of the Israelis' plan.

"With this in mind Israeli commandos launched an attack on Beirut airport in 1968, during which 13 Lebanese civilian aircrafts were destroyed."

"The operation resulted in increased tensions between the Lebanese army and the Palestinian resistance," Abdel Nasser noted.

"These tensions escalated to all-out armed conflict between the two. A cessation of hostilities ensued following the Cairo Accord of 1969, which allowed the Palestinian factions to run the refugee camps and to retain a military presence in some parts of Lebanon's south."

Churchill shot a glance at Rabin and said, "After the events of Black September in Jordan in 1970, the Palestinian guerillas needed to reinforce their positions in southern Lebanon."

Rabin was vexed by the new status quo.

"The Palestinians carried out a series of brazen attacks that left Israel incensed. Particularly gruesome was the 1972 Munich Massacre, in which eleven members of the Israeli Olympic team were killed. In 1973 their activities extended to Cyprus, where they carried out two operations spontaneously, the first against Israel's ambassador to Cyprus and the second against Israel's El Al airline."

The skeleton chuckled on the inside. Worse was yet to come for Israel. Egypt and Syria had outwitted Israel, and the skeleton wanted to be the first to tell everyone of the impending surprise the Arabs had in store for Israel.

"The Egyptian and Syrian Armed Forces launched a surprise joint attack on October 6, 1973."

Rabin's mug fell through his hands.

"They've gone and done it now!" he shouted.

Abdel Nasser felt great pride and esteem in his men.

"The Egyptian armed forces sealed the napalm tubes closed and used a high-pressure water pump to undermine the sand walls the Israelis set up to fortify their positions."

"Soviet surface-to-air (SAM) missiles were instrumental in protecting the skies of Egypt and Syria," Stalin said with a grin.

"Israeli fighter jets dropped out of the sky like birds," Abdel Hamid shouted with joy.

"The first six hours of the lightning Arab advance in the war left the world in a stupor," the skeleton said, commenting on the course of the events.

"The legendary Bar Lev line had been completely breached, which the Israelis had conceitedly claimed could only be ruptured by means of a nuclear weapon. During this time, the Syrians were able to retake Mount Hermon."

"Israel was unable to destroy the enemy's missiles inventory," Hitler said gloatingly.

"Beginning with day four of the war the United States Armed Forces intervened via an airlift that restocked Israel's weapons and supplies, which allowed Israel to reclaim its confidence," Kennedy replied sternly.

Though Israel did not meet its demise just yet, Abdel Nasser was overjoyed to see the roots of Arab cooperation growing and bearing fruit. "Iraq and Algeria were the first nations to provide assistance to the Arab side in the 1973 war, followed by Saudi Arabia, Morocco and Jordan. Kuwait as well provided not only financial support but even sent reinforcements to the front lines. Libya offered its entire air fleet to help serve in the war effort."

"Don't forget the Soviet Union's role in supplying weapons and replacement parts," Stalin said.

"Iran supplied Egypt with petrol, and halted its oil exports to Europe and America, as did Saudi Arabia and the United

Arab Emirates," Churchill said, agitated by the solidarity exhibited by these countries.

The skeleton continued, "Egypt accepted U.N. Security Council resolution 338, which called for a ceasefire, the while Syria rejected it, which persisted in a war of attrition that lasted eighty two days."

The millionaire wondered aloud what the consequences of that war was. De Gaulle answered him by continuing to narrate the details of the ensuing developments on the battlefield:

"Egypt retook control of parts of the Sinai peninsula, and Syria was able to retake the city of Quneitra, which Israel had razed to the ground prior to withdrawing."

In the millionaire's mind, considerations of gains and losses were paramount.

"What did the Palestinians gain from the war?"

Abdel Nasser responded on a positive note, "Arab victory is not specific to a particular group or territory: a victory for Arabs anywhere is a victory for Arabs everywhere. The Palestinians' morale shot through the roof as the myth of the 'army that could never be defeated' became exposed for all to see."

Hitler looked back on his past days of glory, and longed for the return of old times.

"Possessing confidence in one's inevitable victory is a victory all of its own," he said.

The millionaire, smitten with envy, said, "The price of every barrel of oil spiked to $12 per barrel, three times the original amount, due to the use of the oil blockade by the Arabs as a weapon against Israel."

"The Arabian Gulf became distracted by its oil revenues, and the Arab world began to come apart at the seams," Kennedy said.

"The Arabs lied to themselves, believing that they were really more powerful than Israel. Israel, of course, wouldn't allow their delusions to bask in their delusions for long."

Abdel Nasser hit back with like confidence, "We learned from the experiences of Algeria and Vietnam that no matter how wide the colonial power's smile got, resistance would eventually be able to smack the smile off his face."

Kennedy felt his hunger peak following the conclusion of the Paris Peace Accords in 1973 that intended to secure an American withdrawal from Vietnam. He had long forgotten what it felt like to desire food due to the calamitous defeat the Americans were handed, in which some sixty thousand American soldiers lost their lives during the war years in Vietnam.

"I'm in the mood for a light meal," Kennedy told everyone.

"Would anyone like to join me?"

Kennedy's question stimulated the greats' appetites, and the millionaire decided to order a plate consisting only of salad and vegetables.

Gandhi was astonished by the millionaire's seeming solicitousness. But why not remove all doubt? "Are you now a vegetarian?" he asked.

"On the contrary, I love eating meat," the millionaire pouted.

"But the gout forced me to give it up."

Churchill excused himself from the meal, as he was on a strict diet. Rabin, on the other hand, had a craving for fatty foods.

"Let's have some veal, though we can do without cooking its meat in its mother's milk," he suggested.

De Gaulle paused writing his memoirs for a bit, and said, "I'm craving some fried meat, with a side of mashed potatoes and a glass of French red wine."

Abdel Hamid objected angrily to the request for wine, "I cannot join you all in your meal if there's going to be wine."

Abdel Nasser approached Abdel Hamid and whispered in his ear as everyone looked on. Abdel Hamid nodded his head in approval, then Abdel Nasser told everyone:

"Cancel your orders – I'll be preparing a dish that none of you have ever had before. The skeleton and Gandhi will help me put it together."

Abdel Nasser's suggestion was received favorably by everyone involved. Nasser stood up, followed by Gandhi and the skeleton, and went to work preparing the meal.

Churchill looked at Abdel Hamid and asked, "I noticed you didn't offer to help Nasser with the cooking – do you not have much experience in this regard?"

"Quite the contrary, Turkish cuisine has a vast repertoire of delicious dishes, and a rich array of options to choose from. I just don't seem up to the task today, particularly given the worrying conditions in Cyprus."

"But Turkey has covertly offered to arm the Cypriot Turks," De Gaulle retorted.

"The northern parts of Cyprus are autonomous regions that fall under Turkish military control," Abdel Hamid said.

"Why didn't the West intervene to check Turkish influence there?" the skull asked, puzzled.

"Because of the economic crisis of 1974, my friend," the millionaire replied, clarifying the role economics plays in foreign policymaking. "The crisis was caused by the crash of the real estate markets in Britain, with investors' shares losing as much as 42% of their original value."

"While the markets crashed in Britain, an economic revival was underway in the Gulf Arab countries as a result of the oil boom," Rabin said, the comparison being quite intentional.

"London's magnificent buildings lost have their value, and the Gulf was undertaking large-scale construction projects."

"What do you have against construction in the Arabian Gulf?" Abdel Hamid objected.

Churchill came to Rabin's defense, saying, "I think Rabin is referring to the laws the Gulf countries put into place with regards to the presence of foreign labor in their midst. These laws instituted a Kafala system which reduced migrant laborers to semi-slaves. Laborers were required to procure an in-country sponsor, and many of these sponsors began greedily exploiting these workers."

Abdel Hamid was persuaded otherwise.

"But these laborers found opportunities in the Gulf that were simply not available in their home countries. Millions of families lived off of those opportunities!"

"I'm sure Mr. Gandhi would have a different opinion," De Gaulle said.

Abdel Nasser was engrossed in his cooking. The sight of steam rising from his pot was rather pleasing to his eye. He stirred the pot's contents for a bit, lowered the flame and let the food simmer to completion.

Abdel Nasser took off his apron and told his assistants, "The difficult work is now done. Let's go back and reassure our starving colleagues."

"I heard Mr. De Gaulle mention my name," Gandhi said.

"What happens to be the issue?"

"Oh nothing, we were just talking about human rights," De Gaulle replied.

"When it comes to the Palestinians, the world seems to forget all about human rights, sweeping all the relevant laws and regulations under the rug," Abdel Hamid rejoined.

"There's a distinction to be made between the Palestinians as a people and terrorists," Rabin protested.

"If Arab governments were forced to confront the scourge of Palestinian terrorism, then it's only fair that Israel be allowed wipe them off the face of the earth."

"Are you referring to their expulsion from Jordan?" the skeleton asked.

"And the Lebanon's rightist parties' distaste for them as well," Rabin replied.

Abdel Nasser expressed sorrow for the events in Lebanon.

"Lebanon's makeup is very complicated, and foreign interventions in Lebanon's internal affairs only served to make matters more complicated. Lebanon's importance in the Middle East lies in its strategic location, its wondrous natural beauty, the diversity of its sectarian makeup, the tolerance of the Lebanese people for religious difference, and finally its close relations with both the Arab and Western worlds. Lebanon is a measure of where the region stands as a whole: when dark clouds gather over Lebanon's skies, rain comes pouring all over the Arab world. When conditions are sunny, the entire Middle East enjoys it's suns warmth. For this reason it was imperative to keep this tiny nation drowning in war and bloodshed: any two powers that are determined to go to war find Lebanese soil the perfect location to hash out their battles."

Abdel Nasser's contextualizing notwithstanding, Rabin insisted that the Lebanese were not too pleased with the Palestinians.

"The Palestinian factions were one of the belligerents in the civil war in Lebanon that began in 1975, just as they were belligerents in the war against the Jordanian army."

Stalin analyzed the reasons why the Palestinians decided to participate in the war.

"The Palestinians found themselves between a rock and a hard place: either they enter the war on the side of the progressive leftist parties – and this meant risking the intervention of foreign powers, including Israel, who intended to deal a fatal blow to the Palestinian resistance and the Lebanese left – or they sit the war out, which meant risking the loss of the popular support that was integral to their survival. Between these two options, the Palestinians chose the first."

Rabin seemed relaxed.

"I was very pleased they made that choice. It allowed Israel to find a partner who would do the job of killing their enemies and expelling the remaining population for them."

"The option to go to war is a detested, unacceptable one, even if it might help restore Israel's security," Gandhi objected.

"The most disdainful massacres were committed during the Lebanese Civil War. A plethora of different weapons were used, and Lebanon lived its most difficult days during the decade and a half in which the civil war raged on. A general regime of terror reigned supreme: armed snipers hiding on the rooftops of tall buildings targeted passersby as they walked through the streets, food and supplies were perpetually low, barricades lined the roads, and checkpoints were rampant. The notorious "ID-card killings" were widespread: in many cases civilians passing through makeshift checkpoints would be forced to strip down to their underwear in order to reveal their religious affiliation. Many innocent civilians lost their lives. In addition, thousands of families were evicted from their ancestral homelands, while thousands more fled and immigrated to a vast array of world countries, leaving behind their homes and possessions, which were picked off by one militia or the next.

"Lebanon was like Hell on Earth. Mr. Stalin speaks of rightist and leftist fighters – let both of them burn in Hell, and let the people live in peace."

Kennedy was moved by Gandhi's account of the war. He felt his hunger gnaw at his stomach.

"Where's the food?" he asked Abdel Nasser.

"It's ready," Abdel Nasser said, as he and his two assistants rose from their seats.

"Let's set up the table so we can eat."

Abdel Nasser apportioned the soup in everyone's bowl such that everyone in attendance would have a taste. Gandhi and the skeleton began serving those seated at the table. Churchill excused himself from the meal and lit his cigar, while the rest devoured their soup. Gandhi's blood had been lacking in Vitamin B12, of which he found an ample serving in his soup.

"This soup is delicious," De Gaulle said, savoring his meal.

"What's in it?"

"It's the Indian spices," Gandhi immediately answered.

"They're responsible for much of the flavor in the soup."

Rabin sipped his last mouthful of soup and said, "Indeed, it is very delicious. Perhaps we were so hungry that anything might've tasted just as good."

"You have a point, Rabin," Abdel Nasser agreed. "It has been quite a long stupor for us."

Stalin was enmeshed his food and not available for comment, though the way he smacked his lips as he ate made it very clear that he too was relishing the meal.

"What's the name of this soup?" Hitler asked.

"You might say that it's the sum total of our efforts to present a united Arab front during the 1973 war," Nasser replied, just after everyone had finished consuming their meal.

Rabin threw the bowl in his hands aside, and began to listen carefully. Nasser continued, "The soup you all had was rabbit soup."

"If rabbit soup tasted this good, imagine how delicious a meal of rabbit meat must be!" Abdel Hamid exclaimed.

Rabin stood from his place and began purging the contents of his stomach, and the millionaire felt his joints flame up.

Abdel Nasser chuckled as he told Abdel Hamid, "One day, I will invite you all to eat the rabbit itself."

CHAPTER 33
Red Light

Gandhi's humanism made it an ethical requirement to look after the ailing millionaire, whose health had taken a turn for the worse after consuming Nasser's fatty meal. Gandhi was well-versed in the healing benefits of traditional herbs. He used a few herbs to prepare a hot cup of tea which he had the millionaire drink. In less than twenty four hours the millionaire's health had improved considerably, though he remained concerned about his investments in the Arab world in light of worsening conditions.

Rabin had a restless night. His nightmares haunted him ceaselessly, and as early morn broke he shouted angrily, "We must get rid of the menace of Arab cuisine and its repertoire of dishes once and for all! We shall crush every furnace which Arabs use to keep themselves warm, and we shall destroy the pots and pans of Arab reconciliation and unity! Indeed, we ought to lay their cuisine to waste, and have it replaced with another!"

"Take it easy, Rabin," Gandhi said, his eyes half open from exhaustion.

"Assuming what you ask for comes true, what would you have the Arabs eat? Do you think their stomachs will be able to digest the new cuisine?"

"They'll get used to it, I assure you! We must proceed without any further delay!"

Hitler was displeased by the tone of Rabin's voice.

"Seeing you throwing a fit now one might forget that not too long ago all that came out of your moth were sobs and whimpers."

Kennedy gazed fondly on Rabin.

"He's a tough guy now, that's why he raises his voice."

Rabin's shift was nothing out of the ordinary, or so thought the skull.

"His weapons arsenal helped to strengthen his tone of voice."

Gandhi groaned, exasperated by the fact that the voice of war always seems to beat out the voice of reason.

"The only thing that distinguishes human beings from other animals is their intellectual capacity," he said. "When he allows brute force to take the place of reason, the strong dominate the weak, and the law of the jungle will reign supreme."

"In the summer of 1977 Israel's Prime Minister at the time Menachem Begin requested that U.S. Secretary of State Henry Kissinger arrange a meeting with Sadat," Rabin replied, hoping to appease Gandhi. "In the same year, Sadat announced that he was ready to enter into negotiations with Israel."

"Negotiations! Negotiate about what?" Abdel Nasser interrupted.

"To negotiate peace, of course," Rabin replied.

"This is a Zionist conspiracy to divide the Arabs' ranks and to force Egypt into isolation," Nasser said angrily.

"If they desire a just peace, Arabs ought to negotiate as a united front. Each state ought not be left to fend for itself. The only beneficiary of Sadat's visit shall be Israel."

The skeleton described the political atmosphere that preceded Sadat's announcement of his intent to visit Jerusalem:

"The Syrian masses were outraged by Sadat's declaration. Hordes of demonstrators attacked the Egyptian embassy in Damascus and burned its flag. The Syrian President Hafez al-Assad described Sadat as being 'insane,' and yet none of this dissuaded Sadat from visiting Israel."

"Sadat was a man of his word," Rabin rejoined.

"He went through on his pledge to visit Jerusalem, and he gave a speech in the Israeli Knesset."

Churchill remarked, "Many a time diplomacy is a more powerful weapon than a rifle."

Hitler was noticeably vexed.

"Rabin succeeded in going through on his threat to undercut Arab unity by diplomatic means."

"Israel used military means as well," Abdel Hamid added. "It's illegal invasion of Lebanon in 1978 comes to mind here."

"Do you consider Turkey's occupation of northern Cyprus in 1975 'legal?'" Rabin scoffed.

Abdel Hamid fell silent as he lacked a decent counter argument. Abdel Nasser broke the silence and said, "Israel's invasion of Lebanon proves that it is not serious about peace. The invasion left tens of Lebanese villages in ruins, and led more than a quarter million people to flee their homes. If anything, it brings into sharp relief Israel's belligerent intentions towards the Arab people."

"We had no choice but to undertake that invasion so as to bring the Palestine Liberation Organization down to size, particularly when its activities picked up pace in the aftermath of the 1973 war," Rabin shot back imperiously.

"Don't you see that the Israeli reaction was excessive?" Abdel Hamid asked.

Rabin felt Israel's actions were justified.

"Israeli forces withdrew as soon as their mission was accomplished in a mere seven weeks."

"Though it did maintain a presence in southern Lebanon, it was restricted to a fringe of territory slightly north of the Israeli Lebanese border," Churchill added.

"To protect Israel's security," Rabin confirmed.

"What became of the Sadat-Begin talks?" The millionaire asked.

Kennedy proudly replied, "The talks ended in 1979 with the signing of the Camp David Accords."

Stalin shook his head and said, "The Accords were in the interest of the United States and Israel, as they isolated Egypt from the rest of the Arab world, thereby neutralizing one of the strongest fighting forces in the region."

"I was afraid this might happen," Abdel Nasser said despondently.

De Gaulle asked in a loud voice, "Did Israel finally achieve security with this treaty?"

"Israel needs to abandon its racist policies, ease restrictions on Palestinians, and open a new chapter in its relations with its neighbors," Gandhi said.

"It will benefit greatly by doing so, and only then it will live in security."

"It must also allow the Palestinian refugees to return to their homes," Nasser added.

Rabin objected to both Gandhi and Abdel Nasser's recommendations.

"Space is limited – the land simply isn't big enough to house all these people."

Abdel Hamid scoffed at Rabin's argument.

"Ask your friend Mr. Kennedy for advice. I'm certain he'll propose a solution to your problem."

Rabin and Kennedy exchanged puzzled looks. On the other hand, Gandhi suggested a solution to the problem of limited space:

"You ought to consider building vertically. That might solve the problem. Instead of saturating the horizon with Jewish settlements that require large amounts of space, you ought to look towards the sky, and undertake the construction of tall residential buildings, like they did in New York City, Dubai and Malaysia."

Rabin was restive and tense.

"Easier said than done! The problem is not solely territorial in nature. Time is on the Arabs' side, and the future does not bode well for Israel. What frightens us is Islam itself, which permits polygamy and early marriage. Since the Arabs love to procreate, we face a demographic threat as the number of Arabs continues to increase."

"Living in refugee camps does not spur procreation so much as it creates friction and hatred," the skeleton said sardonically.

Rabin replied in all seriousness, "You say this jokingly, but the numbers don't lie. I shall quote from a report prepared by the Israeli Mossad that documents one relevant case that you ought to be aware of. Mahmoud is a young Palestinian man who goes by the nickname 'Abu Munir.' His father trained him to be a barber when he was twelve years old, and had him married off when he was fourteen, around the same time that he had opened a barber shop for him. That was in 1948. When the war broke out, Mahmoud closed up his shop and fled in the company of his wife to the al-Azraq refugee camp in Jordan. He is now seventy years old. The members of his family – including children and grandchildren – amount to about fifty two people. And there are many such Mahmouds with a similar story."

Hitler was pleased that one of his goals was on the verge of being attained.

"I advise the Palestinians to marry six women instead of making do with the ordinary four, as increased procreation is a greater threat to Israel than a weapon of mass destruction. And it comes free of charge – there is no need to spend billions of dollars in order to possess it, nor is it subject to international legal sanctions."

De Gaulle objected to Hitler's advice.

"I find this to be insulting to Palestinian women."

Rabin felt as if De Gaulle had thrown him a lifeline.

"Human rights organizations ought to confront Hitler and his destructive opinions and to come to the defense of Palestinian women by campaigning against polygamy."

Abdel Nasser's temperature flared, and the blood in his forehead began to boil in anger. He scoffed at Rabin's remarks as he spoke to everyone in attendance, saying, "Look at Rabin! Isn't it just delightful for him to be defending the rights of Palestinian women? He must have forgotten the numerous air raids his war planes conducted as they rained down missiles and cluster bombs on Palestinian refugee camps wherever they could be found. Palestinian women would be more than happy to relinquish any rights she might have in order to relieve the suffering brought about by years of exile and the pain of seeing the bodies of her infants being incinerated by the napalm bombs launched by Israeli fighter jets."

He shot a glance at Kennedy and then continued, "It ought not go without mentioning that the fighter jets that rain down hell on our people were manufactured by the United States of America."

Rabin nodded his head in agreement, and added, "But those jets run on Arab oil," he reminded Nasser.

The skull said impetuously, "That very same oil and those very same fighter jets shall be used to conduct air raids on the Arabs' kitchens. We shall begin by striking at the weakest of Israel's Arab neighbors."

"Why do the Americans allow the weapons they manufacture to be used in this fashion?" the skeleton asked.

Kennedy the war hero replied, "Such were the exigencies of the war against Communism: our priorities were to bring about the downfall of the evil empire and to spread democracy in the four corners of the globe."

Hitler saw a stark contradiction between Kennedy's words and his actions.

"The policy of the United States of America is rather puzzling, particularly since they claim to support democratically elected governments."

"Democracy is the worst form of government, except for all the others," Churchill replied.

He then asked Hitler, "What do you find puzzling about the Americans' support for democracy?"

"Perhaps he has in mind the Salvador Allende government which took power in Chile in 1970 by democratic means," Nasser jeered.

"It was a communist regime elected by the people," Stalin added.

"But the Americans funded and backed the fascist General Augusto Pinochet in his bid to overthrow the government and take power in 1973."

Hitler criticized the Americans, saying, "That the government there had been democratically elected meant nothing to them."

Kennedy rebuffed Hitler's accusations, saying, "We respect the democratic process. I am a Democrat, as you all know. But elections or no elections – we simply couldn't accept the prospect of a communist government right in our backyard in Latin America. Here, the democratic process is of little significance. One Castro is enough – One Cuba is enough."

"We've also had enough of you toying with the nations of the world!" Gandhi objected in a harsh tone, directing his remarks at all the greats.

"They say one thing, and do another," Nasser added in Gandhi's support.

Stalin joined the chorus out of spite for capitalism.

"What matters to them is that the people in power are to their liking, elections notwithstanding."

Kennedy calmly responded, "There are priorities, and then there are even greater priorities. As the noose tightens around one's neck, priorities must give way to greater priorities."

De Gaulle was disdained by the Americans' vacillating on the issue of respect for the democratic process.

"America's main fault is that it always seeks after being the lone superpower in the world."

For Kennedy De Gaulle's view felt like a huge lump that he wasn't able to swallow. He gulped down a glass of water that he had in front of him and said, "Mr. De Gaulle, it seems France is constantly arousing their fellow Europeans to stand against American unipolarity. Do you deny the favors that America has done for France in liberating it from Germany's clasp?"

Hitler was fishing in murky waters.

"You're right, Kennedy," he said.

"You were better off leaving the French to fend for themselves. That would have left us in power there."

De Gaulle replied with extreme deference, "For the thousandth time, and in the name of France, I express my gratitude to you for standing by our side at the end of World War II. But an expression of gratitude ought not be taken as a willingness to surrender."

"Who said anything about surrender? You're working against us!"

"We're not working against anyone. We're simply trying to make our mark. We find the prospect of being lackeys to anyone to be demeaning and an insult to our pride."

Churchill noticed Kennedy getting agitated and said, "No worries, Mr. Kennedy. Europe shall always be America's strongest ally. That Great Britain always rushes to stand to your side is sufficient to demonstrate this."

Kennedy's sense of gloom made the burden he shouldered seem unbearable to him.

"The enemies of the United States of America are on the rise, and America must remain in a position to isolate the empire of evil and spread democracy."

The skull empathized with Kennedy's position.

"You must take every precaution and move forward with your weapons development program."

Stalin felt openly defied by the course the conversation had taken.

"Do you believe that the Communist bloc will sit idly by as you accuse it of being the 'empire of evil?'" he asked.

"Of course not," Churchill replied, unperturbed. "I'm sure you shall exert every effort to continue to expand on the world stage."

Stalin, overtaken by a sheer sense of responsibility, said, "Internationalism is a key element in Communism's ideology, and in order to secure this important aim the Soviet Union must continue to stand shoulder to shoulder with liberation movements all over the world."

"In 1975 the Soviet Union backed Angola in its war against South Africa," the skeleton said, providing an example of Soviet policy in this regard.

"Even Castro aided in the war effort, sending a contingent of soldiers to fight alongside the Angolans."

Rabin added, "In 1974 Colonel Mengistu Haile Mariam overthrew the emperor of Ethiopia Haile Selassie. Following the Colonel's assassination in 1977 he was succeeded by General Tafari Benti, who formed a Marxist government backed by the Soviet Union."

"The United States turned something of a blind eye to those interventions – but the Soviet Union began its provocations in the American hemisphere, particularly its support of Chile and its backing in 1979 of the formation of a socialist government in Nicaragua under the leadership of Daniel Ortega," Kennedy said threateningly.

Hitler had expected disagreements between the Allied Powers in World War II to escalate eventually.

"What did the Americans do to put a stop to the Soviet advance?" he asked.

The millionaire replied, "The Americans protested the Soviet Union's aggressive policies by ceasing the sale of grain to them."

Abdel Hamid was pleased with the American strategy.

"For this reason the Soviet Union was unable to come to the aid of Mulla Mustafa Barzani's revolution."

Abdel Hamid was mistaken, or so Stalin thought.

"Barzani was no leftist – he was a staunch Kurdish nationalist. Fostering a relationship with the Iraqi state was more important to us than helping the Kurds, and we maintained excellent relations with Abd al-Karim Qasim. Even Iran cut its support for the Kurds in the Algiers Agreement of 1975 between it and Iraq, and Barzani's revolution was severely weakened as a result."

Stalin continued, "Don't think for a moment, Abdel Hamid, that the Soviet Union's failure to receive American grain shall prevent it from backing Marxist and leftist governments."

Churchill was sick and tired of hearing about Communism's principles.

"Sometimes, obstinacy is like playing with fire. In 1979 the Soviet Union backed the Najibullah government in Afghanistan, this time by sending a mighty army to invade and prop up Najibullah's rule."

Kennedy was outraged by the Soviet Union's behavior.

"In the United States' view, the Soviet Union had crossed all red lines in its invasion of Afghanistan."

Gandhi sighed sorrowfully and said, "What a sad world we live in – everytime a red light flares in some part of the world, the prospect of imminent looms near."

De Gaulle empathized with Gandhi's sorrow.

"There, there, Gandhi. Let's just hope that matters don't escalate more than they already have."

Abdel Hamid asked with intrigue, "What was the American response to the invasion?"

"America avoided a direct confrontation with the Soviet Union," Kennedy replied calculatingly, "it decided to turn Afghanistan into a swamp in which to drown the Soviets."

Churchill knew well the American plan.

"By supporting and encouraging the Communists' sworn enemies."

"You mean the Muslims?" Abdel Nasser predicted.

Kennedy rubbed his hands and said, "That's correct. The Saudis came through with the financial support."

The skelton continued, "Pakistan was charged with overseeing developments and providing logistical support to the mujahideen."

Hitler understood the remainder of the plan.

"The Americans took up the task of training the mujahideen and supplying them with weapons."

"Why would the Americans undertake to train foreign fighters free of charge?" the skeleton wondered.

"Nothing is free in this world," the millionaire answered.

Kennedy explained, "Once they train on American weaponry, then they're going to need to purchase it from us."

The skull, long drawn to strategizing and tactic, asked, "Did the Americans' plan succeed? Did they manage to score a victory against the Soviet Union and deprive the latter of their gains in the Middle East?"

Stalin responded, "Let's not forget the 1979 Islamic Revolution in Iran, and its slogan of 'Death to America.'"

Churchill perceived the looming danger to Western interests.

"Of course, you must have been delighted by this slogan, as it indicated that America's days south of the Soviet Union were now over."

Stalin was, in fact, delighted.

"In 1977 leftist parties in Iran worked to overthrow the Shah, and formed an alliance with religious groups to accomplish this objective. Later on, the religious bloc usurped the revolution. Following the Shah's fall in 1979, Ayatollah Khomeini returned from exile in Paris and established the Islamic Republic of Iran, replacing the feared SAVAK security service with the Iranian Revolutionary Guard which went about cracking down on political opposition much as their predecessors had done before."

Abdel Nasser continued on from where Stalin left off, "Ayatollah Khomeini adopted a new constitution for Iran, which helped the religious clerics to consolidate their chokehold on power. In this way, Khomeini's reworking of the theory of vilayat-i faqih, 'The Guardianship of the Clerics,' which up until then had offered clerics a titular position in government, now allowed for full-fledged theocratic rule to be imposed on the people, the cleric seen as being directly appointed by God to rule in His name."

De Gaulle described conditions in Iran following the revolution:

"Ayatollah Khomeini excised the word 'democracy' from the Iranian people's vocabulary. He prohibited intermingling between men and women and forbade music and dance. I find this rather disdainful – it seems he didn't bother to learn from the European civilization during his stay in Paris, which hosted him graciously and afforded him every opportunity to freely go about his work."

The skull wanted to know more about America's strategy in the aftermath of the revolution.

"Did the United States lick the wounds it incurred as a result of the revolution?"

Kennedy replied with the calmness of a deep thinker, "After we managed to rescue the Americans taken hostage by the revolutionaries at the American embassy in Tehran, our strategy was to take every weakness the enemy had and use it against him. Khomeini's ideology of exporting the revolution abroad left their Iraqi neighbors trembling with fear over their impending fate. Saddam Hussein proceeded to nullify the Algiers Agreement with joint American-Soviet encouragement. America's interests lied in putting the fear of Iran in the hearts of the Gulf countries, which would impel the latter to purchase weapons from us."

The skull remarked, "This sounds more like diplomatic maneuvering than a solid military plan. But what did the Soviet Union get out of all of this?"

The millionaire had commercial considerations in mind.

"In the event that war broke out with Iran, Iraq would need to purchase weapons from the Soviet Union."

He stopped to chuckle for a moment, and then continued, "The war went on for eight years, depleting the economic resources of both countries."

Gandhi was inceased.

"More importantly, that war reaped the lives of more than a million human beings," he said sorrowfully.

CHAPTER 34
Prized Game

For Israel, the Iranian revolution was like a hunting rifle which it used to take down three birds in a single shot. The first bird had a plump body, bringing in its wake an increase in U.S. support for Israel's military capabilities. The shot wounded a second bird, causing it to fall from the sky, as the First Gulf War in 1980 broke out, leading to a depletion in the military strength of Iraq, a country that in a very real sense was an extension of the Syrian front to the north. The last bird to be struck by the shot succumbed to its wounds and crashed over craggy rocks, as the Gulf countries picked up the enormous tab left by the war, forcing them to decrease aid and grants to the Arab states neighboring Israel as well as to the various factions of the Palestine Liberation Organization.

Hitler chided Gandhi for drowning in his sorrows.

"Why is it that I see you weeping and moaning, Gandhi? The million human beings who lost their lives during the eight years of war between Iran and Iraq amounted to a measly ten percent of the amount of people who lost their lives in World War II on the German side alone. I didn't weep over them; rather, I joined them."

Gandhi responded calmly, "There's clearly a difference between you and I. After all, you are Hitler, and I am Gandhi."

Abdel Hamid saw in Hitler and Gandhi's exchange the seeds of full-blown conflict between the two and decided to intervene.

"Mr. Gandhi loves all people, Hitler. I'm sure he meant no offense."

"He has the gall to compare himself to me!" Hitler replied vaingloriously. "What can a mouse do when confronted with a cat's paws?" Hitler then asked.

For a moment it appeared that Gandhi was ready to abandon his principles.

"Don't forget that my descendants are now in possession of a nuclear weapons capability," he said.

"India is set to play a leading role in the next century."

Kennedy empathized with Gandhi as he told him comfortingly, "That's most certainly true, Mr. Gandhi, though I believe India's stature on the world stage will remain beneath that of the great powers. Nevertheless, I'm still convinced India will play an important role in the years to come. As President Nixon once said, the Indians are like 'small trees in a jungle comprised of great powers, but these small trees carry within their roots the possibility that they might one day become gigantic.'

"I thank America for its optimism about India's future," Gandhi replied with extreme deference.

Hitler went back to rabble-rousing.

"Don't get too excited, Gandhi. The Chinese backed Pakistan in their bid to develop a nuclear weapons capability, and therefore India's possession of nuclear weapons will not suffice to transform it into a major power."

"There is a historic enmity at work between India and Pakistan," Churchill noted with a coolness that the English were known for.

"Despite the fact that they are one and the same people!" Abdel Nasser said, as if apprised of the situation at hand.

"One may ignite a short fuse and end up producing a spark mighty enough to consume entire countries whole," Stalin said as he shot the millionaire a glance, indirectly reminding him of the fate that befell his luxury coffin.

Hitler felt as if he had one-upped Gandhi, saying, "And this will relieve humanity of one billion people!"

Gandhi was appalled.

"This is a crime in every moral and ethical sense of the word!" He objected.

De Gaulle clarified his opinion on the matter, "Politics is one thing, morality and ethics quite another," he said.

"You will die as martyrs, monsieur Gandhi," Stalin said reassuringly.

"Martyrs will enjoy paradise and drink from rivers of honey," Abdel Nasser said, apprising Gandhi of a martyrs' reward.

"And every martyr is assigned forty houris," Abdel Hamid added.

"While we're on the subject, Mr. Nasser, might I ask you a question?" Kennedy asked, intrigued.

"Are these houris beautiful?"

"I haven't seen them yet, I'm still waiting my turn to cross into the gates of paradise. There are millions of people standing in line in front of me who await their turn as well."

Stalin told Nasser playfully, "I beg of you, Mr. Nasser, when you get there that you send me a bottle of vodka to help me get through this mercilessly cold weather. You could put the bottle on Mr. Kennedy's tab, of course."

Kennedy was taken aback.

"What am I, your long-lost father? Why do I have to pick up your tab?"

The millionaire intervened in fear that a war between Kennedy and Stalin would threaten his commercial interests.

"Settle down, gentlemen. Your drinks are on me."

Abdel Hamid extolled the millionaire's efforts. For a moment he forgot that he was no longer sultan and appointed the millionaire as vali:

"Afarim, dear vali! Well done! My governors, the sons of my invincible empire, will never disappoint my belief in their grace."

"What else is there, aside from houris?" Kennedy asked with genuine interest.

Abdel Nasser piously cited a verse of the Qur'an that read, 'Rivers of milk, whose taste will never sour, and rivers of wine, pleasing to those who drink thereof.' (47:15)

"If this is true, then I must apprise my descendants of this!" Kennedy said with intense ardor.

"They'll send troops from the 101st Airborne Division to storm this paradise and divert its resources for use by the United States. Paradise will not carry the name of America's fifty first state!"

Abdel Hamid feared for the fate of paradise. He nervously whispered in Nasser's ear, "What are we supposed to do here?"

"Relax. He's just joking."

"He's not joking. In 1961 he announced his support for the Apollo mission with the aim of landing a man on the moon. In 1969 the mission was a success, and Neil Armstrong was the first man to ever walk on the moon's surface. In fact, I believe the Americans have already seized control of paradise, and they're now preventing us from entering it!"

Abdel Nasser was annoyed.

"If Kennedy had the slightest clue where paradise was he wouldn't spend another minute in our midst – he would have simply beaten us there."

Abdel Hamid found Nasser's argument persuasive. Churchill began contemplating Kennedy's intentions and asked him, "Do we have a place in this paradise of yours?"

"As long as you are on our side, then our destinies are tied," Kennedy asserted.

Churchill was overjoyed.

"I shall order the deployment of ten thousand British soldiers backed by aircraft carriers to help the Americans liberate the fifty-first state," he exclaimed.

De Gaulle rejected the American-led campaign to seize control of paradise.

"We object to the illegal invasion and forced occupation of other people's land," he said.

"No matter, Mr. De Gaulle. We will raise the issue before the U.N. Security Council and take a vote on it."

Stalin was terrified, as if he had just lost Moscow to enemy forces.

"This campaign is at odds with Soviet ideology, and we will use our veto power to stop it in its tracks!" he shouted menacingly.

"If you decide instead to use force, then do know that our nuclear warheads are waiting for you."

Kennedy knew he was standing on solid ground, and so he could care less about Stalin's threat.

"You're dreaming, Stalin. We pounded the first nail in your ideology's coffin when we successfully penetrated into the communist nations of Europe by means of the Solidarity trade union in Poland, which announced its first strike in 1980."

Stalin guffawed and said, "The Polish secret police backed by the Soviet Red Army will take up the task of popping this soap bubble."

"The West will never allow the Soviet Union to succeed ideologically, particularly following the rise to power of the Iron Lady Margaret Thatcher in Britain and the strongman Ronald Reagan in the United States," the skeleton said in response to Stalin's boisterous confidence.

"They are intent on exhausting the Soviet Union economically by means of the arm race and preventing you from expanding into other nations."

Abdel Nasser was outraged by that policy.

"The Soviet Union's downfall will bring about a shift in the international balance of power in a manner that will swing the pendulum in Israel's favor."

"The West ought to strengthen its grip on flashpoints all over the world, so as to be able to isolate its enemies wherever they happen to be," the skull responded.

Hitler understood the skull's point of view.

"The United States immediately went about implementing this policy. In 1981, it signed a Strategic Cooperation Agreement with Israel that gave the latter the green light to invade Lebanon."

Abdel Hamid was reminded of Rabin's threat to lay Arab cuisine to waste.

"The second invasion of Lebanon came in 1982, just as Rabin had threatened."

Rabin clarified the objectives of the new Israeli invasion.

"Our aim was to destroy the Palestinian resistance, force it to conclude a peace treaty with Israel, and isolate Syria."

De Gaulle recalled the painful memory of how the Germans managed to occupy the French capital during World War II and said, "It was the second act of aggression against Lebanon by Israel in less than five years. For the first time the Israeli army had occupied an Arab capital."

Rabin replied with resolve, "When an enemy seeks cover in his nest, you must hem him in on all sides and tighten the noose around his neck, cutting his water and electricity and preventing his access to food, until he dies or comes out waving a white flag."

Gandhi was appalled by Rabin's response.

"This is what is known as excessive force!" he exclaimed.

"Indeed, it is nothing short of an intentional campaign of genocide, with malice aforethought," Abdel Hamid added.

The Americans' proposed solution was conveyed by Kennedy, who said, "Ronald Reagan gave the Palestinian fighters a personal guarantee that he would protect their families on condition that the former evacuate Lebanon of their own accord."

Nasser lowered his head in shame.

"The entire world – and the Arab world in particular – witnessed the departure of fourteen thousand Palestinian fighters from Lebanon under joint American-French-Italian protection."

Churchill consoled Nasser, saying, "Don't be too sad, my friend. After all, by their departure the Palestinians escaped certain death."

Abdel Nasser replied, "What saddens me more is that Israel did not fulfill its promise to protect the lives of the fighters' families. More than two thousand unarmed Palestinian refugees, including women, children and the elderly, were slaughtered en masse in the Sabra and Shatila massacre that occurred shortly after their departure."

"It was the extremist right-wing Lebanese militias who were responsible for that massacre," said Rabin, defending the conduct of Israel's armed forces.

The skeleton suggested that a conspiracy was at work between Israel and the extremist Christian militias.

"The camp was surrounded on all sides by the Israeli army, and Israeli General Ariel Sharon was directly involved in coordinating the Israeli army's movements in the area."

Rabin denied that Israel was involved in any such conspiracy.

"The Israeli army did not participate directly or indirectly in that massacre," he said.

"You're right, my dear friend!" Gandhi replied with scorn.

"They did not participate directly in the massacre, but they also did nothing to prevent it or to put a stop to it once it was underway!"

Stalin added, "Gandhi is exactly right. The fact that Israel did not massacre the refugees themselves does not negate their obligation to protect civilians in its capacity as an occupying force."

Kennedy concurred.

"At the request of the Lebanese government, the American Marines and a few French forces stayed on in Lebanon," he said.

Signs of relief appeared on Rabin's face.

"The invasion managed to achieve its objectives: the Palestinian resistance was ejected from Beirut and southern Lebanon. Our achievements in this respect were topped off by the May 17 Agreement which ended the state of war between Israel and Lebanon."

Nasser shot back at Rabin with a tone of defiance, "It is true that Israel was able to expel the Palestinian resistance from Lebanon and to break their back, but a Lebanese resistance took their place, with the aim of expelling the Israeli occupation from Lebanese territory. If you're unaware of his, ask your American and French friends sitting right next to you."

"The Lebanese resistance proved just as fierce and relentless as their Palestinian counterparts," Kennedy answered before Rabin even had the opportunity to ask.

"Hezbollah perpetrated terrorist attacks against the Americans, though the latter did not come as an occupying force but rather to help give safe passage for the Palestinian fighters to leave the country. Hezbollah repaid the favor by killing 241 Americans in a suicide attack on the Marines barracks in Beirut."

De Gaulle added, "And was their act of opening fire and killing the French and American ambassadors to the country resistance? It was most certainly an act of terror. As for the suicide attack on the French Paratroopers barracks, then an attack on soldiers whose orders prevented them from loading their rifles with live bullets were also no occupying force. The terrorist attack against them resulted in the deaths of 56 paratroopers. These men returned to France in coffins containing only their severed limbs and scattered lumps of flesh."

"I detest violence in all its forms," Gandhi said with a resentful sadness.

"I feel sorrow for the loss of these innocent victims."

"American foreign policy bewilders me – how could they condemn terrorism and religious fundamentalism in Lebanon and support it in Afghanistan?" Stalin said with astonishment.

Kennedy replied, "The United States backed the Afghan mujahideen in order to bog the Soviets down in a quagmire, just as they tried to do to us in Vietnam."

"Shame on this world," Gandhi said with sorrow.

"Everytime a soldier – be he of the Western camp or of the Eastern camp – moves a limb, then war is always but an eyelash away. Let the world live in peace and security, and without war!"

Stalin hoped for a resolution that was in line with the dictates of his Communist ideology.

"To be rid of the scourge of war once and for all requires us to work to defeat world imperialism."

"Rather, it requires us to work to defeat communism," Kennedy shot back.

Stalin paid no heed to Kennedy's statement.

"The divergence of interests and the competition for influence will lead to vicious infighting between the Western countries themselves. The United States ought to realize that the true danger to its security is not from us but from other capitalist countries."

Hitler agreed with Stalin's point of view.

"I threw in my hat in World War II with the aim of restoring that which was taken from Germany in the aftermath of World War I. What precludes Britain, France, Holland, even Germany from attempting to take back what the United States took from them, even if those attempts to lead to the renewed outbreak of world war?"

The skull was terrified by the picture Hitler painted. "Most capitalist countries possess nuclear warheads," he said with apprehension. "If war breaks out – well, you all know what will happen as a result!"

De Gaulle calmed the skull's nerves, saying, "No one has an interest in the outbreak of nuclear war, as it will only lead to the destruction of both warring parties. Nuclear weapons do not distinguish between capitalists and socialists."

All this talk of worry about the outbreak of war caused Kennedy to groan in annoyance.

"The capitalists are not foolish enough to bring about their own destruction," he said, sitting on an arsenal of massive advanced weapons systems.

"What interest does anyone have in accumulating a nuclear weapons stockpile when but a few warheads are sufficient to lay the Earth to waste?" the skeleton asked.

"For purposes of stoking terror and blackmail," Rabin replied confidently.

"The Americans weren't satisfied with the enormous weapons arsenal they had at their disposal," Gandhi said with contempt, "so the American administration allocated – under the orders of President Ronald Reagan – some twenty six billion dollars to be spent over a period of five years with the aim of developing what was referred to in the popular media as the 'Star Wars initiative.' The Earth had gotten too constricted for them, and so they looked to continue their war in outer space."

Kennedy shot a glance at Gandhi and said, "You do not understand America or the American people. It is the American people's gall, their resolve, and their hardworking nature that is the secret behind their success and progress. No nation with these characteristics will allow the Soviet Union to defeat it. Its firm policies led to the downfall of Communist rule in Ethiopia, helped expel the Cubans from Angola and brought Panama and its canal – not to mention Nicaragua and Chile and other Latin American nations - back into the fold of the free world. We will not desist until Eastern Europe is free. War is our destiny, and it is our responsibility to wage it, whether on

Earth or from the moon and stars or even the farthest depths of outer space. In the end, victory shall be ours."

"I salute you Margaret Thatcher, Prime Minister of the British government!" the millionaire chanted as loud as he could. "I salute you even more, President Ronald Reagan!"

The millionaire's voice pierced through the skeleton's eardrum.

"Settle down, millionaire!" he shouted back.

"The way you chant with all of your heart, you'd think the two of them gifted you the elixir of life!"

"Why, capital is indeed the elixir of life."

"What did these two leaders do that their predecessors hadn't done?" Hitler asked with genuine curiosity.

The millionaire answered him with pride, "The two of them implemented the ideals of neo-liberalism, preventing the state from interfering in the markets. The World Bank and the International Monetary Fund have also adopted this ideology."

De Gaulle perceived a threat in the new policy.

"Neo-liberalism poses one of the most dangerous threats to economic security, increasing the risk of financial crisis due to a lack of government oversight, the proliferation of securities fraud, and facilitating the obtainment of loans without sufficient screening and monitoring.

"And let's not forget an increase in defense spending," Gandhi added.

The millionaire nevertheless remained overjoyed with the government's new neo-liberal policies.

"Neo-liberalism has opened up new opportunities to invest in new ventures and enterprises, including those that had previously been the sole preserve of the state."

"Who took advantage of these new opportunities?" Abdel Nasser asked with great interest.

"Just the imperialists and the capitalists," Stalin replied.

"Were you able to seize control of the state's coffers?" Abdel Hamid asked the millionare.

"Yes, and legally," the millionaire said, referencing the deregulation bills that passed through Congress beginning in Reagan's administration.

"What is the opinion of Mr. Stalin vis-à-vis this new liberalism?" Gandhi asked.

"It's like robbing a bank in the middle of the day," Stalin answered.

Kennedy defended the deregulation measures, saying, "To allow the elite to manage capital is not robbery."

"I agree," Gandhi said, "but only on condition that this elite abides by ethical and moral boundaries."

"Ethics!" Stalin shouted, shaking his head in disbelief.

"I don't think wealth and ethics go together," Abdel Nasser added.

Churchill objected to these two opinions.

"My friend the millionaire has clarified that his activities were under the cover of the law," he asserted.

Abdel Hamid was not persuaded by Churchill's argument.

"The world must have changed quite a bit, it seems. Now the law permits individuals to plunder the wealth of the people."

Stalin alerted those in attendance to the fact that the phenomenon of private acquisition of public property had continued to intensify in recent years.

"And this all for the sake of the elites, and on the pretext that privatization helps to spur growth in the economy!"

To Gandhi, the word 'privatization' had a kind of pleasing ring to it. "Privatization must be some lesser known cure," he said. "I've never heard of it before?"

"As the popular Arabic saying goes, 'Ask someone with experience, and you can forego a visit to the doctor.' I have personal experience with privatization, and I must say that it is the best cure for economic stagnation. You would do well to add it to your list of natural herbs with the ability to treat chronic diseases."

Abdel Hamid didn't take the millionaire's response seriously.

"What is privatization, gentlemen?"

"Privatization is the act of depriving the state of its resources and redistributing them among the likes of this insolent millionaire," Stalin said, enraged at the millionaire.

"Does it entail the destruction of public companies in much the same way Rabin intended to lay waste to Arab cuisine?" the skull inquired.

"Israel will only be cured when that cuisine is destroyed!" Rabin replied as he gritted his teeth.

Kennedy wanted to ease Rabin's concerns.

"Rest assured, Rabin," he said with full conviction that what he was saying was true, "your wish will one day come true as a result of globalization."

Abdel Hamid opened his eyes in alarm and cleaned out his ears to ensure that he could still see and hear correctly.

"What is globalization? How does it work, and for whose benefit?"

Kennedy sat straight and said, "Globalization is, in a sense, a war on distance and time. With the help of the latest technology, matters of great difficulty have become within the realm of the possible – the increased use of telephones, television sets, fax machines, the Internet, and satellite dishes means that local matters now take on a global significance.

"The impoverished masses stand to lose what little they possess at the hands of this neo-liberal order and the ideas that underlie it," Gandhi said as his heart ached.

Abdel Hamid felt a holy war was in order.

"The impoverished masses and the believers will resist these losses using a variety of methods, including religious conviction," he asserted zealously.

"You're talking about terrorism!" Rabin exclaimed, sensing that he was in danger.

"The main causes of what you call terrorism are poverty and exploitation," Gandhi declared with the calmness of a physician with much experience in the diagnosis of diseases. "In order to eradicate terrorism, you must learn to tolerate the lower rungs of society."

Gandhi then looked at the millionaire and said in a harsh tone, "Cut back on your greed, donate to the poor, and terrorism will vanish!"

The millionaire noticed Gandhi's eyes seething with anger and asked him, "What do I have to do with any of this for you to reproach me so harshly?"

Gandhi responded with determination and defiance, "If the amount of money spent on war or to pay for the arms race was used to develop projects that could help the poor, the scourge of terrorism could be eliminated without a single drop of blood being shed."

CHAPTER 35

Rocky Mountains

The major corporations were the main beneficiaries of privatization as they set about acquiring state-owned enterprises and public institutions. In Stalin's eyes – which saw through the prism of his ideological views – the main losers were the state and the proletariat. Undoubtedly there is more to the whole affair than meets the eye, and opinions can differ quite starkly from the official point of view. As far as the state is concerned there is no absolute win or loss – a loss can be perceived as a win if perceived from a different angle. For one, as enterprises are transferred from state ownership to private ownership, the quality of the services provided to the nation's citizens improve quite considerably, and a company now exerts every effort to improve the quality of its products as well so as to survive and endure in the face of severe market competition. Another major benefit is the increase in profits a company owner sees once the company goes private. As for the losses in revenue sustained by the state, then the latter can more than make up for them by raising taxes on the producers, the buyers and the sellers.

The millionaire was in a cheerful mood, as he had purchased a slew of poorly performing enterprises at a cost of next to nothing.

"I am not insolent as you make me out to be," he told Stalin

"I'm a successful businessman – if you wish to call this insolence, then that's up to you."

"You may be able to buy companies and even the state with your wealth, but you'll never be able to buy a person's humanity," Stalin replied resentfully.

"The fate of any human being who refuses to submit to our will shall be either starvation or death," the millionaire declared with an even temper.

"Take, for instance, the case of Patrice Lumumba, who tried to prevent our companies from extracting uranium from Congolese mines."

Churchill whispered in the millionaire's ear, "Keep silent! Don't draw attention to us! Be diplomatic in how you express your ideas, and don't be so pompous in your choice of diction."

"Death purifies the living of their sins," Gandhi said, commenting on the millionaire's boldness.

"It seems that even now you have not been purified of your attachment to your wealth and investments," Stalin reproached the millionaire angrily.

"That's all you seem able to take into account. You're clearly a man who understands nothing!"

The millionaire took Churchill's advice to heart.

"My apologies, it appears my limited insight has gotten the better of me again," he said sarcastically. "I apologize. Please, let me learn from you all. I beg you all to forgive me."

With that, the millionaire left their circle and made his way over to a corner in which the skeleton and skull were sitting. After taking a deep breath he picked up the skull from the floor and placed him above his knee. He stroked the skull's cranium gently with the palm of his hand as if it were a house kitten and began extolling the many victories the General had won before he was reduced to a mere skull.

"You must have been awarded many highly-valued medals of honor for your valor and courage on the battlefield."

The skull had clinched its eyes shut, enjoying the warmth that he felt as he sat on the millionaire's thigh.

"Unfortunately, the gravedigger took away all my medals."

The millionaire unconsciously picked the skull off of his third and put it back on the floor. The skull felt too heavy for him to carry once he learned that it had lost all of its medals.

Gandhi followed the millionaire to solace him after the latter withdrew in disgrace from the greats' conversation. He placed his hands on the millionaire's shoulder and began to take a seat. The millionaire gazed upon Gandhi's chest and found it bare. "Where are your medals, Gandhi?" he probed.

Gandhi looked on him in pity and said, "I don't have any medals, for when I own more than I need, I am stealing from others."

He then added, "Would that every one of us made do with what he or she deserved. The world would not have suffered from poverty and deprivation, and no one would have died from starvation."

The millionaire pushed out his lips in contempt and bewilderment.

"Mr. Gandhi, I simply can't believe that a famous leader such as yourself is bereft of possessions!"

"You better believe it, Mr. Millionaire!" The skeleton shot back reproachfully.

"When Gandhi died he left nothing to his name but sandals, a pair of glasses, a stick, a floor mattress and a small book collection."

"Do you know, Mr. Millionaire, that I am richer than you?" Gandhi said in a warm, sweet voice.

The millionaire shot Gandhi a glance of disdain.

"How so?" he asked conceitedly.

Gandhi ignored the millionaire's conceited tone and said, "I am in possession of a moral virtue that is capable of revamping economic and material conditions as they stand between human kind. You, however, do not."

The millionaire had no intention of giving up his search.

"What about you, skeleton?" He asked. "Do you have any medals?"

The skeleton answered with self-regard, "I do. I consider the pen which I use to search for and record the truth my medal."

The millionaire jumped with joy. He had finally found a transaction whose value to him was priceless.

"Would you sell it to me?" he asked pushingly.

The skeleton responded indignantly, "It is more precious and more sublime than any medal I have ever bought. I don't see how it can be of any use to you. In fact, I think that you'll simply misuse it. But I do know a way to help you get what you are looking for."

The millionaire had an obsession for buying medals and collecting archaic treasures at a time when the rest of the world was obsessed with preventing the Cold War from escalating any further following the Soviet invasion of Afghanistan.

"What was it about Afghanistan's rocky mountains that drew the Soviets there?" Abdel Hamid asked.

Kennedy recognized what was at stake in the Soviet invasion of Afghanistan.

"The Soviets had devised a well thought out plan for the invasion. In ideological terms, the invasion was conceived as an attempt to expand south in order to spread Communist ideals there. The Soviets knew that these rocky mountains were home to a vast array of natural resources, including a large reserve of oil and natural gas. In addition, Afghanistan was located strategically between the Caspian Sea and and the Arabian Sea. In sum, the red-colored Russian Bear happened to be very fond of warm waters."

Churchill added in Kennedy's support, "The Soviet incursion into territories adjacent to the Gulf countries and its large petroleum reserves poses a threat to Western hegemony over access to this black gold."

Stalin clapped his hands feverishly upon hearing the opinions of Churchill and Kennedy. "This is the capitalist mindset – you allow for yourselves what you forbid for others," he said.

"There are matters more important than natural resources. The main objective behind our entry into Afghanistan revolved around concerns of Soviet national security, considering that Afghanistan is bordered by three Soviet countries: Tajikistan, Uzbekistan and Turkistan. Each of these three countries has a majority Muslim population, and there was a need to check the spread of Islamist movements heralded by the success of the Islamic revolution in Iran."

The millionaire heard the conversation steer into a discussion of economic resources and rejoined the circle.

"The Soviet military intervention in Afghanistan ought to be seen as a threat to world peace," he hastened to add.

"The United States of America announced an immediate ban on grain and technology exports to the Soviet Union," Abdel Nasser said, describing America's initial response to the crisis.

"The American administration also concentrated on promoting enmity to communism and the Soviet Union in the Islamic world," Abdel Hamid added.

"The Americans furnished the Islamic jihadist movements with weapons and trained the mujahideen so as to know how to use them," the skeleton said. "Saudi Arabia provided funding and facilitated the arrival of volunteers to the battle field, while Pakistan and China offered logistical support for the mujahideen's operations."

The skull wanted to put his feet up for a bit. "All this talk of strategy and battle has made me tired. I want to unwind for a bit. I'm going now to get some needed night's rest. I don't know why we're giving the Middle East all this attention."

De Gaulle took pity on the skull.

"So long as there is a need to keep the machines running in our factories and vehicles moving in the streets we're going to need a steady access to oil, the elixir of our economic prosperity. However, the Islamic revolution in Iran, the American hostage crisis, the Arab-Israeli conflict and the conflict between India and Pakistan, the sparring over ideological and economic influence – all of this leaves the region in a state of constant flux."

The skull let out a yawn. He was beginning to feel a kind of drowsy intoxication.

"I want to go to sleep," he said.

Hitler chided the skull, saying, "I advise you to take a trip to Afghanistan's plains, famed for their opium poppy fields, or maybe even Morocco or Lebanon where there is an ample supply of Indian cannabis. I'm sure you'll be tweeting like a bird and sleeping like a baby."

Nasser looked at Hitler.

"The millionaire might not allow him to go there," Abdel Nasser said, commenting on his advice. "It's presence there might negatively affect the millionaire's opium and hashish profits.

Kennedy settled matters once and for all.

"Let the skull sleep wherever it chooses. The Americans, on the other hand, will not rest until they've managed to inflict a defeat on the Soviet armies in Afghanistan by whatever means possible: by military means, financial means, opium, hashish, even by means of Islam. Our objective is clear: to foil the Soviet invasion of Afghanistan."

"Why are you so determined to do so?" Gandhi innocently asked.

"Nations don't have a short memory span, and neither do governments," Kennedy rejoined at once. "The Soviets were behind the awful defeat the Americans suffered in Vietnam, and it is our duty to give the Russians a taste of their own medicine."

"And how did they like the taste of their own medicine?" Hitler asked, relishing in the American-soviet tit-for-tat.

"It's as bitter as gall," Abdel Nasser retorted, having tasted it himself in 1967.

"The dose we took was even more bitter," Stalin said, pained to the core, "as it was forced on us by Gorbachev's boneheaded policies which diverged from the Leninist-Marxist track in neglecting military reform, choosing instead to adopt what he called the 'perestroika' reforms which, though pursued under the pretext of 'restructuring' the Soviet Union, ended up leading to its downfall."

He took a drink of water from the glass that was in front of him, and concluded his remarks as follows: "Ah," he sighed.

"I only wish that I had lived longer, so that I could have had the opportunity to strangle this Gorbachev with my bare hands."

Kennedy was delighted by Stalin's pessimism.

"As for me, I would have shaken his hand with enthusiasm! He was a brave man, taking the courageous step of withdrawing his troops from Afghanistan in 1989 after having suffered the loss of over ten thousand men during the many years of Soviet Union in Afghanistan. In this way not only did he save the lives of his troops, but he was also able to save enormous amounts of money that would have gone to waste had the war effort continued."

"The Soviets went out the door," Abdel Hamid said composedly, "only for the Americans to come in through the same door."

"He was a gracious man," Churchill said, describing Gorbachev, "a very gracious man."

"I'm sure you think he was," Stalin scoffed, "given that he offered the Soviet Union to the West on a silver platter."

Kennedy tried to persuade Stalin that change was necessary, "Rather, he offered the gift of freedom to the Soviet people, and as fate would have it today the Russian Federation celebrates its independence."

Stalin's pupils widened.

"Independence?" He asked. "From whom?"

"From itself," the skeleton replied nervously.

Instead of calming his nerves, the skeleton's reply only made Stalin's rage worse. "Russia celebrating its independence from Greater Russia – it's the biggest farce in the history of man!"

Stalin continued, "You all ought to go and celebrate with Gorbachev and his friends, and have them pour you a drink of Russian vodka in Western-made glasses."

De Gaulle said comfortingly, "Gorbachev believed in Western liberalism, but his reforms were a bit rushed, or perhaps he himself was rushed by the United States and Britain."

Stalin formulated an argument that he believed incriminated the West, "Western liberalism was only successful in creating economic catastrophes and crises. In 1987, the American stock market fell 22% as a result of high-risk long-term transaction deals gone wrong, and the effects of this crash will certainly affect Russia as well. As for freedom, then this is a highly nebulous concept, and everyone has their own view of what freedom ought to mean. Perhaps Gorbachev granted media outlets in Russia a measure of freedom in how they chose to operate in order to further his aims, but he deprived the Soviet people of their strength and independence. The true meaning of freedom is to provide everyone with security and the opportunity to work, as well as furnishing education and health care free of charge."

Gandhi was a firm advocate of the nuclear disarmament and nonproliferation agenda.

"It ended the Cold War and the attendant arms race," he said.

"This occurred in 1989, during President George Bush Sr.'s meeting with Gorbachev in Malta, which relieved the Soviet Union of its financial obligations," the skeleton rejoined.

"This is how America came to have free rein in the four corners of the globe," Stalin hit back in a hostile tone.

Abdel Nasser looked to soothe Stalin's anger.

"The developing countries lost a key backer, and the nations that declared their independence from the Soviet Union began searching for a new benefactor."

Gandhi, also looking to express his sympathy to Stalin, said,

"I mourn the secession of the former Soviet nations just as much as I mourned Pakistan's breaking apart from India."

Abdel Hamid winked at Nasser, and then told Gandhi:

"There are those who like to see flags flutter. Such people must have been overjoyed to see fifteen flags flood the skies of northern Asia with their dazzling colors."

Churchill ignored Abdel Hamid's gag and said, "The same held true for the Eastern European countries, their newfound spirit of independence causing their flags to pulsate with new life, the Solidarity trade union in Poland being the first government to break free from the Communist camp."

Hitler's belief that the German people would be united once more had never wavered.

"On the 9th of November 1989, the Berlin Wall – the dividing line between East and West Germany, which had heretofore made the short distance between the two well-nigh impossible to cross – fell. That was the beginning of the German people's reunification. In the following year, the German flag bearing the colors black, red and gold was raised high over the entire territory of re-unified Germany and planted firmly in the heart of every German."

"The fall of 1989 brought raging winds that uprooted the Communist regimes in Eastern Europe," De Gaulle said, sounding as if he were reading the weather report.

"An atmosphere of calm prevailed in the Middle East," Abdel Nasser added, "as the Lebanese Civil War had come to an end via the Ta'if Agreement."

Calm and serenity began to spread through Gandhi's veins.

"How wonderful it is when peace reigns all over the world," he said.

The millionaire proffered a different point of view.

"The adoption of the capitalist system and the deregulation of the markets was even more wonderful."

Stalin assailed the millionaire with whatever power he had left.

"You are despicable, mr. millionaire, as is your capitalist system."

The millionaire concealed his anger. His stomach pains also seemed to be back, and yet Gorbachev's 1991 announcement that the Soviet Union had been dissolved made him laugh out loud. On the other hand, Stalin saw his strengths dwindle. This house, this Soviet house that he had built with might and resolve over the span of forty years of political activity – all his efforts had been for naught. Stalin's fall coincided with the fall of the Soviet Union.

"Gorbachev could have repaired the home rather than destroy it!" he said as he plunged to the ground.

He then consoled himself, saying, "International conspiracies and various other circumstances converged to bring about the downfall of the Soviet Union's Communist regime. But the cruelty of the capitalists' exploitative system shall bring socialism back to life, and this time we will avoid making the mistakes of yore."

"The former Soviet republics have become flashpoints for international conflict," the skeleton said, dashing Stalin's hopes.

"They still aspire for freedom."

Kennedy concurred with the skeleton's opinion, and said, "Humanity is an indivisible whole. The notions of freedom, justice and equality are the fruits of democracy's tree. Every nation on Earth has a right to these three things."

Kennedy's statement shocked Stalin.

"I see that you're more committed to Communism than the Communists!" he scoffed.

"Give my ideology whatever name you desire," Kennedy responded eagerly. "But what I have said is the basis upon which United States of America was established. As is written in our constitution:

'All men are created equal. . . they have freedom of expression, the freedom to practice their faith and worship God in the manner that they choose. The law is above all – and it protects all.'

The Final Chapter
Hot Ice

There's always a chance that a severe ice storm might strike and re-ignite the Cold War anew between the two erstwhile superpowers. The war between them is not over yet. Like ice submerged in water, the war retains the same physical composition that it always had. The legacy of seventy years of bitter conflict cannot be wiped away by the signing of a treaty or even by the good intentions of one of the two sides.

While it is true that things have loosened up in the relations between the two countries, nevertheless a certain amount of friction and anxiety has been carried over, especially since Russia remains in possession of a vast nuclear arsenal that it inherited in the aftermath of the dissolution of the Soviet Union.

Russia has felt its influence in international affairs wane. It knows what it means to lose parity with the United States on the world stage. Not only did it have to come to terms with its diminished stature among the Great Powers, it saw itself forced to offer an endless series of concessions to the West. It certainly is not pleased to find the bipolarity of yesterday give way to the unipolarity of today, with the United States of America being the only superpower left. The millionaire's fortunes shifted too, but more so in the opposite direction: with Russia now open to free market capitalism, the millionaire stormed

Russia's enormous market of voracious consumers, hungry for such things as fancy automobiles, jeans and hamburgers, and even the enchanting look and feel of the green American dollar, which was now available for purchase to any Russian who so desired to acquire it. Needless to say, the millionaire's assets increased manifold as a result.

"The Soviet Union fell, and the myth of an 'evil empire' fell with it," Hitler said, describing the predicament the Americans had found themselves in. "The Americans' weapons arsenal became meaningless."

Kennedy shot back defiantly, "For capitalism to live, it needs to concoct a new empire of evil."

"Anyone who stands in the face of free market capitalist interests and Big Oil is eligible to take up this position," the millionaire added.

Stalin grinned deviously and quipped, "Who had the honor of succeeding the Soviet Union in this respect?"

"There were many qualified candidates," Kennedy said matter-of-factly.

The skeleton named a few such candidates:

"North-Korea. . .Iran. . .Libya. . .Hezbollah. . .Afghanistan . . .Sudan. . .Somalia. . .Syria. . ."

"Saddam Hussein was chosen to fill the position," Abdel Nasser said, hitting the nail on the head.

"He decided he wanted to exploit his nation's oil reserves – as well as those of neighboring Kuwait – for his own ends."

Kennedy nodded his head in agreement, though he had a glum look on his face.

"We've had quite the difficult time trying to figure out how to deal with the mind sets prevalent in the developing world."

Churchill added in Kennedy's support, "Indeed, it seems as if their ways of thinking are at odds with any standard of reasonableness or fairness."

"We back them with funding, weapons. . .we give them a leg to stand on," Kennedy grumbled. "Once they are able to stand on their own, they turn on us. It's puzzling, really."

"Are we still talking about Saddam Hussein?" the skeleton asked.

Kennedy still seemed noticeably downcast.

"Saddam Hussein is just one of many examples. They are many more where he came from."

Abdel Hamid wondered what criteria America used as it handpicked these leaders. Rabin's response revealed a few secrets that he had picked up in his many years of experience:

"It's a matter of mutual interest. America's interest in Saddam Hussein began in 1959, when he was chosen by the Ba'ath party to carry out an assassination attempt on then-Iraqi president Abd al-Karim Qasim as part of a larger plot by the Ba'ath to seize power in Iraq. When the attempt failed, Saddam Hussein fled the country, first for Syria and then Beirut before finally setting in Cairo.

The skeleton had difficulty putting two and two together.

"I don't get it – where is the mutual interest here?"

Churchill calmly replied, "The two parties shared an interest in seeing Abd al-Karim Qasim disappear. Had the assassination attempt been successful the Ba'ath would've seized power four years quicker than it did."

The skeleton was confused, still unable to see what interest the Americans had in the assassination attempt. He decided to pose a deeper question in hopes of hearing the answer he was looking for: "What interest did the Americans have in the Ba'ath party's coming to power?"

The skeleton's thick-headedness caused Churchill to grumble, but he decided to indulge the skeleton.

"Abdal-Karim Qasim considered Kuwait a part of Iraq. This was perceived by us as a direct attempt to subvert Britain's efforts to cement its partition scheme in the region. Britain had greated cantons, and installed in each of these cantons rulers who, owing to historic tribal differences between them, would rather fight to the death than contemplate the possibility of unity and reconciliation. As these cantons were weak from constant war with one another, the ruler of each canton would take recourse to soliciting support from a foreign power. At the time, this foreign power was none other than Great Britain. In exchange for our support, the ruler promised to adhere to our dictates and to keep his population in check."

Abdel Nasser held the ingenuity of the British plan with contempt.

"These are the fruits sowed by Great Britain in the Arab world. I hope one day that these rulers may resolve their tribal differences and be free of the need for you to protect them."

"You seem to me a greater threat than Abd al-Karim Qasim was," the millionaire said in a hostile tone.

Abdel Nasser shot back with an equally hostile tone:

"Stalin was right when he said you were despicable."

Gandhi intervened to prevent an impending clash between Abdel Nasser and the millionaire.

"How did the United States compensate Saddam Hussein for the indirect service he had done for them?" he asked inquisitively.

Kennedy responded with pride, "The men of our intelligence agencies are generous in their disposition. They offered him their protection, and payed the rent for the apartments he was staying in, just as they sponsored his living expenses in Cairo for five years prior to his return to Iraq in 1964."

"His tab must have been pretty steep," Stalin waxed sardonically.

"Was Saddam Hussein ever able to pay it back?"

The millionaire covered his grin with his hand.

"The tab came with a pretty high interest rate," he said, "and an exorbitant amount was demanded in each installment. The first installment Saddam paid off by foiling the attempt at unity between Syria and Iraq."

"In Israel, we were living in a state of worry, fear and anxiety due to the Syrian-Iraqi rapprochement," Rabin said mindfully.

"The presidents of both countries, Major General Ahmed Hassan al-Bakr of Iraq and Colonel Hafez al-Assad of Syria, had worked to bring the merger to fruition and were quite serious about sealing the deal. The two men shared many similar characteristics, particularly as concerns their intelligence and their belief in Arab unity."

Abdel Nasser was overjoyed to learn that his dream of Arab unity had been revived.

"I never doubted for a moment that the Arab nation was capable of producing courageous and sincere leaders like these two men."

Gandhi pitied Nasser.

"Not so fast, Nasser. Let Rabin finish the story."

Rabin's worries were no more.

"Had they succeeded in forming a unity government it would have posed a greater danger to us than the unity of Syria and Egypt. The selfsame Ba'ath party was in power in both countries, and the shared ideology would mean that the nascent government was being formed with stronger foundations."

De Gaulle picked up from where Rabin left off, "Saddam was on to the two of them. He established a strong security apparatus in Iraq and in 1979 just before the unity was set to go into effect he forced President Ahmed Hassan al-Bakr to tender his resignation and Saddam Hussein announced himself the President of the Republic. In the first meeting of the party's new assembly after he took power he personally oversaw the liquidation of all pro-unity advocates, whom he had denounced as traitors. In this way, the prospect of Syrian-Iraqi unity was nipped in the bud."

Abdel Nasser was incensed.

"Had I known what he was up to I would have never offered him asylum in Egypt!" he said.

Churchill chuckled. He was used to assessing matters dispassionately, taking into account only that which was in lin with reason, his experience and the reports written for him by his secret intelligence agencies.

"As long as the Arabs continue to allow their emotions to barge into their thinking, then Israel and the West will have nothing to worry about. Just because you carry a rifle doesn't mean you're a good hunter – Saddam Hussein ruled in the name of Arab nationalism, and look what he did!"

Hitler was furious with Saddam's actions.

"Removing strong men from one's circle and exiling the learned and cultured from one's court so as to eliminate any threat to his one-man rule and to give himself the appearance of being a leader unsurpassable in his omniscient genius – why, that's what a coward does!" he said.

Stalin followed up the previous question with another one:

"Was Saddam's service sufficient to pay off his debts in full?" he asked.

The millionaire set his sails so as to face his wind, and replied, "It was not long before Saddam rendered a second service, this time by igniting the First Gulf War. By doing so Saddam put an end to the threat posed by Iran to the countries of the Arabian Gulf, and the latter funded the costs of war from its oil revenues. The war, however, destroyed the economic and military infrastructures of both Iran and Iraq, and in this way he opened a door of opportunity for us to in terms of reconstruction projects and weapons sales."

Gandhi loudly rebuked the millionaire:

"You're like a chainsaw – you deal in death, and that's how you make your fortune!"

It appeared the skull had grown weary from a lack of sleep, which made it difficult for him to understand how political positions might change to go along with new developments.

"Why did you nominate Saddam Hussein to take the position of evil emperor when he has been of enormous service to you?" he asked.

De Gaulle volunteered to answer the skull's question, "After the war with Iran, Saddam was in need of enormous sums to replenish his coffers. Failing to secure them, he took a page from Abd al-Karim Qasim's book – or perhaps he went even farther than the latter, when he invaded Kuwait in 1990.

Hitler disputed De Gaulle's reasoning.

"It is true that Iraq had always desired to annex Kuwait ever since its independence in 1961. But no Iraqi leader dared to implement this desire of theirs. Had it not been for the fact that the United States of America gave Saddam Hussein a green light to invade he would not have undertaken that foolish act."

Kennedy responded to Hitler's comment with silence. Rabin watched Kennedy like a hawk, and then said, "Saddam Hussein really believed he had it in him. He was deceived by his weapons arsenal, which he had no qualms with using, even against his own people. In 1988 he launched an attack on the Kurds, and hit the city of Halabja with poison gas."

"More than four thousand people – among whom were the elderly and children – were killed in that attack," Gandhi added.

Rabin continued, "In all honesty, Israel's leaders were quite worried about Saddam Hussein and his chemical weapons program."

Abdel Nasser responded indignantly, "Was Israel not satisfied with it's destruction of the Iraqi Tammuz nuclear reactor in 1981?"

Rabin calmly replied, "The Arabs' problem is that they do not understand that an increase in their strength will be perceived by Israel as a threat to its security and safety, and we will do everything in our power to destroy that strength or any attempt at Arab reconciliation that might threaten our security."

He then continued, "Had not the world moved to force Saddam and his forces out of Kuwait, the state of Israel would have taken up the mission on its own."

Abdel Hamid concluded, "If I understand you correctly, then America's attack on Saddam was precipitated by Israel's desire to see the latter cut down to size."

Hitler was impressed with Abdel Hamid's analytical abilities.

"For this reason, America replaced the green light with a red light which they brandished in the face of Saddam and his forces."

Stalin clenched his fist with contempt and said, "The invasion of Kuwait created an open opportunity for the United States to gain access to new oil fields. They hastened to send their troops to Saudi Arabia and worked to shore up world opinion and the Security Council in favor of an operation to expel the Iraqi army from Kuwait."

The skeleton described the fast paced events:

"In 1991 The Security Council demanded an immediate and unconditional withdrawal of Iraq from Kuwait. Iraq responded by calling for negotiations as a means to buy time. Saudi Arabia and the rest of the Arabian Gulf countries grew increasingly concerned that a potential Iraqi invasion was on its way to them. Saddam Hussein was himself now a threat. Iraq was unmoved by the stringent economic sanctions the Security Council imposed on it, and so the Council gave an ultimatum to Iraq to withdraw within a specified period of time or face military action. The next day following the end of the specified period, the operation to liberate Kuwait began in earnest. An alliance of thirty four countries headed by the United States of America was formed, and the Americans gave the operation the name 'Desert Storm.'"

After his worries had subsided, Rabin said, "Iraq was defeated in that war and was forced to withdraw from Kuwait."

The millionaire was saddened by the oil wasted in that war, though not by the destruction that was wrecked on Kuwait's infrastructure.

"During their withdrawal Iraqi forces set fire to 727 oil wells, which could very well have led to an international oil crisis."

"I see that you are saddened by the burning of the oil wells, but you don't even bat an eye at the environmental pollution that resulted," Gandhi chided him. "Plumes of black smoke rose to the sky with such intensity that its dust spread as far as Greece to the west and India to the east."

"I agree that it was an insane deed and a humanitarian catastrophe," Nasser said with sorrow.

"Perhaps it is partly responsible for climate change on a global scale."

Abdel Hamid evaluated the consequences of the war on Saddam Hussein.

"The Americans must have moved to overthrow him, correct?" he asked.

Kennedy replied, "As then American President George Bush Sr. said in a speech right after the war ended, 'The fate of Saddam Hussein is up to the Iraqi people.'"

The skeleton zealously relayed the Iraqi people's reaction to that remark:

"That statement motivated the Shi'a of Basra and the Kurds of Iraq to stage a rebellion against Saddam's rule, which had left Iraq in tatters."

De Gaulle was critical of American policy in this respect:

"America deceived them into action, and the refused to provide even a modicum of support to them. The Iraqi Republican Guard, however, remained loyal to their President and brutally cracked down on the rebels."

Kennedy defended the American decision not to get involved.

"It was an internal Iraqi matter," he said.

"But the United States supported autonomous rule for the Kurds, with the aim that one day they shall have their own independent state."

Abdel Hamid threw a fit.

"This is something which Turkey will never allow to happen, and I believe Iran shares this opinion with us."

The skeleton explained the situation of the Kurds:

"The Kurds are spread out in five countries. They have a major presence in Turkey, Iraq and Iran as well as a negligible presence in Syria and Armenia. In each of these countries they demand to be allowed to break away and form their own independent state. They have already been granted an autonomous region in Iraq."

"The Kurds of Turkey are an integral part of the Turkish people," Abdel Hamid interrupted.

"Perhaps the United States and Israel might seduce them with weapons and funding – after all, the presence of Kurdish secessionist movements can be used as an effective tactic to strongarm the five countries with a large contingent of Kurds. But any support will be limited to securing this purpose, beyond which America's support for the Kurds will cease once they are no longer needed. Additionally, there are sharp differences among the Kurds in terms of dialectical differences and tribal affiliation that will preclude the possibility of Kurdish unity."

Abdel Nasser concurred with Abdel Hamid's opinion.

"In 1994 a power struggle between the two main Kurdish parties escalated into all out armed conflict. The civil war lasted four years, leaving some two thousand people dead. This confirms that matters will not transgress beyond autonomous self-rule for the Kurds."

Gandhi lamented the state of mutual hostility between the peoples of the region.

"I hope that the voice of reason will be heard, that the world's conscience will be reawakened, that a new page will be turned, and the peoples of the region will live in peace and war and conflict will be a thing of the past."

He paused for a moment, then continued his train of thought.

"If the money spent in the First and Second Gulf Wars – which exceeded $120 Billion – were used for development instead of murder and destruction, we would have been halfway finished with the job of ridding the world of evil. The poor are like soldiers: if you don't keep them busy, then they'll keep you busy. They're also a lot like bankrupt merchants, who search through the pages of their old notebooks looking to find the culprit responsible for their miserable fate. In this way, the poor are prone to radicalization, religious fundamentalism and violent struggle."

"It's an obligation on the United States of America given its status as the only superpower to carry its historic responsibility and lead the world's nations," Kennedy rejoined with due seriousness.

"Following the end of the Second Gulf War in 1991 it called for a peace conference in Madrid which brought Arabs and Israelis together to work directly with one another to resolve the Palestinian issue."

Stalin, desiring to feel useful again, said:

"At the time, the Soviet Union had not crumbled just yet, and it sponsored the conference side-by-side with the United States."

"In keeping with our long-standing interest to see stability reign in the Middle East, Europe hosted the conference in Madrid," De Gaulle said, describing the European role in the whole affair.

The skeleton touched on the works of the conference, saying, "The conference was held on the operating principle of trading 'land for peace,' pursuant to the various United Nations resolutions generated during the long years of the conflict. Bilateral negotiations were conducted Israel and its Arab neighbors. Jordan and the Palestinians pursued independent negotiations with Israel, and in the end each of them concluded agreements with Israel that were separate from one another. Syria and Lebanon committed to a joint track in their negotiations with Israel, and in the end failed to reach an agreement due to Israel's refusal to withdraw from the Golan Heights."

Rabin defended Israel's vision, saying, "I was earmarked to head the government of Israel for the second time in 1992, whereupon I publicly declared that I was committed to achieving peace with all of our neighbors. I admit that the Syrian-Lebanese track was an extremely complicated one, due to the fact that Israel suffers from shortages in its water supply which it makes up for by means of the water it receives from the Golan Heights and Mt. Hermon."

"This is a stark violation of Arab territorial and water rights," Abdel Nasser said, criticizing Israeli recalcitrance. "This clearly demonstrates that Israel is not serious about achieving peace."

Rabin rebuffed Nasser's accusation, saying, "That's not true – the Palestinian track was the most difficult of all negotiative tracks to pursue, and yet we had much success in pushing matters forward with the Palestinians, and in the end I signed an accord with them myself. The signing ceremony took place in the Rose Garden under the auspices of the United States, and the world watched in awe as Arafat and I exchanged our historic handshake and took turns signing the Israeli-Palestinian Declaration of Principles in 1993. On a side note, American President Bill Clinton had startled me a day before the signing was scheduled to take place by informing me that he was seriously considering not showing up to the ceremony. He dreaded the prospect of attending with every fiber in his being!"

"Why did he feel that way?" Kennedy asked with genuine interest.

"I asked him about that," Rabin replied.

"He told me that he wanted to avoid Mr. Arafat's infamous greeting, which usually involved a procession of kisses from his bulging lips."

"How did you respond to him?" De Gaulle asked inquisitively.

"I thought about the matter for quite a while. After turning it over in my head, I suggested that he go through with it. I directed his attention to the fact that Arafat's kisses, particularly in front of the watchful lenses of the news cameras, were intended to be a heartwarming expression of the Palestinian people's gratitude to the United States."

Gandhi applauded Rabin's suggestion.

"I firmly believe that Clinton will agree to graciously accept the Palestinian people's expression of gratitude to him," he said.

Rabin continued his story.

"Clinton lowered his head to think for a moment, and then he said, "I think someone can say thanks in a way that doesn't involve kissing.""

Abdel Hamid empathized with Clinton's reaction.

"The Arabs themselves have a saying, 'A kiss on the cheek is a stab in the back.'"

The skeleton approached Rabin and asked, "Did you all let this golden opportunity pass on a momentous occasion that had the potential to put an end to half a century of conflict?"

Rabin felt like he was at the end of his tether.

"I suggested that Mr. Clinton have his Secretary of State Ms. Madeleine Albright attend the ceremony in his place. My words failed to persuade him, unfortunately, and he left the matter hanging until the next day."

"Were you guys able to work something out?" Kennedy passionately asked.

"Clinton sought the advice of consultants and mental health professionals with experience dealing with situations similar to his, particularly as millions of people all around the world were set to watch him."

Churchill laughed out loud, glad that he never had to deal with such a dilemma during his political career. Finally, he quieted down his laughter and asked, "Did Clinton manage to find a way out of this mess?"

"The solution was proposed by an athlete, who advised the President to place his left hand firmly on Arafat's right shoulder and use his right hand to greet him. That way, Arafat would be physically barred from reaching Clinton's face."

"Did the plan work?" Abdel Hamid asked probingly.

"Indeed it did," Rabin answered.

"But I felt sorry for Arafat. I imagine on his deathbed his heart will ache with the knowledge that Clinton refused a kiss from him."

Stalin inquired as to the content of the Declaration of Principles Agreement, "What were the most important points in that agreement?"

Rabin elaborated, "The Palestine Liberation Organization recognized the 1947 U.N. Resolution 181, which partitioned Palestine into two states: one Arab, and one Jewish. The PLO also promised to remove any clauses from its bylaws that called for the destruction of the state of Israel."

Abdel Nasser was taken aback.

"This Agreement was certainly in Israel's interests – what did the Palestinians get out of it?"

The skeleton beat Rabin to the punch:

"An interim Palestinian self-government authority was formed to rule for a period of time not to surpass five years. In the meantime, final status negotiations are intended be undertaken that will cover the following issues: Jerusalem, refugees, settlements and security and border arrangements. This five-year interim period began with an Israeli military withdrawal from Gaza and Jericho."

Stalin had pessimistic expectations about the outcome of these negotiations.

"I imagine these negotiations will go downhill now that the Soviet Union has disappeared from the world stage following its fall and the dissolution of the Warsaw Pact in 1991. The mediator of these negotiations ought to be impartial and not biased to either of the two sides."

De Gaulle was imbued with hope:

"In 1993 Europe announced the formation of the European Union pursuant to the Maastricht Treaty. The fruit of my loins, which grew and developed in the Common Market years, has finally come of age! The vision that I worked hard to bring about is now complete. It is in Europe's interest that peace reign in the Middle East and that the Mediterranean countries are stable. After all, we consider North Africa a natural extension of Europe."

"It seems Europe yearns again for the old colonial order, and seeks to take back the colonies that were once theirs," Kennedy said, commenting on De Gaulle's vision.

"I believe Turkey ought to have legal precedence over these colonies," Abdel Hamid interposed.

Abdel Nasser clarified the reasons why the Arab peoples hate the West:

"The negative image that the Muslims have of the West was brought about by American and European thirst for the Muslim countries' oil, as well as their biased stance in favor of Israel."

Kennedy astutely replied, "Since Turkey has a more positive image among the Arabs, and since we are eager to respect their feelings and aspirations, we will give them what they desire, and grant our ally Turkey a more prominent role in this important region of the world."

"Sometimes I wonder if oil is a blessing or a curse," De Gaulle said.

"The Arabs possess it, America wants it, and the world needs it. He who controls its production and sale, controls the world economy. For this reason the Middle East is the place where problems fester."

Abdel Nasser groaned from pain.

"Petroleum is a blessing when it is accompanied by strength and justice," he said, answering De Gaulle's question, "and it is a curse when it is a pretext for recurring intervention in the internal affairs of the region. In the end, the peoples of the region detest the Western powers not only for the differences between Eastern and Western ways of thinking, but also because the former covet their national resources."

Kennedy said with firm conviction, "It is our destiny to rule the world. All we are doing is marching towards our destiny."

Stalin overcame his despondent mood and exclaimed, "Russia too will bounce back as a result of its people's efforts and resolve. The rise in oil and natural gas prices will be a big help in this respect as well."

Hitler backed Stalin's opinion. To him, Europe could not remain marginalized for long.

"With the rise of the European Union and its continued expansion, it is likely to become a powerful military and economic force. Perhaps it will align with Russia to bring down America's sole superpower status and create a new balance of power in the world."

Kennedy realized the threat that a Russian-European détente might bring.

"Let the Europeans expand as much as they like," he said angrily, "on condition that they not try to outstrip the United States of America. We will keep our eyes on the world, and bring down any nascent power that thinks of overthrowing our regime of unipolarity."

The extent of America's power began to dawn on Hitler. He recognized America's hand, its powerful, magical hand, in happenings and events all over the globe, which it put to great use for the purpose of solidifying its hegemony on the world scene. "If you ever wanted to know the secret behind world events, then look to America. My, even the Algerian-Moroccan war over the western Sahara was caused by America's efforts to prevent Europe from investing in North Africa."

"American involvement can also explain the rise of radical fundamentalist movements in many countries of the world on the weakest pretenses," Abdel Hamid added.

"Take, for instance, the Algerian Civil War, which broke out in 1992 when elections that brought the Islamists to power were nullified by the army."

Churchill said to Abdel Hamid, "I believe these were democratic elections, so what business are they to the fundamentalists? They believe sovereignty is God's, the while in a democracy sovereignty belongs to the people."

Gandhi denounced the brutal acts of violence that were committed in that civil war.

"These acts of violence targeted civilians - engineers and other laborers. The massacres committed by the Armed Islamic Group of Algeria in 1997 left more than 400 Algerian civilians dead. These attacks not only targeted civilians but even Islamists less radical than they were. They considered every Algerian who did not actively take part in the fight against the Algerian government an infidel worthy of death."

Stalin proffered another example:

"Following the Soviet withdrawal from Afghanistan a civil war broke out between different factions of the mujahideen. The infighting raged on for years, ending only with the Taliban's rise to power in 1996."

"Humanity has grown tired of war," Gandhi said, feeling fatigued himself.

"War has cost it so much - but the pockets of our millionaire friend do not swell without it. Lebanon, Morocco, Algeria, Afghanistan, Yugoslavia, Ethiopia, Eritrea, Somalia, Congo, Angola, Sierra Leone, Mozambique - he loved all of these countries very much, and yet, as we all know, love can kill: that's why he contributed to the outbreak of civil and regional war in them."

Churchill retorted back, "Don't be too concerned over Africa – after all, the racist apartheid regime has come to an end in South Africa."

"Racism came to an end after a long struggle waged by the African National Congress," Gandhi said, raising his voice.

"Nelson Mandela spent twenty seven years of his life in prison, only to be crowned by his election as President of South Africa. Justice triumphed, and racism disappeared, and

Mandela has now become a symbol of freedom and equality claimed by nations the world over."

Gandhi's rant about Africa had no effect on the skeleton, who was engrossed in thinking about the United States' intentions towards Europe. "What did the United States do to remain powerful in Europe?" he asked.

Stalin replied presumptuously, "If you are referring to the Balkan states, then it's only natural that the Socialist Federal Republic of Yugoslavia would splinter in the aftermath of the Soviet Union's collapse."

De Gaulle continued to have doubts about America's intentions in Europe.

"The American presence was well-received by Europe so as to counter the Soviet presence prior to its collapse. The Europeans worked to end that presence following the dissolution of the Socialist Federal Republic of Yugoslavia."

Abdel Hamid had long been interested in the fate of the Balkan countries.

"How did the Americans respond in this game?"

"America backed the Federal Republic of Yugoslavia under the leadership of Slobodan Milosevic," Kennedy replied matter-of-factly.

"Afterwards, the civil war erupted."

"It was a proxy war par excellence that was fought about between the peoples of the Federal Republic themselves," Abdel Nasser said.

Abdel Hamid stretched for a bid, and asked, "Were the Europeans successful in forcing the Americans out of the Balkans?"

De Gaulle replied with renewed hope, "In the beginning of the war, Bosnia, Croatia, Slovenia and Macedonia all broke away from Yugoslavia."

"So the Americans were on the brink of defeat?" Abdel Hamid asked, intrigued.

Kennedy hit back with that trademark American toughness:

"The Americans feared that Europe would exert its influence on Serbia as well, a prospect that would bring about the downfall to America's presence in the area. We needed to come up with a solution."

"America's proposed solution went into effect in 1998," Churchill began explaining, "when it rallied the people in Kosovo to rebel against Serbia. As the majority of Kosovars were Muslims, they encouraged Saudi Arabia and Iran to back the rebels, and the Arab mujahideen who had fought in Afghanistan a new opportunity to earn a living, and they flocked to the area in the thousands."

Kennedy now appeared victorious.

"The Serbs rejected Kosovo's bid for independence, and waged a brutal war against the rebels. They committed the most egregious crimes there, and the war was on the edge of extending to central Europe had not NATO intervened in tandem with the United Nations. In 1999, NATO fighter jets ran air sorties over Serbia, using laser-guided smart bombs in its attacks on Serb positions. The United States no longer had any use for the Serbian president, and so he was forced to abdicate and held for trial before an International Court. Kosovo was placed under international administration."

"With the secession of Montenegro from Serbia, The Federal Republic of Yugoslavia broke up into seven states," Hitler remarked, "and America's powerful hand continued to clutch at the heart of southern Europe."

"This demonstrates that the Americans continue to develop their weapons capacities in order to maintain exclusive hegemony over world affairs," Stalin said, expressing his convictions.

Kennedy angrily responded, "The Americans know quite well that China and Russia send their spies in an attempt to learn the secrets of our latest weapon, which was used for the first time in our attack on Serbia."

"Britain cooperated with the United States in developing a new generation of weapons called 'microwave weapons,' which operate on electricity and are directed at radar and computer systems, vehicle engines, communications networks, and the Internet," Churchill said, speaking as if what he were saying was common knowledge.

"The aim here is to paralyze humans rather than kill them."

Gandhi's heart burned with anger upon hearing Churchill's words.

"You have my gratitude, the two of you," he scoffed.

"Now if the United States and Britain want to occupy any country, they can atleast do it without shedding a single drop of blood."

The skeleton approached the skull, which had secluded itself into a corner and was getting ready for bed.

"Based upon your long years of experience, tell me, what does the Great General predict will happen in the new century?" the skeleton asked with intense interest.

The skull basked in the skeleton's praise of him.

"What would you like me to predict? Be specific?"

"What are the kinds of weapons the great powers will use in World War III?" the skeleton passionately asked.

The skull thought it over for a bit, and responded with puzzlement, "War is a ferocious beast, one that exits the jungle, bares its fangs, and hunts down everything in its path. And that's how war will forever be. To answer your question, I'm sorry but I can't predict what kind of weapons will be used in World War III, although I do know that it will be sparked by large-scale famine in the world, the desire of the great powers to seize sole control over the oil fields, in addition to other factors, such as climate change, water shortages, and religious puritanism that arises out of the contradictions between rational thought and ideological dictates."

The skull then paused for a moment, as he was feeling quite drowsy. He then said, "But I can predict what kind of weapons will be used in World War IV."

"Tell me," the skeleton said unhesitatingly.

The skull overcame an intense desire to yawn.

"With sticks and stones," he said, fully confident in his prediction.

Conclusion

After a heavy monsoon season, the natural landscape became adorned in a jubilant greenish hue. The buds of flowers began to open, and their pleasant scents enticed the greats who, having overcome their fear of the gravedigger, made their way out into the cemetery's main garden, leaving the skull behind immersed in its deep sleep.

The skeleton walked to the middle of the garden and stood underneath the extensive shade of a lush tree. He called out to the greats in a loud voice:

"Leaders of the world, I have important news, and I urge all of you to listen and pay close attention!"

Upon ensuring that everyone was listening attentively, he said, "The millionaire informed me of his desire to purchase the medals of honor hanging on your chests."

"What does the millionaire want of them?" De Gaulle asked, astonished.

"Maybe he wants to decorate the walls of his palace," Kennedy satirized.

"My medals are not for sale!" Stalin protested. "They are public property owned by the people of the Soviet Union."

The millionaire glanced at Hitler, who stared back at him and said, "Why are you looking me in the eye?" He then clenched his fist and said, "How do you even you dare?"

"I think they enchant him," Gandhi said, calming Hitler's anger.

Kennedy, not a man to mince words, said, "I imagine he's inspecting those priceless, lofty medals you have hanging from your chest."

"I'll pay whatever price you ask!" The millionaire blurted out.

Abdel Hamid laughed, and then said to De Gaulle, "He's a rather astute merchant. He'll probably buy them from us and sell them to the Jews."

Abdel Nasser remarked, "The Jews don't lack in medals. Rabin himself procured dozens of them during his long military career."

Gandhi looked at everyone, and said in a sorrowful voice, "Damn these medals, which are but the product of war."

He then raised his voice in order to certify that everyone was hearing him:

"We Orientals are a spiritual people, bedazzled by ideals. You in the West, on the other hand, are materialists. We look at things and explain them through the lens of God and His omnipotence, the while you look at them through the lens of matter and atoms and computers."

The millionaire pompously responded, "This is why we progressed and became the first world. We are the pioneers of civilization in the twentieth century, while the countries of you Orientals remained colonized backwaters."

Gandhi pitied the West's slavery to the material form.

"If General Goebbels were to return to life and order that all books be burned, but gave you the choice of saving one book, which one would it be?" he asked.

The millionaire quickly responded, "Of course, we would pick the Bible."

Gandhi laughed a winner's laugh. "Why, that's an Oriental book," he said cleverly. "Its main character. . . sorry, its prophet was an Oriental. It's also a religious book that is preoccupied with spirituality."

Gandhi stood up and began to walk around, revitalized by the rich, perfurmed aroma that surrounded him. He picked a rose from the garden, lifted it to his face and inhaled deeply. He then turned to face the greats and asked them in a raised voice, "Who is the greatest one of you?"

The question startled the greats.

"I'm the greatest!" Stalin quickly said.

"No, I am!" Hitler shot back.

Churchill waved his hand in negation.

"No one is greater than me!"

Hitler argued that he was the one most worthy of that honor:

"I am the greatest of you all - I was able to do what no one else among you was able to do."

"The greats of the twentieth century pursued the path dictated by their ideological commitments," the skeleton said, as if giving testimony in a court of law.

"Some managed to achieve victories for their nations and people, others brought calamities and disasters on them."

Abdel Nasser submitted his affidavit, in which he exposed the sacred cows of the twentieth century:

"Slavery in its conventional sense has come to an end - though it continues on in the exploitation of the peoples of the Earth under a variety of 'civilized' labels, including the opening of new 'markets,' privatization, globalization, and so forth. This all happens under the rubric of Western cultural and economic invasion."

"Remember the victims of the two World Wars," Gandhi added, his voice hoarse and despondent.

"The Armenian Genocide, the Holocaust, the Palestinian Catastrophe, the wars in Bosnia and Herzegovina, as well as the new slavery - these are issues that concern everyone all around the world. These are all blushes of shame on humanity's collective face."

"It is not too late to save humanity from its rut, and to raise it up to the level of absolute good, the highest standard possible of ethical and humanistic imperative," Stalin said.

"Materialism kills the human being, and it kills values," Gandhi replied, dejected and despondent.

"It does away with ethics, and devalues certain principles and replaces them with others. The discovery of the atom was a leap in scientific achievement. But I ask you, Mr. De Gaulle, how do you think of it now?"

De Gaulle nodded his head knowingly.

"You're referring to the atomic bomb which was dropped on Japan," he said.

Gandhi continued, "Yes, which destroyed two entire cities in its wake, and put an end to all life in them."

"That's how war is, Mr. Wise guy," the millionaire said haplessly.

Gandhi was re-engulfed by sadness, and despite that he said to the millionaire:

"There are no winners in war. The price paid to achieve a so-called 'victory' is a thousand times more costly than the benefits of this false victory."

"Nations still have a lot of work to do in the area of human rights," Churchill exclaimed.

"What protects the world from being cast into a third world war?" The skeleton asked simplemindedly.

"Satyagraha," Gandhi replied, as if resolving the matter once and for all. "The principle of nonviolence."

De Gaulle offered his own solution.

"Democracy must spread to the four corners of the globe. Doing so will put an end to terrorism and extremism, as well as despotism and tyranny. In order to steer clear of the prospect of new war, we must put an end to the idea of eliminating the 'Other,' and build all-embracing and egalitarian relations between all humans."

Kennedy proffered an opinion of his own, saying, "We must work to prevent atomic and hydrogen bombs from falling into the wrong hands."

Abdel Hamid was persuaded by the strength of their opinions. He too had been a witness to the destructive effects war wreaked on the Ottoman sultanate.

"Yes, surely it is war that will bring about humanity's downfall."

Gandhi closed his eyes and conjured images that depict the apocalypse:

"Killing and famine, Poverty and homelessness, misery and hardship. . .diseases, new and old, whose symptoms include pain and whimpering. A whole slew of catastrophes ensue. Women sob, and pregnant women miscarry. Calamities following one after the other, the destruction of all buildings and residences. The Earth becomes a desert wasteland, and drinking water is polluted with atomic radiation. People fall to their deaths like the leaves of autumn. Corpses pile up in the streets, and on that day the gravedigger will not be able to bury him no matter how hard he tries. Instead of decorating the graves of the dead with red roses, cherries will be planted everywhere. This is what humans have sown, and this is what they shall reap."

The eyes of the greats brimmed with tears. Gandhi too, tried to weep, but he couldn't, due to his participation in the Salt March of 1931 which scorched the canthi in his eyes, causing his well of tears to dry up.

Stalin was stoic. He looked at the sorrowful, mourning faces of his colleagues and remained composed and collected. He was suppressing his sobs. Gandhi approached him and said, "It appears, Stalin, that you had no part in the upheavals of the twentieth century. Or perhaps haughtiness has gotten the better of your humanity."

"It is shameful that a great man should weep," Stalin replied.

"Nonsense," Gandhi shot back. "Jesus Christ wept three times."

The millionaire drew a cross on his face and said, "As far as I know, he wept only twice."

The skeleton said, "The first time was when he wept for Lazarus."

"The second time was after giving prophesying that Jerusalem and its temple will be destroyed," Kennedy added.

Gandhi asserted with full confidence, "And the third time was when Stalin was born."

Stalin was moved. His emotions raged between sadness and regret. His eyes welled with tears, and he placed his face between his hands and sobbed profusely.

The skeleton and the millionaire too began to weep. Heartfelt wails could be heard from all those in the cemetery, in regret for what their hands had wrought.

The greats threw off the medals that were hanging on their chests, and cast them into the main square of the cemetery. As their conscience's tormented them, they broke out in sobs. While the millionaire wept over the medals, the greats wept over the calamities they dragged the world into throughout the twentieth century.

The greats' tears flowed through the silky hills, and gathered to form a large, deep lake at the end of the cliff. The rays of the glamorous July sun were reflected off of it, and a soft wind blew carrying away the vapors of the lake to form thick clouds. They treaded through the Earth on wings of air, accompanied by the rattling sound of thunder. The clouds began to pour down in heaves, raining bread and nutrition, peace and stability, medicine, and schools.

The skull was still at rest. A rat snuck into the third wing from a crevice. Its eyes beamed in the catacomb's darkness like those of a cat. Finding the skull alone, the rat lit up with joy, and rushed back to share the good news with his rat comrades, who had been awaiting the opportunity to pounce on the skull and drag it back to their hole so as to nibble on its cranium piece by piece.

Tens of rats, filled with zeal and bent on revenge, began to swarm the catacomb. However, their mission was thwarted by the gravedigger as he walked into the wing.